Whispers in the Tallgrass

Novels by Alexander and Bratcher

Whispering Oaks

The House of M. Lucretius

The Satsang: A Tale of Redemption (forthcoming)

Whispers in the Tallgrass

A Novel by Liz L. Alexander and Jean M. Bratcher

Milldara, Inc.
Publisher
www.milldarainc.com

ACKNOWLEDGEMENTS

We would like to thank the dear friends who read the early version of this book and offered us both criticism and encouragement. Without their help we would have been lost. In particular we owe a great deal of gratitude to Tom Laquidara. Tom, sorry we didn't rip any bodices for you, but your input has certainly earned you a lot of positive karma for your next life. And thanks to Tom Miller for all of the art work and formatting.

And a special thanks to Crissey, Pompeii, Harvey, Pepe, and Angel for not barking often while this book was completed. And to Milton, our cat, for walking across the keyboard and sleeping on the printer. While we were working.

CHAPTER 1

As spring came to Cincinnati, 29 year old Jillian White seemed to have it all. She was extremely busy at Midwest Bank where her work was becoming more and more engrossing. She was building connections and confidence, and finally felt that she deserved the salary she was making.

Since her divorce, she had tried to fill her time with things she enjoyed. For the first time since she'd met her ex-husband, she was taking care of herself. Jillian was 5'6'', with long dark brown hair and emerald green eyes. She was pleased that she had not only maintained her trim figure, after losing weight following her divorce, but had also toned her muscles with her activities. Weeknights, she went to the gym to work out or attend yoga classes.

Jillian had been dating the handsome and extremely eligible Dr. Peter Burke for nearly two months. This delighted Jillian's mother, but was not exactly an ideal situation for Jillian. Peter was busy building his practice and had little free time. This suited Jillian in that she had developed a lifestyle that left her little time for dating or for a relationship. Initially, the schedule was an attempt to avoid the loneliness, but she had come to enjoy her schedule of activities. Although Jillian was willing to occasionally miss a night at the gym for a special occasion, she refused to change her Wednesday night riding lesson and Peter couldn't understand what he called her "obsession." Still, they had fun together and shared many of the same interests.

Yet, while everything was going so well in her life, she was still lonely. She had told no one, not even her best friends, Sally and Anna; she didn't believe they would understand. Since meeting in college, they'd been there for her through her loss of self throughout her caring for her ex-husband, Drake, her painful marriage, and divorce.

It would be easy to adapt her schedule and lifestyle to spend more time with Peter. She had contemplated doing just that in the hope he would drive away the loneliness. However, it wasn't just that Peter wanted nothing to do with the horses and could not understand her love of them--he would not object or interfere with her riding--but rather that she could not see herself with him forever. Their relationship had not chased away her fear of being alone; the fear was too deep. She could not understand where it came from, but she knew that it had paralyzed her in the past and that it kept her running in the present.

As the horse show season started up, her excitement about attending more shows overcame her disappointment about not being able to ride many Saturdays when her instructor, Josie, would be away. She was not interested in competing herself, but she enjoyed watching the process and was proud of the riders from Misty Glen when they did well. Jillian wondered how Peter would react to her going away for a weekend by herself. She enjoyed his company and hoped he would be tolerant; but she knew she'd go whether he was or not. It was part of the reason she knew she and Peter would not last. The fact was she would rather spend a day at a horse show than be with him and was willing to lose him over it.

She fought down the fear. What if no one else came along? What if she ended up alone? She didn't believe she could bear such a fate, and wondered if she was making up her mind about Peter too quickly. She liked him, but how could she have strong feelings for him when she hardly knew him? She only wished she could understand and heal the intense sadness that arose whenever she felt alone. It made no sense to her; she only knew she feared and dreaded it.

Jillian casually mentioned to Peter that she would be away the weekend after next to go to a horse show, and was relieved when Peter did not seem concerned. She was not ready for a confrontation and not sure she was strong enough to let go of the relationship. When she tried to bring up the confusion she was experiencing to Sally, the advice she received ignored her feelings, suggesting she forget about the horses and the past, but hang on to Peter.

Well, she consoled herself; *Sally was always the pragmatic, cut to the chase type. She focused on practical matters.* Jillian knew that her feelings were not something she could be pragmatic about. She refused to get into another long-term relationship that wasn't right for her, one that would make her forget her own needs and desires, and was angry that Sally couldn't understand after what she had been through with Drake. If she wanted someone to empathize with her, it would have to be Anna. She called her friend and arranged to meet for lunch with her.

The two friends made small talk until they had placed their orders, and then, picking up her iced coffee, Anna looked at Jillian and said, "Okay, what's eating you? You look like a month of rainy Mondays."

Jillian laughed humorlessly. "I didn't realize it was that apparent. It's really kind of silly, I guess. I've got what almost anyone would say is a great life. I even think it's a great life, but I'm still not happy. And I don't know why." She sighed and reached for her coffee.

"Have you got any idea what you're unhappy about?" her friend probed.

"I have this...irrational is the only word for it...this irrational fear of being alone. It's ridiculous. I'm almost never alone. Most of my time is filled with doing things I love. It's as if I'm looking for something I've lost, something I had, but don't have now," she explained, waving her hand at the nebulous thoughts that plagued her.

"Do you think this is still about your past life as Ellie?" Anna asked, referring to Jillian's recovered memories of a life lived during the Civil War. They had talked a lot about Jillian's previous incarnation as Ellie and her relationship with her fiancé, Ted. Jillian had realized it was that life that had held her in her unhappy marriage to Drake.

"No...it's not that. At least, it's not about Ted and Ellie. But that's as much as I can say for certain. It has the feel of that kind of loss, however, only much worse. I just can't put my finger on it. I just fear that I will live out my life alone and die alone. And the feeling creeps up on me when I'm least expecting it." She looked up at Anna, hoping her friend would be able to give her some direction or suggestion.

Anna looked down at the table in contemplation, fiddling with her knife. "I wonder what happened to Ellie after Ted died. We don't know what happened to the family during the war. We don't know if Ellie ever married or how she ended up. I think that might be important information to find out, don't you?" Anna cocked her head and looked up at her friend.

Jillian nodded, feeling as if she finally had some way to deal with her problematic emotions. "It might be worth looking into. Heaven knows, there's nothing in this life that should be making me feel this way." She found she was able to smile at Anna. "Thanks for the suggestion. I knew there was a reason I kept you around." Both friends laughed with some relief and proceeded to enjoy their lunch, talking and eating.

CHAPTER 2

The first out of town horse show of the season started on Thursday and would have formal evening equestrian classes Friday night. Jillian left work early; she wanted to get there early enough to see some of the classes. She recognized Lana, whom she'd met at the Christmas party at Misty Glen; the woman was riding a large bay gelding. As the judge approached Lana's horse, Jillian cheered loudly.

Lana came in third in the class. Jillian thought that was great, but she saw the disappointment on Lana's face when she congratulated her. She was surprised to see Ed had come all the way from Pennsylvania and was driving in the Open Fine Harness Class. She had met him at the same party and they had also developed a friendship. She checked the program and discovered the horse he was driving was owned by someone else who also lived in Pennsylvania. By the time she arrived at the hotel to check-in, it was after eleven.

Having missed most of the morning classes Saturday, Jillian went to the stable area before heading to the rings. She was pleased to see an array of ribbons displayed over Misty Glen's tack room door. Lana spotted her. "Are you just getting here?"

"Yes, I slept in," Jillian admitted guiltily. Noticing Lana's jeans, she asked, "Aren't you riding today?"

"Amateur Three-Gaited; it's the last class of the afternoon. There's a children's equitation class for ten year olds left before lunch. They're really cute. Let's watch them, and then go for lunch."

"Sounds good," Jillian agreed.

The two women headed for the bleachers. Jillian thought the children were cute, but she was also impressed by the poise and abilities many of them demonstrated. The two women ate on the show grounds. Lana was curious if Jillian had heard from Ed. She told her about their one lunch together over the winter and her reaction to him. She found him easy to talk to, but could not see him as anything more than a friend. She then told Lana about Peter, but quickly added that she did not expect it to go anywhere. Lana shared that she'd recently broken up with a hunter and jumper trainer. They watched a couple more classes together until Lana headed back to the stable to change and prepare for her class. Jillian wasn't sitting there long before Ed showed up at her side. He stayed with her throughout Lana's class. They both cheered their friend when she came in second.

The exhibiters' party was held in a large tent on the grounds. There was a hot and cold buffet, a cash bar, and an oldies band. The casual atmosphere seemed to foster the group becoming louder and rowdier than the previous party Jillian had attended. Lana started pointing out people from other stables. Since Lana was free again, she was especially interested in describing the men. She rambled on about which ones were married, in serious relationships, players, available, or gay. Jillian felt she should have a notebook; she'd never be able to remember it all. She did, however, notice that there were a few who were particularly good looking. She realized she'd have to pay more attention to the men who rode the jumpers.

Sunday, Jillian stayed to see Lana win the reserve in the Three-Gaited Championship Class. She left around three, wanting to get back to Cincinnati at a reasonable hour. She had a message from her mother. She returned the call, knowing her mother was checking to make sure she was home safely. It was easier than listening to the lecture. However, she received one anyway about never visiting anymore. She agreed to come for dinner Monday after work.

When Jillian walked in the door at her parents' house her brother, Bill, greeted her. "It's about time you got here. I'm starving and Mom's been making us all wait for you."

"You look like you're starving," Jillian responded sarcastically, grinning at her brother.

The table was set, the water poured, and the salad and dressing waiting to be served. "Jilly's here; let's eat." Her mother called to Bill, Sr.

Conversation was lively as the family caught up and discussed the plans for Donna's wedding in August. As the mother of the bride, Fran was getting excited. Jillian was pleased that her younger sister would be coming home from California for a week in June for her fittings and to finalize her wedding plans.

"Jilly, how did Peter like the horse show?" her mother asked, always eager to hear how her daughter's relationship was prospering.

"He didn't go with me," Jillian said, matter-of-factly.

"You went all by yourself? Couldn't he get away?" Her mother sounded upset.

"I didn't ask him, Mom." Jillian found herself getting irritated, knowing what would come next.

"Why not, Jilly? I thought you liked him," Fran queried with concern.

"I do, but he isn't interested in horses. He would have been bored. It was a lot more fun without him." Jillian tried to turn her attention to her dinner.

"Jillian, how could you? He's such a nice man and a doctor, too." Fran shook her head in disapproval.

"I don't know, Mom," she responded, rolling her eyes and feeling more irritated at the pressure she was receiving.

"After Drake, I'd think you'd be happy with someone who could take care of you," Fran stated, pursing her lips in disapproval.

"I don't need to be taken care of!" Jillian declared, slamming down her silverware.

"Now, Jilly, don't get angry. It's not that you haven't been taking care of yourself. It's just that every woman needs a man." Her mother reached out toward her daughter solicitously, trying to calm her.

"Mom, what century are you from?" Jillian demanded, pushing herself back from the table.

"Jillian, don't talk to your mother like that," her father commanded from the other end of the table.

"I'm sorry, but you treat me as if I'm a child and I'm not. Mom, Peter's a nice guy, but..." She couldn't finish her sentence because her mother cut her off.

"Jilly, is this because he doesn't like the horses?" Fran's expression indicated that she was flabbergasted.

"That's part of it," Jillian acknowledged.

"Between the lessons and going away weekends to these shows, you shouldn't be spending so much money on horses," her father inserted.

"Dad, it's my money! In fact, I'm saving money to buy my own horse." Jillian suddenly felt as if she were ten years old.

"I don't understand. What's come over you?" her mother complained.

"It's the one thing that makes me happy." She looked around the table, wanting someone to understand.

"Give her a break! It's about time something made her happy, especially after everything she went through with Drake." Bill didn't really understand, but he knew what it felt like when his parents ganged up on him.

Fran continued to shake her head, but changed the subject to safer topics. Jillian left immediately after dinner, telling her parents she had to get up early.

CHAPTER 3

Jillian had a busy week at work and was glad that she would not be seeing Peter until Saturday. She was looking forward to her Friday night yoga class. She had missed a number of them between going out with Peter and being out of town for the horse show. Joan Fitzgerald, from Human Resources at work, greeted her. "I thought maybe you'd dropped out."

"No, I've just been really busy," Jillian explained, unrolling her mat.

"Let's catch up after class," Joan suggested.

At the end of class, there was a meditation. Anna's words about Ellie came to Jillian during the time of quiet. Tears began to form in the corner of her eyes as she reconnected with the woman she had been. After the meditation, she joined Joan at the juice bar. She initially had trouble talking about the present and attempted to direct the conversation toward Joan, asking about how her antiques obsession was going. The distraction enabled her to regain control of her emotions, only then was she able to tell Joan about her own excitement over the horses and shows.

"If you don't mind my meddling again, there seems to be something you're not happy about. What's going on?" Joan asked her. They had become somewhat friendly since spending several days together on a business trip. Jillian had found her a very supportive listener and confidant at times.

"Since getting divorced from Drake, things have been going very well for me. I love work and I'm doing well there. I have a great new home that I've finally managed to get decorated to my satisfaction. I have my riding lessons and the horse shows, which are the real pleasure of my life. And I'm dating a great guy. So, of course, I'm unhappy and discontented." Jillian laughed at her own foibles.

"If you're unhappy, you're unhappy. You know as well as I do that things can't bring happiness. You seem to feel there's something missing in your life. I'd say that you need to find out what that thing is. You need to follow your heart." She smiled encouragingly at Jillian.

Sighing, Jillian admitted, "The problem is, I don't know what it is my heart wants. I don't seem to have a minute of quiet time to figure it out. Even when I'm alone, I'm distracted with thinking about other things." She shook her head as if she could shake the answer out of it.

"When was the last time you took a vacation? And I don't mean a weekend away at a horse show. Maybe, you need to take some time away by yourself. You could go somewhere peaceful and just give yourself time to search your heart. That's what I would do," the older woman suggested.

"It has been a while. I'll give it a thought. Thanks, Joan. You really are a friend." Jillian hugged the other woman.

"My pleasure. I'm always glad to be of help. Now, I'd better get going or George will sell all my favorite antiques." She picked up her gym bag and left.

After riding Saturday, Jillian drove to Eden Park. She wasn't sure how she ended up there. It was more difficult finding parking than the last time she was there. Normally, she would have felt self-conscious walking around in her riding pants and boots, smelling like horses, but the thought never even crossed her mind. She walked by children playing, couples sitting on blankets, and teenagers roller blading and skate boarding. The air was clear and fresh with the aroma of spring blossoms. She needed to think; she realized that if she'd gone home she would have become involved in the minutia of living and avoided her own thoughts. She found a relatively quiet place to sit and closed her eyes, taking in a deep breath of air.

The smell of magnolias in bloom brought her back to the memory of Ellie sitting on the bench overlooking a pond in South Carolina. She could almost hear Ted saying her name at a time when they were still just friends. She felt as stuck as she was when she made that trip to Sheldon. However, now there was no anger or hurt, just the fear of being alone.

Jillian couldn't remember having experienced loneliness or fear of it as Ellie. Rather, she seemed to prefer being alone to being with the wrong person. She didn't believe knowledge of the rest of Ellie's life would help her in her current dilemma. And even if she wanted to learn more, she had no idea how. The last experience had occurred by accident. Even if she went back to the old farm in Sheldon, she doubted she'd learn more. However, it might be interesting to trace the history of the old place and see if she could verify any of her memories. If she were going to Sheldon, she'd have to go soon before the summer heat and humidity set in. This was one trip she definitely wanted to make alone; she did not want any distractions. She laughed to herself, thinking how rare that was.

That night Peter picked Jillian up at seven for dinner. Halfway through dinner he commented, "You seem distracted tonight."

"Uh…I'm sorry. I guess maybe I am." Jillian squirmed in her chair, wondering how to tell him about her plans.

"What's going on in that pretty head? Is there something I should know about?" Peter reached across the table, putting his hand on hers.

"No, actually I was thinking about taking a vacation." Jillian tried to sound casual about the trip.

"Umm…that's a word I seem to have forgotten the meaning of." Peter laughed.

"Me, too. I can't remember when the last one was. How about you?" she asked, trying to postpone the moment when she told him she wanted to go alone.

"Probably between my residency and starting to practice. What did you have in mind?" he asked, picking up his wine glass.

"I was in Savannah about a year and a half ago on business. I thought I'd like to go back to the Old South and explore some." She was not ready to share more with him.

"You're not one of those Civil War buffs, are you?" He grimaced with distaste.

"No," she laughed. "But things seemed strangely familiar. This time I'd like to go to Charleston and the lowlands."

"When were you thinking of going?" he questioned.

"I'm not sure, but soon or it will be too hot." She held her breath, waiting to hear him invite himself along.

"There's no way I could get away for more than a weekend without plenty of notice." Peter seemed genuinely disappointed.

"Oh…" Jillian was relieved she didn't have to tell him she was not inviting him. "Maybe the next time." She tried to make her face show disappointment, rather than her relief.

"And how many years away will that be?" he teased.

"Well, I guess that would depend on the invitation." She smiled coyly, relieved that he had not caught on that she did not want him along.

"We'll have to see about that. How was your horse show anyhow?" he asked, just recalling that she had gone.

"It was very exciting. Some of my friends won ribbons and Lana won the three gaited Reserve Championship! The evening classes were so…" She stopped, changing the subject when she realized by his expression that she had lost him. After dinner, they went to the Blue Wisp Jazz Club, and then back to Jillian's place where Peter spent the night. The sex was warm and comforting, but very predictable. She was glad he couldn't stay for breakfast in the morning.

Monday, Jillian reviewed her upcoming appointments. She then went to Jerry's office and asked if she could take the first week of May off. She was prepared to plead for it, but received an immediate approval. She began making travel arrangements the same day.

CHAPTER 4

Jillian flew out of Cincinnati into Charleston, South Carolina. As she stood in line at the rental car agency, she wondered if she was crazy. Her parents had been positive that she was when she told them of her plan to vacation alone in South Carolina. Sally thought she was on a wild goose chase, but felt that taking a vacation would be good for her. However, she could not understand why Jillian wouldn't prefer to wait and vacation with the handsome doctor.

Anna and Joan were the only ones who seemed to understand her need for this vacation and encouraged her to take it. Anna knew the entire story and believed it was important for her to find out more about her past. She also seemed sure Jillian would discover some kind of factual data that would confirm Ellie's existence and Jillian's memories of her past life.

But Joan was another matter. The older woman seemed to understand there was more to the trip than Jillian had expressed. She hadn't dared to tell Joan about the experience she'd had. The woman had been on the same business trip to Savannah, Georgia and the two of them had traveled to South Carolina together. Her business companion had never asked Jillian about her strange behavior there; she had just been accepting. Yet, Jillian couldn't shake the feeling that Joan knew much more than she'd ever verbalized. Mostly she would ask poignant questions, the only advice she ever gave was to trust herself and follow her heart. Her style reminded Jillian of the old slave woman, Mama Noli. She shook her head, pushing away the thought.

Jillian drove into Charleston. She had made reservations at the King George IV Inn in the heart of the historic district. She had decided to spend a couple of days there before going on to Beaufort, where she would stay at the Rhett House. It was an expensive treat, but she had felt so comfortable there last time, she felt it was well worth it. She was unsure how she would feel on this trip. Although she had traveled alone, for business and horse shows, there had been people she knew from work or the stable staying in the same hotel. This would be the first time in her life that she would be completely on her own.

Jillian checked in and went to her room. She opened her suitcase to hang up a couple of dresses and blouses. The first thing that came into view was the antique, silver hand-mirror. She had packed it on an impulse. She fingered the molded magnolias on the back of the mirror. After Drake had broken the mirror glass, she'd kept it as the only tangible reminder of Ted and Ellie. She had wondered what had become of the matching comb and brush, but she had not made this trip looking for any more information about the couple. The mirror was a reminder of another time and another way of life. She sighed and put it aside, hanging up her clothing. She took a walk and picked up some takeout food for dinner, eating alone in public was too uncomfortable. She brought the food back to her room to eat, and then turned in early.

Jillian started out right after breakfast for the visitors' center. She perused and collected numerous pamphlets, and then decided to begin her exploration with a horse-drawn carriage tour. She walked to Pinckney and Anson Streets, bought a ticket and climbed on board. The covered cart soon filled up with other tourists and they moved out at a slow pace. The guide seemed knowledgeable and was able to answer most of the questions put to him. Jillian rode along noting the changes, occasionally, spotting a house that looked familiar. When they got to the waterfront area, it seemed strange to see that the old warehouses had been converted into luxurious properties, bed and breakfasts, apartments, and storefronts.

After the tour, she took the trolley back down to the historic district. She wandered the streets looking for anything familiar. It started getting hot in the sun, so she found a sidewalk café on the shady side of the street and ordered an iced tea, and then went through the brochures she had picked up, trying to decide how to spend the afternoon. She chose a harbor tour, paid for the tea, and then headed to the docks. When the ship passed Fort Sumter, the only thing she could think about was how a string of tragedies had all started there. Once the ship docked, she headed for the antique shops on King Street. She strolled through the shops, looking at small items, rationalizing that she could pack only something small. When she saw the prices, she realized that Joan had been right about the prices at the auctions being so much better than in the stores. She started laughing when it occurred to her that she really had been looking for the silver comb and brush that had been part of the original set that matched her mirror. She continued exploring the shops until her feet were aching, so went back to her room at the bed and breakfast, kicked off her shoes, and rubbed her feet. That night, she dreamt of walking down hot, dirty streets with long skirts and high-top shoes, twirling a parasol.

The next day, Jillian took her time over breakfast, and then packed up her things. She checked out, but left her rental car in the inn's parking lot. She wanted to go on the walking tour of the old houses of Charleston before leaving the city. Jillian recognized many of the houses from the outside from her past life memories. The guide led the tour group through each one, explaining what furnishings and decorations were original to the homes and what had been added. He explained that attempts had been made to restore the homes to their original condition. On a couple of occasions, Jillian almost corrected him when he attributed colors and wallpaper patterns to the 1850s when she knew that they were much later. She stopped herself, unable to explain to him how she knew or to tell exactly which period they actually were. For all she knew, they could have been 1900 or 1960. She had not re-experienced anything after 1861. Jillian realized she felt comfortable in the environment of these homes and especially enjoyed the gardens that were in full bloom. At the end of the tour, she sat at a café and ordered a salad. Sighing with pleasure, she realized she was enjoying the city in a way she never had before and she relished the time relaxing before she needed to return for her rental car and leave for Beaufort.

She followed the directions she had printed off the internet before leaving home that directed her out of Charleston to Beaufort. The route took her by a number of small towns. On the outskirts of Sheldon, she felt drawn to turn right toward Whispering Oaks Farm, but she wasn't ready. Instead, she turned left toward the coast and the safety of Beaufort. She had been driving almost two hours when she realized that she knew the rest of the way without the directions. As the road turned into Boundary Street, she had no trouble finding her way to the Rhett House. Jillian felt as though she had come home. The man at the front desk welcomed her back and called for the same young woman as the last time to escort her to her room. She stretched out on the bed relaxing, pleased that she had budgeted for the luxury of the place. She dozed for a while, and then threw on a brightly colored cotton dress that came just below her knees and a pair of sandals. She was curious what other guests she might meet over wine and hors d'oeuvres in the living room.

The front room was already filled with laughter and conversation. Jillian poured a glass of wine and stood on the outskirts of a small group made up of four women and two men. One of the women introduced herself and the rest followed suit. They all chatted about what they had seen in Beaufort so far, the many movies that had been filmed in the area, where they had come from, how they had heard about the Rhett House, and where they were going next. When they discovered that Jillian was traveling alone, two of the women invited her to join them for dinner. In the restaurant book on the cocktail table, the three found a seafood restaurant in Port Royal. Jillian drove, wondering how much of the area might be familiar. Anything that had been there before the Civil War was gone, if not from the war, then from hurricanes that had ravaged the area, or the building of modern military bases. Her companions were planning to leave for Charleston the next day and bombarded Jillian with questions when they heard she had just come from there. Having noticed a shrimp boat docked at the restaurant, Jillian decided to try the mixed shrimp platter. It turned out to be an excellent choice. Throughout the meal, she kept telling the others, she'd never had such fresh, flavorful shrimp. Several jokes were made about *Forrest Gump* and the ways one might enjoy shrimp. All three passed on dessert, knowing what would be waiting for them back at the Rhett House.

Jillian parked behind the bed and breakfast. The women agreed a long walk was in order before going to the kitchen for dessert. It was already dark and the temperature had dropped. They went down to the waterfront, walking under the lights and listening to the sounds of jazz coming from one of the restaurants on Bay Street. They had strolled for an hour, working up their appetites by the time they arrived at the back door of the Rhett House. Jillian led the way up the steep steps to the kitchen door. There was an older couple sitting at the table sipping tea and eating homemade apple pie. Jillian had trouble deciding between the lemon meringue pie and the double chocolate cake. She ended up cutting half slices of each and poured a mug of coffee to go with it, promising herself she would walk it off the next day.

That night Jillian found herself dreaming of sailing along the coast in an old masted schooner. She could see the heavy clothes she was wearing, long skirts, and strange, heavy feeling shoes that laced up high. She even thought she could feel the pressure of whalebone in a corset. The wind on her face was invigorating and she loved the smell of the sea. Jillian felt that it was her, yet not her on the ship. There was something very familiar about the experience, something that she knew and had done many times, even though she had never sailed in her life. The experience was so tangible that she was confused when she awoke to find herself lying in a strange bed. It took her a few minutes to remember where she was.

Jillian turned on the bedside lamp and walked over to the desk in the room to find a pad of paper and a pen. She wanted to write down what she could remember of the dream while it was still vivid. When she looked at the clock, she realized that she had only been asleep for a few hours and she pushed herself back to bed.

Again dreaming, she found herself in a strange setting. She was young, maybe only nine or ten years old, playing in a yard of a large Federal style house. She could see the warm sunlight sparkling on a large body of water partially hidden by trees and bushes, and could smell the sea once again. When she looked down at her body, Jillian saw a long dress, coming down to just above her ankles, with high-topped boots that were buttoned up the sides. As she ran, she could feel long curls bouncing against her neck and back. She felt very free and happy playing. Somewhere behind her she heard a voice calling, "Ellie, wait for me! Mamma said you had to play with me!" Jillian felt herself slow and turn to see who was calling to her. As she did this, she awoke, once more in her hotel room.

Jillian wondered if these dreams were memories of her life as Ellie Peters. *Could being in Beaufort be calling up lost memories?* Looking at her travel clock once more, she knew that she would have to try to sleep. It was far too early to get up and move about the building. Her mind swam with questions, as she tried to relax and let herself drift back to sleep.

This time the images were even more surreal. She was in a rowboat out on the water, drifting without direction. She was looking for someone, but wasn't sure who it was. She struggled to call out to the person, but had no voice. There was no one else around and it was growing dark and foggy. Jillian felt frightened, not for herself, but for the person she was seeking. She wanted to move the boat more quickly, but there were no oars. She felt an urgency to find the missing person before something happened to...him. Yes, it was definitely a man. Where was he? Why could no one else help her? Why did she have to be responsible for saving him? She struggled to paddle the boat forward with her hands. As she reached into the cold water, her fingers brushed something. She looked down and saw the body of a man floating face down in the water. She reached out to grab him, but he floated away from her. She reached out farther, managing to grab his boot. As she tugged with all her strength, all she accomplished was to turn the body over so that she could see his face. She was struck with recognition even though the face was hideously bloated and blue. Jillian awoke with a start, screaming, "Ted!"

Breathing heavily, and very disturbed by the dream, Jillian got out of bed. She slipped on her robe and went to the bathroom to wash her face, hoping to wash away the dream as well. She could still vividly see the face of the drowned man. What really disturbed her, even more than the helplessness, was that he looked like the man from her recovered memories, but now in her mind's eye, she could see Drake's features there as well. Going back to the bed, Jillian knew she wouldn't get any more sleep that night. She turned toward the window where she thought she could see daylight starting to seep around the edges of the curtains. She crossed the room and pulled them open to look out on the brightening day. A low-lying fog clung around the ground, swirling in places as a passing breeze stirred it, like the moving shreds of the nightmare that had awakened her. Jillian decided to take a warm, leisurely bath and get dressed for the day. By the time she had finished, she could hear other guests stirring, and smelled fresh coffee and baked goods being prepared in the kitchen. The nightmare had sufficiently faded so that she could face the morning.

CHAPTER 5

Jillian started her day with a walk to St. Helena's Church. So much had happened to her since she was last there. She wanted to take her time reading the names in the graveyard. As she respectfully walked the pathways between the gravestones and above ground tombs, she recognized many surnames. At one point, a groundskeeper approached and asked her if she needed help. She just shook her head; overcome with emotion, she was afraid she would not be able to choke out that she was just paying her respects. Eventually, she made her way back to the entrance to the churchyard, bowed her head, and exited onto North Street.

She walked to Scott Street and turned right; she could see the old arsenal ahead on the left. She turned the corner onto Craven Street and entered the courtyard of the old arsenal. The grounds and building had been turned into a museum. She went through a narrow doorway on the right that led to a dark stairway going up to the second floor. The stairs opened into a sparsely filled gift shop with an attractive, middle aged woman sitting at a desk. She asked Jillian to sign the guest book and collected a small donation to enter the museum. Jillian stopped before each plaque and poster to read the descriptions and historical background of the displays. She took her time and, once she reached the information on the 1840s, found herself slowing down even more. This coincided with the beginning of Ellie's life. Toward the end of the exhibit were a few typical outfits worn by widows of the Civil War. There were also display cases showing accessories used by these women. Jillian's hand went to the glass. There was a delicate black hand-fan that she desperately wanted to hold. For a brief moment, she had a flash of herself as Ellie fingering the fan. She shook her head, trying to push away the vision. It made no sense to her. It seemed to have something to do with Ted and Ellie, but she wasn't sure what that might be. She knew that Ellie and Ted had never married. She'd never been his widow; he had died three weeks before their wedding day.

Dazed, Jillian left the museum, thanked the woman at the desk, and felt her way down the dark stairway. She needed to get outside into the air. She stood in the warm, May noontime sun, breathing deeply. She wandered out of the courtyard, and then learned against the outer wall of the old arsenal. Once she got hold of herself, she noticed a patio with tables and umbrellas across the street on the corner. A cold drink seemed appealing; she crossed Craven Street and found an opening to the patio. She discovered that it was a combination bookstore and restaurant, the Firehouse Books and Espresso Bar. She ordered a fresh vegetable wrap and iced tea, and then started to peruse the books while she waited. She came across a book on the history of Beaufort County through 1861. She sat on a bench at a table with the book and read the introduction as she ate. After several minutes of flipping through its pages, she decided she needed the book, paid, and left.

Jillian walked down Craven Street toward the neighborhood of the Point. The last time she was there, she had been mesmerized by a couple of homes. At that time, when she walked the neighborhood, she had not understood why they pulled her so much. Having learned of her life as Ellie Maitland Peters, she now knew that the small house had been her family's summer home and the big house on the water had belonged to the Campbells, the family of her fiancé. She wanted to take a closer look. She wandered through the neighborhood, noting which houses had been replaced by newer ones and which ones had been modified since 1861. She stopped in front of the Peters' house. It seemed even smaller than she had remembered and the landscaping was completely different, but it was definitely the house where Ellie had spent the first twenty summers of her life. Jillian quickly took a couple of pictures, feeling uncomfortable photographing someone else's home in the middle of a residential area.

She walked on through the neighborhood until she arrived at Ted Campbell's family house. The property was bordered by streets on two sides, a neighbor's house on the third side, and water on the fourth. She meandered slowly along the front, taking a quick photo. At the corner, she turned right, staying on the street, trying to see through the thick foliage running along the side of the property. The street came to a dead end about twenty feet short of the sound. She crossed the grass to a bench at the edge of the water. It was obviously placed there for public use. Jillian sat, relieved that she'd be able to spend time there without drawing attention to herself. She could see the side and back of the house as well as the dock. It was not the same one, but appeared to be located in the same spot. She could envision the Campbell schooner tied up there. She smiled, remembering the good times she had spent on that boat with Ted, and then shivered recalling the dream she'd had of trying to find him.

The knowledge seemed completely natural. She laughed, thinking how she would have reacted if someone else had told her such a fantastic story before she'd gone to Sheldon. It had only been a year and a half ago, but she would have thought they were crazy or lying. She had changed her entire life based primarily on what she had learned. Other than Anna, who believed in reincarnation, she thought everyone she knew would think she was crazy if they knew the reason for this trip. She wanted to understand and overcome her fear of being alone. She hoped that she could learn about the rest of her life as Ellie and that it would help her stop the panic.

Yet, Jillian realized she was procrastinating. She was so close, but instead of going straight to Sheldon, she had spent two days in Charleston and, now that she was in Beaufort, she was sitting and reminiscing about happy times in Ellie's life. She was afraid. The joys of the last visit had also been accompanied by pain, humiliation, and guilt.

The last she remembered about Beaufort was that it had been invaded by Union troops in November of 1861. Nothing newer had come to her as she had wandered the streets. She couldn't imagine Ellie not having returned. She decided to explore Beaufort more and put off Sheldon for another day. She sat for a while longer enjoying the gentle breeze off the water. Finally, she forced herself to get up and walk through more of the Point neighborhood. She came across the Chamber of Commerce and went in, thinking to collect some brochures and information on historical Beaufort and possibly Prince William Parish where Sheldon was located. The staff was very friendly and helpful. They also suggested she go to the library's resource center, where they kept copies of maps, photos, newspapers, and nearly any other type of information she might want. She was given a map of the city and directions to the library. She realized it was practically next door to the bookstore where she had lunch. By the time she reached Bay and Scott Streets, it was nearly four. The library would have to wait another day. Instead, she continued on Bay Street to Newcastle Street and went to her room to freshen up for the cocktail hour at the Rhett House.

Jillian participated in small talk with the other guests. She skipped dinner, relaxing in the garden by the side of the house. At nine, she went to the kitchen and sat at the table with a piece of pecan pie and a cup of coffee. Others strolled in and joined her. Conversation was lively. She enjoyed the travel stories of wonderful experiences and the humor with which they described the disasters.

After all the walking she had done that day, Jillian quickly drifted off to sleep. She found herself mounted on a high stepping bay, galloping through the woods toward a beautiful, green meadow filled with sunshine and wild flowers. She heard the sound of another horse racing along behind her. She laughed at the thrill of the race and knew that Ted was trying his best to catch her, but she was far too good a horsewoman for that. She heard his laughter as he rushed to catch up. Her eyes were momentarily blinded by the warm sunlight as she and her mount burst from the woods into the meadow and she slowed their pace to allow the horse to cool down. She turned her horse and saw Ted pulling up as well. Still laughing, he slid from the saddle and came to help her dismount. She felt his hands at her waist and her body slid down along his. Their bodies pressed against each other. Ted's head bent to hers. Their lips met, and as Ellie, Jillian felt the fire of their first kiss course through her body. She shivered with pleasure at the experience, but pushed away before anything more could happen. She awoke with a start, realizing that her body was responding to the intensity of the dream.

Jillian lingered over breakfast. She considered going to the library, but knew if she did it would take too much time away from Sheldon. She went back upstairs to her room, brushed her teeth thoroughly, and then was about to re-brush her hair. She stopped, realizing what she was really doing. She grabbed her purse and keys and started out the door. She turned back and, on impulse, took the broken mirror with her. Within thirty minutes, she was pulling over in front of the Old Sheldon Church. She walked inside the gate and stopped, trying to remember where she had seen the tombstones that had upset her when she was there before. She followed the pathway that led to the right of the church, slowing alongside of it. She stopped when she saw the headstone that read "Peters."

The small incised stones of Ellie's grandparents and great-grandparents were barely legible. However, the stone that read "John Augustus Peters" was clear. Jillian gasped when she saw the date of his death, "March 30, 1862." Next to the stone was another, "Charlotte Maitland Peters, wife of John Peters, January 10, 1863." On the other side of John's stone was one that read, "James Lucius Peters, March 23, 1862." Jillian was shocked; they had all died during the Civil War. She looked frantically for Ellie's and her sister, Suzanne's headstones, but they were nowhere nearby. While looking, she came across the headstone that had upset her so last time, "Daniel Proctor, February 11, 1906." The tears flowed down her cheeks. She couldn't explain them and had no idea who this man had been. In confusion, she went back to John's grave and sat down. Aloud, she asked, "What happened? Did you all die and leave Ellie alone?" The only answer she received was her own thought, *Take the mirror and go back to the farm.* Reaching out to stroke Ellie's father's headstone, she whispered, "Thank you for passing on to me a love for horses." She rose and walked back to her car; the answers she'd found only created new questions.

Jillian made a U-turn. As she drove to Whispering Oaks, the horse farm that Ellie had grown up on, she wondered what reason she would give the present owners for showing up on their property. The auctions they held to support the farm were only held on Sunday afternoons. She had purchased the mirror that Ted had given to Ellie for Christmas one year at another auction nearby. The gift had signaled a turning point in their relationship. Their childhood friendship took on new implications. Ellie had only been eighteen years old at the time. The location of the matching comb and brush was unknown. She took a deep breath and turned into the driveway. No one seemed to be around. She pulled up in front of the house, turned off the engine, and got out of the car. Her anxiety rose as she approached the stairs. She climbed the steps and walked across the porch to the door.

Before Jillian could knock, a tall, thin, blond woman with piercing green eyes, about ten years older than Jillian, opened the door, "May I help you?"

"Uh...I hope so." Jillian notice the woman was examining her intently with suspicion. Yet, there was something familiar about her. "I don't mean to disturb you," Jillian began, still not certain how to even explain her presence there.

"Are you selling something?" the woman asked bluntly.

"Oh, no!" Jillian laughed nervously. "Actually, I'm trying to buy something." She hesitated, and then added, "I know you only hold your auctions on Sundays, but I have to go back to Ohio before then, and I'm looking for something specific."

"I don't know if I can help you. What are you looking for?" the owner asked, crossing her arms over her stomach, but looking slightly less suspicious.

Jillian thought, *she would think I was crazy if she knew what I was really looking for.* "I bought an antique hand-mirror not far from here. I'd like to find the matching comb and brush."

The woman seemed to be searching her memory as she stared at Jillian. Finally, she responded. "Please, come in. It's getting hot out here and for something like that I'd have to check our inventory lists." She swung the screen door open and stepped back so Jillian could enter.

Jillian followed the woman through the house to the kitchen in back. She attempted to steal looks into each room as they passed. "We've been working on computerizing our inventory, but it still doesn't seem to be working right." She pointed to a chair at the table. "Have a seat." She poured two iced teas and put them on the table. She then picked up a large, black ledger off the counter and sat down across from Jillian.

"You've kept the original table." Jillian rubbed the wood with affection.

She looked at Jillian strangely, "Yes, the house was furnished when we bought it. We refurbished and kept most of the contents."

"I noticed as we walked down the hall," Jillian stated, not realizing how that might sound.

The woman raised an eyebrow, but did not comment. She started flipping through pages.

"How long have you been in this house?" Jillian hoped she wouldn't alienate the woman, but she desperately wanted to find out some of the history that she didn't recall.

"Oh, about fifteen years now." She kept turning pages.

"Do you know anything about the history of this old place?" She tried to keep her voice light and casual.

"There was an old lady living here when we first saw the place. It was very run down. She said the place had been in her family since the early 1800s. She said they used to have slaves here." The woman shivered. "I don't like to think about that; I just know I had to own the place. I knew I would from the moment I saw it."

"There couldn't have been slaves here during her lifetime?" Jillian couldn't imagine the previous owner being that old.

"A lot of what she said didn't make much sense. She did apparently inherit the place from her mother, but after the Civil War, it had been bought for taxes by a Daniel Proctor. He left it to her mother."

"Suzanne Peters?" Jillian ventured tentatively.

"No...but how did you know the name? The Peters were the original owners." The woman seemed to become suspicious of her again.

"I...I don't exactly know. It's a confusing story." Jillian blushed, realizing she was pushing too hard. She considered telling her that it was a branch of her family and she was just trying to find out about their history. But, she had already said she was looking for the brush and comb. She feared the woman would know she was lying and just throw her out.

The woman had been looking though the ledger throughout their conversation. "Here's a brush and comb. They're ivory."

"No, the set I'm looking for is silver, molded silver." Jillian gestured, trying to express the idea.

"You better describe it to me in more detail." She looked at Jillian with such intensity that Jillian felt she did not believe her.

"I have the mirror with me." Jillian reached into her large shoulder bag and pulled out the magnolia molded, silver mirror. "I should have shown it to you right away."

The woman reached across the table and picked up the mirror. She seemed to be moving in slow motion. "What's your name?" she asked, looking startled as she examined the mirror.

"Jillian." She was confused by the woman's reaction to the mirror. "Jillian White."

"I always felt part of the set was missing." She closed the ledger. "June. I'm June." She handed the mirror back. "Come, I have something to show you." She led the way up the back stairs and down the hall to one of the front rooms.

Jillian blurted out, "The furnishing are all the same, even the armoire." She realized it was Ellie's room.

June laughed. "I should think you were strange, but I felt the same way when I walked in here." She walked to the dressing table, picked something up and turned toward Jillian, hands outstretched. The matching comb was in one and the brush in the other.

Jillian started feeling dizzy. She held out the mirror. The two women looked at the three pieces, seeing that they matched perfectly. Before either could say anything, the phone rang. June put the comb and brush back down on the dressing table. "Excuse me while I get that. Go ahead and take a look at them." She ran out of the room.

Jillian heard the phone stop ringing and June say, "Hello?"

Jillian sat down at the dressing table. She put the mirror on the table and picked up the brush. Without thinking, she started brushing her hair.

CHAPTER 6

Ellie sat at her dressing table brushing her long dark auburn hair, holding back the tears that glistened in her green eyes. Studying her reflection, she thought that her high cheekbones looked pale and her long narrow face appeared weary. She was dressed in black, listening to her mother wailing in her own room. She sighed, realizing she needed to take control of the household. Her father had charged her to run the farm while he was away, but she had always expected him to visit when he could get leave from the cavalry and advise her. Now, at twenty-one, she was entirely on her own. She still blamed herself for her fiancé Ted's death. She had just started to accept her father's and her brother's belief that Ted would have had to return to Port Royal even if she had married him earlier as he had wanted. Then news came that her brother had been killed on the twenty-third of March in Kernstown, Virginia. One week later, her father was killed at Fort Macon. She wondered if the news of her brother's death had even reached him before his own. She knew their deaths were in no way her fault or responsibility, but she couldn't shake the feeling that she was being punished for Ted's death.

Ellie sighed as she got up, sleeked her dress down over her tall, slender frame, and went to her mother's room. Her sister had been trying to calm their mother since their father's burial two weeks ago. Suzanne had stayed with her all day and most of the nights. Ellie felt she should relieve her sister, but she'd been so busy trying to run the household and the farm that she'd had no time. Although not as many mares had been bred, there were still fifteen foals to tend. Also, Mr. Barton, the overseer, had informed her the day before that five slaves had run off. She told him this time he was to do nothing; she would handle it herself. The argument that had ensued left a bad taste in her mouth. She told him to focus on getting the best price he could for the horses. She gave him a list of forty horses and told him to only accept gold or silver, no Blue Back Confederate paper money without checking with her first. She didn't want to be unpatriotic, but she remembered her father's words. The overseer had walked out disgusted with her. She knew she had to get rid of him, but when she did there would be no white man left on the farm.

She found her mother in bed, with Suzanne sitting by her holding her hand. "Suzanne, I'll sit with Mother for a while," Ellie offered, seeing how exhausted her sister was.

Suzanne rolled her eyes and mouthed, "Thank you." She slipped her hand out of her mother's and quietly left the room.

"Mother, we need to talk," Ellie stated, sitting down on the small chair next to the bed.

Charlotte turned away, "My life is over." She began weeping again, her body wracked with the sobbing.

"Mother, Suzanne needs you; I need you." Ellie raised her voice to be heard over the loud crying. She felt great sympathy for her mother's grief, but they just didn't have the luxury of wallowing in their pain.

"You do not need anyone!" Her mother sobbed out accusingly.

"That is not true. Mother, please. Summer is almost here, we have to make plans." She desperately wanted her mother to take the responsibility off her shoulders, or at least take some of it. She needed Charlotte to return to running the house. Ellie knew she couldn't do it all.

"There is nothing to plan. There is no reason to plan anymore." Charlotte moaned, rolling her head about on her pillow in despair.

"Stop it!" Ellie had no patience left for her mother's melodrama. "You have to get a hold of yourself, if not for yourself, for Suzanne. You do not see her crying, but she needs you. We are all grieving."

"What do you expect me to do without a husband?" Charlotte snarled, sitting up to glare at her heartless daughter.

Ellie was startled by her mother's anger. She had been about to plead with her to take up her role of manager of the house, but she realized that Charlotte was not capable of assuming that role just yet. She considered her options, and then hit on an idea that would please her mother and reduce some of her own worries. "Go to Aunt Felicity's in Savannah. You always loved Savannah. Take Suzanne so she can finish school. There are too many memories here right now."

Charlotte seemed to brighten at the thought. "You will have to come, too," she stated, seeing this as a perfect solution. Her sister and brother-in-law would care for all of them.

Ellie looked at Charlotte, realizing that her mother had no idea of what she needed to do to keep the farm afloat. "No mother. At least not right away."

"I cannot leave you here, not without a husband to protect you," Charlotte stated with alarm.

"We have to keep the farm running." She was going to tell her about the guns her father had given her, but realized that she'd be even more upset about the idea of her daughter using a gun. "I shall come soon."

"But, Ellie, the only white man will be Mr. Barton. You cannot stay here with him, alone. What will the neighbors think? It would not be proper! I cannot allow that." Charlotte sat up on the side of the bed, her tears forgotten in her maternal indignation.

"Mother, you have to be reasonable about this. Mr. Barton cannot be the only one running the farm. Someone has to make the decisions about what horses to sell, which ones to train. And someone must be here to take care of our people. I just do not trust Philip Barton to treat them well without some supervision. It was different when we were all just going to Beaufort. Father and James could come back to check on things and Mr. Barton knew it." Charlotte began to tear up at the mention of her lost men. Ellie knew she had to persuade her mother quickly, before she fell back into her despair.

"I will not have to stay here long, but I must put plans into place and see that everything is prepared before I leave. You and Suzanne do not have to be here for all of that. You will be so much happier when you are with Aunt Felicity. You should be with your family in your time of sorrow." Ellie thought that was just a bit dramatic, but she knew it would work with Charlotte. She watched as her mother struggled with her desire to leave the farm and go to Savannah and her fear of leaving Ellie behind.

"With those terrible Yankees all over Beaufort and the port, how will we ever get there?" Charlotte Peters was a bright woman, but she'd never had to take care of herself. With her son and her husband so recently killed, she was overwhelmed.

"Mr. Barton can escort you on the inland route." It occurred to Ellie it would give her a chance to see how things would go on the farm without him for a couple of weeks.

"But, Ellie, there would be no man here." Charlotte was appalled at the idea of leaving a defenseless woman alone with only the slaves.

"It would only be a couple of weeks." Ellie did her best to minimize the time and her mother's objections.

"But Ellie, will you be able to manage the slaves? Since the war started they have been so...so uppity." Charlotte waved her damp handkerchief to emphasize her words.

"Mother, we have always been good to our slaves and we have never had any problems with them." She was glad her mother hadn't heard about the recent runaways. She'd have to make sure the overseer didn't tell her. "I shall send a telegram to Aunt Felicity. Now, get up. You have a lot of organizing to do."

"Ellie, I know I have often been frustrated with you for not being more like other Southern ladies, but I am proud of you," Charlotte stated, hugging her daughter. She smiled with relief, having made up her mind to go. Suddenly, all objections were swept aside.

Ellie returned her mother's hug and left the room to inform the household. Charlotte managed to get out of bed and direct her maid in making preparations to leave for Savannah. She started coming down for dinner with her two daughters; however, she mostly pushed her food around on her plate.

CHAPTER 7

By the first of May, the days were hot and humid. Mr. Barton had sold twenty of the available forty horses. Ellie reviewed the list, selected ten of the remaining twenty, and instructed him to take them to Savannah and sell them there. He was to give half the proceeds to Charlotte and bring the rest back to Whispering Oaks. Again, she warned him against taking Blue Backs. Ellie told her mother to be careful with the funds, with the war going on, she did not know when or how much more she'd be able to get to her.

Ellie watched with sadness and anxiety as her mother and sister rode off in the carriage driven by Mr. Barton with four horses tied behind. They were followed by a wagon with their two maids, a driver, two grooms, trunks and six more horses. She hoped that her mother would survive her grief. She knew she would have a better chance in Savannah under Aunt Felicity's care. With her mother and sister gone, she would not have to worry about them and could focus on the farm. She walked to the barn to check on the foals. Their antics had always cheered her, but today it wasn't working.

Ellie knew she needed to check the fields that had been planted, but it was approaching noon and too hot. She'd put it off until the next morning. She was already feeling lonely and had wanted to talk to Mama Noli about the runaway slaves. The old lady was sitting in her rocker on the small porch of her hut.

The African-born woman greeted Ellie with apparent affection.

"Howdy do, Miz Ellie. It sho is good ta see ya. C'mon up an' set a spell. Ah got some clover tea inside ef ya's thirsty," the old woman offered.

"Thank you, Mama Noli. I would love some, but only if you will allow me to get it myself." When the old slave smiled and nodded, Ellie went into the hut, found the tea in a jar and poured two cups full. She brought one out to her hostess, and then sat down on the bench near the door with the other.

The two women sipped the sweet, herbal tea in companionable silence for several minutes, Mama Noli waiting patiently until Ellie was ready to talk.

At last Ellie spoke. "Mama Noli, I am sure you know that several of our people have run off seeking their freedom. And I hope you know that I sympathize with their desire to be free." The old woman smiled and nodded without interrupting.

"I wish that I could give all of you your freedom and pay you to stay here to work. But that simply is not possible at this time. Perhaps once the war is over, things will be different. I pray they will be. But I have a more immediate concern, and that is keeping the farm running and tending to the horses we still have here. I need the people to stay here and to keep working. I will not stop anyone who chooses to leave, but I would hope that they would choose to stay. But I do not know how to keep them here. Mama Noli, how can I persuade them to stay?" She looked to the wise old woman, hoping to hear some sage advice that would help her.

Mama Noli continued to rock while she contemplated the problem.

"Dat dere is a knotty problem, Miz Ellie. Ef sumun gits da idea ta take off dey's gonna do it. Dem what stays is mos' likely ta have fambly here what cain't go wit dem. Ah knows ya cain't pay dem no moneys 'cause ya ain't got none ta pay wit. So ya needs ta gib dem sumpin dey wants jist 'bout as much as money o' freedom. Could be ya could gib dem land what is truly deres, or ya could gib dem knowledge so dey have sumpin' fo' dey future an' dey chillens' future. It would have ta be sumpin' dey cain't git away from here. But dey lifes got ta be better dan dey is now, ya see?" She looked searchingly into Ellie's eyes.

"Yes, ma'am, Mama Noli. I think I do see what you mean. If their lives are better here than they could be away from here, and they had a real hope of freedom, it would give them some reason to stay and keep the farm going." Ellie leaned back against the wall of the hut, thinking about what she could do that might help her people feel more valued and hopeful.

Mama Noli sipped her tea and continued rocking, still patient with her young mistress.

"Thank you, Mama Noli, for giving me so much to think about. I will come back to visit you soon," she stated, standing up from the bench. "I need to get back to the house. Thank you for talking with me and for the tea. Is there anything you need before I leave?" She stood, ready to run any errands the old woman might have."

"No, Miz Ellie. You git on wit ya, now. Lily'll be along presently an' she kin tend ta me ef Ah need sumpin," the old woman said, smiling. Ellie bent to give the wrinkled cheek a kiss and left.

CHAPTER 8

The next morning, Ellie saddled up Princess. The three-year old still had a lot to learn; Ellie told one of the grooms, Joey, to saddle up one of the mares. He was going to accompany her. The teenager claimed he didn't know how to ride, but Ellie knew most of the boys who worked directly with the horses often rode bareback out in the back pastures. He made a big show of not knowing what he was doing when he first mounted, but he had trouble hiding his grin. Ellie led the way up the hill. From now on, it would be her responsibility to keep track of the corn and hay fields, to check the fencing and the horses in the far pastures. She wondered how often she needed to do it.

"Joey, how often did Mr. Barton make rounds?" she asked the youth.

"Ah don' know, Miz Ellie," the young man replied.

"Well, how often did you saddle a horse up for him?" Ellie demanded, frustrated by the slave's seeming ignorance.

"Maybe two times durin' plantin' an' dat many agin durin' harvest," he finally admitted.

"That was all?" Ellie was appalled at the overseer's laxity.

"Well, unless yo papa was here." The young man looked uncomfortable.

"How often then?" she pressed.

"Ever day, but he don' check much," he told her.

Ellie considered this for a while, and then changed the subject. "Joey, why are you still here?"

"What ya mean, Miz Ellie?" he asked, puzzled by her question.

"Others have run away; you are young and healthy. Why have you stayed and not gone with the others?" she explained.

"Old Joe is mah grandfather an' Ah belongs ta yo papa, or...who does Ah belong ta now?" He turned to her, confusion showing on his face.

"Charlotte." She hesitated; she needed some young slaves to stay; she just wished she could give them their freedom and had the money to hire them. "Joey, I am going to need your help. Will you check the fences every week? You can ride one of the horses to do it."

"Miz Ellie, thank ya...Miz Ellie, Mista Barton gonna be real mad." The young man seemed torn between the offer to ride horses and have some autonomy and the fear of the overseer.

"Mr. Barton will not be a problem," Ellie assured him.

"Ah hopes ya's right; he's..." The young man hesitated to finish the sentence, fearing to criticize a white man before his young mistress.

Ellie laughed. "I never liked him either."

By the time Ellie and Joey got back to the barn, it had grown hot. She realized she would have to get up early on the days she was going to ride the farm. She didn't remember when she'd last been on the farm after the first of May; by this time each year she'd always been in Beaufort for the hot summer months. The family always tried to escape the humidity and mosquitoes for the soft summer breezes off the sound. Summer had always been a time of learning and socializing. She wondered whether she'd ever see their summer cottage again, since the Yankees took over Beaufort. Before she returned to the house, she turned to Joey, "Have you been learning to read?"

"No, Miz Ellie." His face reflected his fear that he would get into trouble if he said he had been.

"Maybe, it is time you did." Ellie turned and went up to the house. She washed her face and hands and sat down at the kitchen table. Lottie seemed to know what she needed, having brought up some cool tea from the cellar. Ellie sat, trying to gather her thoughts. She felt that she had too much to learn too quickly. When her father had attempted to prepare her to run the farm, they both had expected that she'd have help or at least someone to advise her from time to time. She knew she couldn't do it alone. She needed to find out who would stay and start training them to take over some of the responsibility. She'd start by holding reading and arithmetic classes for anyone who wanted to learn for an hour every day when it was too hot to do anything else. It would help them, give them a reason to stay, and give her a chance to get to know some of them better. Lela and Mattie had learned the basics; together the three of them could teach everyone.

Lottie continued about her work while Ellie sat sipping her tea, deep in thought. Lela came in with some early spring vegetables and strawberries for her grandmother. Ellie shared her idea about teaching anyone who wanted to learn with Lela. The woman was excited about the idea, but questioned how Charlotte and Mr. Barton would react. Ellie just shrugged. Mattie joined them; she had been looking for Ellie. When she heard the plan, she left to draw Ellie a bath, shaking her head and mumbling, "We is all gonna git in trouble."

Lela spread the word that anyone interested in learning to read should come to the porch of the main house the next day by mid-afternoon. When the butler, Peter, heard, he approached Ellie to express his concern. "May Ah speak with ya, Miz Ellie?"

"Of course, Peter. Is there a problem?" Ellie asked, concerned.

"Ah heared of yo plan ta teach ever body. It may be dangerous, Miz," Peter stated solemnly, frowning with apprehension.

"You know it is the right thing to do," Ellie stated, hoping to win him over to her side.

"Miz Charlotte might not think so," the young black man stated, shaking his head.

"Miz Charlotte is not here; it is a new time. You know my father would have agreed under the circumstances." Ellie felt exasperated with this unexpected opposition.

"Yes, um; he probably would have," Peter admitted grudgingly.

"I know you read. Will you help?" Ellie needed everyone she could recruit for this project.

"Miz Ellie, Ah'd be honored." Peter's expression showed that he was indeed surprised and pleased with the request. Ellie smiled, feeling that she had made another convert to her cause.

Ellie started eating dinner by herself in the dining room. Halfway through the meal, she picked up her plate and glass; she carried them into the kitchen. Lela, Lottie, Mattie, and Peter were sitting at the table. She put her plate down on the table, sat next to Lela, and resumed eating. The slaves exchanged looks and quietly returned to their meals. Before going upstairs, Ellie informed Lottie that she'd be eating her meals with them in the kitchen until Charlotte and Suzanne returned, unless she had company.

She knew that, if she were going to meet her goals for the farm, she'd need to be organized and set a schedule for herself. Over the next few days, she started developing a routine. The mornings varied between riding with Joey to check the outer areas of the farm and working with the young horses, handling and training them. She was relieved that she did not have to take over the management of the farm during the breeding and foaling season; Mr. Barton had at least overseen that much. Late mornings and afternoons, she spent working on the books and her usual household tasks. Later in the afternoon, she joined the slaves on the porch for their lessons. Eight of the adult slaves regularly showed up, along with the three who were helping teach. In addition, all the children came. Some only wanted to watch, but several of them actively participated. Before too many days had passed, all the children were learning and outstripping the adults. Even Mama Noli came to sit in a rocking chair and observe her people learning to read. She beamed with pride as her great-grandchildren took turns trying to read aloud from some of Ellie's old childhood readers.

During the second week, Ellie and the slaves were studying on the porch. It was a particularly hot afternoon. Lottie had taken the liberty of bringing a pitcher of cooled tea and glasses to the porch. Ellie quickly saw that her lessons could not compete with the cool drinks and gave up on the day's teaching. As they sat relaxing, a wagon was heard coming down the road. When it turned in the drive the slaves became suddenly quiet, looks of fear came over their faces. Then someone spoke, "It's Nathaniel."

Another stated, "Mista Barton should be close behind."

Nathaniel pulled the wagon up to the house instead of the barn and yelled up, "Miz Ellie, Miz Ellie, Ah gots ta talk ta ya."

"Joey, get that horse. He is overheated." Ellie called down. "Nathaniel, where is Mr. Barton?"

"He ain't comin', Miz Ellie. Dat's why Ah gots ta talk ta ya." Nathaniel stood with his head hanging, and his hands clasping his battered hat.

"Come up here." Ellie waved him up the steps to the porch.

The man ran up the stairs. He was too upset to even notice the other slaves or their sighs of relief. It didn't even seem odd when Ellie handed him a glass of tea. He gulped it down, and then blurted out. "He stole da money." His eyes were wide with fear that he would be punished for the overseer's wrongdoing.

"Nathaniel, what happened?" Ellie gestured for the man to have a seat on one of the stools vacated by a child.

"Mista Barton was goin' west wit da money," the man explained, seating himself.

"Start at the beginning and tell me everything that happened." Ellie offered him more tea. She could see that he was overheated and sweating profusely.

"We got ta Savannah an' took Miz Charlotte and Miz Suzanne ta Miz Felicity's. We stabled da hosses at Miz Felicity's. Den Mista Barton say we gots ta sell da hosses. We sell all o' dem da fust couple a days 'cept one. He 'fused ta sell dat one. Ah tries askin' him 'bout it." The slave hesitated and rubbed his face. "He gib da paper money ta Miz Charlotte an' kept da coins. He tol' Miz Charlotte, he's comin' back here da next day. He say he gonna visit some friends. When he don't come back, Ah goes lookin' fo' him. People say he gone west. Miz Felicity tell me she tell Miz Charlotte an' give me dis fo' you. Tell me ta go home fast as Ah kin. So Ah's here." He stopped his narrative to gulp down the tea once more.

Ellie opened the letter from her aunt. The letter informed her that her uncle Walker would start looking for a new overseer and that he'd come if she needed him. They were not telling Charlotte about it.

She looked up at the expectant face. "Thank you, Nathaniel. Lottie will give you something to eat. You must be hungry." Ellie went inside and sat at her father's desk. Any doubts she had about Mister Barton were gone. She was relieved that she no longer had to get rid of him herself, but angry that he had stolen from her and her family. She'd been counting on that money. She now needed to sell the ten horses left on her list.

CHAPTER 9

The next morning, Ellie went to the barn and told Joey to saddle up a horse while she got out the tack for Princess. They'd been out the day before, but Joey didn't ask any questions. Ellie led the way down the drive; she needed to get the word out that she had ten saddle horses for sale. She felt the general store was a good place to start.

Ellie dismounted in front of the store and handed Princess' rein to Joey. She started up the steps, and then turned around, "Joey, you had better dismount and just hold the horses." She didn't like to remind him of his status, but she couldn't afford any unnecessary problems.

"Miss Peters, it is so good to see you. It has been a long time." Lucas Franks was a middle aged, balding man with a growing paunch and warm smile.

"Yes, it has been, Mr. Franks," Ellie responded, smiling up at the man she had known all her life.

"How are Mrs. Peters and your little sister?" he enquired pleasantly.

"They are stronger than even they know, Mr. Franks. Thank you for asking." Ellie was not going to let anyone know that she was alone with the slaves on the farm.

"How may I help you today?" he asked, ushering her into his store.

"I have a few things to pick up, but I also wanted to post a list of horses we have for sale," Ellie explained, pulling the list from her reticule.

"Where is Mr. Barton?" Mr. Franks was surprised that a daughter of the family would be performing a business task.

"Mr. Barton is tending a sick foal, Mr. Franks. I wanted to come and pick out a few things. May I post the list?" She smiled at the shopkeeper and waved the list at him.

"I will do that for you, Miss Peters," he offered, reaching out for the paper.

"Thank you, Mr. Franks." Ellie handed over the list of horses and their descriptions and asking prices.

"Did you hear that the Elton girl got married? Her young captain got leave last month and they got married in the church. Mrs. Franks went to the service. She said Molly Elton looked quite the picture. Of course, her new husband had to leave two days later. He was headed back to Richmond. Miss Elton, or I should say, the new Mrs. Harper plans to join her husband in Richmond as long as it is still safe to travel. Oh, that reminds me, Miss Peters. You need to take care traveling about the county. There are rumors of Yankee scouts roaming about the countryside. And you know that not all our Southern soldiers are gentlemen, sad to say," the shop owner warned her.

"Thank you for your advice, Mr. Franks. I shall take care not to go about unescorted in the future." She smiled up at him, appreciating his concern for her safety.

"Oh, Miss Peters. Uh...there is one other thing I need to mention. I hesitate to bring it up, but no one has made any payment on your family's account since

January when your late father was here." Mr. Franks looked uncomfortable in having to bring up such a subject to a lady.

"I am so sorry, Mr. Franks. I had no idea. Mr. Barton did not mention it. I will have to pay you the next time I come to town. I did not bring any money with me this trip. I hope that will not be too inconvenient for you," she asked, looking up with mournful eyes. The storeowner looked at her sad face and nodded his acceptance of the situation, but handed her a statement of the account.

Ellie stood on the mounting steps and slipped onto the sidesaddle. She felt unsettled as she and Joey trotted off toward Whispering Oaks. She decided she had better clean the guns her father had given her, check the amount of ammunition and practice handling them. She only hoped she remembered how to do it all; it had been years since her father had shown her or she had actually handled them. Before he left for the war, he had shown her where they were. At the time, she hadn't thought she would need to know. He'd told her it might be necessary to arm some of the slaves, but to choose carefully. She also considered her father's words about hiding the family silver and her ring. She hadn't been willing to take off the engagement ring that Ted had given her. She still didn't feel she was ready.

She hoped that Mr. Franks was overreacting, but decided to clean two of the pistols right away. She left one loaded in her father's desk and the other she took up to her bedroom. She went to her mother's room to see if she had left any jewelry behind. There was a pearl and ruby broach, a cameo pendent, an emerald ring, and her father's gold pocket watch. She held the watch to her heart. Her eyes filled with tears as she thought of how much she missed him. She missed his guidance, and then smiled, realizing that his words would always be with her. She never would have been going through her parents' room this way if it hadn't been for him. She continued searching her father's things. His dress boots were stuffed with socks. She was about to put them back in place, but stopped, questioning why he would have had his man put so many pairs of socks in one pair of boots. She began empting them. The sock in the toe of the left boot held coins. She dumped them on the floor and counted out three hundred dollars in gold coins. She put the empty socks back and pocketed the money for hiding later.

She then headed to Suzanne's room. She found nothing of value. The only thing left in the room was her sister's winter clothing. She then entered her brother's room at the other end of the hall. When she opened his armoire; she started laughing. She had not realized how much clothing James had. It was packed solid. The laughter stopped as quickly as it started when the thought struck her that he'd never wear any of them again. She found nothing else she needed to hide. She returned to her room and put her father's money in her dresser. She decided she would hide it later outside of the house.

Ellie joined the slaves on the porch. They had already begun their lessons. She was disappointed to see that Nathaniel was not among them. They seemed to be doing well without her. She went in search of Nathaniel. She hardly knew the man, yet he had exhausted himself to bring her word of Philip Barton's theft when he could have just run away. She knew he worked with the horses and, as all the able-bodied slaves did, the hay and corn fields during planting and harvest. She found him in the tack room cleaning harnesses.

"Nathaniel, I wanted to thank you for coming back with the news of Mr. Barton. In all the excitement the other day, I do not believe I thanked you." She smiled warmly at the man.

"Ah's jist' doin' mah job, Miz Ellie." He blushed at her attention.

"Why did you come back?" she asked him bluntly.

The man looked surprised by her question. "Ah belongs here."

"With the war going on, not everyone thinks that way anymore," Ellie explained.

"Ah has a wife an' chillens here. Mama Noli, she mah grandmama. Ah couldn't never leave her," he explained to her.

"Nathaniel, with Mr. Barton gone, I will need your help." Ellie was unsure how much to tell him, but she had to trust someone. "My uncle may not be able to find another overseer for a long time and I am not sure how I feel about a stranger coming here."

Nathaniel drew himself up to stand as tall as he could, puffing out his chest some as well. "What ya want me ta do? Ah'll hep. Ya been good ta mah little Lily an' Mama Noli."

"I need for you to be my eyes and ears. I need for you to direct the harvests when it is time." She waited to see his reaction to this offer of greater responsibility.

Nathaniel was quiet for a minute. "Miz Ellie, three mo' slaves left since dey foun' out Mista Barton not here no more."

"Thank you for telling me." She sighed. "I also need for you to learn more numbers and to read."

"Miz Ellie, Ah's too ol' fo' dat." He made a face that expressed the impossibility of her request.

"You are never too old to learn," she told him, shaking her head at him.

"Yes, Miz Ellie." The large black man hung his head as if he had been castigated, showing his submission to her will.

As Ellie walked back to the house, she wondered how long it would take her people to say "no" once they had their freedom. She was hopeful that the Confederate States would win the war to leave the Union. However, she continued to also believe that slavery would end. She hated that her family owned these people. She would not try to stop anyone from running away, but she had to admit she hoped enough of them would stay to help her run the place. Once the war was over, she would try to talk Charlotte into rewarding them with freedom and offering them employment.

It had only been three days since she'd posted the list of horses for sale, when four Confederate soldiers came to the farm in a wagon. Ellie was walking from the barn where they approached her.

"May I help you gentlemen?" she asked politely, smiling at them.

"We're looking for the overseer, a Mr. Barton, Miss," the sergeant stated, tucking his gloves into his belt.

"I am Miss Peters. Any business you have with Mr. Barton, I can handle. He is out in the back pasture." She tried to make her voice sound steady and to look competent.

"We'll wait, Miss," the sergeant stated, signaling his men to climb off of the wagon

"Are you here about buying horses?" she demanded.

"Yes, Miss," he responded with a sigh.

"Any horses sold here, I will need to approve." Ellie pursed her lips and crossed her arms, trying to look stern. "What type of horses are you looking for and how many?" she demanded.

"Our captain sent us to buy two saddle horses, Miss," the man explained, giving in to her assertiveness.

"If you will follow me?" Ellie turned back toward the barn.

As she walked ahead, she overheard one of the soldiers comment to the others, "I'd follow that one anywheres." The others tried stifling their laughter.

"Joey, get the bay mare and the chestnut gelding out and bring them to the north paddock. Nathaniel, get the grey and roan mares." The men scrambled to complete their mistress' bidding.

"What about that one?" The man pointed to Princess.

"She is not for sale," Ellie stated definitively.

"Our captain would be very pleased with that mare," the sergeant suggested, smiling broadly.

"Your captain…. She is lame. We do not sell any lame horses at Whispering Oaks. We have a reputation to maintain." Ellie felt her heart pounding with fear that someone would challenge her statement.

"Why ain't ya shot her?" the soldier questioned suspiciously.

"She can still carry foals," Ellie replied, trying to think as quickly as possible. She was about to protest as the sergeant began walking toward Princess when the slaves brought in the other horses.

Nathaniel and Joey brought the four horses to the paddock area. Ellie had them long line each one and asked if any of the soldiers would like to mount up. Each looked at the other and Ellie realized that none had much riding experience and did not want to embarrass themselves in front of each other or her. They quickly picked out the bay and roan mares.

Ellie invited the men back to the house and offered them seats on the back porch. She was certainly not going to invite them inside after they had behaved so badly. She called to Peter to bring the men some cooled tea, and then she and the sergeant got down to negotiations for the horses. She let it be known that she was insulted by his first offer of $10 Confederate per horse.

"I am quite willing to do my part for the cause, Sergeant, but I will not allow the cavalry to rob me blind. I can only assume that you believe that I am bad at business because I am a woman. I assure you, I am fully aware of the value of these animals. And, I am also aware of the current value of Blue Backs. Make me a sincere offer or we are finished here." Ellie crossed her arms and glared at the man. His men laughed and complimented Ellie in a rather crude way for her business acumen.

"She got ya there, Sarge! That little lady has some balls on her. She ain't no delicate flower." The men laughed again, leering at Ellie, apparently aroused by her assertiveness. Ellie turned her glare on them and they laughed once more.

"You boys finish your tea and go on down to the barn and wait for me," the sergeant snarled at them. Peter collected the empty glasses and stood watching as the men ambled away from the porch, whispering and nudging each other, looking back at Ellie. He remained at attention while his mistress and the soldier conducted their business. Finally, Ellie accepted an offer, despite the loss she would be taking by accepting the Confederate Blue Backs. She went inside and brought out the bill of sale for the two mares, folding it, and handing it to the sergeant after he had given her the cash. As she watched the men tie the horses behind their wagon and ride away, Ellie felt sullied by having been in their presence.

Peter remarked, "Beggin' yo pardon, Miz Ellie, but dey sho weren't no gentlemen. Ah doan know what ah army is comin' ta wit da lacks a dem in it."

"You are absolutely right about that, Peter. And my father and brother both lost their lives while they live. There is something unutterably unfair in that," Ellie responded, turning to go inside.

"Yes, um. Dere sho is," he added, holding the door for his mistress.

Ellie was angry and upset after the soldiers left. She had been insulted by the way they had looked at her and the comments she had heard. It also concerned her; she had believed that no Southern man would behave in such a manner toward her. She needed to do something to get rid of her anger. She paced from room to room for a half hour, and then went out the front door and walked around the house. Lela was cleaning the chicken pen. Ellie thought, *that's odd,* and then she realized the person who normally did it had run off. When she got to the vegetable garden, she saw it needed weeding. This was Lela's domain. She looked around and saw no one in sight. She directed her anger at the weeds and started pulling. It wasn't long before she was dripping wet from the noonday sun. She kept weeding.

That night, when she removed her black mourning dress, she realized that the black dye had bled out all over her and her underclothing. Mattie exclaimed at the damage that had been done to Ellie's linens, complaining that they were no longer even fit to give to the slaves. Sighing, Ellie told her to take the clothing and to prepare a bath for her. She would have to try to scrub off some of the color. Ellie wrapped herself in her robe and went down to the laundry room. Mattie had water heating on the stove. She helped Ellie pin her hair on top of her head, and then poured cool water into the tub and added hot water to it. Ellie sat in the tub and began rubbing the soap over her tinted skin. Mattie picked up a scrub brush and took the soap. She began scrubbing Ellie's back. Ellie was startled when Mattie began laughing.

"What is so funny? I see little to laugh at in this situation," Ellie said with disgust, wincing as Mattie scrubbed harder.

"Ah'm sorry, Miz Ellie. Ah was jist thinkin' you is mo' black dan any o' yo slaves is." She laughed again. Ellie tried to be angry, but quickly joined in the laughter.

"I have had to scrub off dye before, but this is terrible. I cannot keep doing this. I will have no under things left, and no skin. I believe I will have to give up wearing mourning as long as I have to be outside in this heat working," Ellie sighed, once she had stopped laughing. "I will keep it for going into town or to church."

"Yes, um. Ah think dat would be best," Mattie agreed.

CHAPTER 10

The next day, Ellie cleaned one of the shotguns, took the pistol out of her father's desk, and ammunition for both. She called Peter, handed him the shotgun and the ammunition, and lead the way out of the back of the house. She wanted to practice loading and firing both weapons. She then turned to Peter. "I know you have loaded the guns for my father. Have you ever shot one?"

"No! Miz Ellie, ya know dat's not sumpin' Ah kin't do." Peter looked appalled at the idea.

"Peter, you may have to protect the house." She handed the loaded pistol to him. "Look where you want the bullet to go and point it. Go ahead."

"Are ya sure, Miz Ellie? We could get in trouble." He gingerly took the weapon, looking at it with some trepidation.

"If you do not learn to use them, the trouble could be much worse." She patted him on the shoulder encouragingly.

Peter fired at a nearby tree branch and hit it twice after reloading both guns a number of times. They went back into the house and together replaced the two weapons in John's study. She retrieved another pistol and brought it to the barn. She was relieved that Joey was out checking the fences and that Old Joe and Nathaniel were the only people in the barn. She wanted to show Nathaniel how to clean, load, and fire the pistol. He was more reluctant than Peter. However, with Old Joe's encouragement, Nathaniel followed Ellie's directions. After he loaded and fired the pistol twice, he reloaded it again. The three of them found a safe place for it in the tack room. Ellie informed them that Peter was the only other one trained with the guns and that he had access to some in the house. Before going back to the house, she told Nathaniel that she needed the wagon hitched up in the morning, that she wanted him to accompany her to the general store. Ellie did not like owing money and she wanted to spend the Blue Backs while they were of some value.

Ellie wrapped the pistol she'd hidden in her bedroom in cloth and took it with her along with the Blue Backs when she went down to the barn the next morning. She put the weapon on the floorboard under her feet. Nathaniel noticed, but said nothing.

"Good morning, Mr. Franks," she called as she stepped down from the wagon.

"Good day to you, Miss Peters. How can I help you today?" he asked, wiping his hands on his apron.

"I have a list of supplies that I would like to stock up on. Also, I need to scratch off two of the horses on the list I gave to you," she stated, opening her reticule and pulling out her list of needed supplies.

"Did Mr. Barton sell them, Miss Peters?" he asked hopefully.

"Yes, he did." Ellie could see the look of relief on his face. He expected that he would be paid. She smiled to herself, thinking how she must remind him of his patriotism so that he would not be reluctant to accept the Confederate money. "It was an honor to provide horses to our fighting men. We must support our new country in any way we can."

"You have given so much already, Miss Peters. It is good to hear you have not become discouraged. Now, let me see your list." Mr. Franks sent his slave boy out to help Nathaniel load up the wagon with bags of flour, a barrel of molasses, boxes of ammunition, a pound of sugar, several salt licks, and a box of salt. Mr. Franks added these items to the previous bill. She counted out the money in Confederate currency. She pretended not to notice the look of disappointment on his face. She was glad that she had reminded him of his patriotism and dedication to the Confederacy. Mr. Franks walked Ellie out to the wagon and offered his hand, assisting her into the vehicle. "Be careful, Miss Peters. There are more rumors of Yankees in the area. I do not know how true they are, but to be quite honest I am surprised we have not seen any of them already. They have had control of Port Royal Sound for months now."

"Thank you. I will. Good day, Mr. Franks." She nodded to Nathaniel and he started up the horses.

CHAPTER 11

It was the twenty-ninth of May, 1862. Ellie and Joey had been out riding, checking the upper fields and horses in the back pastures. It was already hot as the two rode back to the barn, even though it was only mid-morning when they unsaddled their mounts. A booming echoed in the distance. A rapid, intermittent cracking noise made it quickly apparent that it was not thunder, but the sounds of war. Princess pranced nervously in place, rolling her eyes in fear. The other horses also became anxious and restless.

The teenaged slave moved closer to his mistress, staring through the open barn door. "Miz Ellie, what we gonna do?" Joey was obviously frightened.

Ellie did not know what to answer. Her first thoughts were for the horses. She did not know if they would be safer in the barns or out in the fields. She thought of the woods and considered hiding the herd there, but she had to protect her people. She heard cries of fear coming from all directions. It was probably too late to get the animals into the woods without risking the lives of the slaves. She couldn't tell how far away the battle was and had no any way of knowing what direction they were heading.

"Miz Ellie?" Joey called to her again, looking for some direction.

"Get Old Joe and Nathaniel in here and anyone else good with the horses. Stay inside. I will send everyone else to the house." She ran out of the barn yelling, "Everyone go to the house."

She ran to the house, grabbed the pistol from her father's desk and ran back to the barn with it. She handed it to Old Joe. "You can reload for Nathaniel if he needs it."

Ellie ran back to the house. It was rapidly filling with nervous slaves milling about uncomfortably in their mistress' house, but more afraid of what might be happening outside. Out of breath, she called Peter and told him to clean the other hunting rifle while she got the pistol from upstairs. She came back down and counted heads. "Where is Mama Noli?"

Lela spoke up. "She refuse ta leave her cabin. She say no one gonna bother wit da lacks o' her."

Ellie started mumbling and pacing. She stopped, "Peter, go get her."

He returned alone ten minutes later. "She say if dey kill her, she gonna die in her own home." He shrugged.

Ellie prayed the old woman would at least stay inside. She and Peter watched the drive for any sign of movement from behind the curtains, each holding a loaded rifle. Several of the women were huddled with the children in a corner, trying to keep them quiet and calm. Lottie was too big and too old to sit on the floor, but she had turned one of the settees around close to a wall so that she could sit on it and be partially hidden. The male slaves who weren't armed sought weapons of any type they could use. Pots, pans, and knives from the kitchen were passed out among them and they took up posts at the windows and doors. Two of the younger women were kneeling and praying out loud that God would save them from the Yankees who were coming to kill them. Hearing their words, Ellie couldn't help adding a silent "Amen" to their prayer.

The silence fell shortly after one in the afternoon. However, the tension did not ease. They did not know where the fighting had been or if either army might be heading in their direction. Ellie did not know what to expect. She feared the Yankees would kill, loot, and burn. Yet, after the contact she'd had with the Confederate rank and file, she was not sure how much better they'd be. She remembered her father's warning to hide most valuables, but leave something for them to plunder.

"It seems to be over for now." She opened the front door, implying they should leave the house. "If any of you hear anything or see anyone, come quickly to tell me."

After everyone left, with the exception of the household staff, Ellie slumped down on the settee, still holding the rifle. "Peter, Lottie, Mattie, we need to hide most of this." She indicated the silver sets on the sideboard.

"Where we ta put it, Miz Ellie?" Peter asked, picking up several pieces.

"Mattie, remember the box of big books in the attic?" Ellie spoke decisively.

"Yes, Miz Ellie." Mattie waited for more instruction.

"Take that tea set, put it in the bottom of the box, and cover it up with as many books as will fit. You can bring the leftover books down here." Ellie rose from the settee and moved to the sideboard.

She then turned to Lottie, "Hide those in the cellar." She pointed to a set of silver goblets on a silver tray.

"Peter, would you gather half of the silverware? I will meet you at the front door." She handed him the rifle and walked slowly up the stairs.

Ellie retrieved the gold coins she had found in her father's boots. She had more money, but her father had obviously meant this to be kept for an emergency. She had to hide it out of the house. Ellie pushed the heavy pistol deep into her skirt pocket, and then shoved the bag of coins into the other pocket. She went back downstairs and met Peter at the front door. "Let's find a place in the barn to hide it."

Peter carried the silverware on a silver tray as if he were about to serve honored guests. Ellie tried not to snicker as she led the way to the barn. She wondered if he'd ever been inside of it. She couldn't remember such an occurrence. She almost laughed aloud at the incongruity of the formally attired slave, carrying himself like a haughty duke, hiding the family silverware from two armies in a barn. Collecting herself, she called for Nathaniel and instructed him to remove one of the lowest boards in the stallion's stall while she held the animal. They wrapped the silver in burlap, put it into the wall, and then nailed the board back in place.

After dismissing Peter, Ellie picked out five mares with nursing foals. Having gathered extra ropes, she and Joey led Princess and the mares out behind the house and down the path leading to the shelter that had been built in the woods to assist runaway slaves. The foals trotted behind their dams. They tied the ropes to trees, while they set up a temporary paddock. Ellie entered the shelter; while Joey continued to work on the ropes, she dug out some of the hard packed mud in one of the corners. She started to place the bag of coins in, but stopped and removed the engagement ring Ted had given her, adding it to the bag, then covered the bag with mud. She realized the shelter would be a good place to keep more supplies. She had never expected to use the hiding place for animals when she had helped build it to shelter runaway slaves on their long journey north. As she and Joey walked back, she asked him to bring some hay out and put it in the shelter.

Just as they arrived at the rear of the house, the booming began again. Ellie heard women's screams and children crying. She took Joey's hand and ran up the back steps of the house, pulling him along. It was late in the afternoon and many of the slaves had already been gathering on the front porch. They came scurrying into the house. Peter handed her one of the rifles and she took up her position at the window behind the curtain. Time passed slowly; the perspiration dripped off her forehead, puddling in her eyes and blurring her vision. Ellie pulled her skirt up to mop away the moisture while she continued to survey the farm.

Lottie came into the front room with food and drinks, supplying the terrified women and children with some comfort. The distressed slaves settled into numbed groups, sitting silently, some of the women rocking their babies to try to quiet them. The sounds of cannon fire and gunshots continued into the evening. During the night, the gunfire became more sporadic. Ellie had identified the sounds as coming from north of the farm and seemed to be moving toward the east. By morning, the rumbling was far in the distance. At last there was silence.

No one had slept much through the night. Ellie took the rifle with her to the kitchen; Lottie, Lela, and Mattie followed. Ellie silently started cutting slices of bread. Lottie fired up the stove for coffee, and Lela and Mattie started to help with the preparations. Ellie spread jam on the bread and carried the slices on a plate to the front room, offering it to the children first. She told everyone to eat and that, other than feeding the animals, everyone was to take the day off and rest. Lela and Mattie began bringing in coffee and more bread with butter and jam. As they started to leave, Ellie stopped Lily, gave her a cup of coffee with cream and sugar, and wrapped some bread with jam in a linen napkin. She instructed the child to take it to Mama Noli. She fixed another tray and asked Lela to help her. They carried the food to the men in the barn. Before returning to the house, she pulled Joey aside. "Please check Princess, and bring some hay and sweet feed to the horses in the woods."

"But, Miz Ellie..." The fear was evident in his voice.

"It is safe now. Just cover your tracks on the way back." She gave him a gentle shove to start him on his way. The young man sighed and nodded.

Back at the house, Ellie doused her face with water and stretched out on the couch with the rifle on the floor by her side. She slept fitfully in the day's heat. At the sound of a door slamming, she jumped up, reaching for the rifle. When she realized what it had been, she berated herself.

Ellie dragged herself into her father's study and sat at his desk. She understood it was up to her to set an example and hold the farm together. She hoped she would not lose too many more slaves. She needed the manpower to keep things going. Sitting in her father's chair she recognized was an attempt to attain his wisdom. She was aware that she needed to appear as if she knew what she was doing and to make everyone believe they were safer on the farm, even if she didn't feel safe herself.

CHAPTER 12

The next morning, Ellie decided she needed to act as if everything was back to normal, regardless of how nervous and scared she actually felt. She ate lightly and went to the barn where she gathered up more ropes, filled the wheelbarrow with sweet feed and hay, placed a salt lick on top, and then headed out to the woods. They hadn't left much water and the trough was dry. Ellie had been concerned about this and planned to expand the roped area to include a small nearby stream. She broke up the wheel tracks as she pushed the wheelbarrow back to the barn. Finally, she sat on the front porch rubbing her arms, attempting to message sore muscles, ones she hadn't even known she'd had. Peter appeared with a glass of tea on a tray.

"Miz Ellie, ya shouldn't be goin' out inta da woods by yo sef," he reprimanded her.

"I took a pistol with me," she responded, drinking deeply of the refreshing tea.

"It ain't propa. What would Miz Charlotte say?" he asked sternly.

"She is not here to say. If you are so concerned, Peter, you can feed the horses." She was too tired to put up with his elevated sense of propriety and prejudices.

"Ah don't know nothin' 'bout hosses. Ah works inside, Miz Ellie. Ya knows dat." His dignity was definitely wounded.

Ellie started laughing. She looked at the dirt on her own hands and arms. She could only imagine what her face looked like. Yet, standing before her was this black man, dressed so elegantly, holding a silver tray.

Peter smiled tentatively, unsure why his mistress was laughing. He did not recognize the irony of the situation.

She stopped laughing as suddenly as she started. "Peter, get a rifle and stay hidden." She stood and strained to make out who was riding slowly down the drive. The horse seemed to be meandering. As it neared, she could see a rider was on it. "A blue coat," she mumbled.

"It's a Yankee. Oh Lord, it's a Yankee, Miz Ellie." Peter stood rooted to the spot, his eyes wide with terror.

"Do not just stand there. Get the rifle!" She pushed him toward the door.

Ellie watched as the horse continued slowly down the drive toward the house. She could see the rider slumped in the saddle and that the horse was not being directed. She held the pistol tightly, hiding it behind her back as she swallowed her fear and walked down the steps. The horse sniffed the air, and then made a sudden turn and trotted toward the barn. As the horse jerked right, the rider fell off to the left, being dragged with his left foot stuck in the stirrup. Seeing the man not respond as he bounced on the ground, she forgot momentarily that he was the enemy. "Joey, stop that horse!"

She walked quietly up from behind, not wanting to startle the animal. Joey cautiously approached from the front until he could snatch the reins. Ellie shoved the pistol into her waistband and unhooked the rider's foot from the stirrup. Her hands were covered in his blood.

"Oh, good lord all mighty!" she exclaimed, looking at the dark stains on her hands. "Joey, wash the animal down. Check carefully, make sure none of this blood is from him, and then feed him. The poor thing looks as though he is starving." She shook her head, mumbling, "With all this spring grass, there is no good reason for any horse to go hungry, even the enemy's."

Peter came up behind her. He had been watching from the safety of the house. He held the rifle out before him, ready to shoot if the man made any sudden moves. Ellie pushed the barrel aside. "He is not about to harm anyone, Peter. He seems to be unconscious. Now, what are we going to do with him?"

"Miz Ellie, we got ta git sumun here from da army. Dey need ta come git him. We cain't watch no Yankee," Peter lectured, prodding the unconscious man with his foot.

"Right now I am not going to send any of you men away from the farm looking for help. If the Yankees are around us, you could be captured. We have no idea where the Southern troops are. We will have to keep him locked up until we know what is happening out there. But where can we put him? He is going to need some attention for his injuries. I cannot have him out in the woods. There is no way to lock him in out there and it is too far away to keep an eye on him. I have no men to spare to set a guard on him." Ellie chewed her lip trying to think of a place that would be safe. She ruled out the barn. There were no empty tack rooms there, and he might escape from an empty stall. Finally, she got an idea.

"Peter, go down to the barn. Tell Nathaniel and Old Joe to bring a ladder and some old horse blankets up here. We will use it as a stretcher to carry him to that slave cabin near the barn. No one is living there now. We can nail the windows closed, just enough so that he cannot climb out, but air can get in. We can put a lock on the door to keep him safely inside. There is a bed and table there already, so we will not have to furnish it." She looked at the butler who continued to stand staring at the enemy soldier.

"Do not just stand there gawking, Peter! Get moving before he comes to." She grabbed his arm and tugged to get him moving, and then turned toward the house, calling to Lela to bring towels, soap, water, and bandages. Ellie stood over the unconscious body, wondering what had brought him to their doorstep.

The men arrived with the ladder and dragged the soldier onto it. Ellie directed them into the cabin while she waited outside, pacing and trying to think. *He is the enemy. If I leave him locked up, he will probably die, if not from blood loss, from the heat and infection. He is no threat. But he is a Yankee. They killed my father, my brother, Ted, all the men. I should let him rot. Damn! Then I would be no better than a Yankee.* She sighed and walked back to the cabin. Nathaniel was keeping watch. She opened the door to find the man crumpled on the floor. The slaves had not even bothered to put him up on the wooden pallet that was attached to the far wall. She pulled off his right boot and when she started working on the left one he moaned. As she yanked it off, he cried out in pain without regaining consciousness.

Lela arrived first with the soap, towels, bandages, and water. She shook her head. "He doan look so good." The slaves helped her get him off the floor onto the crude bed, and then Nathaniel silently backed out of the cabin. Without a word, the women worked, stripping him of his clothes, and washing away the dried and oozing blood. The source became apparent. A bullet had torn into the muscle of his left thigh and infection had set in around the wound. As they examined the leg, they realized the bullet was still in him. Ellie left Lela to finish cleaning him while she went to the house for more supplies.

As she gathered the linens, sewing box, scissors, knife, and whiskey, she thought of the last time she and Lela had tended to a wounded man. It had been dangerous and they'd had to hide what they were doing. This time, she did not have to hide her actions, but the consequences could be even graver.

Nathaniel was still sitting in front of the cabin with a pistol by his side. She sent him for more water and some witch hazel. Lela had finished bathing the soldier. They sat him up and poured some whiskey in his mouth. He coughed and choked, but seemed to get most of it down. They then went to work on his leg. Ellie realized as she dug the bullet out that the bone had been broken too. Once they'd finished with the wound, Ellie sat with the man while Lela went to the barn to get wood to splint the leg. With the work done, she suddenly felt herself blushing as she realized she was sitting with a completely naked man, and that she had seen more of his body than she'd ever seen of any man, even Ted. She was relieved when Lela returned and they could go back to working on him. Hot, tired, and hungry, she returned to the house while Nathaniel hammered the lock into place on the outside of the cabin.

Mattie stripped the blood stained, dirty clothing off Ellie's body. She had already drawn a bath. Ellie slipped into the cool water, sinking down, wetting her hair. She wanted to soak off every morsel of the stench she felt covered her. However, Mattie did not leave her time to relax. She came in, mumbling about the condition of her clothes and the dirt under her nails. Ellie wondered if either of them would ever get used to the rigors of this war. Her mind slipped back to the man in the shed. *Had he killed any good Confederate men? Am I doing the right thing trying to save him? When will his mother get the news her son is missing?* She wondered, *Does he have a sister, too? A wife?* She didn't even know his name, but she had seen him naked. If she were to continue to nurse him, she'd have to do something about that, too.

After she finished eating, she turned to Lottie. "The Yankee has lost a lot of blood. I suppose we have to feed him. Would you fix him a tray?"

"Ya want me ta feed dat man?" She was incredulous that Ellie would direct an old lady to go near a dangerous man.

"No, Lottie. I will take it to him." She went up the back stairs and down the hall to her brother's room. She went through his dresser drawers until she found a light cotton nightshirt. She pushed away the fleeting thought that this man could have been her brother's murderer. She put a pillow under her arm and took some sheets. By the time she went back downstairs, Lottie had a tray ready. She called Peter to help her. She could tell by the expression on his face that he did not like caring for the man, even if one of the reasons Yankees were invading was to free men like Peter.

The place looked as if the slave who had previously occupied it had never bothered to clean it. The torn, bloody, blue uniform was still lying in a heap on the floor. There was a small, rickety, wooden table in the cabin. Peter put the tray on it. Lela had spread a towel over the man before they had left. Seeing his condition, Peter let down his guard and struggled to put the nightshirt on the man, not wanting his mistress to be exposed to such a sight. At times, he still thought of Ellie as the little girl that his master had expected him to watch out for. John Peters had been good to him, as far as masters went, and he felt a responsibility toward his daughter. Ellie fiddled with the tray, pretending to be busy in order to keep her back to the man while Peter dressed him.

Together, the two rolled him back and forth in order to get a sheet under him on the pallet. Ellie covered him with the second sheet. As she slipped the pillow under his head, Peter asked, "Do I have ta feed him, too?"

"No, Peter. That will be all. Thank you. I know you do not want him here. Take that uniform with you and burn it. We do not need anyone discovering a Yankee uniform," she ordered, waving at the pile of clothing on the floor.

Peter picked it up, holding it out as if he might be contaminated by it. Ellie wiped clean the only chair, and then set it next to the pallet. She picked up the bowl, a spoon, and napkin off the tray. She sat and stirred the contents; she wasn't sure what was in the broth, but trusted Lottie's cooking and judgment. She gently shook the man's shoulder. "You have to eat something, sir."

He moaned in response. She shook him some more. He mumbled something, but she could not make it out. "You do not have to talk, but you do have to eat." She pushed a small spoonful into his mouth. Without opening his eyes, he woke enough to eat half the bowl before reaching up and pushing her hand away. The effort seemed to exhaust him and he drifted back to sleep. She put the bowl back on the tray, and then sat back down on the chair. She didn't know what she expected of him, but she sat staring at him. He was the first young, white man she had seen in months. He had a sharp narrow nose, high cheekbones, and the longest eyelashes she'd ever seen on a man. She wondered what color his eyes were. His hair was thick, medium brown with light highlights. Ellie shook her head; what was she thinking? She giggled, embarrassed. She dragged the table over next to the pallet, left a glass, pitcher of water, and the bottle of whiskey where he could reach it should he wake, picked up the tray and left, latching the door from the outside.

She brought the tray back to the kitchen. "Don't Yankees know good food?" Lottie demanded, seeing that he had not finished her soup.

"He did not really wake up." Ellie laughed when she saw the insulted look on Lottie's face.

The next morning, Ellie ate, and then took a tray down to her patient. She reminded herself that he was also a prisoner and that President Davis had made it clear that all prisoners were to be treated properly. Some Southerners had been complaining that the Yankee prisoners were actually served better food than the Confederate soldiers. She did not know if that was true, but she was determined to show this Northerner that, for all the horrors of slavery, Southerners were moral, God-fearing people.

She unlocked the door, knocked, and entered without waiting for a response. The man was sleeping fitfully; beads of perspiration covered his face. It was still early morning. She set down the tray and touched his forehead. He was burning up with fever. She tried waking him, but he did not seem aware of her presence. She doubted that she would get much food into him. She attempted to get him to drink. She ended up pouring more water on him than he swallowed. Frustrated, she put down the glass and moved back the sheet, thinking to check the bandage. As she did, she nearly gagged at the smell coming from the wound. It explained the fever. She knew how to treat this type of infection. She thought, *It is better that he has not fully wakened.* She used the pump near the barn, refilling the bucket and pitcher. Joey attempted to take the bucket, but she refused his offer, sending him in search of Lela.

Lela arrived to find her swabbing the young man's face with fresh water. "Miz Ellie, ya want me?"

Ellie and Lela grew up together and could hide very little from each other. "I interrupted your work. I am sorry."

"Ah was collectin' eggs. Wit everbody leavin', Ah gots lots ta do. Ah got da chickens, da hogs, an' mah garden." Lela ticked off her chores on her fingers, wanting Ellie to appreciate how hard she was already working.

"I know. You have been doing so much, and now here I am asking you to help me with this Yankee." Ellie looked at the other woman with sympathy and apology.

Mollified, Lela peered at their patient. "He's lookin' worse."

"The wound is infected." Ellie hesitated. "Lela, I know you will help me if I ask, but I also know you are doing the work of three people already."

"Dat Ah is!" she agreed.

"I will weed the garden, water it if it gets dry, and pick the bugs, even if you will not, but will you help me tend him?" Ellie was pleading with her slave.

"Why ya do dat?" Lela screwed her face up in an expression of surprise and confusion.

"I do not want you leaving, too." As she said it, the emotions welled up. For the first time, she realized how very important Lela was to her. Softly, she added, "You are my friend."

Lela was not sure how to react. When they were little children, they had played together. However, once Ellie had started school, it became apparent to Lela that her childhood friend was the daughter of her owner. Yet, Ellie had taught her to read and helped her with escaped slaves. She understood that their relationship was complicated. Finally, she responded, "Ah'll go git more linen."

Together, the two women cleaned, packed with a drawing poultice, and re-dressed the wound. They took turns, one holding him in a semi-sitting position while the other forced broth or water into him. They bathed him and changed his nightshirt. For two days, he still did not come to full consciousness even when he cried out or moaned. During that time, Ellie had worked in the garden and scrubbed the prisoner's cabin. There had been no more sounds of warfare.

Lela and Ellie had gone through their morning ritual and Ellie had worked in the garden. The day seemed especially hot and humid. She bathed and changed into clean clothes before lunch. After eating, she took a tray down to the cabin. She noticed that he seemed to be sleeping peacefully. She sat by his pallet, reluctant to disturb him. The work and heat had tired her; she closed her eyes, thinking to relax for just a minute, listening to the rhythm of his breathing. She started when she heard him move. She opened her eyes to return the stare of his intense green eyes. She blushed, but couldn't look away from his eyes. There was something about them that she couldn't help feel she knew.

"I am sorry if I woke you, ma'am." His voice was soft and gentle.

"I was just resting my eyes." She was annoyed that he had seen her vulnerable and was determined not to allow it to happen again.

"Ma'am, where is Victor?" he asked, politely but with some concern.

"Victor?"

Yes, ma'am. My horse."

"Your horse is fine, no thanks to you. Do you not believe it is important to feed your animals? He was starving when you rode in here."

"I raised that horse, but they have been pushing us and he did not seem to be doing well in this God awful heat," the man explained.

"Our horses do fine in this heat. You should take better care of him." Ellie pursed her lips in disapproval and tugged at the sheet to remove a crease.

He smiled at her ire, "Do you care as much about your slaves as you do about my horse?"

"I know what you all think; I have read your newspapers." She was about to lecture him about something she did not believe in herself, but stopped. "Do you think you can feed yourself?"

He started to try to pull himself up into a sitting position, but the pain and weakness stopped him. He looked down at his leg and noticed for the first time that he was in a nightshirt. "Where did my uniform go?"

"I burned it," she responded with satisfaction.

"Did you also..." He didn't seem able to say more and his pale face brightened with color.

She enjoyed his apparent embarrassment. How different he was from Ted. "Would you have preferred I let you die?"

"No, ma'am." He wiggled in discomfort, trying to find a position where his leg did not hurt.

Ellie rearranged the pillows to elevate him. "You lost a lot of blood and had a fever." She handed him a glass of water, "Drink!"

His hands were shaking and he needed both of them to get the glass to his mouth. She allowed him to struggle with it; however, she decided she had better feed him the soup or it would be all over him. She picked up the bowl and offered a spoonful. He started to reach for the spoon. "Please, let me; your hands are shaking." He looked at his hand and silently acquiesced.

"Thank you, ma'am. I am sorry to be such trouble," he managed to state between mouthfuls of soup.

"You have been no trouble." She hesitated. "Other than coming here and killing our men." She bit her lip and continued to feed him. Toward the end, he was starting to fall back to sleep. She took the tray and silently left, latching the door behind her. She had forgotten to ask his name.

She returned to check on him just before dinner. As she opened the door, she was struck by the heat. She poured more water and woke him to drink it. She left without saying anything as he dozed, leaving the door open behind her. For the moment, she was not worried about her prisoner being able to get very far.

During dinner with the house staff, she brought up the problem. She explained her concerns for the life of their prisoner. When Lottie and Peter objected to the idea of taking care of him, Ellie pointed out that they were civilized, Christian people who did not just let someone, even an enemy, die. Nor was she willing to actively take part in his murder through neglect. She pointed out that bringing him into the house would make it easier for all of them to watch him as well as take care of his physical needs. Ellie added that he was far too weak to be a danger to anyone. They would have to worry more about that when he was healed. She had to admit that bringing him inside the house would place them at a higher risk if Southern troops came. Although she planned on turning him over to the Confederates, she could not put the man's life at risk by handing him over while he was so ill. Ellie pointed out that they would be less likely to find him in the cellar than in the cabin by the barn because soldiers were more likely to go down to the barn than into their cellar. She won them all over when she pointed out that they could more easily lock him into the cellar than in that rickety old cabin that was close to falling down already. It was agreed that he would be moved into the cellar the next day.

Lottie, who had to go to the cellar several times a day to bring up supplies for meals, expressed her fear. She wanted to know more about the man, hoping to hear something that would alleviate her anxiety. She asked if they had found anything on his person that would tell them something about him. Peter stated that they had found the man's Union Army commission papers in his saddlebags. He was

Second Lieutenant Daniel Proctor. They really didn't know anything else about him.

Mattie offered to take the tray down and assist Ellie with his dinner. Laughing, she accepted the offer; she knew it was out of curiosity and not a true desire to be helpful. The two women entered the cabin after knocking; their movements and Mattie's whispers seemed to wake him.

"Marster, we brought ya dinner," Mattie called out to him.

"Please, ma'am. Do not call me master," a deep, yet gentle, male voice responded.

Ellie hid a smile behind her hand at Mattie's confusion. Ellie put out her hand, "I am Eloise Maitland Peters."

"Proctor, Second Lieutenant Daniel Proctor, ma'am." He reached for her hand, grunting with the exertion and the strain on his wound.

"Lieutenant, this is Mattie." Ellie smiled at her maid. "She came to see if Yankees have horns."

"Miz Ellie, doan ya go sayin' dat. Ah knows dey doan have no horns." Mattie was blushing at the teasing she was receiving in front of the stranger.

"I hope Mrs. Peters knows it too, Mattie." His eyes twinkled, yet his voice remained serious.

"She ain't married, Lieutenant," Mattie corrected him innocently.

Ellie blushed.

"Excuse me, please, Miss Peters." He gave her a small bow with his head and smiled.

"You need your strength. It is time that you ate." She sat on the chair next to his bed, while Mattie stood, arms folded, watching and grinning. Ellie wanted to tell her to get out before she said anything more, but was unwilling to have him hear her giving the slave an order. She left him with a pitcher of water and a glass, again latching the door behind her.

"Miz Ellie, ya see dem eyes?" Mattie giggled as they walked back to the house.

"Mattie, he is the enemy!" Ellie tried to sound indignant, but she too had been moved by his eyes.

CHAPTER 13

The next morning, Lela and Ellie cleaned and re-dressed the wound. He did not cry out, but the pain was evident on his face. While still weak, he was able to feed himself with minimal assistance. Ellie informed him that he would be moved, due to the heat, after he was cleaned up.

Peter and Nathaniel entered as the two women left. Once they had washed, shaved, and changed him, they transported him to the house. They entered through the outside cellar door, thus minimizing the number of stairs down which they had to carry him. A mattress and bedding had been set up on one of the old pallets. The room had sufficient light from two small windows and was considerably cooler than the cabin had been. Once he was settled, Ellie appeared with fresh water, an oil lamp, and a box of matches. "I do not know what you are accustomed to; however, Mr. Proctor, we are at war and you are an enemy of South Carolina." Ellie was attempting to stay firm and remind herself. "President Davis demands that all prisoners of war be treated well. When you are well enough to travel, the authorities will be notified of your presence here."

"You do not like me very much, do you, Miss Peters?" he asked, trying to sound disinterested, but sounding a bit wounded by her attitude.

"Mr. Proctor, there is nothing to like about you or to dislike. You are a Yankee; that is all that matters." She spun around and, restraining herself from running, walked up the stairs.

Ellie's prisoner continued to sleep much of the day. Lela and Ellie changed his dressing daily. She'd checked the horses in the woods and rode up to the upper fields with Joey. She had also kept her commitment to Lela and worked in the garden regularly. She had been reluctant to leave the farm, missing church one Sunday; however, she felt she needed to find out what was happening in the rest of the world. She dressed in black, put a pistol in her purse, and had Nathaniel drive her to church. It was difficult to sort out the facts from the rumors, but it was evident that the Yankees had been pushed back to Port Royal Sound and out of the area.

She returned home after services, feeling somewhat relieved. She had been sending Mattie down with Mr. Proctor's lunches, but decided to take it to him herself and share the war news. She told him what she had heard. When she noticed that he had stopped eating and was just staring at her, she stopped. "Did I upset you, Mr. Proctor? I was so pleased by the news; I did not even think how it might affect you."

"You are wearing black. Whom did you lose, Miss Peters?" he asked quietly.

Ellie looked down; she could barely whisper, "My father, my brother, and my fiancé."

"I am terribly sorry. It must be very difficult for you."

Ellie could see his sympathy was genuine. "I wish it could have been for something I believed in; maybe then I would not feel so…" her voice trailed off.

"You do not believe in what, Miss Peters?" He attempted to encourage her to talk; it was the first time that she had shown any emotion other than anger.

"It does not matter now, anyway. They are gone and we are at war. You know that, no matter who wins, none of us will be the same: North or South."

"Do you have any family left?" he asked, hoping to keep her talking a bit longer.

"Oh, yes! My mother and little sister. They are in Savannah. We never stay here during the summer," she expanded.

"Do you usually go to Savannah, too?" He hurried to get a few bites in while she talked so that he would be ready to ask another question when she stopped.

"No, we have...we had a home in Beaufort. But you have taken it over." Once again, she was the angry Southern lady speaking to her prisoner.

"Why are you here and not with them in Savannah?" He was not about to comment on the loss of her Beaufort home.

"Someone has to run the farm." She smiled. "It is a good thing for you, Mr. Proctor, that I am here. If Peter did not kill you himself, he would have turned you over to the first Confederate soldier he could find."

"Why did you stop him?" He was genuinely interested in her answer to this question.

"I do not know... You were wounded; harmless...It just did not seem to be the right thing to do." Ellie felt confused by his question. She really wasn't certain why she had hesitated, despite what she had said at the time about the Yankees being in the area.

"I thank you, whatever your reason, Miss Peters. The wound seems to be healing well and I am starting to feel stronger." He shifted his position in the bed, lifting his leg slightly trying to show that such movement no longer hurt him.

"I hope your bone heals as well," she offered, trying to be humane.

He nodded in agreement. "Miss Peters, I vaguely remember you chastising me for the treatment of my horse. Has he recovered as well?"

"A little grain, hay, water, and rest were all that it took. He looks fine now, Mr. Proctor. Of course, he could never meet our expectations." Ellie knew she was bragging a bit, but she was so very proud of their horses.

"Oh, really! And what expectations are those, Miss Peters?" His attitude appeared somewhat haughty.

"At Whispering Oaks, we breed and raise Saddlebreds. We have the best riding horses in the world. They have such wonderful gaits; you could sit in the saddle for hours and never feel as if you left the front porch." Ellie continued for some time talking of the wonders of the breed and the special care her family had made to bring out the best qualities. She was so involved in her passion she did not notice him smiling at her.

When she finally stopped for air, he interjected, "I hope that I will be permitted to see your magnificent horses before you turn me over to the local authorities."

"Do not flatter me, Mr. Proctor." His statement startled her. While she needed to make sales, she wanted to hide the best of her horses.

"It was not intended as flattery, Miss Peters. My family is not in the business of raising horses, but I have come to appreciate a good one."

"What is your family in the business of?" She wanted to change the subject.

"We have a farm in Pennsylvania. We mostly grow wheat, and corn, but we also keep some dairy cows and supply the neighboring town with milk. And of course, we grow the usual vegetables and animals for the family."

The two continued an animated conversation, discussing the farms and the business of running them. The afternoon passed without either being aware of the time until Lottie came clomping down the stairs. "Miz Ellie, ya comin' up fo' supper o' ya stayin' down here all night?"

"I will be right up, Lottie." She laughed at Daniel's expression when he heard the slave speaking in such a manner to her mistress.

"Give me dat tray!" Lottie shot an unfriendly look at the Yankee soldier.

"I will bring it up." Ellie stood up and picked up the tray.

"Miss Peters, thank you for the conversation. Now that I am starting to feel better, the time down here passes slowly." She smiled sadly and left.

CHAPTER 14

At dinner, she was unusually quiet and absorbed little of the chatter. It distressed her that she had enjoyed the afternoon. He had listened to her ideas about the horse business as if he accepted that she might have something of value to say. He did not seem to think it odd that she held her own opinions, and seemed to consider hers when she disagreed with him. She sent his dinner down with Mattie. She delivered breakfast, asked about his reading preferences, and then abruptly excused herself. She selected a couple of books to accompany his lunch. She avoided going down to the cellar for the next couple of days.

She wanted to talk more with him, but he was the enemy. She wanted to talk with someone who treated her as an equal. The slaves viewed her either as a child to protect or someone to appease. Mama Noli was the only one who seemed to recognize her for who she was. It was time for another visit. She raided Lottie's pantry, finding treats for the old lady, and went straight to her cabin.

Mama Noli was sitting on the front porch in the rocking chair that John Peters had given her the previous Christmas. She smiled broadly when she saw Ellie approaching. "Miz Ellie, Ah wish yo daddy was here ta thank agin. Dis chair's givin' me much comfort."

"I miss him terribly, Mama Noli. I miss him and James and Ted." She forced a smile. "Right now, I even miss Suzanne. I guess I am lonely. I just hope Mother will feel better and they will come back well in the fall."

"Ya mama git better, but ya's gonna have ta care fo' her. She never care fo' hersef." The old woman sighed and shook her head.

"Father knew that about mother, too." She smiled at the wisdom of the old woman.

The two spoke openly with one another for some time. As Ellie started to leave, the old woman stopped her. "Miz Ellie, ya got ta git da pris'ner out in da sun. No light bein' in da cella' is gonna' git 'im sick."

"How do I get him up and down?" Ellie asked, waving her hands helplessly.

She laughed. "Ya figure it out. Does ya think he's gonna run away?"

"No, his leg is broken." She shook her head in acknowledgment of that point.

"Are ya 'fraid o' him? Ah heared he's good lookin' fo' a white man." The old woman grinned lasciviously, her toothless pink gums showing.

"Mama Noli!" Ellie blushed at the woman's insinuation.

"Git 'im in da sun." She waved her hand at Ellie as if she was shooing chickens away.

"Yes, ma'am." Ellie walked back to the house thinking, *I am not afraid of him. I am afraid of myself!* She didn't know anyone who had gotten sick from no sunlight. Yet, she remembered Mama Noli telling her about her trip in the bowels of a ship from Africa to America. She could never forget the woman's story. She trusted her experience and judgment.

It was nearly time for the afternoon lessons on the front porch. Ellie handed Peter a set of James' clothes and instructed him to assist Mr. Proctor to dress. Nathaniel had reluctantly been attending. When he showed up at the house, she told him to go to the cellar and help Peter bring the prisoner up to the porch. Ellie smile to herself. Now, she would find out if this Northerner believed what the Northern papers claimed about the South and their Negroes. She was interested in his reactions.

Ellie was busy with two of the youngest children, helping them learn addition, when the men brought Daniel up onto the porch and settled him into a comfortable chair. She nonchalantly maneuvered her position so that she could observe him without him realizing she was doing so. As she watched, Ellie saw Daniel looking at all the eager, dark faces working on different tasks. She saw him shaking his head in disbelief as Lela encouraged one of the adult slaves who had just started learning simple words. He smiled broadly as he took in the sight of the camaraderie of the informal school where those who had learned a skill aided those who were just beginning. A small girl approached Daniel hesitantly and asked him if he could read. When he acknowledged that he could, the little girl drew a book out from behind her and extended it to him. Daniel accepted the book, tucked it in beside him in the chair, and cautiously lifted the child onto his lap, careful not to rest her on his injured leg. Ellie smiled as he pulled the book out and began reading it to the delighted girl. Several of the other little ones joined the pair to listen to the story. Before long, Lottie came out onto the porch with three tall pitchers of cool tea and fruit juices. There was a stack of cups and mugs on a table waiting to be used. Some of the older children were recruited to help distribute the beverages. Two boys were sent to the kitchen to bring out trays of sandwiches and cookies Lottie had prepared for the crowd. One of the children brought Daniel a mug of tea that he sipped gratefully. Ellie leaned back in her chair, smiling smugly. Her Yankee prisoner would have to rethink his beliefs about the South now. She nibbled her cookie with great satisfaction, and then returned to her labors.

"I would like to thank you, Miss Peters, for sending the books. They have helped me pass the time," he told her with some warmth when they had time to chat.

"We have many books in the house, when you are ready for more, Mr. Proctor." Her tone was especially cool.

"I would also like to thank you for having me brought up here today." His smile had shrunk to superficially pleasant in response to her coldness.

"You may thank Mama Noli. She said that you needed sunlight to continue to heal and be healthy." Ellie was playing the grand Southern lady in order to keep Daniel at a distance.

"Is she here to thank?" he enquired pleasantly.

"No, she is not." Ellie offered no further explanation.

"Have I insulted you, Miss Peters?" he asked, uncertain as to what her attitude was caused by.

"No, Mr. Proctor, you have been nearly as polite as any Southern gentleman. I cannot imagine what would give you such an idea." Her tone was sharp. Mattie and Lela exchanged looks of disbelief. He had said none of the things that their mistress usually became angry over with gentlemen.

"I have seen nothing of you since your visit on Sunday, Miss Peters, and now…" he began explaining, only to be interrupted by Ellie.

Ellie stood. "I have a farm to run. I do not have time to entertain Yankees." She turned abruptly and entered the house.

Lottie waddled in after her. "Miz Ellie, what would Miz Charlotte say, hearin' ya talk ta a guest in dis house lack dat? What kine a Southern lady is ya?"

"What would Miz Charlotte say?" Ellie responded, mimicking the older woman. "What would Miss Charlotte say about having a Yankee in her house after they killed her husband and her son? What would she say about teaching slaves to read?"

"Ah doan know what's got inta ya, girl," the old cook responded, hurt by her mistress' mockery.

Ellie drew breath to respond, but held her tongue. Instead, she looked out the door at Daniel sitting peacefully in the late afternoon sun coming onto the porch. "He has had enough sunshine for the day."

The two women had been very loud. Everyone on the porch had stopped talking to listen. Most seemed shocked at their mistress' behavior. Peter shook his head, mumbling, "Dat girl's gonna git us all in trouble." Lela and Mattie made eye contact and started giggling; they understood it, too

CHAPTER 15

Ellie continued to avoid seeing Daniel Proctor. However, she had him carried up every day to the porch during the slaves' lessons. She rationalized that, if he needed sunlight, it would be safest when so many slaves were present and he could be of some use by helping to teach reading and numbers. She sat inside, next to an open window, out of sight, listening. Lottie glared at her, shaking her head in disapproval as she walked by carrying the refreshments.

On the third day, little Lily stuck her head in the window, "Miz Ellie, Mama Noli wanna see ya, right away."

Ellie had been afraid for the old woman's health for many years. She ran out the front door, down the steps, and straight to Mama Noli's cabin. She was sitting in the shade of her porch, rocking. "Mama Noli, what is wrong?"

"Miz Ellie, have ya se'f a seat." The old black woman spoke slowly, indicating the chair next to her. She continued rocking. "Ah does love dis here chair."

"How are you feeling?" Ellie's concern was turning to impatience as she watched the elderly woman.

"Ah is fine," she responded, turning her head toward the younger woman and smiling contentedly.

"Why did you want to see me, Mama Noli? I was afraid you might be ill," Ellie questioned.

"Ah is ol', but dere's a lot a life lef' in dis ol' body." She sighed. "Miz Ellie, ya ain't bein' ya se'f. Ya's not usin' ya head." Mama Noli wrinkled her brow with concern as she looked at her mistress.

"What do you mean?" Ellie asked, very confused by the old slave's words.

"Ya ain't teachin' da lessons; ya's makin' da mens carry dat man up an' down. He's not goin' nowhere! Dat man is da fust one what agree wit ya an' you is 'fraid o' him." She ticked off her points on her gnarled fingers, shaking her head sadly as she did so.

"I am not afraid of him!" Ellie stated emphatically, rising from her seat to challenge the other woman's words. But as she looked into the wise old face, she had to look into her own heart as well. "I…Oh, Mama Noli, I am so confused." She slumped back down onto the chair.

"What ya confused 'bout?" Mama Noli asked gently.

"We are at war and he is the enemy." Ellie shook her head, attempting to cancel out anything that conflicted with that position.

"He a man. We ain't gwan ta be at war fo'ever." She looked sympathetically at Ellie, understanding her pain and her emotional struggle.

Ellie just sighed.

"Ah is here, child, effin' ya needs me," she stated softly, reaching out to touch the young woman on the knee.

Ellie gently patted the old hand. "Thank you, Mama Noli." Ellie stood and walked slowly back to the house. She joined the group on the front porch, sitting next to Joey; she began helping him with his letters. No one dared comment that she had returned, but everyone noticed. When Lottie brought out the afternoon refreshment, everyone stopped their studies and began to socialize. She remained subdued, as she felt his eyes on her from across the porch. She continued to ignore him until the slaves began to disperse, and then approached him.

"Forgive me for not standing, Miss Peters." He cocked his head and the green eyes twinkled above the sarcasm in his voice.

"How is your leg feeling today, Mr. Proctor?" she enquired politely, but as neutrally as she could manage.

"Not bad," he hesitated, "unless I move." He couldn't seem to hide his smile when he looked at her.

Before she could respond, Nathaniel interrupted. "Miz Ellie will ya be needin' me? Ah gots ta feed da hosses soon."

"Yes, Nathaniel." She walked into the house to find Peter and instructed him to help Nathaniel bring Mr. Proctor into the living room.

Peter grumbled. "Ah carries him up an' down. Now, Ah gots ta carry him in an' out."

Ellie smile, "No, you do not have to carry him downstairs anymore."

"Miz Ellie, ya gonna leave him in da house?" He was obviously worried about this turn of events.

"Yes, and you can thank Mama Noli for saving your back." She chose to ignore his concern.

"Miz Ellie, he a trained soldier; what 'bout da guns?" Peter reached out and put his hand on his mistress' arm, something he would never have done except in extreme distress or to physically assist her in some way.

"They are hidden, and right now he is unable to get around by himself." She smiled reassuringly at him, and patted his hand.

Realizing what he had done, Peter pulled back his hand, and then enquired cautiously, "Does Ah got ta guard him?"

Ellie shook her head. "No. We will lock the study at night."

"An' you, Miz Ellie?" he asked, hesitantly.

"I have a gun next to my bed. It will be safe for now, Peter." Ellie was becoming slightly annoyed with her butler and his need for reassurance.

"Ah hopes ya's right," he mumbled, shaking his head

"Bring him in and put him on the couch. We will bring up the bedding after dinner." Ellie went into her father's study, closing the door behind her. She sat curled up in one of the arm chairs as she used to do when her father was still alive. She hoped she was doing the right thing. She had never been around many Yankees. She knew she agreed with them that slavery was wrong, but she did not really understand much more about them. Eventually, he would have to be turned over as a prisoner; she could not just let him go free. She wondered how long it would take for the bone to heal. The bullet wound seemed all healed, but she had no idea about the muscle where she had dug the bullet out.

It bothered her that she found him attractive. She believed it would be wrong to like the enemy. Not wrong, she corrected herself, but dangerous. It could interfere with her better judgment. Maybe, if she got to know him, she would find his flaws and get over the attraction she was feeling. She decided to take a walk and check on Princess; she wanted to get away from everyone and always felt better with the mare.

It was hot and buggy in the woods. All of the horses seemed to be feeling the effects of the insects. She wondered if she should bring them back to the barn. She would talk to Old Joe to find out if he knew any remedies. By the time she returned to the house, Mattie, Lottie, and Peter were frantically looking for her.

As she entered through the back door, Lottie called to her. "Miz Ellie, where ya been? We been worried sick 'bout ya."

"Lottie, there is no reason for you to worry about me. I went to see Princess." Ellie was amazed by their extreme response when she had been gone for such a short time. She wasn't accustomed to having to answer to anyone but her parents about her whereabouts.

"Supper's ready. We been waitin' fo' ya; less ya gonna eat wit dat man." She made the last two word of the sentence sound like an accusation of murder.

"That man has a name, Lottie. Mr. Proctor," she instructed the cook with some asperity.

Lottie humphed as she started ladling out the soup. She handed a bowl to Peter, "Dis is fo' 'Marster Proctor'." Her tone was sarcastic.

Lela and Mattie began teasing Ellie about her decision to move him upstairs to protect Peter's back. Neither believed it. Ellie noticed Peter going back and forth to the living room throughout the meal to attend to the injured man's needs. "Peter, you should be able to eat supper. We need to find an easier way. If only we could move him around more easily."

"Miz Ellie, Ah seen a chair wit wheels in Savannah once," Mattie suggested.

"What a good idea, Mattie. Maybe Old Joe could put something together until Mr. Proctor can use crutches. Joe has always been good at fixing the carts and such." Ellie smiled at such a creative way to deal with the problem.

"How long will dat take fo' him ta use crutches?" Peter asked, apparently feeling insecure once again.

"I do not know," Ellie replied, not wanting to have to reassure him again.

"Ah'll talk ta Ol' Joe tonight 'bout it," Lela volunteered.

Ellie locked her door that night, laughed at herself for doing it, and slept soundly. She came down the back stairs in the morning, ate breakfast in the kitchen, and slipped out the back door. She knew it would be more difficult to avoid him, since they moved him into the living room. A part of her wanted to spend as much time as possible with him, yet she was uncomfortable being near him.

Old Joe excitedly met her when she arrived at the barn. He was proud of his invention. He only needed to know which leg was broken to finish it. By the time

Ellie and Joey had returned from their ride to the upper fields, the job was complete. He had taken two wheels from an old training cart and two smaller ones from a broken wheelbarrow, put the smaller ones onto swivels and the larger ones on an axle, attached them to a plain wooden spindle chair that he reinforced to support the axle, and then added a board to support the splinted left leg.

She invited Old Joe to come up to the house for lunch. Her unusual decision was reinforced by the grin that came over his face. In the past, he would have been given a few coins as a token of appreciation for his extra work, but that was a different time. She still wanted to reward him for his efforts and to give him the opportunity to see his product in use. He walked away mumbling, "Ah gots ta clean up. Ah's goin' ta da big house fo' lunch."

Ellie pushed the wheel chair to the front steps, and then called for Peter to carry it up. She was excited and hoped that Mr. Proctor would like their surprise. She held the front door for Peter and followed him into the living room. The Yankee was lying on his side on the mattress on the floor reading when they entered. Ellie held the chair steady while Peter assisted him into it. He tried it out around the living room and found he could maneuver well in a straight line, but had difficulty making turns. Ellie hid her smile as she watched him experiment with it. After the third collision into the furniture, she blurted out, "Remind me never to let you drive any of our horses." She couldn't hold back the laughter.

He smiled at her sheepishly. She blushed in response, quickly exiting, hoping he had not noticed. She came back just before lunch and invited him to join her in the kitchen. He wheeled himself awkwardly down the hall behind her. The table was set for seven; Lela and Mattie were helping set the food on the table. Old Joe came to the back door, removing his straw hat as he entered the house. Lottie made a fuss over him, recognizing that it was a special privilege for the old man. She ushered him to a seat at the table and had to push on his shoulder to get him to sit down in the presence of the white folks.

"Old Joe, it is a pleasure to have you here with us today. You have done such a wonderful job making the chair for Mr. Proctor," Ellie stated before they began eating. She smiled at the old man who was blushing at this acknowledgment of his skill.

"I would like to second that statement, Joe. You have given me an incredible gift with this chair. It is so pleasurable to be able to get about the house and to be involved in this companionable group. I thank you for your inventiveness and skill," Daniel added.

Joe's blush deepened as the other slaves cheered for him. Ellie called for him to say a few words, which caused him to demur shyly, but the others encouraged him to speak up.

"Ah doan know what ta say. Miz Ellie yo fambly's allas been good ta me an' mah fambly. Ah'm jist grateful ta ya fo' gibben us all a safe place ta work an' lib. Ah allas tried ta do mah best fo' yo' daddy. Ah sho miss him, Miz Ellie. But Ah know he watchin' ober all us here an' Ah is honored ta be settin' here wit ya'll taday," he finished, ducking his head to hide the tears that had started down his cheeks. Mattie leaned over to hug the old man, while Ellie and the other women dabbed at their own tears.

"Well now," Ellie began when everyone was back in control of their emotions, "this is meant to be a celebration. What do we have for our lunch, Lottie?" She turned to the big cook who brought over a heaping platter of fried chicken and a bowl of rice and peas. The group began passing platters and bowls around, passing compliments back to the cook for the work she had done.

"An' dey's pie fo' dessert, so ya'll save some room, now. Ya hear?" Lottie ordered, seating herself at the table and reaching for a bowl to serve herself.

Old Joe ate heartily, but silently, listening to the teasing and banter passed among the others along with the food. His eyes glittered with enjoyment and humor, but he was too unaccustomed to such interactions with the "Family" to be able to participate. Ellie noticed he often stole looks at the Yankee soldier who had so readily become a part of the inner circle. Daniel laughed easily and teased all the women, even teasing Peter when the butler seemed to become too pompous at one point. Old Joe had never laughed at any of the house slaves in his life. Their station was so far above his that he would not have thought of it, yet here these people were treating him like one of them. Looking at the old man, Ellie saw tears in his eyes once again.

"Old Joe, what ever is the matter? Are you unwell?" she asked him with great concern.

The old man hung his head and shook it, saying quietly, "No, ma'am. Ah's jist fine. Ah jist never thought Ah'd be settin' here wit da lacks o' ya'll. It do mah heart good ta see da color' folks an' da white folks settin' tagedder an' laughin' lack dis. It sho do." He wiped away the tears with the sleeve of his shirt. His statement was followed by a silence as each person considered his words.

"It does my heart good as well, Joe," Daniel stated quietly. "I had always believed that the white and Negro people of the South had to hate each other. I am happy to see that there can be love and affection between them, instead of cruelty and discrimination. I can only hope that this attitude will spread throughout the North and the South some day."

Ellie smiled at Daniel and said, "Amen to that." This sentiment was echoed by all the others present in the kitchen. It took a few minutes for the level of emotion to return to the jollity that had prevailed before, but it did. Finally, Lottie brought the rhubarb pie to the table to acclaim from all.

"Old Joe, I have been meaning to ask you, if you know of anything we can do to protect the horses up in the woods from the flies and mosquitoes. The bugs are driving those poor animals to despair," Ellie told the old man.

"Well, Miz Ellie, we could start up some smudge fires. Smoke would keep da bugs off," Joe suggested.

"I would rather not call attention to the horses up there," Ellie explained, shaking her head with a worried frown.

"Den we gonna haf ta make up some oil from cedar an' marigolds. Dat ought ta hep dem some," he said after some consideration. "Dem hosses gonna smell like fine ladies," he added with a laugh. The others joined in with his joke, causing the old man to blush at his temerity in making a joke.

Ellie went to the study to work on the books after eating. It was too hot to do much of anything else. After an hour or so, she felt as if someone were staring at her. She looked up to see Daniel Proctor sitting in the doorway. "May I help you with something, Mr. Proctor?"

"No. ...Well, yes. ...You are very different from what I expected." He knitted his brow and shifted his jaw to the left, pondering the incongruity.

Ellie was surprised by his statement, wondering what expectations he had held and almost fearing to hear them in case she was not meeting up to them. She arched her eyebrows and asked, "Oh, and what was it that you were expecting?"

"You are nearly always working, Miss Peters. I had been led to believe that Southern women were ladies of leisure unless they were Negroes." For once, he wasn't smiling or being sarcastic.

Stung by his implied criticism of her culture, she snapped back, "You really should know more about the people whose land you are invading."

He nodded his head, not in agreement, but to acknowledge that she had scored a point. "Are all Southerners as single minded?"

"Mr. Proctor, this war..." She had started angrily, and then hesitated. "Maybe we are. This war did not have to happen. Slavery is wrong and it would have ended soon anyway. However, I am a Southerner and the people in my life are dying. I live here; you Northerners have invaded my home. Why are you here?" The question was genuine and not hostile.

"I am not sure I know anymore. It started as wanting to save the Union and free the Negroes. There were some who had escaped who worked for my father. I remembered as a child seeing the scars on their backs. But the things I have seen..." His voice trailed off and he seemed to stare past her as if he were seeing it all over again. He brought himself back, "Am I what you expected of a 'Yankee'?"

Shaping her expression into one of exaggerated honesty, she stated, "Oh, yes. I just knew you would all be rude monsters with two heads." She laughed to show him she was joking, trying to lighten the mood. She was not about to tell him what she saw in him.

He tried to sound serious. "I would tell you we all have three heads, but you have seen too much of me to believe me."

"Mr. Proctor!" Ellie was aghast, one hand rising to her bosom, and the other covering her mouth, her eyes wide with amazement. She felt her cheeks burning with embarrassment.

He backed his chair out, laughing, and wheeled himself away down the hall.

She wanted to throw something at him. How dare he bring up, in such a cavalier way, that she had stripped him when he arrived wounded! He was infuriating. She had been honest with him. He had briefly shown her his own pain and vulnerability. Then, just when she was feeling that she might be able to relate to him, he said something so very rude. She couldn't focus on the books. He had her totally confused; she couldn't imagine anyone other than Ted having been so forward. Was this typical of Northerners or could he be attracted to her? Or was he this forward with all women? Was this the flaw?

Ellie went to the porch at four o'clock to help teach. She blushed every time she felt Daniel's eyes on her or when she looked at him. Between him and the heat, she had trouble concentrating. She just wanted to sit in a cool tub. The children had arrived with wet heads and she fondly remembered when she was little and had splashed in the pond out back on a hot spring day or during Indian summer. Yet, she couldn't remember such heat as this and it was only the end of June. How she missed Beaufort!

At dinner she ate sparingly; the heat had taken her appetite. She was unusually quiet, listening as others pried Daniel with questions about the North and his family. In the process, she discovered he had never been to New York, but had spent time in Philadelphia; his family farm was about fifty miles west of the great city. He had an older brother who was married with two children. His brother had recently joined the army, much to his wife's dismay. He also had a younger sister, who was engaged to a man from New Jersey. He reported they planned to be married next Christmas, adding he hoped the war would be over by then, so that he would be free to attend.

Mattie's next question, Ellie realized, was for her benefit. "An' Marster Proctor, what' do yo wife say 'bout you goin' off ta war?"

"I am not married, Miss Mattie," he replied, smiling crookedly at her.

"Well, Ah was sho a good lookin' man lack you would a had a lady waitin' fo' ya!" she exclaimed exaggeratedly, looking in Ellie's direction and smiling broadly.

"No, sadly, Miss Mattie, there is no one." He sighed, and then smiled devilishly at her. "Miss Mattie, are you flirting with me?"

"Marster Proctor, ya knows Ah ain't! Ah ain't dat type a girl." She blushed. "Ah gots a man."

"Mattie, who is he? You never told me." Ellie was genuinely surprised. This new piece of information helped her to forget about herself.

"No one ya knows, Miz Ellie." Mattie suddenly seemed to get shy.

"Yes, Miss Mattie, tell us about him." Mr. Proctor added.

"When ya stops callin' me Miz Mattie. Ah ain't no 'Miz.' Ah works too hard ta be called 'Miz!'" she stated, laughing so that Ellie would not take offense.

"What do you prefer? ...Mrs. Mattie?" he asked her.

"Mattie, jist Mattie." She emphasized the name with a firm nod of her head.

Lela and Ellie were trying hard to keep back the laughter, but the tears were coming to both their eyes.

"You stop calling me 'Master Proctor' and I will stop calling you 'Miss,'" he offered.

"What Ah supposed ta call ya den?" she asked, totally without a clue as to what would be acceptable.

"Daniel," he stated with a shrug of his shoulders.

"Marster Daniel den." She smiled, feeling that the problem was settled.

"No!" He laughed in frustration. "No, just Daniel."

"Dat doan seem right, but ef dat's what ya want, …Daniel." She darted her eyes toward Ellie to see how she was responding to this situation. Ellie just smiled and shrugged her shoulders as well.

"So, Mattie, now that we have that settled. Tell us about your man." His eyes twinkled with mischief once again.

When Mattie hesitated, Lela added. "Tell dem, Mattie."

"He live a fo hour walk away. He got big muscles, but he gentle as a lamb. He work in de fields." She smiled shyly and blushed while she talked about him.

"How did you meet?" Daniel asked. Ellie was also curious.

"He come ta thank Lela fo' heppin' his brudder George."

Without thinking, Ellie blurted out, "Our George!"

Peter looked confused. "We doan have no George."

The three younger women exchanged looks and Lela interjected, "It a long story. Go on, Mattie. Tell dem more 'bout Henry."

"He walks here mos' Sundays." She smiled and her eyes shown with pleasure and pride that he would travel so far to be with her.

"He must care for you very much, Mattie, to walk eight hours to see you." Ellie was impressed; she couldn't imagine Ted having done such a thing just to see her for a couple of hours. She felt a bittersweet sadness. She noticed Daniel had become quiet and seemed deep in thought. Lela and Mattie carried the conversation throughout the rest of the meal.

CHAPTER 16

Ellie turned in early, sending everyone off to their families. She would have to be careful. It was one thing if Lottie and Peter were to know about her activities helping slaves escape; however, she could not risk letting this stranger know. While he probably would have approved of her actions, he would not be confined to the farm forever. Once he was in Confederate custody, if he were to say anything, she would have serious problems.

She couldn't fall asleep. It was too hot and her mind kept going over everything Daniel had said and how he had said it throughout dinner. She fluctuated from being annoyed by his comment to Mattie, to defending him for not understanding Southern ways. She tried opening her bedroom door, hoping to improve the airflow. But she continued tossing and turning; she was hot and agitated.

Finally, she could stand it no longer. The moonlight was sufficient for her to make her way down the front stairs. She pumped a glass of cool water and sat quietly on the couch with her feet up, trying to cool down. She listened to his rhythmic breathing deep in sleep. She tried to watch him, but he was in the shadows. She dozed on and off until nearly morning, and then slipped back upstairs to her own room.

Over the next few days, Ellie spent her mornings out of the house, working. Daniel joined them in the kitchen for lunch and dinner. He'd visit her briefly in the study before going to the porch to assist with the teaching. At night, she would slip downstairs and sleep on the couch for a while, avoiding the hotter rooms upstairs. She'd listen to his breathing, interspersed with an occasional moan when he'd turn.

One morning, Ellie had been working late in the vegetable garden. She came up the back steps covered with sweat and dirt, carrying cucumbers, lettuce, and ears of corn in her apron. She stopped short upon entering the kitchen. Daniel was sitting at the kitchen table rolling dough with such efficiency that it was evident he'd done it many times before this. His back was to the door, but Lottie spotted her. "Stop starin' an' bring dem vegetables here."

She kept staring, but walked across the room, dumping them on the sideboard.

"Miss Peters," he was unsuccessfully attempting to hide his smile, "what are you staring at? You look as if you have never seen a man in the kitchen."

Trying to redeem herself, she replied, "You have flour on your face."

"If you are concerned about my face, I suggest you take a look in the mirror," he stated, looking back at his dough.

She didn't have to see to imagine how she must appear. Her hands went to her hair, "Oh…" As she ran out of the room, she heard him and Lottie laughing. Mattie was already in the tub room, fixing her bath.

"He saw ya, din't he?" Mattie asked, shaking her head at the untidy mess that was her mistress.

"Oh yes, Mattie, he did. Did you hear him laughing?" Ellie was scrubbing at her face with the dirty apron, torn between humiliation and anger.

"Ah doan know why you is workin' in da dirt den lettin' dat nice man see ya lack dis." She was shaking her head in disapproval. "He ain't married; he don't got no lady, an' you needs a man."

"Mattie, he is not for me," Ellie stated definitively, straightening her back and lifting her chin.

"Ya allas say dat. How ya know?" Mattie pursed her lips in disapproval as she helped her mistress out of her filthy clothing.

"We are at war and he is the enemy," Ellie stated, certain that should finish the discussion.

"Ah doan know no Suddern gent'man dat hep Lottie, o' teach us ta read, o 'grees wit ya 'bout thins," Mattie argued, pouring a bucket of warm water over her mistress' head as she sat in the tub.

"I wish things could be that simple," Ellie stated, wiping water out of her face and reaching for the soap to wash her hair and body.

"Try him out," Mattie suggested, picking up the scrub brush and starting in on Ellie's back.

"Try him out?" Ellie wasn't certain what Mattie meant by her statement, but she was certain she did not approve of the idea.

"Yessum. Dat's what ya gots ta do." Mattie rose and brought over another bucket of warm water, pouring it over Ellie and rinsing off the soap. It also effectively stopped the discussion for a few minutes. By the time Ellie could talk again, Mattie was prepared to wrap her head in a fluffy towel. Then she began rubbing Ellie dry. Ellie felt so relaxed and refreshed by the end that she decided to let the discussion drop.

Mattie, however, had no intension of letting up. When they went upstairs after the bath, she was insistent that Ellie dress for company and fussed over her hair. By the time she returned to the kitchen, Daniel had washed off the flour and was rolling about the room in his chair setting the table. He stopped and looked her over carefully. It was the first time she'd noticed him paying attention to her figure. "You do clean up quite well." He smiled pleasantly, but his eyes kept roving over her body.

She pretended not to notice. "Thank you, Mr. Proctor."

He turned to Lottie. "Is everyone in South Carolina so formal?"

"Yes, dey is, ...Daniel." She emphasized his name for Ellie's sake.

Her response was to make a face at Lottie and roll her eyes. She knew that if he'd been a Confederate or not at war, they would be on a first name basis, considering the amount of time they'd spent together. However, she was not ready to let down her guard or imply that they were friends.

His eyes followed her throughout the day. She was relieved to go to bed that night and to remove her corset. However, the heat drove her back downstairs again. As she entered the living room, clouds obscured any light from the moon and she crashed into his wheelchair. He responded to the sound, "Who's there?" He also let out a short groan as he turned quickly on his mattress toward the sound.

"It is just me. I am sorry if I woke you," she hurriedly whispered.

"No. I could not sleep. Is something wrong that you came down?" He sounded a bit groggy, but concerned.

"Yes, it is too hot upstairs. I thought it might be cooler." She bumped into something else.

"Why not light a lamp or candle?" he suggested.

"I do not think that is a good idea." She was only in her nightgown without even a robe. Wanting to change the subject, she enquired, "I heard you groan. Are you in pain?"

"The leg seems to be throbbing for some reason; probably, from the doorway that jumped out in front of me this afternoon." He grunted as he sat up and rubbed the injured leg.

"Yes, the doorways in this house can be tricky. Would you like a drink? Maybe it would ease the pain some," Ellie offered, concerned for him.

"I do not drink alone. If you join me, it might help the pain." His voice sounded warm and friendly in the darkness, like an old friend.

She felt her way over to the cabinet that held the liquors. She could feel the glasses. "I do not even know what you drink."

"Bourbon, but anything that is not sweet will do," he grunted, trying to shift into a comfortable position.

She opened bottles, sniffing in the dark. She found some Dubonnet for herself and the bourbon for him. "I found it." She laughed. "Peter will be upset with me in the morning; I spilled some."

"You could light a lamp," he suggested once again.

She ignored his statement, gingerly walked toward him, and lowered herself to the floor. He took the glass from her hand. "You could sit next to me on the mattress. I do not bite."

"Are you sure?" She laughed nervously. She thought of Ted biting her breasts and quickly pushed away the memories of pain and humiliation. She stayed on the floor, afraid that, in the dark, they might touch, and worse, she might like it.

"If you think I might take advantage of you, I assure you, I am not that type of man," he said quietly, wanting her to feel safe with him.

"I was under the impression that all men were that type of man and that the man who did not act on it was a rare exception." She couldn't keep a hint of bitterness out of her voice.

"I could be one of your exceptions," he wheedled, teasingly.

"I find that difficult to believe. Any man so forward, in my experience, wants much more." She shifted just slightly so that there was a bit more distance between them, and a bit more nightgown as well.

"Wanting and taking are very different. I just like it when you turn bright red. You are fun to tease, Miss Peters." She was struck again by the warmth of his voice in the darkness.

"And Mattie?" she challenged him, thinking of how he liked to tease the slave woman as well. Ellie felt a twinge of jealousy.

"Mattie? Mattie is of no interest to me." His voice was no longer a gentle whisper. He sounded puzzled by her statement.

"Because she is a Negro?" Ellie was preparing to attack him for hypocrisy.

"Not at all; because she is a flirt." He humphed at the idea of being interested in such a woman.

"A flirt?" Ellie started laughing. "You are right. She really is."

"I prefer a woman of substance, beauty, intelligence, determination, one with a wonderful laugh. And of course, she would have to be fun to tease." He sipped his bourbon. "And now, I am her prisoner and can take no action."

She wanted to lean forward and kiss him. She was responding to his words in a way that was totally different from what she had felt for Ted. Frightened, she mumbled, "I had better go upstairs to bed." She quickly rose and fled upstairs.

As she was leaving, however, she thought she heard him say, "Yes, leave me with your image to sweeten my dreams

CHAPTER 17

Ellie took Nathaniel and rode into Sheldon to pick up some supplies and to see if there was any mail. There were two letters waiting for her, one from her Aunt Felicity and one from Suzanne. When she got back to the farm, she took the letters into the study to read them. Suzanne's was full of news about school and all the beaus she was collecting about her. She barely mentioned their mother and didn't bother to ask how things were going on the farm. Ellie thought Suzanne's intent was to make her jealous because she couldn't be in Savannah with them. She couldn't help thinking that Suzanne had succeeded to some extent. It would be nice to be away from the hard labor involved in taking care of the farm and the unremitting heat and humidity there. However, Ellie was glad to be productive, to be continuing her family's horse breeding enterprise. She couldn't see herself sitting around playing at being a belle with suitors coming to her door. She laid the letter aside to share with the others at dinner.

Next, she opened her Aunt Felicity's letter. Felicity reported that Ellie's Uncle Walker was having difficulty finding a suitable overseer for the farm. She explained that most of the men who could have done the job were already in the army. Those who were left were either infirm or were men of low character who could not be trusted with such responsibility. She hoped that Ellie was coping adequately and could hold out for a while longer. Felicity was certain that someone would turn up soon. She went on to report that Charlotte was still quite unwell, seldom leaving her bed and never leaving the house. Felicity had brought in the doctor several times. He had left tonics for Charlotte and encouraged her to rest. He had told Felicity that the strain of the losses she had suffered and her fears for the future had taken a toll on Charlotte. He feared that she would remain an invalid for the rest of her life, but was not in fear for her immediate well-being. Felicity assured Ellie that everything possible was being done for her mother and that she did not have to feel pressed to come to Savannah if it was not convenient at this time.

Ellie sighed and folded the letter. She was concerned for her mother's prolonged illness and slow recovery, but was relieved that she was in no immediate danger. Part of Ellie felt guilty that she was not there to help nurse Charlotte, but she had to remind herself that there was no one else to take care of the farm and there were family members and slaves in Savannah to tend to her mother. Besides, Ellie told herself, she was not her mother's favorite daughter and would not be missed all that much. If her mother got worse, she would leave right away, but she could postpone that decision for now. She looked out the window at her beloved farm and knew that she would not leave it unless there was no other alternative.

There seemed no end to the overbearing heat. Ellie looked forward to the rain that fell almost daily. It seemed to bring the temperature down slightly, but it did not relieve the humidity any. She attempted to keep up with her work. Afternoons, she envied the children their swim. She got into the habit of dismissing everyone immediately after the evening meal. She and Daniel would talk for hours about the day, their lives before the war, politics, religion, and their goals for the future. Occasionally, they'd play card games, chess, or backgammon. He often made suggestive comments, but never moved on them. The most he ever did was touch her hand or hair. They continued to call each other by their proper names. And at the end of the evening, Ellie would reluctantly leave for bed. She tossed and turned, frequently sneaking back down after she thought he was asleep. While she truly wanted to be in one of the cooler rooms downstairs, she found it soothing to doze off to the sound of his deep breathing as he slept. When she would go back upstairs, she'd dream of being with him or telling Charlotte she'd found the right one. During the day, the slaves frequently caught them staring at each other. Mattie and Lela would tease her and ask if he'd tried anything. She'd blush and shake her head.

It had become their custom for Ellie to hold his chair still while he slid out of it onto the mattress. One evening, he seemed to land harder than usual, and then grabbed his left leg, rocking.

"Are you all right?" she asked anxiously.

"I will be, just give me a minute," he huffed out, gritting his teeth.

She rushed over to the cabinet. "Let me pour a bourbon for you."

"I do not drink alone," he stated firmly.

She thought this was probably true because he had turned down any offers of a drink over the past week that they'd spent the evenings together. "Maybe one would help me sleep." She did not like to see him in pain.

"Have I been keeping you up in your dreams?" he teased, gently rubbing his leg.

"You and the heat." She couldn't believe she had actually said it.

"I am sure I could improve on your dreams." He smiled provocatively at her, his green eyes stealing her breath away. She took a deep breath, hoping her own thoughts would not show. Instead, she put on a disapproving look.

She sat on the floor next to him, handing him the drink. "I am constantly amazed by your rudeness, Mr. Proctor."

He reached over and touched her hair. "Ah, but it gives such beautiful color to your cheeks."

Neither had touched their drinks, but they continued to stare into each others' eyes. Ellie found herself drawn in, leaning forward, until her lips met his. She felt the softness of them as they just brushed against hers very gently. He slid his hand to the back of her neck holding her to him as he parted her lips with his tongue. She responded to his gentleness, allowing herself to be lost in the moment. Nothing else mattered, but the slow lingering kiss. As he released her, she felt dizzy. He continued to curl her hair in his fingers. Slowly, she reached up, releasing his hand from her hair, holding it. She looked away from his eyes, fearful that if she did not she would kiss him again. "I had better leave."

He kissed her hand as she rose to leave. He asked, "Does this mean I may call you Ellie?"

She turned and smiled, "Good night, Daniel."

That night she lay on the bed in a thin, cotton nightgown, grinning. She dreamt of what could have happened next. In the morning, she was humming as she did her chores. There was lightness in her step that she'd rarely had. At lunch, she addressed him as Mr. Proctor. Other than raising an eyebrow, he made no comment about the formality. However, as soon as she entered her father's study, he showed up, closing the door behind him. "Are you having regrets?"

"No," she stated emphatically. "What would make you think so?"

"'Mr. Proctor'?" He seemed genuinely confused.

"Oh, that!" She giggled. "A Southern gentleman would understand." She hesitated. "The slaves talk. It is actually one of the best ways to find out about your neighbors if you are so inclined."

Daniel frowned. He considered her words and the implication of them. "Ellie, I am much better; soon I will be able to stand on this leg. You had better turn me in to the authorities. If I stay much longer, you will be in danger. As you say, the slaves talk. The wrong word, in the wrong ear and they might decide you are giving aid and comfort to the enemy."

"You are not well yet." She was upset and confused by his statement. He was suggesting that he go to a prison camp to protect her!

"Will you keep my horse? I know you will take good care of him. I do not want him back on any battlefield." He took her hand, looking earnestly into her eyes for her promise.

She did not answer him, but stood abruptly and paced the study. He kept his silence, already recognizing her habit. "I need to go see Mama Noli." She walked out, saying no more, and went straight to the old woman's cabin.

As usual, she found her elderly friend and counselor seated in her rocker on her porch. The old woman smiled welcomingly at her and waved her to the bench in the shade of the porch.

"What kin Ah do fo' ya, Miz Ellie? Must be impo'tent ta bring ya out in dis heat." She waited quietly for Ellie to speak.

"Mama Noli, I need your help with a very serious problem. You know that, if Southern soldiers come here, we could have some real trouble having Lieutenant Proctor here on the farm. I am worried that someone might say the wrong thing and give him away. I need our people to tell anyone who asks about him that Lieutenant Proctor is a friend of James' from school who was wounded while fighting for the Confederacy. They all have to understand that this is vital for the safety of all of us. If the Confederate soldiers were to learn that I am harboring a Yankee soldier, they would certainly take me to prison. They might take the farm and sell all of you off. Please, Mama Noli, can you help me make the others understand how important this is?" She looked pleadingly at the old woman.

Mama Noli nodded her head and patted Ellie on the knee. "You jist leave it ta me, chile. Won't nobody say nuthin' ta nobody 'cept dat he a wounded Confed'rate soldier an' a frien' o' yo dead brudder James." She smiled again.

"Thank you, Mama Noli. I knew I could count on you." Ellie stood, hugged the wizened body, and took her leave.

Walking back to the house, she began to doubt that she would be able to turn him in to the Confederates. Neither could she let him return to fight against her people. She did not know what she should do.

That night he sat with her on the couch, talking as if nothing had happened and nothing had been said. However, she was unusually quiet. Eventually, he took her hand in his, caressing it. "Ellie, what is on your mind?"

She did not answer, but responded with the pain in her eyes of what was to come. She was unwilling to tell him of her dilemma.

"I understand what you have to do." He brought her hand to his mouth kissing it. "I have heard from our Confederate prisoners that General Lee treats his prisoners better than his own soldiers." There was sadness in his voice. "My only regret is that I have had such little time with you."

She took his other hand, "You do not have to leave yet; at least not until you have completely healed."

"I will not put you in harm's way anymore than you already are." He squeezed her hands to add emphasis to his words.

"It has been taken care of by Mama Noli," she told him.

"The wizened old lady who sometimes comes to watch the children during the lessons?" he asked, surprised.

"Yes. You are a friend of my brother's from the western territories who was injured fighting for the South. No one will tell that there is a Yankee here." She smiled at the cleverness of the lie she had concocted and the collusion of the slaves in maintaining it.

"But, Ellie, what will your neighbors say about you keeping an unrelated man in the house without a chaperone? I will not soil your reputation!" He seemed determined that she would not suffer from association with him.

"Daniel, we are at war. As long as they believe you are a wounded soldier, they may talk, but they will not dare condemn me," she reassured him, drawing his hands closer to her as if she could keep him there with her by force.

"You mean as long as they do not know that I am a Yankee!" He shook his head, smiling at her. "Have you always been so devious, my dear Ellie?"

She laughed, thinking of the hut in the woods, "Oh, yes, especially if it is for a greater good."

"And kissing an enemy soldier is definitely for the greater good." He kissed her hand again. "I like the way you think."

"You are so infuriating sometimes. Teaching slaves to read in South Carolina is illegal. How do you think Mattie and Lela learned? What do you think my brother, the law student, would have done if he had found out?" Her anger was only half playful as she enumerated her "crimes against the State" for him.

"Probably he would have had you locked up in your room where you belong." He shook his head at her vehemence, not recognizing the true heroism in her actions.

"You would like that I suppose." Ellie was pouting at not being appreciated.

"Only if I had the key," he said wickedly, leaning in toward her.

"My brother would have shot you before he would let you have the key." She had been speaking so casually about James, and then she remembered. Her eyes filled with tears. "You are wearing one of his suits."

He put his arm around her. It was the first time since James and John had died that she felt she was not alone with the weight of the farm and her family on her shoulders. She sobbed, pushing her face into his chest while he gently held her. The sobs turned to quiet tears; she sat up, pulling a handkerchief out of her sleeve. "I am sorry. I do not know what came over me."

"Ellie, you do not have to be strong all of the time." He pushed himself up off the couch and gingerly transferred to the chair on wheels. Having rolled himself to the cabinet, he poured a Dubonnet for her and rolled back.

She accepted the glass. He did not pour anything for himself, but encouraged her to drink it down. "Now, go to bed. You need the rest."

"Let me help you first." She stood and moved to the back of the chair to assist him.

"I will be fine. Go!" He reached back to pull her head down to him.

She kissed him on the cheek and slowly went upstairs. She wanted to go back down, but could not trust herself. Also, she remembered her brother's words about a man's needs. She did not want to tease or test him as she had Ted.

CHAPTER 18

Over the next few days, their daily routine continued. While they were with the others they addressed one another formally. While alone, they used first names. They held hands; he played with her hair. They kissed good night passionately; however, he made no attempt to touch her inappropriately. If she had any complaint, it was the knots he made of her hair.

She blushed when Mattie commented about the mess one morning. Seeing her response, Mattie laughed, "Daniel's made dis mess! Ah ain't blind, an' we knows ya calls him Daniel."

He raised his eye brow and smiled gently the first time she called him Daniel in front of Lottie. The older woman snickered, "Ah guess, ya kin call her Ellie."

It was that same day that she came up from the barn with a pair of crutches that Old Joe had made. The two spent the afternoon testing them out. Daniel's leg was extremely weak from the muscle damage and from being off of it for two months. Ellie insisted he keep it splinted. He found that the slightest weight on it was painful and gave in to her fairly quickly. Getting up and down was still the hardest. She had tried to get him to use the chair part of the time, but he had refused, being determined to walk.

By evening, he was exhausted. He sat down hard on the couch, rubbing his leg. She kept shaking her head, but poured a bourbon and a Dubonnet, and then joined him on the couch. "Daniel, it will take time to build that leg back up. It will not heal well if you do again what you did to yourself today."

"Are you always this stern with the men in your life?" His eyes were twinkling.

"Stern? You have not seen stern," she humphed in response.

"I am all yours. Be stern with me." He leaned in to her.

She swatted his arm. "Is that all you think about?"

"When I am near you, when I see you, when I think about you, yes." His eyes were burning emeralds in his face, so deep she could have fallen into them and been lost.

She put down her glass, took his from him, and put it down. She touched his cheek, turning his face toward hers; slipping her fingers up through his hair, she leaned in toward him. He met her part way, kissing her as he put his arm around her, pulling her closer to him. He explored her tongue and mouth with his. He wrapped his other arm around her, holding her close. Gently, he ran his hand up and down her side. She felt as if she could melt into him. He broke the kiss, continuing to hold her close. She did not want the moment ever to end. When it did, they snuggled close, finishing their drinks in silence. She wrapped herself around him, placing her head on his chest, listening to his heart beat. He played with her hair, her ear, ran his fingers over her neck and face. She shivered with pleasure at his touch and heard a sound like a purr coming from her own throat. She smiled as she thought of herself as a contented and pampered cat. Eventually, he shooed her off to bed.

August passed slowly. Daniel had become proficient in the use of his crutches. Other than during an occasional rain storm, the days, as well as the nights, remained hot and steamy. The summer on the farm seemed peaceful. There had been no sounds of battles in the distance nor had Ellie heard of any Yankees in the area on her rare trips to the general store. The remaining slaves had slowed their pace, accustomed to the need to adjust to the heat. Eventually, Ellie followed their lead. The only ones who seemed to enjoy the climate were the children as they frolicked in the pond out back. Ellie watched with envy.

One afternoon the heat seemed unbearable. She went out back and sat on the bench watching them splash and listening to the laughter; however, with no air moving, sitting in the sun only aggravated her discomfort. As the sweat beaded on her forehead, she walked to the edge of the pond and scooped some water onto her face and arms. The children stopped splashing and laughing, unsure if their behavior would be acceptable to their mistress. Rather than tell them to continue playing, she started splashing them. They froze momentarily, not knowing what to do, but once she laughed, Lily splashed her back. Ellie laughed and kept up the game. The other children joined back in, splashing each other and their mistress. As the water battle continued, Ellie slipped, falling into the pond in her enthusiasm for the game. They continued to play loudly and Ellie was drenched with pond water from head to toe.

She was unaware that the noise had attracted the attention of Lottie and Daniel who had been in the kitchen. They had been watching out the window. When he saw her leave the pond and start up the back lawn, Daniel went to the tub room for a towel. He greeted her on top of the back steps. He was about to hand her the towel, but was stopped short by the view. Ellie was wearing one of her lightest and oldest cotton skirts and blouses for working outside in the heat. In addition, she had taken to wearing very few undergarments, settling for an old cotton shift under her clothing. The result of the drenching in the pond was that her thin cotton coverings were clinging very suggestively to every curve of her body, and the bodice of her blouse was unbuttoned sufficiently to offer him an excellent view of her cleavage, especially from his higher position on the porch. Daniel couldn't seem to stop himself from admiring the view wholeheartedly. When Ellie realize what he was staring at, she grabbed the towel out of his hands and tried to cover herself. She glared at him, and Daniel had the good grace to look down rather than continue to stare; but a huge grin painted his face as Ellie stormed by and he turned his head to catch the rear view of her retreating figure.

"Horseback riding has certainly given you some fine muscles, Ellie," he called after her appreciatively. Her only response was to slam the back door.

Lottie followed her as she passed through the kitchen toward the laundry room. "What ya think ya doin', Miz Ellie? Traipsin' 'round here near nekkid in front o' dat man! What'd Miz Charlotte say?" The big black cook pursued her mistress, hands on hips.

Coming into the kitchen, Daniel called after her, "Lottie, she needs to do something besides work."

"Ya Northern ladies do dat?" she snapped at him, swinging around to glare at him.

"They swim sometimes, when there are no men around."

"Ah doan know. Lord hep us all!" She went into the kitchen and put some water on, and then she called out, "Mattie, Miz Ellie smells lack da pond."

Ellie could hear Daniel laughing. "Oh, but the smell was worth it for the view."

She yelled out from the tub room. "You just stop that right now, Daniel Proctor."

He laughed harder in response.

Once the house emptied for the night, they sat on the couch talking, laughing, and kissing. As the kisses became longer and deeper, his hand moved slowly from her hip to her arm. When he moved it back down, his fingers brushed the side of her breast. His hand slowly moved over her breast, gently caressing the nipple between his fingers. She stiffened, expecting pain, but none came. Instead, she felt tingling throughout her body and wanted him to touch her all over. She ran one hand up his back and neck responding to his tongue with hers. Her other hand slid down to his hip. She held it tight, afraid she might reach for him. She knew she was already teasing him, but she would not stop him and ignore the feelings she had for him. He released her breast and stopped the kiss. He sat back, closing his eyes and bringing her hand to his mouth, gently kissing it. Once again leaving her breathless, they parted for the night.

The first she saw him afterward was at lunch the next day. He was unusually quiet and looked down when she smiled at him. She did not know why he was upset. He followed her into the study, closing the door behind him.

"Ellie, I am so sorry. It was wrong of me to touch you. Can you forgive me?" His voice trembled as he fought to keep his emotions in check.

"There is nothing to forgive." She was amazed to see him so upset over his behavior. It crossed her mind that Ted would never have apologized in the same circumstances, but would have taken it as a sign that he could be even more aggressive with her.

"After seeing you all wet…" He shook his head, stopping himself mid-sentence. "There is no excuse. It was wrong of me."

"Daniel, I would have stopped you if… Please do not be sorry it happened. I am not sorry." She stood and walked to him, extending her open arms to him.

They hugged and he left her to her book work. However, over the next couple of weeks he was extremely careful not to touch her in what might be thought an inappropriate way, and only kissed her gently on the cheek good night. She began to feel he might be losing interest or felt her behavior with him was immoral. She wanted him to want her, to touch her with his gentle hands.

During this time, he had stopped using the splint and worked on putting more and more weight on his left leg. Ellie suspected that it was no longer the bone that was the problem he was having, but the muscle. Not only had the bullet torn it up going in, but she had dug the lead out causing more damage to the muscle, and then it had been immobilized for weeks while the bone healed. She understood he needed to use his leg more and suggested he accompany her to the barn. He seemed enthusiastic about getting out of the house. He struggled down the front steps, but had no trouble on his crutches keeping up with her. Other than Old Joe, everyone was working in the upper fields. She told him about each horse in the barn, and together they watched the weanlings and yearlings that she had not hidden in the woods or back pasture. Finally, he asked, "Where is my horse?"

"He is in a safe place," she responded mysteriously and smiled at him.

"What are you talking about? Where is he?" Daniel laughed at her antics.

"Before you showed up, there had been soldiers here to buy horses. They wanted my horse, but I told them she was lame. After that incident, I decided I needed to hide some of the mares. He is with them. Do you want me to bring him back to the barn or can you wait a little longer?"

He smiled at her and took her hand. She smiled in return, but a sigh slipped out. It reminded her that soon he would be completely healed and would leave her.

"What is wrong?" he asked her, tilting her chin up so he could study her face.

She dropped her eyes to hide her emotions and lied to him about her thoughts. "It is not right that horses are not safe in their own barn!" She was not about to tell him she wanted him to stay when he had been so distant. He had never said anything about a future.

They went back to the house and he worked his way up the stairs. Once they sat on the couch in the living room, he suddenly noticed his bedding was gone from the room. "What is going on Ellie?"

She heard concern in his voice and decided to tease. "You are getting around too well now."

"Are you afraid of what I might do?" He smirked lecherously at her.

"I think, I am afraid of what …you will not do." She stifled a giggle.

"I do not…what are you up to?" He was catching on, but still confused.

She swatted him. "The nights are comfortable now and you can make the stairs. I thought you might like a real bed."

"I certainly would like to try yours!" The twinkle was back.

"No!" She hit him playfully again. "I thought you would be more comfortable in my brother's room."

"More comfortable? More comfortable than what?" he asked, moving closer to her.

Before she could comment, he pulled her toward him and kissed her long and hard. "Daniel, the slaves!" she protested, pushing gently against his chest with little effect.

After dinner, Daniel made his first trip to the second floor. She showed him the way to James' old room. She had already brought up glasses, a bottle of bourbon, and one of Dubonnet.

"What is all this?" he asked, amazed by her preparations.

"I thought we could toast your progress and your new room." She smiled broadly at him.

"Come here!" he commanded, his deep voice making her feel week in the knees.

She turned toward him and he grabbed her hand and pulled her close. It was the first they stood alone, face to face. She looked up at his eyes, remembering the first time she had noticed his lashes. She wrapped her arms around his neck. Leaning the crutches on the bed, he held her by the waist, pulled her toward him, and kissed her neck and throat, tasting her skin with his tongue; he worked his way to the other side and up to her ear. He kissed her cheek and eyes and nose, and then her lips. She opened them to him. His right hand slid up her side, easing his thumb onto her breast. If his tongue had not been in her mouth, she would have sighed in contentment. His other hand had slipped around her lower back and pulled her hard against him. Through their clothing, she could feel him grow hard against her stomach. She felt relief that he wanted her; then she remembered they were standing in his bedroom. While she did not want it to stop, she was afraid to encourage him any further. She broke the kiss, "Maybe, we should have that toast now."

His hand lingered momentarily on her breast. He watched his own fingers as they gently squeezed and messaged, noting her low deep breathing in response. Smiling up at her, he said, "I suppose, we had better."

He hobbled with one crutch over to the chairs by the window, lowered himself slowly, and poured the bourbon and Dubonnet. Saluting her with the glass, he proclaimed, "Here is to my beautiful Ellie and the day her breasts are unencumbered."

Smiling, she shook her head and sat in the chair facing him. She was not sure whether to laugh or to hit him. They talked awhile, and then she showed him where the nightshirts were kept. "These are all my brother's things," she said sadly. "He has no use for them anymore and they seem to fit you." She left, closing the door gently on her way out

CHAPTER 19

Daniel spent the next few mornings walking between the house, the barns, and the slave cabins. Ellie was otherwise occupied with her routine. One morning as he was coming down the front steps, Ellie rode up on a large chestnut mare leading a bay. "Do you think you are up for a ride?"

He took the reins of the bay and led her to the steps. It required that he put considerable weight on his bad leg, but he managed to clumsily mount from the third step. She trotted off, calling over her shoulder, "First stop, your horse!"

Daniel followed along as well as he could. Ellie, hearing a few grunts and a subdued curse, slowed her horse to a walk. He came up beside her and, together, they walked their horses through the woods.

When they reached the roped area, Ellie dismounted. Turning to Daniel, she called, "Do not get off yet; we still have a way to go." She was concerned that he might not be able to get back on without a mounting step. When they came upon the cabin, Daniel slid off his horse before she could stop him. "Now, where do you think you are going to go?"

They both started laughing. He had left his crutches back on the front steps. She called out to Princess. The young mare bounded up to her mistress looking for treats. A number of other horses followed, including Daniel's gelding. He was pleased to see his horse and the condition Victor was in. He was also surprised at the size of the herd: one stallion, ten mares, five weanlings, five yearlings, Princess, and his gelding. He was intrigued by the cabin. "Ellie, your mare is beautiful. I understand why they wanted her and why you have hidden her. I thank you for taking such good care of my old horse."

"He is not old. I checked," she stated a bit indignantly.

He laughed. "I should have known. What about the structure? It was not built for horses. What was it?"

Ellie steeled herself to lie to Daniel. Drawing in her breath and shrugging, she replied, "I would not know. It was just here." Then, quickly changing the topic, she reached out to pat the neck of another horse. "What do you think of our stallion?"

"You do not trust me!" Daniel exclaimed, surprised by her obvious prevarication.

Ellie, angered by her own lie and stung by his statement, rounded on him. "How can you say such a thing to me? You can go anywhere in my house. You are riding one of my horses. If I did not trust you, would I do these things?"

"You know very well what this building was. When you hushed everyone up about that George fellow, I knew you were hiding something from me. However, I was not offended. After all, we hardly knew each other. But now..." He scowled at her, hurt painting his visage.

Ellie was suddenly filled with anxiety. He had uncovered her secret. "Daniel, you can never mention it to anyone. I could go to jail; my family would lose the farm. Even, if you Yankees win this war, which you will not, my neighbors…well I do not know what they would do. I…"

Daniel, seeing her panic, interrupted her. "Ellie, I would never do anything to harm you. If you are that afraid, you do not have to tell me." He took her hand and kissed it. "Let us check over your horses, and then figure out how I will get back on this horse." He laughed, attempting to lighten the mood.

Ellie handed him the reins of her horse and started moving about the herd, running her hands over the animals. She spent extra time with the young ones, recognizing that they were not being handled nearly enough. She finished and walked back, taking the reins from Daniel. "Have you ever heard of the Underground Railroad?"

"Of course! …Ellie, you are part of it?"

She avoided making eye contact with him and answering his question. "There is a tree stump over here; maybe you can mount more easily from it."

He understood the risk she had taken in telling him as much as she had. He put his arm over the saddle to take some of the weight as he walked to the stump. Ellie held the bay still so that he could use the mare to get up on the stump, and then onto the horse. "Now, how are you going to mount?" he asked her, a pained grin on his face.

"Notice, I am not using a side saddle." She put her foot in the stirrup and gracefully swung up onto the saddle.

He smiled, shook his head and jokingly said, "What would Miz Charlotte say?"

Ellie realized he was not ready for any hard riding and led them back to the house. The upper fields she had wanted to check would have to wait.

The next morning, Ellie rode out to the back pasture to check the small herd she had hidden there. She did not see any need to tell Daniel that she had another stallion and some twenty odd more horses separated out. She realized that she might have mares foaling at the wrong time of year, but protecting the stock was crucial. She had carefully picked which horses would be pastured with each stallion in order to prevent in-breeding. She still had three stallions stabled in the barn and the remainder of the herd in the front pastures and paddocks. She was not sure whether to be relieved that she had not been bothered by any military men over the summer months that the farm had been forgotten or concerned that, with the end of the summer heat, there would be more activity in the area. The last year, it had been October before the Confederate cavalry had come in search of horses. The Union troops had waited until November to attack and kill Ted. She hoped they would have another month or two of calm. She did not want to think any farther ahead. She could only foresee pain. Daniel would be healed and she would have to let him go. And then Christmas! She could not imagine what that would be like without her father and James. There would be no party this year unless Charlotte insisted.

Charlotte! The summer was over; when would she return from Savannah? The wrath of Union invaders would be nothing compared to Charlotte's when she discovered a Yankee was living in her house and wearing her son's clothing! She loved her mother and missed her, but Daniel... She remained distant, lost in thought upon her return from the back pastures.

She unsaddled and groomed the horse she had been riding, methodically brushing down the mare, relieved to have a mindless task that gave her an excuse to be alone. She finally turned the mare out and started walking toward the house. She had just made it to the front steps when she heard horses galloping. She stopped anxiously to listen and realized the sound was coming from the road and not any of the pastures. It was then she saw mounted horses at the end of the drive. She yelled, "Peter, someone is coming! Take your post!"

She watched them approach, finally able to count four horsemen wearing gray. She stood her ground, waiting. When they stopped before her, she greeted them with a smile, "Captain, good day." She nodded to the other men. "It certainly is good to see some of our fine fighting men. It has been a long time since we were honored with a visit. After your long ride, may I offer you some refreshment?"

"That would be very kind of you, ma'am, but we are here on business," the captain responded brusquely.

"Nonsense now! Since when have Southern gentlemen been unable to enjoy refreshment while conducting business?" She turned and walked up the stairs. She did not want to leave Peter's sight until she found out their business. Also, she wanted to warn Daniel. "Please have a seat. It is such a lovely afternoon; I will have us served on the porch."

The men reluctantly dismounted and climbed the stairs. Ellie left the door open and yelled, "Lottie, please bring some refreshment to the front porch. We have four fine Confederate soldiers visiting." She turned and joined the men. Sitting, she indicated some chairs, "Please, gentlemen." As soon as they sat she asked, "Captain, what business brings you here today?"

"We are looking for horses, ma'am. We were told you had horses to sell here."

"Yes, we have about eight horses that are ready for sale. How many are you looking to buy?" Ellie smiled pleasantly at the officer.

The captain frowned. "We need twenty, ma'am."

"Oh... We certainly can help you get a good start on it." She realized she had more to worry about than just Daniel. Before the man could comment, Lottie appeared with a tray and began serving the men.

"Captain, we get so little news out here. How have our troops been doing?" She kept them talking for the better part of an hour while they ate.

The captain became impatient with the delay and interrupted the conversation. "Ma'am, we need those horses. On the way in, I noticed many horses, certainly more than eight."

Ellie nodded agreement, but temporized, explaining, "Some are weanlings, some yearlings, mares carrying foals; none of those would be of any use to you, Captain."

"Certainly, the young ones would be of no use."

"Are you in need of riding horses or driving?" she asked, hoping to talk him out of taking all her stock.

"Mostly riding."

"I do have three horses that have been trained to cart, but are not saddle broken. If that would be of help, it would make eleven," she offered.

Pressing to complete the business, the captain stated, "If you would call your overseer, ma'am, I would like to take a look at them."

"My overseer is away on business. Unfortunately for you, sir, he took ten horses to be delivered to Savannah. I will be glad to have our grooms bring some of the horses up for you to examine."

"That will not be necessary, ma'am. We will go to your barns and look ourselves."

Realizing that she had no choice, Ellie quickly conceded. "If you would prefer. I will accompany you."

The captain stood, offering his hand to Ellie. She took it, trying to behave as she knew Charlotte would have. She led the way, walking slowly. As they walked through the barn, one of the soldiers took some paper and a pencil stub out of his pocket. He started taking dictation as his superior officer made comments about each horse. It became evident to Ellie that the man wanted twenty and was not about to be turned down. He started asking for various horses to be moved out so that he could check them more closely. When he asked to see the first stallion, Ellie objected. "The stallions are not for sale."

Stubbornly, the officer responded, "Ma'am, we all have to make sacrifices to win this war."

"You do not have to tell me about sacrifices," Ellie responded, drawing herself up with indignation. "My father and my brother have been killed already in this war. If I do not have stallions, I cannot breed mares, and then there will be no more horses."

Looking a bit sheepish, but remaining firm, the captain responded, "Ma'am, I am sorry for your loss. However, you have a couple of colts out there. I need those horses now." He turned to the man writing. "How many do you have now?"

"Eighteen, Captain," the man stated.

"We will also take those two," the officer commanded, pointing at two other animals.

"How will I get to the store or church?" Ellie demanded, frustrated with his determination.

"You have some young ones that can pull a cart soon enough." It had taken all afternoon. His business finished, the captain looked at Ellie and said, "I believe there were more sandwiches." He turned and walked back toward the house, his men following along. Ellie hurried to catch up.

While the Captain had remained polite and there had been no rude asides from his men, he was going to be much more difficult to deal with than the sergeant the previous spring. He seemed as determined to take her stallions as she was to keep them. She was becoming angrier, but she knew she had to hide it. Pleading to his honor might go farther. The tray and dirty dishes had been removed; there was no trace of their previous refreshments.

"Lottie, where are those sandwiches?" Ellie called into the house.

The older woman waddled out to the porch. "Dey's all gone, Miz Ellie. Ah thought ya'll was done." She looked at her mistress' face, seeing she was unhappy.

No longer feeling very hospitable toward the soldiers, Ellie shooed Lottie toward the kitchen. "These men are still hungry. Please fix them some more."

The portly cook protested, "It's nearly suppa time, Miz Ellie."

The captain, on the other hand, satisfied with the livestock he had managed to obtain, was delighted with the idea of home cooking. "Thank you. We would be pleased to join you for supper. It has been a long time since we have had a home cooked meal." He held the door open for Ellie, and then he and his men followed her into the house.

She nervously led them to the living room. Giving them a stiff smile, she stated, "Please have a seat, gentlemen. I need to check on preparations."

"I am sure your Negro knows how to prepare a meal, ma'am. I will need a bill of sale for those horses."

"Captain, we have not even discussed prices." She felt she would do better separating him from his men. "Please come with me to the study, I am sure your men will be comfortable in here."

She led the way to the study and flung opened to the door. To her shock, Daniel was sitting at the desk, writing. "Daniel!" She realized she needed to cover her surprise. "I thought you were resting." She turned to the man at her heels. "Captain, this is my husband, Daniel Proctor." Turning back to Daniel, "The captain is here to buy some of our horses."

"Excuse me for not getting up to greet you." He patted the crutches that were leaning up against the desk. "Please have a seat."

The man walked up to the desk and extended his hand. He looked suspiciously at Daniel and around the room. He sat, after noting the chair with wheels sitting in the corner of the room. "You are not from around here, are you, Mr. Proctor?"

Daniel forced a laugh. "No, I grew up out west in the new territories"

"How did you come to meet your wife? She is a most unusual woman."

Daniel smiled and looked affectionately at Ellie. "Her brother and I were in school together."

"At Beaufort?" The captain appeared to making casual conversation, but Ellie could see the wariness in his eyes as he asked his question.

Daniel had been listening to every word Ellie had said since he met her. He knew this was a trap. "No, Columbia Law School."

"Did you practice law in Columbia, too?"

"No, the war began before I finished school. James, Ellie's brother, and I signed up right away."

"What unit were you with Mr. Proctor?" The captain was obviously still suspicious of Daniel.

"Were you at Kernstown, Captain?" Ellie quickly interrupted.

"No, Mrs. Proctor, I was not." He seemed annoyed by her interruption.

"That is were my brother was killed and, nearly, my husband." Pulling a handkerchief out of her sleeve, she dabbed her eyes and added some sniffling.

"Captain, such talk upsets my wife. She lost her father and brother within a week of each other, and it only reminds her that I will be well again and returning to war."

"Daniel, please do no talk of it." Ellie didn't have to force the hurt that echoed in her voice.

Daniel looked at the captain and shrugged. The man seemed to accept the situation and changed the subject. "Maybe we should discuss the horses I want."

"Daniel, he wants all three of our stallions, the brood mares that are not with foal, and my carriage horse. I tried to explain to him that we cannot sell any stallions." Ellie protested, hoping he might be able to persuade the captain to change his mind since he had not responded to her feminine persuasions.

"Mrs. Proctor, I am sure your husband understands the need of the Confederacy, even if you do not."

"How dare..." She was about to lose control of her temper.

"Ellie, please!" Daniel's voice remained gentle, but firm.

She flashed him an angry look.

"I am sure your husband and I can handle this transaction to both our satisfaction." He had essentially dismissed her.

"Ellie, go ahead. I know you need time to prepare for dinner and would like to check on our other guests."

Ellie wanted to throw something at him; however, she realized he was right. She needed to trust him and to check on the three soldiers. They might not be so well behaved without the supervision of their officer. She closed the door behind her and tended to the other men, offering them some of the scotch she had so hated, yet had kept for Ted. He no longer had a need of it. As the thought hit her, she felt a brief pang of guilt. He was not even dead a full year and she was protecting his enemy by pretending to be his wife. No, she would not make the same mistake with this man as she had with Ted. This war would take him from her too, one way or the other, but she would not regret their time together; she would deny Daniel nothing. She left the men for the kitchen.

"Peter, please set the dining room table for six," she instructed the butler.

"Miz Ellie, Ah's glad ya ain't turnin' Daniel in ta dose men. He's a good man," Peter whispered as he walked past her.

Laying her hand on his arm, she stopped him. "Peter, in front of the soldiers, make sure you call him Master Daniel."

"Ah know; we all knows," the slave stated, nodding his head at the others.

"Also," she blushed, "I told them he is my husband."

"We knows dat, too." Peter seemed indignant that she would think he was not aware of what had happened.

"Miz Ellie, dose men ain't goin' no wheres tonight. Dey gonna think it funny ya doan sleep wit yo husband," Lottie offered.

"Oh, Lottie, I had not thought about that. I just did not know how to explain him when we walked into the study."

"It's betta' she spend da night wit Daniel. At least, he's a gent'man; dat udder man he ain't no gent'man, da way he look at Miz Ellie," Peter told Lottie.

Ellie hadn't noticed. It hadn't occurred to her that Daniel might actually protect her; she had though she was protecting him. She went up the back stairs to her room to change. Mattie was already there, laying out her clothes for dinner.

Ellie looked over the choices before her, considering her predicament. She had to appear to be a proper Southern wife, but she had never had the opportunity to dress up for Daniel, and she wanted to display her "charms" for him. She considered carefully, wanting just enough shoulder and bosom to be revealed without starting the soldiers to thinking. Ellie decided to compromise, selecting a dress with a gauzy bodice that covered her completely, but allowed a hint of contour to show through. The dark green complimented her coloring. She also decided it would be unwise to show off any valuable jewelry, and opted to wear a cameo pendant that had been in the family for generations. Mattie quickly dressed Ellie's hair. While she was doing this, Ellie said, "Mattie, I need you to get some clothes out of James' room and bring them in here."

"Ya not gonna let 'im sleep in here?" the maid asked, shocked at the idea.

Ellie blushed and hurried to explain, "They have to believe he is my husband."

Mattie frowned at Ellie's reflection in the vanity mirror. "Ya wan' me ta stay here an' protect ya?"

Ellie looked up in irritation at the slave woman's reflection. "No, Mattie. I do not want you to stay here to protect me. Daniel is a gentleman."

"He may not be a houn' lack Marster Ted, but he a man. An' he got it bad fo' ya," Mattie told her.

Ellie turned to look directly at her maid. "You think so, Mattie?"

"Oh, lordy! Ah knows ya lacks 'im, but you is in love. Not like wit Marster Ted, dis time ya's really in love." She smiled sympathetically at her mistress.

Ellie sighed in response, slumping in her seat at the new complication to her life.

"Ya be careful, Miz Ellie," Mattie said, laying her hand on Ellie's shoulder. "I will, Mattie. But I think it may be too late." She sighed again and straightened her spine. "Go get those clothes, please. I had better get downstairs to our guests. I do not like leaving Daniel alone with them." She rose, took one quick look at her image in the peer glass, and hurried out of the room.

As she descended the stairs, she found all the men waiting for her. She looked for Daniel immediately, wanting to see if he was coping adequately, and to see how he responded to her appearance. She was gratified by the broad smile that spread over his face as he saw her. She returned his smile warmly, and then turned to smile less sincerely at their guests.

"You look lovely tonight, my dear," Daniel stated as she reached the landing. Ellie felt herself blush at his compliment and moved to take his arm, squeezing it affectionately. The assembled soldiers nodded and smiled respectfully.

"Captain," Daniel said, turning to the officer, "would you be good enough to do the honors and escort my wife in to dinner. As you can see, I am not equal to the task with these crutches in the way."

"I would be honored, sir," the captain responded, offering Ellie his arm. She slipped her hand over his arm and they turned toward the dining room, the soldiers following, with Daniel bringing up the rear, limping more than was necessary to exaggerate his disability.

Once they were seated, Peter and Lela began bringing in the plates of food. Lottie had not gone out of her way to impress the visitors, but the food was sufficiently abundant and tasty that the men were very happy with the fare.

"Captain, my husband was not present this afternoon when you were telling me about the war news. I wonder if you would be so good as to repeat what you were telling me earlier." She smiled at the officer who was seated at her right hand.

"Yes, Captain. We hear so little here. How are things going for the South?" Daniel asked, revealing nothing of his own sentiments about the success or failure of the Confederacy.

"Certainly, sir. I would be happy to oblige you. Back at the end of May, General Joe Johnston was severely wounded at the Battle of Seven Pines. General Robert E. Lee took command of the Army of Northern Virginia at that time. General Johnston will be sorely missed, but there is a great deal of faith in General Lee. Lee forced McClellan to retreat from the area of Richmond during the Seven Days Campaign, as the papers are calling it. That happened back on June 25 through July 1. Everyone in Richmond is breathing a lot easier after that victory. Then last month, the end of August, our Southern troops beat General Pope at the Second Battle of Manassas. Their General Fitz-John Porter just sat back and watched what was going on. He had his troops ready, but he would not send them into battle until it was too late." The captain shook his head and smirked at the stupidity of the Northern general. He looked at his audience to see their responses. Daniel had carefully schooled his face so that it reflected only proper Southern sentiment.

"Do go on, Captain. Tell my husband about the most recent news. Oh, Daniel, it is too hideous. I swear you will not believe it." Ellie was proud of the way Daniel had heard the bad news for the Yankee side. She knew what other report was to be made, and wanted to be certain he would be prepared for it as well.

The captain took a sip of his wine and proceeded with his narrative. "Back on the seventeenth of September there was a huge battle at Antietam, up near Sharpsburg in Maryland. The Yankees got as good as they gave, and both sides lost a great many men. However, Lee withdrew to Virginia where his wounded could get better care. The Yankees are claiming a victory at Antietam because he left. There are rumors that the English and French have decided to wait on recognizing the Confederacy because of it. Then just the other day, on September twenty-second, that damned Lincoln sent word that he intends to free all the slaves in areas that remain 'in rebellion' as of January 1, 1863. Can you believe the gall of this man, thinking he can steal our property right out from under our noses? He must recognize that the North is losing the war; nothing else could explain his temerity in trying to do this. Why he could as well have told us that he is freeing all our livestock on January first if we remain at war with the North!" The captain ended his tirade, shaking his head in disbelief, and then drained his wine as if to calm his spirit.

"Absolutely unbelievable!" Daniel agreed, frowning deeply. "What does the man think the South will do in response to such a challenge? Can he really believe that slave owners will lay down their weapons, because they fear that their slaves will suddenly decide to walk off the plantations? Or does he think that the freed slaves would then fill the regiments of the North to fight against their former 'oppressors?'" Daniel questioned with a straight face, looking at Peter standing passively behind the captain as if he had heard none of the conversation.

Conversation shifted to other matters and interests. The soldiers ate heartily and drained several bottles of Ellie's wine. By the end of meal, the men were stifling yawns and gratefully thanking their hosts for the wonderful dinner. Daniel stated their pleasure at being able to entertain the brave men of the South. Ellie stood and proceeded from the room toward the stairs, followed closely by Daniel and Peter.

Peter helped Daniel up the stairs with exaggerated difficulty. At the top, Ellie touched his arm and carefully indicated to him the opposite hallway. He silently followed while Peter led the soldiers to the guest rooms. As soon as they entered her room and the door closed, he softly spoke in jest, "I should have known; you just wanted to get me into your room."

She shook her head, smiling. "I thought I had given you plenty of time to hide."

He leaned one crutch against the wall and reached out to play with one of her curls. "I thought my Confederate nurse was determined to turn me in to the authorities."

"Daniel," she protested, moving closer to him. "I could not, not now."

"Thank you, Ellie." He caressed her cheek with his fingers, a smile playing across his face.

She handed him back his crutch. "Have a seat."

He sat in an armchair; she sat at her dressing table and started taking down her hair. She felt his eyes on her as she ran the brush quickly through her hair, and then started unlacing her boots. She looked up, meeting his eyes. "Do you plan on sleeping in your boots?"

His only response was to start unlacing his own boots; however, his eyes did not leave her, watching as she wiggled her toes. She looked deep in thought. "I am sorry; I was only able to save one of the stallions for you."

"No, Daniel, you did a wonderful job. That man was terrible and you got him to pay more than I ever would have expected, even if it is only Blue Backs. Thank you." She looked up at him, her gratitude shining in her eyes.

"Anytime, you want me to play your husband, I would be pleased to oblige you. However, if that is not the problem, what is?"

She blushed. "I was trying to figure out how to get out of this thing," she yanked on her dress, "with you here and without Mattie's assistance."

"Hmm, you certainly do seem to have a problem." He smiled.

"You are enjoying this too much." She stood and walked to the other side of the bed and pulled down her petticoats. "You cannot sleep in those clothes, either. So what are you going to do about it?" she asked him, laughing at his predicament.

"Have you forgotten so soon?" He feigned being hurt. "I believe you have already seen everything I might have to show." He cockily started unbuttoning his shirt.

She walked over to the lamp and turned it down as low as possible without extinguishing it, and then struggled with the buttons she could reach. She found the string to untie her corset and yanked it, letting out a breath of relief. Out of the corner of her eye, she saw him stand as he dropped his trousers, and then sat back down. She guessed that if she could see him, he would be in his underwear. She was determined not to sleep in her gown and corset. She continued to struggle to get the last two buttons undone. She could hear him fiddling with something. "What are you doing?" she questioned, surprised at the activity she heard.

"Folding my clothes," he responded as if she were mentally challenged.

"Do you do that every night?"

"Yes, I have never had slaves to take care of my things," he responded matter-of-factly.

"You do not have to be nasty!" Ellie snapped back, stung by his words.

"It was a statement of fact, Ellie. I meant nothing more by it." He wondered why she had reacted so strongly. "Let me help you with those buttons."

She walked over to him and knelt down, turning her back to him. He unbuttoned two buttons, and then ran his hand up her back and neck to her hair. She turned, still kneeling between his legs and reached up, touching his covered chest, moving her hand to his throat and neck. She leaned toward him. They kissed for a moment, and then he pushed her away. "Do you have an extra blanket and something I could put my feet up on?"

"No," she said, simply.

"No?" He looked at her, surprised that she would refuse him this comfort.

"There is no reason you cannot share my bed. I trust you would not do anything ungentlemanly. Now, please close your eyes while I finish changing." She walked over to the bed, found his nightshirt and threw it at him, and began changing into her nightgown. When he did not move, she added, "We both have to sleep." She put out the lamp and crawled into bed, pulling down the covers on the other side. She couldn't help but smile in the dark when she felt him sit on the bed. As she felt him lie down beside her, she pulled the covers up over him and then reached out in the dark, caressing his face. She snuggled up next to him, lying on her side; she put her head on his shoulder. He continued lying on his back, holding her close. He seemed afraid to move, as if he were holding his breath.

She started to giggle. "Do you always wear your underwear under your nightshirt?"

"I thought it would be safer," he answered, chagrinned.

"Safer?" She giggled softly again. "Are you afraid of me?"

"No, but maybe you should be of me." He turned on his side, facing her. He touched her face, and then slid his hand behind her head, leaning in to kissing her. She responded by parting her lips and moving her tongue between his. He opened his mouth and met her tongue with his, playfully teasing. As they continued kissing, he began gently rubbing his hand up and down her side. She waited each time for his thumb as it passed slowly over the outer part of her breast. The anticipation of his touch had distracted her from noticing that each time his hand went up so did her nightgown. She realized what he had done when his hand came in contact with her flesh at her waist. While continuing to kiss her, his hand hesitated. She realized he was waiting for a signal from her that he had her consent to go on. She gently started working at his nightshirt in order to slip her hand underneath. She discovered that he had left his drawers on, but was wearing no undershirt. She slowly slid her hand across his stomach and up the center of his chest. As she ran her fingers through his hair, she thought it was just right. He was not especially hairy, but had enough to accentuate his masculinity. In response, he moved his hand slowly up to her bare breast. His hand remained gentle while his kiss became more ardent. He slid his hand to her shoulder, and then pushed her onto her back, continuing to kiss her. His hand then slid back down to her breast while his other hand yanked on her nightgown, pulling it up to expose her. She shivered, tingling throughout her body and mind. He broke the kiss and leaned over her, kissing her breast and running his tongue over and around her nipple. By this time, both nipples were hard, pointing and inviting him. He continued to explore her with his tongue. She breathed deeply, arching, offering more of herself to him. Holding one breast in his hand, he climbed over her, moving back up to kiss her neck and face. She held his nightshirt up, and then slid her hand around his back, encouraging him to rest his bare chest against her breasts. With flesh on flesh, he pushed his tongue deeply into her mouth. As he moved it in and out, she could feel the tip of his penis through his underwear pressing hard between her legs as if it would drive into her, cloth and all. Suddenly he stopped, rolling off of her onto his back, breathing hard. "Ellie, I am so s…"

She interrupted, placing one finger over his lips, "Shh…" She rolled to her side, snuggling next to him, putting her head on his shoulder. He gently pulled her nightgown back down, covering her nakedness. They slept intertwined.

Accustomed to waking early, she quietly slipped out of his arms at first light and dressed. Before leaving the room, she gently kissed his forehead and, believing him to be asleep, whispered, "I love you, Daniel Proctor." She missed his smile as she left the room.

She went down the back stairs to find Lottie cooking and Lela sitting at the table drinking coffee. She poured herself a cup of coffee and started to sit. "Miz Ellie, dem soldiers startin' ta move 'round up dere," Lottie pointed out to her.

Ellie sighed. "I had almost forgotten about them. I will see you later." She sadly left for the dining room, coffee in hand. It wasn't long before she heard footsteps coming down the front stairs. She took a deep breath and straightened her shoulders, preparing herself to be the grand Southern lady of the house. She greeted them cordially and had Peter begin serving them. Soon, they heard the clumping of Daniel coming down the stairs with his crutches. He smiled broadly as he saw them all seated at the table.

"Good morning, gentlemen. I trust you slept well," he greeted them. There were general sounds of agreement. Peter hurried to pull out Daniel's chair. Once Daniel was seated, the butler continued serving the breakfast. They filled themselves on ham and fried eggs, biscuits and sausage gravy, corn bread with fresh butter and fruit jam, and all the fresh coffee and buttermilk they could consume. At last, the captain thanked them again for their kind hospitality, but insisted that it was time to collect their livestock and get back on the road. Ellie and Daniel accompanied them to the barn, purportedly to be social, but neither of them wanted to take the risk that the soldiers would decide to collect more animals than they had purchased. Ellie was especially concerned that the captain would decide to take the last stallion.

They watched in relief as the men rode off with the horses tied together. She touched his arm. "Thank you. I do not want to think what might have happened if you had not been here."

Daniel smiled and patted her hand where it rested on his arm. After a moment, he said, "Ellie, you need to get the list of horses down at the general store. You also need to get word out that they took everything or others will be back."

"I will take one of the brood mares and ride in this afternoon," she assured him.

"No," he cautioned. "Wait until tomorrow; you are liable to catch up with them."

"You are right. Traveling with that many un-mounted horses, their progress may be slow." She began walking slowly back to the house.

"Ellie, you cannot go alone. It is not safe out there. Take a couple of the men with you," he told her firmly, as he too walked back.

"But…" she began, about to debate this with him.

"Ellie, please do not argue with me about this. You do not seem to be aware of the impact you have on men. It is not safe." He stood still, frowning with frustration at her disregard for her own safety and her naïveté about how the world had changed from what she had known.

She wanted to object, but she knew he was right. It seemed strange how things had changed. She had taken care of him and now he was protecting and helping her. They went back to their own rooms as if nothing more had happened between them. However, there was a new understanding and a new closeness.

CHAPTER 20

Lela and Mattie knew not to question her in front of Lottie or within Daniel's hearing, but both were curious. They waited until she was outside picking vegetables to approach her. Mattie brought up a few empty baskets, handing one to Ellie and one to Lela, and then proceeded to pull up some carrots. She found one that was particularly long and wide. Holding it up, she called for the attention of the other women.

"Looky here, ya'll. Look at how big dis here carrot is. Miz Ellie, ain't dis a big carrot? You ever seed anythin' big as dis here carrot afore?" She waved it suggestively in the air. Lela laughed out loud, but Ellie only blushed.

"Ah think Ah done seed sumpin' dat big afore, but Ah ain't rightly sho," Mattie continued. "Do dis carrot look familiar ta ya, Miz Ellie? Maybe it was some diff'rent color o' sumpin'. Maybe it was all red, o' purple, o' sumpin'? What cha think?" She laughed, bringing the carrot closer to Ellie, waving it in front of her.

Ellie stopped picking beans and stood up straight. "I am sure, I have no idea what you could be talking about, Mattie," she stated with great dignity, but found she couldn't stop staring at the waving carrot.

"Now, Mattie," Lela jumped in, still laughing, "Miz Ellie doan know nuthin' 'bout...carrots. She wouldn't know nuthin' 'bout...carrots even ef she was ta sleep next ta one all night long. Miz Charlotte done raised her not to take no notice of...carrots, 'cept she married ta one." Both slaves laughed at that comment. Ellie struggled to keep from joining them in their laughter.

"I ought to sell the both of you down to Mississippi right this minute!" she exclaimed, trying to sound angry, but losing the battle.

"Naw, Lela. Dat ain't necessarily da case. Miz Ellie's had some doin's wid...carrots afore. But she only wants ta look at...carrots. She only wants ta tease...carrots. She doan never let no nasty carrot do what carrots is want ta do...bury demselfs in dark holes!" Mattie doubled over with laughter, almost falling to the ground. Lela put a hand over her own mouth to stifle the screams of laughter coming out of her as she jumped up and down and pointed with the other hand at Ellie's blushing face. Ellie bent down, picked up a clod of loose dirt, and flung it at Mattie just hard enough to reach the other woman. Mattie was caught off guard and fell to the ground, where she continued to roll around and hug herself as she laughed. Ellie rushed over and began tickling the recumbent woman, who only screeched louder. Lela quickly joined in with the other two. It was several minutes before the three of them finally had to stop their foolery in order to catch their breath.

As they lay in a bunch in the middle of the garden, gasping, Lela finally asked, "Well, Miz Ellie? Did ya let da man do some gardenin' last night or didn't ya?" This sent Mattie into another paroxysm of laughter. Ellie pushed Lela over, laughing and gasping along with them, but she didn't answer their questions. She struggled to her feet and began brushing some of the dirt off her clothes. She extended her hands to help the other two women up. They all picked up their baskets and returned to their tasks. After a few minutes, Mattie called to Lela, "Ah doan think she let dat po' man plant nothin' last night. Jist as well. Root crops planted at night bear a lot of fruit!"

Once again, Lela covered her mouth with one hand to stifle a screech and pointed with the other at Mattie. Ellie turned bright red, and then burst out laughing once again. "I swear," she gasped out when she could breath again, "I do not know who is worse! You two have no respect for me at all." She wiped the tears from her eyes and surveyed the remnants of the garden. "If you think you can concentrate for half an hour, we can clear out the rest of the vegetables before lunch. And I really do not want to hear another word about…carrots!" The other two women tried very hard to look chastened and penitent, but found it difficult to suppress their giggles.

After lunch, Ellie had Joey hook up one of the brood mares that would not be foaling until late spring. She had both Joey and Nathaniel accompany her, taking a hunting rifle under the seat, as well as a pistol and a wad of Blue Backs in her bag. They drove quickly into Sheldon and tied up at the store.

Mr. Franks came to the door to greet Ellie, smiling broadly. "Well, if it isn't Miss Ellie, or should I say, Mrs. Proctor? I heard tell you got married and no one the wiser here abouts. Any truth to that rumor, Miss Ellie?"

Ellie was taken aback by his greeting. She saw other neighbors inside the store maneuvering to hear how she responded. "Why, Mr. Franks, you should know better than to listen to idle gossip." She smiled to show that she was not offended. "I would never marry without inviting you to the service. Who were the little magpies that made such accusations?"

The storekeeper had the good grace to look embarrassed. "Why a troop of our boys came through here with a string of the finest horses in the parish. They said they had just bought twenty horses from Whispering Oaks Farm. The captain said that he had negotiated with a Mr. Proctor. I corrected him, figuring that Mr. Barton had come back and he must have dealt with him. But he insisted that he had spoken with both Mr. and Mrs. Proctor. What was I to think, knowing your mother and sister were both away?"

Ellie patted the rotund man's arm reassuringly. "The soldiers did, indeed, buy twenty of my horses. As a matter of fact, I have come to remove my advertisement because they took all my available stock. They wanted to take all of my stallions as well. I, of course, protested that I would not be able to run the farm without at least one stallion, but that captain did not care to listen to a mere woman. When he saw Mr. Proctor, he assumed that he was my husband and began doing business with him. I was not about to disabuse the captain of his notion; if it meant that a better deal would be negotiated. I trust you think I did the right thing. I had no one to consult at the time." She looked up at him with the most pitiful, helpless female expression she could conjure up. Out of the corner of her eye, she saw some of the other customers bending their heads together in discussion. There were one or two nods of approval, but there were also several scowls of consternation.

"Of course you did, Miss Ellie. I am relieved to hear that there is a man about the premises. Have you hired a new overseer? Is that who this Mr. Proctor is? And why did he not come to town for you?" Mr. Franks asked with some concern.

"Oh, silly me," Ellie responded. "Of course you do not know Mr. Proctor. He's been a friend of James' for so long. We heard about him for years before meeting him. He and James studied the law together up in Columbia. He enlisted at the same time as James, and was wounded at the battle of Kernstown. His family is all the way out west in the territories, so we had him come to us to recuperate. Mr. Proctor does not get around well on his own, as yet, or I would certainly have brought him in to see our little town." Ellie found she was running out of lies to add to the story and hoped that her audience would be content with what she had said without requesting further details.

"One of our own boys, wounded in battle, and you nursing him and running the farm. And not a word of complaint. I declare, Ellie, you are a fine example to the women of the South," one of the women told her, smiling and patting her arm. Ellie blushed at the commendation, knowing how they would respond if they only knew the truth. She could see many of the others seemed contented with her explanation and accepted the situation; however, one or two of the women, the worst gossips in the area, looked suspicious. Ellie feared there would be trouble. She put on her bravest smile and proceeded to make her purchases. She had just finished and was directing Joey to take the supplies out to the wagon when she was approached by the priest of the Old Sheldon Church.

"Good afternoon, Ellie," he said, smiling warmly at her.

"Good afternoon, Father Burton. What a lovely surprise to see you here." Ellie returned his smile with genuine pleasure.

"We have missed you at mass. I understand that you have been very busy with the farm and, apparently, with nursing duties. I will not keep you standing and chatting. I know you will want to get back home. Do be careful. The area is hip deep in Confederate troops, and some of them are less than the gentlemen you have been accustomed to seeing." He raised a cautionary finger.

"Thank you, Father. I shall certainly take great care. And I hope to come back to services in the near future. I am sure Mother and Suzanne will be returning soon, now that the weather is starting to cool."

"We look forward to having you at church again. And I hope to see Mr. Proctor there as well, once he has recovered. Take care, now." He tipped his hat at her and left the store. As he walked out of hearing, Ellie slowly let out a sigh of relief and proceeded out the door in his wake.

Ellie was lost in thought on the drive back to Whispering Oaks. The word was out that she had an unmarried man in her house. She knew that if it were not for the war her reputation would be completely destroyed. As it was, it was already in question. She contemplated whether she had made a mistake not saying it was true that they had been married. However, Charlotte would never believe it. She was not sure she could even pass him off as one of James' friends to her. In business and politics, her mother might be naïve; however, not much got by her when it came to Ellie or men. To ask Daniel to keep up the façade of being her husband would be too presumptuous on her part. Yet,…if he asked… How long before he would want to go back to being a Yankee and fighting against her people? He was getting stronger and probably only really needed one crutch. She sighed, not wanting to think about losing him. She hoped he would survive the war, whether he came back to her afterwards or not. She reprimanded herself for being presumptuous again. Neither had spoken of any kind of future. Maybe war did not permit thoughts of tomorrow; there may not be one.

She came out of her reverie as they were on the last stretch of the drive before coming to the entrance of the farm. She noticed the whitewash on the fencing had faded and the brush was overgrown. The reduction of man power was showing. She pointed it out to Nathaniel, asking that when things were slow he assign someone to working on it. As they came down the drive, she could see the porch was filled with slaves. Daniel was among them and Lottie was serving refreshments. The trip had taken longer than she thought. She realized how she liked their current life style. As long as she did not think about the past or the future, she was content.

She walked up the stairs, carrying her bag and the rifle. Peter took the weapon from her and Lottie replaced it with a hot cup of tea. She sat in the chair next to Daniel, feeling suddenly tired.

"Did you run into any problems on the trip?" he asked with concern, having noted her expression.

"No, the drive was fine. There was no need for concern." She leaned her head back and closed her eyes.

"See, Ah tol' ya. She's allas doin' thins no lady should do an' she come back jist fine," Lottie commented.

Ellie just smiled and shook her head. It was obvious that they had been talking about her and Daniel had been worried for her safety. "The town knows you are here and probably half of the Parish."

"Why have they not come to take me away?" he asked, sounding more surprised than anxious.

"There is considerable speculation as to who you are; however, the idea that I could be harboring a Yankee is beyond their imagination." She hesitated. "Daniel, these people are good people. It is just that they are…" she fumbled for the right words, "…attached to their traditions and way of life."

"I should leave," he said quietly, frowning at the predicament.

"No one is stopping you!" She knew the anger she was feeling was unreasonable. "Do you think you are capable of walking to Beaufort on crutches? Or have you changed your mind about letting your horse return to battle?"

"Ellie, I am not a deserter. I will go back to my regiment if I am not a prisoner. It is only a matter of when I will go."

The slaves became quiet at the tone between Ellie and Daniel. It seemed to make them uncomfortable. Ellie noticed their reaction and decided to discuss it later in private. "I know."

Before anything else could be said, Nathaniel joined them on the porch. Not knowing what had been happening, he approached Ellie. "Miz Ellie, ef it doan rain, we kin start ta clearin' out da front next week."

"That will be fine, Nathaniel," Ellie responded distractedly.

"Clearing out what, Nathaniel?" Daniel asked.

"You do not need to…" She turned away from Daniel. "Go ahead and tell him." The annoyance was still evident in her voice.

"Miz Ellie noticed da fencin' by da road needs paintin' an' it's all overgrowed," the slave explained.

Trying his best to keep the sound of command out of his voice, Daniel said, "Ellie, you need to let it grow even more."

"What? What interest is it to you?" she demanded, rounding on him.

"Ellie, when I was injured, I was looking for food, water, and a place to hide and rest. I was following that white fence. It was what led me here. Do you want more Yankees at your door? Or Confederates who will take the rest of your horses?"

"No. …I am sorry I snapped at you." She wanted to escape. She knew she had behaved badly, she also knew she was hurt and angry and had more to say; however, she did not want an audience. She held up her bag. "I need to put some things away."

She went straight to her father's study, closing the door behind her. She took the remaining Blue Backs out of her purse and opened the middle drawer to put them away. There was a half written letter sitting in it. She took the letter out. It began, "My dearest Ellie." She realized this must have been what Daniel was writing when she had walked in on him with the Confederate officer. She read it quickly, feeling as if she had invaded someone else's secret. It was evident that he had expected that she might have to turn him over to protect herself and her honor and that he had accepted his fate. He asked that she write to him in Pennsylvania once the war was over. He wanted her to be a part of his life. She put the letter back, putting the money in a different drawer. He wasn't running from her; he was trying to protect her. She put her head in her hands; she had to stop doubting him. She opened the door and saw Peter in the hall. She asked him to send Daniel to the study.

"You summoned me?" He was still annoyed by her attitude toward him.

She walked over and closed the door. "Daniel, I am so sorry. You…when you said you would leave, I…I was hurt. You do not have to leave to protect me. I know you will go, but it does not have to be now." She returned to stand before him, pleading with him.

He grasped her outstretched hand, looking earnestly into her eyes. "Ellie, you have to live here. Your neighbors will be important to you in getting through this war."

"I know that. If my sister, Suzanne, was to tell the story, everyone would question it. Everyone expects me to tell the truth, regardless of the consequences." She smiled. "In fact, I have a reputation for chasing men away."

"But you were engaged?" he responded, very surprised.

"Ted and I were friends since childhood. I do not think anyone ever saw us as anything but friends."

"Did you love him?" he asked very quietly.

"In a way. He was the only one who accepted my ideas, not that he agreed; he just did not judge me for them." She looked down at their intertwined fingers.

"You sound as if you did not expect much from your marriage."

"Oh, I had my dreams; but after a while…well, everyone seemed against me. Ted and I understood each other and he agreed to live here. It made our families happy."

Squeezing her fingers, Daniel stated, "Ellie, you should never give up on your dreams."

The tears started flowing down her cheeks. Here her dream was standing before her, preparing to leave. "Please, do not leave yet. You are not ready and I need you."

"What would you need me for? Have I not caused you enough difficulty?" He moved closer to her, moved by her tears.

"If you really want to help me, you will stay and go to church on Sunday." She was trying to contain her emotions; she had already shown him more weakness than she wanted anyone to see.

Daniel shook his head in negation. "Ellie, it would only make things worse."

"I did not tell you everything that happened at the store. They know the overseer left. The idea of a white woman being alone with no one to control the slaves or protect her from the slaves or Yankees is unthinkable. To them it is better that I be a harlot, than killed or raped by a Negro."

"These people are kind, God fearing people; how could anyone think they might hurt you?" Daniel frowned in disbelief.

"I do not believe anyone here would, but my neighbors know in their hearts that owning someone is wrong. They would try to kill their masters, if they were owned. They are afraid." She gave him a moment to let it sink in, but before he could respond, she mumbled, "Besides, the priest wants to meet you."

Daniel stared at her for several seconds in silence. "Did I hear you correctly?"

"I think he believes he can divine your intentions." She tried to laugh. She was nervous about the risk of exposing him and that she might not be able to hide her feelings.

"I do not know how wise this is, Ellie. However, if you believe it will help you, I will go with you to church."

She did not answer. She was still too sad, knowing he would leave and that their time together was getting shorter. He sensed her emotion and asked no more, but took her into his arms and held her. The tears returned, wetting his shirt. He just held her tighter, stroking her head, waiting for them to subside. When they finally did, he teased her about the streaks of dirt on her face from the drive and sent her off to clean up and rest before dinner. While Mattie scrubbed her back, she joked, "We could break da udder leg." Ellie splashed her with bath water in response. For a moment, the two women laughed.

At dinner, there was no anger between them; however, they were both unusually subdued. Ellie retired to her room early, forgoing their usual evening. She lay in bed, staring into the darkness. In the quiet, she heard his crutches coming up the stairs, walking to his room, and then coming back down the hall. He stopped in front of her door. After another minute, she heard his crutches heading back down the hall to his room. She didn't bother to wipe away the silent tears.

CHAPTER 21

The next morning, Ellie rode to the upper fields. She saw that Nathaniel had things well in hand, but she stayed visiting with the workers, delaying her return to the house. She didn't know what to say to Daniel. She wanted to ask him to stay longer; she wanted to ask him to come back for her after the war. His letter had given her hope, but he hadn't finished it. He hadn't said enough. She was unsure where he was going with it. She did not know if he truly wanted her to share his life or was being kind in response to her aid. Once he left, would he be forced to fight against her friends and neighbors, or would he do it willingly? Would he survive it? If only it would end before he had to leave. She remained quiet throughout lunch, afterwards going into the study, closing the door behind her. She opened the desk drawer, wanting to read the letter again, but it was gone. She realized she could not let him leave without getting some answers. She believed he cared about her; however, she had no idea in what way or to what extent.

Over the next few days, she made an effort to ease the tension between them. She was unable to ask what she wanted to know. She did not want to put him in an awkward position if he did not have feelings for her. Nor did she want to admit her feelings. The conversations remained superficial. There were no good night kisses. Ellie avoided them, afraid she might want him even more, or worse, he might not respond.

Sunday morning, Mattie woke Ellie with a cup of coffee in hand and pulled out a black dress and a dark russet one. "Which are ya wearin' ta church?" the maid enquired.

"The black," Ellie responded, stretching and yawning.

"Ya look better in da russet," Mattie stated unequivocally.

"Mattie, it has not been a year yet. I am still in mourning. I will not embarrass the family."

Mattie shrugged and said, "Daniel's dressed an' waitin' fo' ya ta take ya ta church."

"So soon?" The color drained from Ellie's cheeks and she felt a terrible sadness settle on her chest.

Misunderstanding her mistress' response to her statement, Mattie explained, "Ya slep' late, Miz Ellie."

"No, Mattie. ...He is going to leave." Her desperation was plain in her countenance.

"Den stop chasin' him away," Mattie responded, looking at Ellie as if she were a child.

Ellie knew Mattie was right. "I will wear the russet one." The first step would be to stop wearing black for a man she had not married. It was not required of her for Ted, and would not change her feelings for her brother or her father. She dressed and took her bag.

"Ya's takin' a gun to church?" Mattie was appalled at the idea.

"It is not safe to leave the farm without protection, these days." She quickly left the room and nearly ran down the stairs. Daniel was waiting in the living room. Without saying a word, she straightened his jacket when he stood to meet her. She then took the pistol out of her purse and slipped it into his pocket.

Joey had the small carriage waiting for them at the foot of the steps. Ellie accepted Daniel's hand as she climbed up. Once he settled in on the seat next to her, she handed him the reins. When they came to the end of the drive, he stopped the horse. "Have you changed your mind?" she asked him, surprised by the stop.

He looked at her briefly, letting her worry for a moment, and then replied, "No. I do not know which way to go."

"Left!" She smiled. They had spent so much time together, it had seemed normal that he would know the way. It had not even occurred to her that they had never before been off of the farm together. Half-way there she started giggling.

"What is so funny?"

"I was just thinking that you drive horses better than chairs." She laughed and hugged his arm.

"As long as no trees jump out in front of us, I will get you to church safely." He kept a straight face, but his eyes were smiling.

She stroked his arm. "Thank you, Daniel. I know the risk you are taking."

"I am afraid, you may be taking the bigger risk," he replied, his voice quiet and serious, all trace of humor gone from it.

She was silent until they arrived at the church grounds. She was relieved to see that her neighbors were already filing into the church and that they would not have to talk to anyone until after the service. She felt eyes following her and Daniel as they walked up the aisle to her family's pew. Once the service began, she was surprised at the quality of Daniel's singing and that he knew the words to most of the songs. The priest looked at her as he began his sermon. She feared he might rail against immoral behaviors, but instead he spoke of Christian charity and how, during these times of war, it was especially important to care for our fallen soldiers and their families. Ellie realized he was defending her actions to the community. She blushed at the thought that this soldier was a Yankee and wondered if the priest would defend her if he knew the truth. She had convinced herself the words still applied regardless of the side an injured man was on: North or South. She had not planned on falling in love with him.

At the end of the service, Ellie squeezed Daniel's hand, careful that no one saw. He was more of a gentleman than many she knew in the parish. She just hoped no one would recognize that he was also a Yankee. They waited for the other parishioners to pass, so that Daniel could follow slowly behind on his crutches. Ellie found herself holding her breath as they approached the smiling priest. She could see the priest greeting his parishioners. She was concerned about what questions he might put to Daniel and whether Daniel was prepared for them. After all, for all she knew, he was some heathen who had no religion. It was their turn all too soon.

"Ah, hello Ellie. I am so very glad you were able to make it to mass today." He smiled affably and waited for her to make the introduction.

"Father Burton, I would like to introduce you to Lieutenant Daniel Proctor, the gentleman I spoke of at the store. You may recall that he is a friend of my late brother James, and went to school with him in Columbia. We have been very fortunate to be able to provide him with some comforts while he recuperates from the injuries he suffered at the battle of Kernstown." Ellie heard herself running on and thought she sounded just a bit hysterical, but she wanted to be sure that Daniel had the story correct.

"A pleasure to meet you, sir. It is good to see that your recovery is progressing so well. And, of course, we are delighted to have you here in our little church. Are you a member of the Episcopalian congregation?" The priest was smiling, but it seemed to Ellie that he was staring straight into Daniel's soul. She tried to wait quietly for his response, but found that she was pushing her fingernails into the palms of her hands.

"Thank you for the warm welcome, Father. I am, in fact, a member of the Methodist Church, but our people have always gotten along well with the Episcopalians in our town," Daniel told him.

"Well, we are all children of the Lord, certainly. And you seem to be a respectable gentleman. I am certain that the families of Prince William Parish would welcome you if you were to settle here after the war," the priest stated, hoping to get some indication of Daniel's intentions toward Ellie.

"This is certainly a lovely area of the country, and has many qualities to recommend it to someone looking for a place to settle. I can imagine that a man could be very happy living here," Daniel replied, turning to look at Ellie.

"Absolutely true!" Father Burton exclaimed. "And a marvelous place to raise children, wouldn't you say?"

Ellie felt herself blushing, but waited with bated breath for Daniel's response.

"I could not imagine any place better, sir," Daniel concurred.

"Of course, the children of a family where the parents are of mixed religions should preferably be raised in the mother's faith. After all, she is the one who would spend the most time with them and would, therefore, have the greatest influence over them. Would you not agree?" Father Burton raised a challenging eyebrow as he looked to Daniel for this most important response.

"Indeed, I feel you are correct again, Father. Provided, of course, that the mother is a Christian woman." Daniel's response shocked the priest a bit. Just the hint that a Christian man would think of marrying outside of his faith was appalling. Ellie knew that it was time to get him away from the churchman, before Daniel's playfulness created a scandal.

"Goodness, Father. We have been taking far too much of your time. I see there are several others waiting to speak with you. I am certain we will see you next Sunday. Have a good week." And with that she tugged Daniel by the arm to start him moving away from temptation. They were quickly approached by neighbors with varying agendas. All of them wanted to get a good look at Daniel and make an attempt to discern what the relationship between him and Ellie really was. Some of them were truly concerned for her and for her recovering patient; some were attracted by the presence of a handsome young man; others were just looking for a juicy tidbit of gossip to pass on elsewhere. Ellie did her best to keep her impatience in check and be polite toward everyone. Daniel smiled and made appropriate responses to offers of support. He was less responsive to the more obvious invasions of privacy. They were almost to the carriage again, when Ellie heard her name called in a giddy feminine voice. She stiffened as she realized that the voice was that of the biggest flirt in the parish.

"Why, Ellie Peters! I declare, we have all been so worried about you out there on your farm with no man around to protect you. Now here you turn up at church with this dashing beau on your arm. You absolutely must introduce me to him!" The blond curled head bounced as punctuation to her demand.

"Hello, Betty Jane," Ellie said through clenched teeth and a very stiff smile. "It is so nice to see you again, as well. This is Lieutenant Daniel Proctor. He went to school with James and has been recuperating from wounds at Whispering Oaks. Daniel, this is Elizabeth Jane Stuart."

Daniel made an abbreviated bow to the young woman and said, "A pleasure Miss Stuart."

"Oh, Lieutenant Proctor, what a pleasure. We get so few eligible men in the area since the war started. All our beaus have marched off to war, leaving us behind to live lives of abject loneliness. It is truly wonderful to see a handsome man who is over fourteen and under sixty. You seem to be recovering very nicely. Perhaps, once you are feeling up to it, you might consider coming to pay a call on my family. I know my mother would get great pleasure out of hearing about your experiences in the war." Betty Jane offered her most persuasive smile, tilting her head and batting her lovely blue eyes at him. She didn't even bother to look at Ellie when she added, "Oh, you must come, too, Ellie."

"I am flattered at your invitation, Miss Stuart, but I fear that I will have little time for visiting once I am recovered." The smile on his face was just barely definable as polite. "I hope you will excuse us. I fear I have been standing too long and need to sit down. Good day, ma'am." He reached up to tug at the brim of his hat, turned to look at Ellie to see if she was ready to move on, and proceeded to the carriage without so much as a backward glance. He assisted Ellie into the carriage, and then handed his crutches to her and climbed in next to her. Picking up the reins, he guided the horse out of the churchyard and through the traffic.

Once they were well away from any other carriages, Ellie poked him. "I do not know whatever made me think you might not be accepted as a proper Confederate gentleman." She started laughing in an attempt to hide her jealousy and concern. "Your biggest problem will be the number of women chasing you. After all, there are no other prospects left in the area."

Daniel responded defensively, "I did not encourage any of those women."

"Really?" Ellie asked, archly.

"Damn it, Ellie Peters! You are the only one I want," he exclaimed, dropping the reins to turn and argue with her.

She grabbed the reins and stopped the mare. She did not know whether to castigate him for his language or throw her arms around him. "Daniel Proctor, do you really mean what you just said?"

"Ellie, what do I have to do to convince you?" he asked helplessly.

She mumbled softly, "Do not die."

"Oh, Ellie. I am too stubborn to die," he reassured her.

"You almost died. Were you not stubborn then?" She sounded like a frightened child, but she couldn't help it. She so desperately wanted to keep him with her and to keep him safe.

"I had no plans then." He tried to hide his smile.

She looked up at him doubtfully. "And now, suddenly, you do?"

He took the reins away from her, clucked to the mare to get her moving, and started humming.

"You are infuriating." She crossed her arms, realizing she was not going to get any more out of him.

He kept humming until they pulled up in front of the house. Lottie had prepared lunch and had been waiting anxiously. Over the meal, it became apparent that all the slaves had been worried the entire time they were gone.

CHAPTER 22

The days fell back into their routine. Evenings, Ellie remained in the living room with Daniel, talking, reading, and playing chess. They walked up the stairs together, kissed good night at the top, and walked down opposite halls to their rooms. The kisses were tender and prolonged. Ellie often stopped at her door, watching him as he walked the rest of the way to his room. He looked back at her each night before going through the doorway. She believed his eyes were expressing the same longing she felt, until he'd wink or toss out a sarcastically suggestive comment. She'd blush and slip into her room. She would lie in bed nights, trying to understand him. He had not touched her since the night they had slept in the same bed. He led her to believe he wanted her, but he took no action. She did not want to tease him as she had Ted. She was not looking to test him. She wanted to be in his arms; she wanted to be close to him.

After nearly a week, she decided she would not wait any longer for him to make another advance. Saturday evening, Ellie brought over two glasses, a bottle of wine, and a corkscrew and sat down on the couch next to Daniel. She interrupted his reading with a poke in the side, and then handed him the unopened bottle. He put down his book, "If you would like me to play your husband again, please hand me the corkscrew."

"If you are going to play my husband, are you sure this is the corkscrew you want?" She waved the corkscrew, holding it far out of his reach.

"Mrs. Proctor, please give that to me if you would like some wine."

She giggled, "Come get it."

He slowly put the bottle down on the table in front of him, and then turned on the couch to face her. "Hmm. You are not playing fair."

She just gave him a big smile, waving the bottle opener. He tried reaching past her, but she leaned back, keeping it out of reach. He leaned in toward her. When he recognized he was not going to get it that way, he grabbed her other hand, pulling her toward him. She started laughing. He slipped his arm around her waist, trying to pull her closer, and then put his other hand on her shoulder. She wiggled, trying to keep her arm free and continued to laugh. As he leaned farther forward, she became pinned between him and the arm of the couch.

"Ah, you are not going to get away now." As he said it, he looked away from the object and into her eyes. She tilted her head and slightly parted her lips. Daniel lowered his head until his mouth brushed hers. He teased his tongue across her lips and back, slipping it in as he began to kiss her. He had one arm still around her waist and his hand moved slowly down below the bottom of her corset; the other hand moved up through her hair, holding her head while he kissed her passionately. The corkscrew fell out of her hand, landing with a clunk. After another moment, he broke the kiss and climbed over her and snatched it off the floor. He was still on top of her, "Did you really think you could keep me from getting it?"

He opened the bottle and, as he filled the glasses, she responded, "It is not over yet."

He turned to smile provocatively at her. "I certainly hope not."

She talked, pestered, and distracted him the rest of the evening. When they got to the top of the stairs, he leaned one crutch against the wall, pulling her close to him with his free arm, kissing her good-night. In the morning, he was dressed for church and waiting for her when she came downstairs.

Both were concerned by the number of soldiers they had seen on the road and officers who had attended church. They remained quiet, each in their own thoughts as they were driving back from church. In her concern, Ellie could not stop herself from staring at him. She became distracted by thoughts of how their day had started; she felt as if she were married to him already, and realized, as she visually examined him, that she would not have the strength or desire to stop him from exercising his marital rights. She blushed at the thought.

When they arrived home, they joined Lottie, Peter, and Lela for lunch. They found out that Mattie was off entertaining Henry. For a brief moment, she envied them. When they finished eating, she sent Lottie and Peter off for the rest of the day, wanting to be alone in the house with Daniel. She asked Lela to help her with her dress and corset before she left and changed into a more casual dress. She had come to enjoy the freedom of not wearing a corset when she had given it up in the summer heat. When she came back downstairs, she found Daniel sitting on the couch; he appeared to be deep in thought. She moved his crutches in order to sit down next to him. "Daniel, is there something bothering you?"

He sighed dramatically. "Yes, I was trying to decide what to fix for supper, since you do not know how to cook and you dismissed the staff."

"I do so know how to cook!" She told him, pinching his arm. "But you are not going to get away with avoiding my question."

Daniel became the picture of outraged innocence. "I answered your question. Are you sure you can cook?"

Ellie became suddenly serious. "Daniel, I know you better than you think."

"Now, I had forgotten you undressed me," he responded with a lecherous smile, and reached out to try to embrace her.

Ellie pushed him back to arm's length and said, "You are concerned about the number of soldiers we saw today."

Daniel gave up his amorous attack and responded seriously. "Ellie, something is going to happen soon. By the number of Confederate troops we saw today, my guess is there are hundreds more. Add that to the sudden need for horses and your military believes there are Union troops on their way into the area."

Ellie drew in a deep breath, trying to extinguish the fear that boiled up into her stomach. "I hate this war."

Daniel leaned down over her, willing her to understand and comply. "Ellie, promise me you will not leave the farm and that you will stay close to the house."

"I will not leave the farm, but I do have to check on things," she temporized.

Daniel frowned at her stubbornness. "Not without me going with you."

"Then, I guess I need to tell you my last secret." She looked up at him, trying to gauge his reaction.

His playfulness reasserted itself. "Only one more?" he asked doubtfully.

"Yes." She swatted his arm. "I have another stallion hidden with twenty more horses out in one of the back pastures."

Daniel immediately looked crestfallen. "I am disappointed. I thought for sure it would be something more...personal."

"You already know everything else."

"Not quite!" He took her into his arms and kissed her.

She thought, *Sunday afternoon on the couch?* She was glad she'd sent the staff away. She wished she could have him to herself all the time. She understood honeymoons for the first time. When Ted had suggested Paris, it was the trip she had been excited about, the time alone with him had not even crossed her mind. They cuddled on the couch, talking and reading to each other. As the shadows lengthened with the late afternoon sun, the room cooled; Ellie went to the fireplace and tried to get it started.

"Ellie, stop!" Daniel commanded.

"It is getting chilly in here." She was confused by his unreasonable demand.

"No more day time fires, unless it is raining. It may draw troops from both sides."

She stopped, turning back to the fireplace in thought. She then jumped up, grabbed her shawl, and headed toward the door.

"Where are you going?" he called after her as she hurried away.

"I have to tell the slaves," she called back to him, hardly slowing down.

"Ellie, tell them no more lamps at night; one candle if they absolutely have to see something."

She stopped and turned to look at him. "I never would have thought of these things."

"Ellie, if you were in a strange place looking for food and a dry, warm shelter, the first time you saw light in the darkness or smoke from a fireplace, you would have thought of it."

"But from this house, I would not have seen it." She ran out the door and went knocking on cabins. She left her shawl wrapped around Mama Noli and ran back to the house.

"Ellie, you left me stranded." His crutches were leaning against a chair across the room.

"I just wanted to make sure you could not escape." She laughed, but thought how she wished it would be that easy to keep him; however, she also knew she wanted him to want to stay with her, not because he was trapped by his situation. She brought the crutches to him.

"You are cold." He was holding her hand, but staring at her breasts.

She sat close to him. He wrapped his arms around her, rubbing her arms and holding her close. They sat together waiting for the sun to go down before going to the kitchen to heat some food and make some tea. He teased her and directed her preparations by the light of a single candle. At times, he stood behind her, making contact as he looked over her shoulder, making comments. She elbowed him in the stomach after one particularly snide comment; however, he had been prepared and it had no effect. He had been leaning with one hand on each side of her on the table. She could feel his penis growing hard against her back. She looked over her shoulder and quickly kissed him on the lips. She wanted to reach back and touch him, but she did not know what he would think of her. Instead, she turned around between his arms, facing him, waiting for his response. He continued leaning toward her, kissing her face and neck, gliding his tongue up to her ear, tickling her. He moved one hand off the table, putting it on her waist. He watched his hand in the dim light as he gently moved it over her stomach and her breast, moving his finger tips around and over her nipple. Even through her dress and camisole, her body began to tingle, and she sighed out her pleasure, letting her head roll back, effectively pushing her breasts toward him.

Daniel suddenly stopped. "I doubt your cooking will taste as good as you."

"With all these distractions, it probably is not my best," she responded a bit breathlessly, smoothing stray hair out of her face with the back of her hand.

"Mmmmm. Are you feeling distracted, Ellie?" he murmured in her ear.

"As if you are not." She quickly brushed her hand over the bulge in his trousers.

Daniel jumped back, nearly losing his balance. She grabbed his arm in an attempt to offer support, and they started laughing simultaneously. They sat at the table, ate dinner, and played cards just like an old married couple. At last, each yawning, they rose. Taking the stub of burning candle, Ellie led Daniel up the back stairs and down the hallway to his room. The mid-October nights were cool, but they decided extra blankets would suffice. Ellie found one in the bottom of her brother's armoire and spread it on the bed. She warmly kissed him and started to leave, but Daniel pulled her back for a second good-night.

Ellie snuck back in during the night and stole one crutch.

CHAPTER 23

She woke just before sunrise, hearing sounds from downstairs. Ellie put on her robe and, taking the pistol, tiptoed down the back stairs in her bare feet. She began to smell coffee as she came around the corner into the kitchen. "Lottie, why are you here so early?"

"Ya gonna shoot me?" the portly cook asked, eyes wide in alarm.

Ellie put the weapon down on the table.

"Ef ya's gonna have a hot brekfuss, it had ta be cooked afore light."

"Thank you, Lottie." She gave the old woman a hug, and then sat at the table. Mattie and Lela soon joined her. Each noted the gun, but made no comment. They were discussing how to get around cooking and heating difficulties when they heard Daniel's deep male voice bellowing from upstairs. "Ellie! Ellie Maitland Peters!"

She started laughing.

"Miz Ellie, what ya do ta dat man now?" Lottie looked sternly at her mistress.

"I stole one crutch during the night." She was quite proud of herself.

"Dat's not nice ta do." The portly cook shook her finger at Ellie. "How he gonna walk?" Lottie put her hands on her hips and glared at Ellie as if she were a mischievous child.

"Lottie, he is much better," Ellie reassured her. "It is time for him to start giving up the crutches. Soon I will give him my grandfather's old cane. It is still in the attic."

"Lela, go git Peter ta hep him," Lottie instructed, swinging a towel at the other slave.

"No! He needs to do it himself," Ellie commanded.

"Ah neva' seen dis mean streak in ya afore, Miz Ellie," the cook stated, somewhat alarmed by the discovery.

"I am trying to help him, Lottie… What I would really like to do is keep him in the wheelchair until this war is over." Suddenly, the humor fled from her eyes, and her fear for Daniel became apparent.

The other women saw her sadness and attempted to distract her. By the time Daniel made his way down the back stairs on one crutch, the women were laughing so hard they did not hear his approach. "If the theft of my crutch was an attempt to keep me out of this raucous gathering, it did not work," he announced indignantly from the doorway.

They laughed all the harder. Ellie made room at the table, pushing the pistol out of his way. Lottie put a cup of hot coffee in front of him. His annoyance turned to confusion, "Were you all in on it?"

Lela and Mattie giggled, but Ellie spoke up. "I did it. You are a very sound sleeper."

"Do you sneak into my room regularly, Miss Peters?" he asked with just a hint of arousal at the idea in his voice.

She smiled and raised her eyebrows as if to say, "Wouldn't you like to know?"

Lottie, witnessing this exchange, widened her eyes as if terrified and stated, "Lordy, Miz Ellie, ya betta not be goin' in dat room nights. Yo mama will wup me when she git back."

Lela and Mattie tried to hold back their giggles. "Oh, Lottie, ya's in trouble fo' da night da soldiers was here. Ah'll be da one what gits wupped fo' her goin' in his room," Mattie teased.

Lela laughed aloud when she saw Daniel's startled face and pointed at him.

"Stop it, you two. He does not understand." Ellie joined in the laughter, when she saw him frown at her statement. She turned to him, "Mother would not know which end of a whip to hold."

He was visibly relieved, realizing Lottie hadn't really meant it and the others were teasing him. The look he then gave Ellie made her realize he would try getting her back. As she wondered what he might do, it occurred to her that she was sitting at the table in her nightgown and robe. No one had mentioned it. Despite the fact that he had seen her in this outfit before, she felt uncomfortable with him seeing her dishabille in front of the slaves. She thought that, if she were to remain sitting, maybe he would not notice. Peter arrived, raised an eyebrow, but did not comment. Ellie was unsure what the silent comment was about, her night clothes, the pistol, or the early morning gathering. When no one seemed to be leaving the table, Ellie needed to figure out how to get Daniel out of the room. Finally, she came up with something. "Peter, will you take Daniel to the study and give him his papers and saddlebag. We may need for him to identify himself for who he really is."

"Ya think dem Yankees may come here?" Lottie was visibly upset.

"No, but they are his things," Ellie reassured her.

"If you think I am going to leave this table before you do," he patted her hand, "you are wrong. She is just trying to get me out of the room, Lottie. There is no reason for you to worry."

"Ah thought you was a gent'man. Ya gonna make Miz Ellie sit dere all day?"

"Yes!" He smiled smugly.

"This is for the crutch. Now we are even." She put her hand on the pistol and stood.

As she walked head up, out of the room, he called after her. "It is not over yet." She could hear him and the others laughing.

When she came back downstairs, she informed him that she needed to check the horses in the back pasture and asked if he still wanted to accompany her. He nodded and wobbled along behind her. He was still trying to get accustomed to walking with one crutch. Joey helped Ellie saddle up a couple of horses. They walked on horseback out toward the back pasture; Ellie quickly legged her horse into an easy canter. She felt Daniel's leg could handle that gait better than a trot.

She stopped to open the gate without dismounting, waited for Daniel to go through and re-closed it. They both dismounted when they arrived at the small herd. He assisted in examining the horses, also spending extra time with the young ones. "Ellie, they need shelter. The winter rains are cold, especially for the weanlings."

"The other shelter took Lela, her brother, and me months to complete. I do not have the time or the manpower now." She shrugged helplessly.

"It does not have to be as elaborate. I will work on it."

"How are you..." she began, and then realized how he might feel about her lack of belief in his abilities. "We will find someone to help you. Thank you."

"Those two trees will make a good start." He paced it, counting it out, continuing to use the horse in lieu of a crutch. He surveyed the area, nodding. "It will not take long."

Without a stump, he awkwardly mounted from the opposite side than was the custom in order to favor his leg. They walked their horses to the gate; Daniel opened and closed it for Ellie this time. Joey opened the barn door and took Daniel's horse from him, offering him his crutch. Daniel went to Ellie's horse and unsaddled the mare. With the crutch under one arm, he put the saddle under the other, carrying it to the tack room. Ellie smiled as she watched him take back his independence.

Over the next couple of days, Ellie saw little of Daniel. After dinner, he shared with her what he had accomplished during the day, describing the lean-to he and one of the teenaged slaves had constructed to give the horses some shelter from the harsh weather. He faithfully reported on any materials he had taken from other projects on the farm, so that they would be accounted for and no one would be blamed for theft. As he talked, he paced, still hobbling with one crutch, but no longer seeming to notice it. Ellie could see by the glow on his face as he talked about the work that he was filled with pride and satisfaction because he was once again contributing something "manly." Ellie praised him for his contribution, recognizing his need to feel needed and valued. However, she also felt a greater attraction and affection for him because of his enthusiasm and willingness to jump in and get his hands dirty than for anything he had actually done. She found herself smiling at him dotingly, and had to acknowledge that her feelings for him were deepening.

Ellie started writing a letter to her mother; she hadn't heard from Savannah in a few weeks and was beginning to worry. She also wanted to know when Charlotte and Suzanne would be returning for the winter. She was struggling with how much to tell her mother when she heard the sound of artillery fire in the distance. Her first thought was that Daniel was out on the edge of the farm. She grabbed her pistol and called for Peter. She wanted to go looking for Daniel, but knew it would insult him. The children came into the house, asking if they could stay.

It wasn't long before Daniel came walking with his crutch up to the house and started up the stairs. Ellie left her post and ran to the front door, opening it for him. He looked around at the gathering of slaves in the front parlor and noted Peter at his post with the loaded rifle.

"Ellie, if the Union Army comes down your drive, you are not going to hold them off with six weapons and four people who know how to use them," he stated, shaking his head at the futility of the gesture, but smiling at its bravery.

"We need to defend ourselves!" Ellie exclaimed.

"If a few stray soldiers show up, this could work. Otherwise…" He shook his head.

She stiffened, refusing to be helpless in the situation. "We have to do something."

"If they are Confederates, you will handle them just as you did the men looking for horses; however, it will cost you the rest of the horses not hidden and nearly all the food and farm animals."

"And if it is the Union Army?" She had been trying not to call them Yankees in front of him.

"Then Peter will go out and tell them the truth about me and invite the officers in to dine. It will still cost you horses, food, and farm animals."

"What should we do?" she queried, wanting to feel she had some power over the problem.

"Tell everyone to try to hide some of the animals, and then to go about their business. The artillery is far enough away," he ordered, pulling aside the curtain to look out.

Ellie was unsure about Daniel's directions, but did as he suggested. She recognized that he was much more knowledgeable about the ways of war and the military. She was beginning to trust his judgment. The slaves reluctantly left the house.

Daniel seemed to be the only one to eat much at dinner that night. Lottie grumbled that no one appreciated her cooking, but ate little herself. When darkness fell, the sounds of gun fire became more sporadic; however, every time Ellie began to relax a little, it would be interrupted by another volley. When they kissed goodnight, Daniel attempted to reassure her that they were in no immediate danger.

Ellie slipped her pistol under her pillow and changed into her nightgown in the dark. She crawled into bed and pulled the covers up over her head. It did not block out the noise; it did not reduce her fear; it did not help her sleep. Finally, she got out of bed, taking the gun, and felt her way down the hall to Daniel's room. She listened at the door for any sounds of movement; hearing none, she opened the door as quietly as possible. She closed the door behind her, and picturing the room in her mind, slowly moved forward until she came to the bed. Finding the nightstand, she quietly placed the gun on it, and then slipped under the covers, cuddling up close to Daniel. She was relieved that she had not awakened him and was comforted by his closeness. She woke early, hearing his deep rhythmic breathing in her ear. He had his arm wrapped tightly around her. She smiled, sighed, and went back to sleep. The next time she woke, it was full day light and she was alone in his bed.

CHAPTER 24

The cannon fire was ferocious. The sounds of war boomed throughout the day. When darkness fell, the cannons seemed to stop, but it was not silent. The gunfire continued through much of the night. Daniel was awake and seemed to be expecting Ellie when she slipped into his room. He pulled the covers down for her, and then covered her once she got into his bed. He kissed her on the forehead and gently held her close. Before long, she heard the change in his breathing as he fell asleep. On the night of the third day, there was silence. Daniel made no comment, but held her close to him when she crawled into bed.

When she showed up in his room the next night without there having been any gunfire all day, he asked, "Ellie, do you think you should be sleeping here again?"

"If you do not want me here..." her voice trailed off. She was confused, unsure if he was concerned what the slaves might say or if he truly did not want her in his bed.

"Oh, I want you here; maybe too much. I would never take advantage of you, Ellie, but it is not easy."

"Oh!" It had not occurred to Ellie that her presence in his bed might be disturbing to him. "I did not mean to tease you."

She started to get up, but he grabbed her wrist, pulling her back toward him. "Do not leave yet," he pleaded, his voice husky with emotion.

Daniel's voice sent a shiver of arousal through her. She slipped back under the covers, cuddling up to him and wrapping one leg over one of his legs. She had no intention of teasing him. He pulled her nightgown partially up as he kissed her, and then slid his right hand up under it. He reached her breast, caressing it until the nipple became hard. She climbed half-way on to him, giving him access to her other breast. He reached for it with his left hand. For a moment, he played with both breasts, and then moved his right hand down her side and over her buttocks. He bent his knee, separating her legs more, and then rolled her over to his other side. She slowly lowered her hand down his side, and then over his stomach. Her hand then came in contact with his warm, hard member. She gently fingered him, gliding over the head of it. She explored the tiny slit, arousing a drop of moisture. He grabbed her hand, moving it away from his penis and placing it on his hip. He began running his fingers through her mound of hair, curling it between them. She experienced a tingling between her legs and felt the pressure building. When his hand moved lower, allowing his fingers to squeeze the lip of her vulva, a small amount of fluid flowed. He followed the trail of liquid up and in with one finger, gently separating the lips, opening her up so that he could rub her clitoris. She lost all sense of control, feeling that her entire body was an extension of his fingers to do with as he pleased. She dug the fingers of one hand into the bed and the other into his hip as two of his fingers moved in and out of her and his thumb pressed firmly above the opening, holding her in place. He pushed her onto her back with his body. He kept her pinned down with his shoulder and kissed her, pushing his tongue deeply into her mouth, just as his fingers were in her body, until he felt the out pouring of her juices. His mouth was all that prevented her cries of pleasure from filling the room as her body experienced its first complete release.

Daniel held her close as she clung to him. She had been taken unaware by the experience. She had not known that such pleasure could be had by the touch of a man. After snuggling for a while, she realized that he had gone soft without having had any satisfaction. She started to reach for him, but he stopped her. She whispered, "But what about you?"

"Not tonight," he whispered back, continuing to hold her tightly.

Her last thought before drifting off to sleep was that she hadn't known a man could be so selfless.

She woke in the morning feeling contented. She kissed him on the cheek, waking him, and then slipped out of bed and went back to her own room to dress for the day. She had trouble keeping her eyes off of him. Her feelings for him were strengthening. She questioned herself, wondering if they were only an illusion produced by lust. Yet, it was his desire to please her at his own expense that drew her closer to him. She wanted to please him, too.

CHAPTER 25

Over the next couple of weeks, their bed time trysts were more subdued. Daniel maintained a self-control that Ellie no longer had with him. However, after another night of similar passion, Ellie became more determined to pleasure him as well. She found it difficult to accept when he told her he found great satisfaction in the pleasure he gave her. She knew by his physical reactions that he needed more. Ellie felt that she was being very selfish and self-indulgent in accepting his attentions without reciprocation; yet she had to admit that she was not willing to give up the pleasure that Daniel was providing to her. She knew she had to accept his withholding himself until he was ready.

It was during this period of mutual sexual exploration that a letter arrived from Ellie's Aunt Felicity. Ellie hurried to open it, wondering that neither Charlotte nor Suzanne had written. She read it alone at first, wondering what news it might contain. She decided she would share the contents with the others later, at dinner.

My Dearest Niece,

I trust this letter finds you well and safe. We were quite relieved to hear that so many of the slaves were still on the farm with you, to help make the work easier; however, your mother, your uncle, and I are very concerned that you continue without benefit of an overseer. I wish to assure you that your uncle continues his efforts to find someone appropriate to fill that position. It has been most difficult to find candidates to interview, much less hire. But these are difficult times and we all have to make sacrifices. It is fortunate that you are such a clever and dedicated young woman and are doing so very well for now.

We have heard from friends in the parish that you have a male house guest by the name of Daniel Proctor, a wounded soldier who went to school with James. We all agree that it was the right thing for you to take him in to be nursed, Ellie. It is the duty of all Southern women to minister to our brave lads wherever possible; however, it really is uncomely of you not to inform us of this action yourself, rather than to have us hear about it from those outside the family. Your mother reports to have some recollection of such a young man from your brother, and so is completely unconcerned for your safety with him. She asked me to convey to you that she knows that you are all that a mother could hope for in a daughter and will conduct yourself in a manner that would bring pride to your dead father and brother.

Speaking of my dear sister, your mother, she also has requested that I inform you that she is still not ready to come home yet. She and Suzanne will remain as our guests for an indeterminate time. Suzanne, especially, wishes to remain among the gaiety and good company to be had here in Savannah during the holidays. I would attempt to encourage you to join us as well; however, I know that you are still burdened with the farm and with an invalid to care for at this time.

    Wishing you a very pleasant Christmas and New Year, I am:

    Your loving aunt,
    Felicity Maitland Hamilton

On the first of December, Ellie realized that a full year had passed since Ted had been killed and she had not noticed. The day should have been their first anniversary. She felt guilty for not having remembered and for her feelings toward Daniel. She was distant throughout the day and did not go to his room that night. She lay in bed crying, confused by her emotions. Neither mentioned the lack of contact over the next few days; however, she frequently noticed him watching her.

Finally he asked, "Ellie, are you disturbed about what we have done? We are not married."

She smiled sadly at him, but did not answer.

"It will not happen again." He seemed hopeful that this would make her more comfortable in his presence.

Her response was to cry. She could not explain herself in her confusion and was unwilling to talk to him about her feelings regarding Ted. He gingerly put his arms around her, letting the tears fall onto his shirt. Once the sobs subsided, he added, "Ellie, talk to me. Tell me what is wrong."

She blurted out, "Christmas!"

"Christmas?"

"Yes, Christmas!" It was something that had been on her mind and definitely safer to talk about with him. "It was always so wonderful. Everyone home together, decorating the tree, searching for special gifts, then watching their faces when they opened them. We had a big party here every Christmas Eve. And now…they are all gone." She slowly shook her head. "James, Father…" she stopped herself from even saying Ted's name to him, "…so many dead. Now, Mother and Suzanne will not be here this year, either."

He stroked her hair for a few minutes. "Ellie, this is our first Christmas. We will start our own traditions. Someday, we will have our own family to share them."

He startled her out of her reverie. Seeing the look on her face, he asked, "Ellie, you do want children?"

"Yes!" It was the first time that he had brought up any kind of future for them together. Ted had never even mentioned children; the guilt began to fade.

He looked relieved. "Maybe, we can use some of my family's traditions, some of yours, and create some new ones?"

The tension had been released and the conversations and laughter returned. However, Ellie continued to sleep in her own room. She wanted to be close to him, but did not trust herself in his presence. They began planning a new Christmas.

The Peters were still in mourning and there would be no party this year. They agreed to take on a Proctor tradition: invite their employees and their families from the past year for Christmas Eve dinner. Knowing Charlotte and Suzanne would not be there to object, they would have all the slaves for a buffet dinner in the house. The planning and preparations kept Ellie busy. It gave her little time to think about her losses. Instead, she thought about the unspoken hopes for their future. She wanted to ask him so many things, but felt it was not her place to bring them up.

When nearly a week had passed and he had said nothing, she inquired, "You asked me if I want children someday, but you never said what you want."

"I always thought two of each would be good. My brother and I had each other, but my sister never seemed to find anyone to play dolls with her."

"Four?"

"Is four too may? Would you mind if we had four children?" He seemed to fear he had offended her, perhaps been too demanding.

She started giggling, "No, I would not mind having four children with you."

Still not understanding her levity, he asked, "Why are you giggling?"

"I am sorry. It is just…well, we are talking about how many children we want to have, but we have never talked about marriage."

He laughed as well. "I guess we should if we are going to have four children." He hugged her, and then changed the subject.

Christmas came quickly; together they decorated a small tree. Ellie was quiet as she helped set the candles on the branches, and then the ornaments. They lit the candles and sat on the couch, staring at the magic they had created. Daniel was impressed by the ornaments, explaining that they only had bows and popcorn strings on the Proctor tree. Ellie listened intently, but remained quiet. Eventually he asked, with a hint of frustration in his question, "What is wrong?"

She teared up, mumbling, "Everyone is missing and Suzanne is not playing 'Oh Christmas Tree'."

He kissed her cheek, stood, and walked to the pianoforte. He sat and opened the keyboard, took a deep breath, and began playing the song. "You have to sing it with me," he called to her between verses.

Ellie smiled and joined him at the pianoforte. She realized she had so much more to learn about this man she loved. It was not until she was alone in bed that night that she realized he had walked to the pianoforte without the cane. She was happy that he could now move on his own accord and wondered how much he would still improve. She smiled at the thought of waltzing in his arms. His health and happiness gave her joy.

While Lottie and Lela prepared most of the food, Ellie and Daniel pitched in as well. Once preparations were well underway, Ellie excused herself and climbed to the attic to see what might make good Christmas presents for the guests at the party. She hadn't had time to go into town, and she felt it wouldn't be right to give away her mother's or sister's property without their permission. She selected a pair of her own earrings as a gift for Mattie, and a fine gold chain for Lela. She chose one of James' warm coats as a gift for Peter. Ellie wanted something personal and special for Mama Noli, but she wasn't sure what to give the old woman, and then it came to her. She didn't have the power to free the ancient slave, but she could give her enough money to buy her freedom from the family. Ellie slipped into her cache and pulled out several hundred dollars in Blue Backs. She understood that they had little value, but her mother would accept them, loyal Southerner that she was. She wrapped the money in a silk handkerchief and added it to her bundle of gifts. With some effort, she was able to find a gift for every one of the guests coming to the party that night. She spent an hour in her father's study wrapping them and putting names on them. When she was done, she carried her packages out to the front parlor and placed them on or under the tree.

They got the good silver out and set up the dining room with as much pomp as if it were the first families of Prince William Parish coming to dinner rather than the family slaves. The food was laid out on the table and the desserts on the sideboard. There were pine boughs and wreaths festooning every doorway and window. The entire house glittered with candles. Ellie and Daniel stood at the front door as the slaves began coming in, shaking hands with each of them, thanking them for coming, and asking them to make themselves at home. The children rushed to look at the Christmas tree with its glowing candles and glittering ornaments. Ellie heard screams of delight as this or that child recognized his name on a package, but each one of them held back with great patience. Ellie's greatest joy was seeing Mama Noli come through the front door, escorted by her family members. Ellie stepped forward to greet the old woman and to personally escort her to a comfortable chair near the fireplace where she could watch all the festivities in comfort. Huge amounts of food were consumed at the dinner. At last Ellie called them all together to receive their gifts. The children rushed over, cheering and jockeying for positions. Ellie selected one of the youngest children to read the names on the gifts, and then to hand them out. She could see the joy and pride on the child's face as she read the names aloud; the tears of happiness on the child's mother's face as she watched her baby reading in public without fear of punishment. Ellie had held on to Mama Noli's gift; she wanted to give it to her personally, and to explain what she wanted done with the money. While the others were distracted with showing off their gifts and singing Christmas hymns, Ellie made her way to the old woman's feet. Sitting on the floor, Ellie offered the bundle to her.

"This is for you alone, Mama Noli. You have to promise me that you will use it to buy your freedom when Mother and Suzanne return to the farm. I want to see you free again before you die." She looked up into the wrinkled old face and saw tears streaking the ebony cheek.

"Oh, Miz Ellie. Ya shouldn' a done dis fo' me. Ah ain't got enough time left ta make no difference wedder Ah is free o' slave. Ah have all eternity ta be free. Gib dis here ta some young folks what need a chance at bein' free. Ah had mah chance onest. Doan waist dis on me." The old slave woman folded the money up inside the handkerchief and tried to give it back to the younger woman.

"No, Mama Noli. I have made up my mind. You will die as you were born, a free human being." Ellie closed her hands over the elderly woman's and gently pushed the package back to her.

Mama Noli looked down at the money in her lap, and then over at Ellie. "May da good Lord bless ya, allahs, Miz Ellie, fo' yo' kindness ta me an' mine." She leaned down and planted a kiss on Ellie's cheek.

Not long after that, tired mothers and fathers began collecting peacefully slumbering children and their gifts. They called their good nights and their thanks as they made their way back to their cabins and their beds. Once everyone had left, Ellie drew on her cloak and joined Daniel in the carriage for the drive to the midnight mass at the church. The air was chilly and helped to wake them both. They traveled in relative quiet, snuggling for contact more than for warmth. They had almost reached the church when Daniel turned to Ellie and asked, "Are you feeling better about Christmas now?" She nodded her answer silently but contentedly, leaning against his chest. Ellie heard him sigh and knew he was contented with the moment as well.

They returned from church, tired and cold, each helping the other up the stairs. When they parted at the top of the stairs, Ellie felt it was wrong that they were maintaining separate rooms.

In the morning, Ellie woke late to the smell of coffee. She put on a robe and went down the back stairs. She had given all the slaves Christmas off and was surprised that Lottie had come in to cook. However, she discovered Daniel puttering in the kitchen, wearing a robe and a pair of heavy socks. She came up behind him, giving him a big hug. They worked together in the kitchen, and then spent the day alone, uninterrupted. They ate leftovers from the party of the night before; sitting on the couch, cuddling and feeding each other. They had slept late and the sun set early. When they went upstairs for the night, they kissed good night passionately. However, Daniel did not move toward his room as he usually did, but stood holding Ellie's hands, looking intently into her eyes. She took a step toward her room, "Come and cuddle with me," she invited.

He moved along with her. "We are only going to cuddle," he told her firmly.

She changed into her nightgown. He tried not to watch while he took off his shoes. Once she was in bed, he blew out the candle, took off his pants, and crawled in next to her. They snuggled and kissed. Ellie explored his face in the moonlight with her fingertips.

"Ellie, I love you. But...you know I will have to leave soon." His face was filled with shadows and dark edges. She thought it matched his words.

"I know. You did not need the cane at all today. You will be able to make the trip to Beaufort by foot soon."

"I thought the war would have ended by now. Lord knows how long it will last. Will you wait for me?" His eyes caught reflected moonlight as he gazed into hers. It was as if God had sent silver fire to fill her beloved's eyes.

Looking there, she felt she could wait eternally for him. "Yes, Daniel. I could never love anyone else."

He kissed her passionately, pulling her close. As they lay on their sides facing each other, she could feel him growing hard against her stomach. She wanted to merge with him; she wanted them to be one, to be inseparable. When his hand slid down her back and over her buttocks, she felt as if she were melting into him. He pulled her nightgown up with a jerk, and then slid his hand underneath. She understood at that moment that she was his and that she would not ever say "no" to him. As he pushed his tongue deeper into her mouth, she imagined what it might be like to have his erect penis within her, taking her as his own. She began to unbutton his long-johns, releasing him. She noticed how he became larger as his hand explored her breasts. She slid her hand between them, easing it over him, gently touching his full length with her fingertips. His hand left her breast and moved down, and from her backside reached between her legs, separating them slightly. As he touched her moistness, she felt him harden more. She wrapped her hand around him, slowly moving it over the smoothened skin. She repositioned her leg over his, opening herself more for his fingers. She moved her hand off of him, sliding it up his side, allowing his engorged, naked penis to touch her clitoris, while his fingers slid in and out of her. She would have screamed in pleasure as a torrent of fluid was released except that throughout the kiss had not been broken. He rolled with her, maintaining the points of contact, over him, to her other side, and then resting her on her back. Hovering, he broke the kiss, "Are you sure? I can wait."

She would not deprive him; she would not regret not having given herself to him. In the dim moonlight, they stared into one another's eyes. "You are my husband now." She knew in her heart, it was true. There was a brief moment of pain as he broke his way through into her, kissing her, their eyes locked until the moment when they both let go. She clung to him and he collapsed on her. They slept wrapped in each other's arms.

CHAPTER 26

Ellie woke smiling; she tickled his ear, waking him too. They kissed good morning, and Daniel grabbed his clothes and snuck down the hall to his own room. Ellie dressed quickly and went down the back stairs to the kitchen. Lela and Mattie were already at the table drinking coffee. Accepting a cup from Lottie, she joined the two women, sure that they would know what had occurred between her and Daniel if she made eye contact. She grinned into the cup avoiding them.

Daniel came down the front stairs without his cane. It was noticed immediately as he entered the kitchen. Everyone offered their congratulations. Ellie realized that she was blushing every time she looked at him and, when their eyes met, he did too. After breakfast, Daniel asked her to join him in the study. She followed him in, closing the door behind her. He took her into his arms, "Ellie, last night was the best night of my life, but we cannot do it again…at least not until after we are married."

"You are right." She stroked his cheek sadly.

"Two or three more weeks and this leg should be able to get me to Beaufort," he stated, patting the offending limb.

Ellie sighed and leaned into his body, looking longingly into his eyes. "I know, but I wish you did not have to leave."

"I will come back for you after the war. We will get married and start working on those children." He winked and ruffled her hair.

She did not answer, but put her head on his chest and let him hold her. She knew he had to leave, but she did not want to think about life on the farm without him. She also understood that, if he did not leave soon, they would not be able to resist each other for very long. After Ted had been killed, she had felt terribly guilty for denying him and delaying their marriage. She did not regret having shared herself with Daniel, knowing him; she knew if he asked, she would not resist him; however, she could not take the risk of it happening again.

Over the next couple of weeks, they assumed their regular routine. He spent the mornings walking and both were weighted down by the knowledge of his departure. As the time came closer, both became quieter. They had agreed not to tell anyone until the day before he would leave. When they were alone and did talk, it was about the future they would eventually have.

On January 11, 1863, everything changed. Ellie received a telegram. As she stood staring at it in apparent shock, Daniel tipped the boy who had ridden in with it. "Ellie, what does it say?"

Her response was to hand it to him. Daniel quickly scanned the contents. Charlotte had died on the tenth and the family would be arriving in two days with her mother's body. He led Ellie to the living room and sat her on the couch. He poured a brandy and put it in her hands, encouraging her to sip on it, and then left momentarily to call Peter. By the time Peter arrived, Daniel was sitting with her on the couch stroking her hair, waiting for her to start crying. He handed the telegram to Peter.

"Oh, my gracious God! Miz Charlotte's dead!" the butler exclaimed as he read the message.

Ellie turned to look at Peter, having heard it aloud, the tears started to flow. Daniel held her as she sobbed. The house went into mourning, awaiting the return of Miz Charlotte.

The day before the family was to arrive, Ellie seemed to be in a nervous frenzy. She snapped at everyone, wanting the house to be in perfect order before her relatives arrived. When she attempted to oversee Lottie's preparations in the kitchen, Lottie snapped back. "Ah knows ya jist loss yo mama, but ya know we knows what we's doin'…. What is ya 'fraid of?" she demanded of Ellie, her hands planted firmly on her broad hips.

Ellie seemed to droop as she realized how she had been behaving. "Lottie, I am sorry. I have to show them I can run this place the way Mama would have."

"Ya mama let us do it. She trust us ta do it right." Lottie wasn't quite placated.

Ellie sank into a chair, completely deflated. "Oh, Lottie, what will I do without her?"

Seeing Ellie appear so helpless and lost melted Lottie's heart. She leaned over her mistress and hugged her, saying, "Chile, you has been doin' since ya papa died."

"Lottie, if anyone tells the truth about Daniel…if Mattie tells Emmy's girl he is a Yankee or…" She hesitated. "Should I tell him to leave now?"

Lottie patted Ellie's arm, continuing to embrace her. "We won' talk. Ef dey do, dey not gonna eat agin."

"They would think it strange if he were to leave now…" Ellie started.

"Doan you fret so, chile. We won' do nothin' ta hurt ya Daniel. He da best white man we knows…next ta ya papa."

"Thank you, Lottie. I do not know what I would do without you." Ellie leaned her head back against the ample black bosom and allowed herself to feel the comfort of the embrace.

The Hamiltons arrived with Suzanne, puffy-eyed and pale. Ellie greeted her aunt, uncle, and cousin quietly, but with genuine affection for them. She embraced her sister with true empathy for her feelings. They were orphans now and needed to support each other. She briefly introduced Daniel to them, but they were all too distracted by the sad drama taking place. They stood stiffly on the porch, watching as several of the men carried Charlotte's coffin into the parlor and set it down on the bier that had been prepared. Ellie had had pine boughs cut to place around the coffin because there were no flowers blooming. She asked that the coffin be opened so that she might take a last look at her mother's face before saying good-by. Suzanne couldn't face seeing the body again and quickly excused herself. Felicity and Walker came to stand on either side of their niece, not only to offer emotional support, but also to provide actual physical support if needed. Ellie longed to have Daniel at her side to embrace her, but she knew that would be unwise and would cause far too much disruption when they needed to be united. Ellie looked down at the much loved face, seeing her mother there, but not seeing her. It was a stranger's face in the coffin, wearing her mother's hair and lips. Ellie took a lock of her own hair and placed it in the coffin with her mother, and cut a single curl from Charlotte's head to keep for herself. When she finished, she signaled that the lid should be replaced. The men screwed the lid tightly closed and placed the pine boughs on the box while Ellie turned and walked to the sofa. Word had been sent out through the church about the death. Friends and neighbors would be arriving soon, some bearing food for the family. The servants knew what to do. Ellie had the luxury of not having to think about anything for a while. She could allow herself the time she needed to mourn. As she looked around the room, she saw Daniel speaking quietly to family and servants. The sight of him there gave her strength to face the rest of the ordeal.

She wanted, desperately, to run out of the house and go hide in the fields somewhere, where she wouldn't be surrounded by so many dead. Her father, her brother, and Ted all seemed to be standing in the shadows of the room, looking sad. Emmy was very solicitous of both Ellie and Felicity. Emmy and Daniel took special pains to see that their every need was met while they accepted the condolences of the parish. Suzanne was genuinely tearful, not seeking to be the center of attention for a change.

Father Burton arrived among the earliest of the guests. He hurried to offer his condolences and any comfort he could to the family. Ellie was pleased to see him and grateful for his kind words. He was especially helpful with Suzanne who required more comforting than the others.

Ellie paid little notice of how time passed until she became aware that the room was filled with people milling about. The staff was efficiently passing out refreshments and looking appropriately saddened by the loss of their old mistress. As Ellie was watching Peter and Lottie circulating through the crowd, she noticed that there was a bit of a disturbance in one corner of the room where several male neighbors had gathered. Ellie could see Peter listening attentively while trying to appear disinterested. Daniel happened to be nearby, and Ellie signaled to him.

"Daniel, something is going on over there. Would you go find out what it is? It seems to be of great interest to Peter. Oh, look. He's rushing off to the kitchen. Please, Daniel. Something is definitely happening." She looked up to him, pleading for his assistance. Daniel patted her hand, gave her a wink, and moved off in the direction of the commotion. Ellie tried not to stare after him, but she could see that a couple of the men were getting very upset, despite their keeping their voices quiet. She watched as Daniel addressed them, questioning the cause of the agitation. She saw the look of surprise on his face when he received their response, and his attempt to quiet them as he indicated they should take the discussion outdoors. Several of the men looked in Ellie's direction, bowed, and moved out of the room. Once they had left, Daniel hurried to Ellie's side.

Ellie sighed and rested her head on his shoulder.

"Ellie, I want to talk with your uncle. I want to ask him for your hand before he returns to Savannah."

She sat up straight. "No! No you cannot ask him now!"

"Why not?" he inquired, confused by her refusal.

"I will tell you why you may not ask my father now," a voice responded from the doorway.

Both were startled, and Ellie moved away from Daniel on the couch as she turned to see her cousin standing behind them. "Emmy!"

Emmeline laughed. "I knew you were hiding something!" She walked over to the side table and poured a brandy, and then sat in a chair next to the couch.

"Emmy, you know I had given up on ever finding the right man for me." She put her hand on Daniel's hand. "I love him."

Daniel blushed. "Emmy, why do you say I should not ask your father for his consent for Ellie and me to be married?"

"The two of you have been in this house alone for months. We have all noticed you are well, other than the limp. Everyone knows Ellie is very proper with men, but he does not know you." She giggled. "He would lock Ellie up in Savannah until your wedding day."

"I do not want to do anything that might hurt Ellie; however, I do not want the family to force her into marrying someone else."

Emmy laughed at that thought. "If Ellie has decided to marry you, she will chase everyone else away."

Ellie squeezed Daniel's hand. "Daniel, I will be here waiting for you."

"Maybe you can stop avoiding me now, Ellie." Emmy smiled and rose to her feet. She finished the last of her brandy, set the glass down on the table, and extended her hand to Ellie. "Come, Cousin, it is late and I am not leaving you down here for my father to find."

Ellie allowed Emmy to take her hand and lead her out of the room. As they started up the stairs, Emmy asked, "Does he know you are an Abolitionist?"

Having overheard, Daniel called from the living room, "Yes, I know."

Ellie laughed, thinking, if only Emmy knew everything that Daniel knew, she would be shocked.

The next day, Walker asked Daniel to join him in the study. Walker settled behind the desk and indicated that Daniel take one of the chairs opposite him.

"Mr. Proctor, I recognize that you have made an excellent recovery, due in large measure to my niece's excellent nursing, no doubt. And I am sure you are thinking about getting back to your unit and your duty." He paused to allow Daniel to respond.

"Indeed, sir, I do feel that I must soon take my leave of the kind hospitality of your niece. I cannot justify my prolonging my stay in safety when so many of my brothers are giving their lives in this war," Daniel acknowledged.

"I wish to say that I recognize you to be a man of honor, Mr. Proctor; however, there is something I would presume to ask of you." Once again, he paused. Daniel nodded his willingness to hear the older man out. "As you are aware, I have had no luck in finding an appropriate overseer to take over the physical running of this farm. I am impressed with the excellent work that Ellie has done here, undoubtedly with your assistance." Daniel began to protest this suggestion, but Walker raised his hand to stop the protest. "No matter, sir. I would ask that you consider remaining through the spring, at the very least, to help Ellie get through the spring foaling and planting. I would feel so much more comfortable knowing there was a competent man on the farm to oversee these duties that should not be left to a young woman of Ellie's sensibilities and upbringing. Do you think this would be possible, Mr. Proctor? Have you had word from your commanding officer requiring your return as yet?"

"No, sir. I have not been recalled to my unit as yet. I would consider it an honor to be of service to your niece. It is the least I can do to repay all her kindnesses to me during my recovery. I will do my best to remain until the heavy activity of the spring season on the farm has passed before I take my leave, assuming that Ellie is in agreement, of course," Daniel added, thinking that would be easy to obtain. The two men shook hands in agreement, both feeling very satisfied with the outcome of the conversation. Walker soon took the opportunity to request that Ellie speak with him in the study where he related the entirety of the conversation to her, asking her consent to the agreement which she readily and happily gave.

Emmy and Ellie spent more time together talking. She told her cousin about Daniel, her feelings and hopes. She wanted to tell her how wonderful he was with her, how gentle, how loving, and how selfless he was in bed, but she could not share this with anyone since they were not married. Emmy was surprised that Daniel was in agreement with so many of Ellie's ideas; she questioned his sincerity, or if he was just trying to win Ellie's affections. Ellie could not tell her the truth, that he was a Northerner, which would have explained his agreement. Having found an ally in Daniel, she was somewhat disappointed in her cousin's thinking. She asked herself why Emmy couldn't accept some of her ideas; it was no longer enough that she didn't judge her.

Emmy had found a beau as well. Like nearly all the other young men in the South, he was fighting for the Confederacy. He had not yet asked her father, but she was sure on his next leave he would ask to marry her. She was timidly excited about the prospect, but admitted to Ellie that she was fearful of their wedding night. Ellie wanted to reassure her, yet was unsure how to do so without giving herself away. The best she could do was to tell her what Charlotte had told her about her father's patience and tenderness. Repeating her mother's story made her cry. For so many years, she had dreamed of the day she could share with her mother the excitement of finding the "One". Now, Charlotte would never know about her joy.

Emmy had been privy to enough discussions between her Aunt Charlotte and her cousin to understand the source of her cousin's pain. She held Ellie while she cried.

Once the tears let up, she suggested, "Ellie, you need to be with family now. Come back to Savannah with us. Let Daniel run things here for awhile."

"No, I will not leave him…or the farm," Ellie stated, vehemently shaking her head.

Emmy continued to persuade, "Just for a little while, Ellie."

"He will have to go back to war eventually. He was going to leave, but then the news about Mama came. If only this damned war would end!" Ellie stood and began pacing in agitation.

"Ellie!" Emmy reprimanded, surprised at her cousin's profanity.

"Emmy, he might die, too! I am going to spend every moment with him that I possibly can. As long as he is here, I am not leaving." She looked wildly at her cousin, her desperation and determination blazing in her eyes.

Emmy's concern erupted in response. "You should not be here with him without a chaperone. What will everyone say?"

"You are not going to say anything to anyone and it will be no different than before you knew as far as anyone else is concerned." Her words were both a threat and a plea for Emmy's cooperation.

Emmy sighed in resignation. "Be careful."

Ellie returned to sit next to her cousin, taking her arm. "He would never hurt me."

Emmy raised her eyebrow and quirked her lips into a smile. "He is not the one I am worried about." Ellie gently slapped Emmy's arm and managed a laugh.

Unfortunately, Emmy was not the last one to try to persuade Ellie to go to Savannah. Both her aunt and uncle applied their considerable persuasive powers to get her to return with them. The discussion took place after dinner, while the entire family was gathered in the parlor. Suzanne was busy playing the piano, trying desperately to impress Daniel with her skill at playing and with her voice, which was quite good although untrained. Daniel had willingly agreed to turn the pages of her music for her, but became distracted when Felicity and Walker raised the subject of Ellie's leaving the farm. Daniel wisely kept quiet and tried not to look at Ellie while she adamantly refused to leave Whispering Oaks. Suzanne must have heard Daniel release his breath when Ellie made her refusal, because she looked at him sharply, and then turned to announce that she, too, would be staying on at the farm. She felt it unfair of her "to continue to impose on Ellie's good nature and generosity" by staying away when she could be contributing to the work that had to be done. Ellie immediately saw through Suzanne's pose, but their aunt and uncle were touched by their young niece's maturity. Emmy exchanged a humorous look with Ellie, who was trying not to cringe at the idea of Suzanne staying. And so it was agreed that the young women would remain on the family's farm, assisted by the chivalrous Mr. Proctor.

The Hamilton's left early the next morning for Savannah. Ellie was truly sorry to see them leave, but also felt some relief that there were fewer people left to deceive about Daniel. Still, she feared that the one remaining would present quite a challenge. The carriage had barely cleared the farm yard when Suzanne was fawning on Daniel. She took his arm, commenting on the chill in the air and asking if he would care to sit by her near the fire in the parlor. When he declined, stating that he had work to see to in the barn, Suzanne solicitously cautioned him to be certain to dress warmly; they would not want their protector taking a chill. Daniel smiled politely down at Suzanne and assured her he would take every precaution, and then he extricated himself from her grasp and sauntered off toward the barn. Ellie did her best not to snap at Suzanne for her behavior toward Daniel.

Lottie and Peter served lunch in the dining room. Ellie sat uncomfortably, playing with her food. "Suzanne, we have been much more relaxed over the past few months. With just the three of us here some of the formalities seem...a bit pretentious."

"Whatever do you mean?" her younger sister asked, genuinely confused.

Ellie explained, "Well, for one thing, unless we have company, we have not been dressing for dinner."

"You never did like to dress, but I believe I will continue to do so. After all, we do have a guest in the house." She turned, smiling at Daniel.

"In fact, Suzanne, we usually do not eat in the dining room," Daniel added.

"What? You eat in the kitchen?" She was appalled at the idea, her hand clutching her throat in horror.

"Yes, we do," he responded quietly.

Ellie tried to explain so that her sister would understand why she had broken with convention. "Suzanne, for a long time I was alone. I do not like to eat alone."

"You are not alone now!" She was becoming more agitated.

Neither pushed any farther, but exchanged looks, agreeing to set things in motion, to return to the routine they previously had. The next morning, Daniel and Ellie ate breakfast in the kitchen with the slaves, allowing Suzanne to eat alone. Neither did they join her for lunch. They decided they would forego the reading and arithmetic lessons for a few days, fearful that she would be sending off telegrams reporting their scandalous behaviors if they were to overwhelm her with everything at once.

They joined her in the dining room for supper; however, they informed her that many slaves had run off and that the remaining slaves were doing twice their normal work and would no longer have the time to serve her. If she wanted to eat in the dining room, her personal maid would need to do the extra work. Her initial reaction was to state that Sally Ann would serve her. Knowing her fascination with Daniel, Ellie did not think it would last long, once she discovered he would prefer to be in the kitchen.

Sally Ann ate in the kitchen with the rest of the household slaves. Ellie noticed her watching quietly, somewhat confused by the comfortable interactions between Daniel, Ellie, and the others. At lunch the next day, they all laughed as she nearly choked on her tea when Lottie neglected to use "Master" before Daniel's name. Once the laughter subsided, Ellie explained, "Sally Ann, there have been many changes here."

"Ah noticed, Miz Ellie. Ya allus been full o' surprises, but...Marster Daniel's lettin' ya...?" She turned her wide-eyed stare toward Daniel.

"Sally Ann, I am in full agreement with nearly all the decisions that Ellie has made," he assured her.

"Nearly?" Ellie enquired, raising an eyebrow in surprise.

"Well...everyone still calls you 'Miss.'" He knew not to bring up his other objections in front of the others.

"What do your help call you and your parents?" she asked him a bit defensively.

"They call me Daniel, and my parents Mr. and Mrs. Proctor."

"Your parents run your farm; I run this one now! At least, no one calls me Miss Peters!"

"Your point is well taken," he conceded with a slight bow to her.

Lela and Mattie were snickering while Lottie gave them warning looks. They had all been close to Sally Ann and had known her for years, but they remembered their own first reactions to having a Yankee in the house. They also knew that Suzanne was in the habit of bribing her for information. They realized it was important that she had the opportunity to get to know him as they did before she found out anything more about him.

"Ef ya doan mind, Ah'll keep callin' ya Marster Daniel," Sally Ann offered tentatively.

"That will be fine, if you prefer, Miss Sally Ann."

Everyone burst out laughing, but Sally Ann looked very confused. Mattie turned to her, "Gib up now an' jist call him Daniel." The others laughed harder.

"Will he really keep callin' me Miz?" she asked of the other slaves.

"Yes!" Mattie replied.

Ellie knew that Daniel had other objections, but they never seemed to have more than a minute or two alone when Suzanne or one of the slaves showed up. They no longer had their evenings alone. Although she continued to dress for dinner, Suzanne joined them in the kitchen; meals became more subdued. Ellie announced that she would be riding to check on the fencing and that they should not wait lunch for her. She gave Daniel a quick look. He nodded in response. He slipped out and down to the barn before Ellie left the house. Realizing what was going on, Mattie distracted Suzanne until it was too late for her to realize Daniel had left the house and insist upon going too.

As the two cantered off, Ellie informed him she really wanted to check the mares that had been hidden, some were getting close to their foaling time. When they dismounted by the lean-to, Daniel grabbed Ellie by the waist, pulling her close and kissing her passionately.

"I am so glad you understood the invitation to ride with me," she told him breathlessly, clinging tightly to him.

"I have missed our time together." He pulled her closer to him, enjoying the feel of her body pressed against his. He gazed into her eyes for a moment, and then a cloud seemed to pass across his vision. "Suzanne seems to be on my heels all of the time."

Ellie sighed her own frustration with her sister. "She is! I have wanted to talk to you for days."

He distracted her, playing with her hair, still holding her in his arms, "Yes?"

"I want to free all of the slaves, but Suzanne owns half of everything."

She felt him shrug. "Buy them from her."

Ellie leaned her head against his chest. "I do not think I can afford to do that and pay them a wage, too."

Daniel considered this for a moment, and then suggested, "Pay her in Blue Backs."

Ellie pushed back from him slightly so she could look in his face. "She is my sister; how can I cheat her that way?"

Daniel looked her in the eye. "She does not own any of them anyway and neither do you."

Ellie tilted her head to the side. "In theory, but that is not the law."

Loosening his hold on her, Daniel stated, "They are already free according to President Lincoln and they know it."

Ellie pursed her lips and stated, "South Carolina does not abide by Mr. Lincoln's proclamations."

"Beaufort is only a day's walk away," Daniel reminded her.

"Will you try to help me convince Suzanne?" Ellie looked up at him, wanting his support.

"You know I will." He smiled down at her, his love shining in his eyes.

She did not need to ask what else he disapproved; she knew this was the issue. They checked over the horses, and then rode to the other herd hidden in the woods. Before returning, they agreed to make more time to be alone and came up with a couple of plans. They asked Suzanne to join them in the study after dinner.

As soon as the door closed, Ellie announced, "Suzanne, I want to set our slaves free."

Suzanne sat down in one of the chairs and fluffed out her skirt. "I have always known you were a fool. How do you expect to run this place?"

"Pay them a wage," Ellie stated simply.

"Well, they are half mine and I will not consent to you throwing away my money." She clasped her hands in her lap, straightened her spine, and set her jaw. She was quite prepared to fight if need be.

"Suzanne, you would be better off to free them now. Most of those who have not run off already will stay. And once the war is over, they will have much kinder feelings toward you," Daniel suggested to her.

She looked at him with surprise and disdain. "They are valuable property. What would I care of their feelings toward me?"

"When this war is over, there will be no more slavery," Ellie stated firmly.

"Do not be ridiculous! South Carolina will never give up her slaves!" Suzanne put as much derision into her statement as she could.

"The Confederacy will not win this war," Daniel told her flatly.

"Daniel!" Ellie tried to warn him, afraid Suzanne would see him for who he really was.

"Ladies, I do not mean to shock or upset you. You forget, I have seen the forces of the South, as well as the North. The Southern states fight valiantly, but in a protracted war, they will not win. The North has more and better equipment and more men."

"How can you say such terrible things?" Suzanne snapped at him.

"It has been nearly two years since the first shots were fired, and the news we have heard of late does not make me think it will be over soon."

"You are wrong! It is a good thing the Confederacy does not have many officers from the new territories." Suzanne's face was beet red with anger and indignation.

"Suzanne, I have heard such talk from others. God help us if he is right. However, this is not about the war, but about what is right." Ellie interjected, trying to get her sister off of Daniel's treasonous statement.

"You will have to buy them from me and pay these wages you talk about from your share of the profits and not mine. And you cannot have Sally Ann, she is mine and I will not give her up," Suzanne stated huffily.

"I will make a list of who is still here and give you fair market value. I understand your feelings, Suzanne. Think more about Sally Ann. How will she feel if everyone else is free?" Ellie tried to persuade her sister.

"Her feelings! What about mine? At least Daniel is taking my feelings into consideration, even if he is misguided."

Ellie realized that her sister's last statement was an attempt not to alienate Daniel. While she hated her sister's behavior toward him, she accepted that he was safer as long as Suzanne was still interested in him. It was agreed that the slaves would be bought from Suzanne.

Ellie disappeared into the study immediately after breakfast the next morning. When she did not come out for lunch, Daniel brought her a plate.

"I cannot do it," she told him mournfully, indicating the jumble of crumpled papers littering the desk and the floor.

"Let me see." He took the sheet she was working on and studied it for several minutes. "Ellie, remember no one truly owns another person. Price them in silver and pay her in Blue Backs."

She sighed in frustration. "I still have to pay wages."

"The cost of labor these days is nothing compared to the price of a good horse. I will help you figure it out; first you need to buy them from Suzanne."

After dinner that night, Ellie presented Suzanne with the list of slaves and a dollar value for each. She included Sally Ann on the list. Suzanne crossed Sally Ann off the list. Ellie reached over and crossed Mattie off the list. Suzanne added the rest up, and then divided it by two. She handed it back to Ellie. "I will sign the bill of sale when you pay me with your own money."

"I will get it now," Ellie stated, beginning to rise.

"Suzanne, your sister is being very generous with you," Daniel told her.

Refusing to acknowledge this sentiment, Suzanne looked away from Daniel and stated, "I deserve to be paid for my property!"

"Remember, Ellie has agreed to pay their wages. It will not change anything for you, other than putting a lot of money in your pocket."

"Thank you, Daniel. I am sure it is your influence or she would have just let them all go. Those others probably ran away because of her."

Ellie abruptly left the room to get Suzanne's money. She could not listen to her sister any longer. She was disappointed that Suzanne had not matured and continued to be selfish and manipulative. As she was walking back in, she over heard Suzanne saying to Daniel, "It is so lovely and warm here by the fire. Just the right place to cuddle up with someone special. Will you not have a seat next to me, Daniel? Ellie could be gone a while."

Hearing this, Ellie cleared her throat as she came back into the room. Suzanne pretended to blush and tried to look as if she and Daniel had been caught doing something naughty. Ellie attempted to hide the disdain she felt for her sister and handed her a stack of papers to sign. The last one was partially filled out for Sally Ann. "What is this?"

"I need to sign my share of Sally Ann over to you, unless you have changed your mind."

Suzanne handed the stack of papers to her sister without signing the last one. "Sign it!"

Ellie sadly signed the paper, and then handed her sister a large stack of Blue Backs.

"What is this?" Suzanne demanded, waving the paper money at her sister.

"The currency of the Confederacy. You said nothing of being unwilling to accept it. Have you suddenly lost your patriotism and confidence in our young country?"

"Not at all." She smiled at Daniel.

Ellie rolled her eyes. Daniel's hand went to his face, covering his mouth. Ellie knew he was trying to hide a grin at Suzanne's expense.

"Suzanne, maybe you should put that money away someplace safe," Daniel suggested.

"You are so thoughtful, Daniel." Suzanne stood and, taking the Blue Backs with her, left the room.

"Well, that went well." Daniel smiled at Ellie.

"I just wish I could do something about Sally Ann. After tomorrow, she will be the only slave on the property." Ellie sat chewing her lip and staring into the fire.

"I will take care of Sally Ann," Daniel reassured her, reaching out to pat her hand.

"How?" she asked, looking up from her reverie. "Do not worry about it, trust me." He smiled warmly at her, his eyes catching the firelight.

Ellie returned his smile, her eyes sliding over his features, looking into his eyes. "I do trust you." The warmth of that knowledge filled her.

He leaned over and kissed her, long and slow; however, both were distracted, having their attention directed at listening for footsteps, not wanting to be caught. They stopped as soon as they heard Suzanne on the stairs. Later that night, Ellie slipped down the hall in the dark to Daniel's room. She did not knock, but entered unannounced. He was in his nightshirt, sitting in the chair, reading. He smiled up at her and motioned to the other chair. She closed the door behind her and sat down. "I would like for you to be with me when I tell everyone the news. If it were not for you, I do not know if I would have had the courage to do what I know is right. I have been talking about it for years, but it is easy to talk when you do not have the power to follow through with it."

"Ellie, your previous activities were much more dangerous than what you are doing now. You would have done the right thing." He reached out for her, pulling her over to his lap. He held her gently, messaging her breast. When she sighed in contentment, he said, "You had better get out of here while you can." They kissed good night and she slipped out into the hall, making it back to her room without anyone noticing.

Once Sally Ann went upstairs to assist Suzanne the next morning, Ellie and Daniel stopped Lela from leaving, stating they had an announcement. Ellie pulled some papers from the satchel she had brought with her to breakfast and handed them out. Peter, Lela, and Mattie slowly read the papers, gradually the smiles spread across their faces. "What dey say?" Lottie asked.

"Dey freed us!" Lela answered.

"We would like to tell everyone ourselves. Everyone except Sally Ann is now free," Ellie stated.

"Why ya not free her?" Mattie enquired.

"Suzanne would not give up her share of Sally Ann to Ellie. Please give me a chance to talk to her." Daniel smiled, making eye contact with each one.

"What we gonna do now?" Lottie asked.

"I hope you will all stay on at Whispering Oaks. Of course, you will be paid for your labor," Ellie responded.

"It's a good thing ya doin'." Lottie gave Ellie a hug, and then Daniel. Mattie and Lela followed her example. Peter offered his hand.

As soon as Suzanne entered, Daniel slipped out, going up the back stairs in search of Sally Ann. Ellie sat in the kitchen, drinking an extra cup of coffee while she waited for his return. As soon as he walked in, Ellie stood, "Are you ready to tell the others?"

"Yes, let us go now, before this bunch ruins your surprise."

Suzanne made a face and kept eating her breakfast.

Their first stop was Mama Noli's hut. The old woman cried when Daniel read the paper to her while Ellie messaged her gnarled hands. "Thank ya, Miz Ellie. But where's Ah ta go?"

"Mama Noli, you will always have a home here. You worked long and hard for my family and we will continue to care for you."

"Ah's gonna die a free woman, as Ah was borned. Ya made me very happy." She patted Ellie's hand and contemplated this great change in her life. At last she nodded, smiled at her former mistress, and said, "Now, go tell da udders."

Ellie and Daniel made the rounds. Between homes, Daniel informed her that he had given Sally Ann some Green Backs as wages to work and protect Suzanne for the next six months and that Ellie would give her more and would continue to pay her for her services until the war was over. He handed Ellie an envelope full of Green Backs that had been in his saddle bag. He added that he had reassured her that she would be free by the end of the war.

That night Ellie lay in bed thinking about Daniel's generosity. She had known he had considerable money in his saddlebag for a mere second lieutenant, but never expected him to share it. His consideration for Sally Ann did not surprise her, yet to use it to protect Suzanne did. Her sister had demonstrated nothing but the worst qualities she had, and Daniel had seen through all of her manipulations. She yawned and sighed, wishing she could snuggle in close to him and sleep.

CHAPTER 27

The next morning, when Mattie came to help her dress, Ellie noticed that she was quieter than usual. Ellie was worried that it had something to do with Mattie's new status as a freedwoman, so she asked her what was wrong.

"It ain't nothin' ta fret about, Ah doan guess," Mattie stated. Ellie pressed her about it further. Finally, Mattie gave in and explained. "Miz Ellie, las' night yo sister done went ta Daniel's bedroom after ever'body was asleep. Sally Ann tole us all 'bout it dis mornin' on account Miz Suzanne was so put out an' angry las' night when she come back ta her room. It look lack she went dere ta git wit Daniel, ef ya unnerstands mah meanin'." Mattie paused in her narrative to see how Ellie was responding. Ellie was tight lipped and pale, but she nodded for Mattie to continue.

"It din't do her no good, 'cause Daniel tole her ta go on back ta her own bed. Guess he said he weren't interested in messin' about wit her. Sally Ann said Miz Suzanne was poundin' her bed an' ragin' around, but kept it quiet so nobody would know what she done. She slapped Sally Ann around a bit, too. Dat gal has a black eye dis mornin'." Mattie shook her head, disgusted with Suzanne's behavior.

Ellie sat at her dressing table, thinking about what Mattie had said. "We must not mention this to anyone, Mattie. Suzanne can be very vindictive when she gets angry. No matter how kindly Daniel turned her down, I am certain she will want to hurt him if she can. We must not let on that we know what happened. That would certainly set her off. I fear what trouble she might make for him if she were to find out the truth about who he is." She looked at her maid to see that she understood and agreed. Mattie nodded and finished Ellie's hair. The two women went downstairs to breakfast and kept their counsel.

Daniel was too much of a gentleman to mention Suzanne's behavior to Ellie the next day; however, she noticed that he barely looked at Suzanne and when he did, he seemed to have trouble hiding his distain. She was about to mention checking the upper fields when Joey came running in. "Miz Ellie, da bay's tryin' ta foal an' sumptin's wrong!"

Being early March, many of the mares were getting close to foaling. Ellie grabbed her sweater and ran out of the front door. Daniel ran as best he could after her. They found the mare down, thrashing. Ellie wasn't sure what to do, but Daniel started yelling orders. "Hold her head down, Ellie, so Nathaniel can help me. See if you can calm her some." He had taken off his jacket and rolled up his sleeves.

She watched as he lay on his side and his arm seemed to disappear inside the mare. "What are you doing?" she demanded, confused.

"Repositioning the foal so we can get it out," he explained, continuing to tug and push.

"Do you know what you are doing?"

"I have had to do it with calves." He continued to struggle. After what seemed like an eternity to Ellie, he pulled back and the foal slid out on top of him. Joey had been watching, shifting his weight from foot to foot. He ran for towels and joined them in the stall. Ellie started to let go of the mare's head. "Not yet!"

He checked the mare. "She's pretty torn up." Nathaniel ran for more supplies, and then he and Daniel worked on her. Finally, Daniel said, "You can let go of her now."

The mare struggled to her feet. Exhausted, the four sat on the ground against one wall of the stall, watching the mare finish cleaning and nuzzling the newborn. Ellie and Daniel held hands, admiring the new life. Joey and Nathaniel left to go about their other chores. While they had always been hard workers, Ellie sensed that both had a new sense of dedication now that they were being paid for their work, regardless of how small their wages were. She felt Daniel's eyes on her and turned to meet them; he touched her face gently, leaning toward her. They kissed tenderly. Ellie was filled with emotions, hopeful that someday they would bring their own into the world, and sad that by the end of foaling season he would be leaving. He wiped away the tears that silently fell on her cheeks, but did not ask why. She believed he knew. The moment passed and they walked back to the house, laughing at each other, both covered in blood and dirt.

Suzanne called out from the sewing room, "To hear the two of you laughing, I guess the mare is well?"

"Fortunately, Daniel knew what to do." Ellie thought it odd that Suzanne bothered to ask.

"Oh my...you both look...all that blood." Suzanne covered her mouth, looking a bit green and queasy.

The two laughed harder. Ellie headed toward the wash room, calling for Mattie, and Daniel went up the back stairs. Suzanne barged in while Ellie was soaking in the tub. "How did you get all that blood on you?"

Ellie looked up at her sister and laughed. "Suzanne, maybe you should watch the next foaling."

"What does a law student know about these things?" Suzanne asked suspiciously.

"Nothing! But if you are asking how Daniel knew what to do, his family has a farm," Ellie responded, scrubbing at the blood on her arms.

"I do not remember James talking about any Daniel," she stated skeptically.

"James had many friends. I am sure you do not remember all of them, Suzanne. You were much younger; you were not privy to every conversation. Mother remembered him." Ellie felt guilty about this statement, but if necessary, she would show Aunt Felicity's letter to her.

"I do not remember James having any religious friends," Suzanne continued to argue.

"What are you trying to say?" she demanded, rising from the tub and toweling off.

"Nothing," Suzanne responded with an insincere smile and a shrug. She turned on her heel and left the room, leaving Ellie standing there feeling very apprehensive.

Ellie felt uncomfortable with Suzanne's statements. She questioned whether her sister was becoming suspicious of his origins or what else he might have said to reject or criticize her. Ellie knew how her sister could turn if she felt either, whether her perception was accurate or not. She needed to warn him to be careful. She was unable to catch him alone the rest of the day. At breakfast, she mentioned that she needed to check on the upper fields. Suzanne commented that she would not need to do such things if she hadn't freed all of the slaves. Ellie did not respond; it only reminded her that Suzanne had no understanding of their current situation. Again, Daniel slipped out before Ellie left the house and Mattie slowed Sally Ann down in assisting Suzanne with her preparations.

Ellie and Daniel went to check the horses in the woods instead. Their time alone had become precious, not only was it hard to come by, but both knew it would be ending soon, at least for a while. Their contact in conversation became more and more important. Each had so much to say and ask, and time was running out.

In the house, it was becoming more difficult. They stole brief touches, long stares, and private jokes, regardless of who was in the room. Nothing ever went so far as to be considered inappropriate, but their feelings for each other were hard to miss. They had started slipping into each other's rooms again once everyone else was asleep. They talked, kissed, and giggled, careful to keep their voices low, not wanting to be caught. Although Suzanne and Sally Ann were the only others in the house that late, Suzanne was the last person they would want to know.

By mid-April, eight more foals had been born without incident. During dinner, Joey came knocking on the back door. "We gots a problem wit da mare out back."

Daniel and Ellie rose from the table. "No, Ellie, finish eating. I will take care of it."

She started to object, but the look of determination on his face gave her second thoughts. She understood that he needed to know she trusted him to handle the situation. He left with Joey. She tried to distract herself after the meal, reading old letters and writing to Emmy. As the hours passed, she began pacing. Suzanne finally went to bed, annoyed with Ellie's agitation. When Daniel still did not return, she took a lamp and went to the barn. Old Joe was napping in the tack room, waiting for the men to return from the back pasture. The old man attempted to reassure her that Daniel and Nathaniel knew what they were doing and that, if they needed more help, they would send Joey. He entertained her with tales of other foalings; he compared Daniel to her father in the way he took charge and helped the bay mare foal. After two hours of stories, the three men came riding in. Daniel and Nathaniel were covered with dirt and blood.

"What happened?" Ellie asked as soon as they dismounted.

"Whispering Oaks has a healthy new colt and the mare is fine, too!" Daniel announced, smiling broadly.

Old Joe took the horse from Daniel. The couple walked hand in hand back to the house. Lottie had boiled water before she left for the night and it had cooled, leaving luke warm water for Daniel to wash in. Together, they filled the tub and Ellie went up to his room to get him a nightshirt and robe while he stripped and got into the tub. When she came back down, she knocked on the door, "May I come in?"

"No!"

She giggled. "What would you like me to do with your things?"

"Just leave them outside the door, please!"

She continued giggling at his modesty, but put them on the floor as he requested. "I will be in the kitchen."

He entered the kitchen, wearing the nightshirt and robe, rubbing his hair with a towel. She had made some tea and set out some biscuits with jam and canned fruits. They sat talking, laughing, and drinking tea for hours. It was nearly dawn when they headed upstairs to bed. The next morning, they were both slow to wake and rushed to leave with Suzanne for church in the morning. Ellie noticed it was the first time Suzanne did not hang on Daniel's arm, but socialized with some of the other young women instead. However, when they returned to the house, she did not leave Daniel and Ellie alone for a moment. She sat between them on the couch and was careful to be more appropriate with him. Ellie could not help but feel she had been missing something.

When they had turned in to bed, Ellie lay staring at the ceiling, unable to sleep. She felt cheated of her time with Daniel by Suzanne's presence. She finally got up and went down the hall. She stood in front of his door trying to decide if she should knock, slip in unannounced, or go back to her room. She had to talk to him; she was beginning to get angry, yet tried to stop herself from feeling she had any right. She eventually opened the door a crack and whispered, "Daniel, I need to ask you something."

When she received no response, she opened the door further. She heard the familiar sound of his deep, rhythmic breathing in sleep. She tiptoed in, closing the door behind her. She climbed up on the bed and, kneeling, shook his shoulder. "Daniel," she called quietly, shaking him gently. "Daniel."

"Ellie?" he responded sleepily. "Is something wrong?"

"What happened between you and Suzanne?"

"What?"

Ellie repeated the question.

"In the morning." He pulled her down to him and kissed her longingly.

"That is very nice," she told him when he released her. She kissed him again. "Now, not in the morning."

He rolled onto his side and pulled her down next to him.

"Well?" she demanded, pushing him away.

"You will just be angry at her and she is your sister. It does not matter."

"Daniel, I know that she came to your room," Ellie informed him.

Daniel looked at her for a moment. "I should have known you would find out. I turned her down. She did not have a chance to do anything."

"Be careful, Daniel. She does not like being rejected." Ellie's fear was easily read in her voice.

Daniel hugged her to him. "I tried not to insult her."

Ellie suddenly understood Suzanne's comment about religion and why she had stayed away from him in the churchyard. "I love you, Daniel Proctor."

"I know." He kissed her. "You know you are the only woman I want."

She kissed him. He held her tightly with one arm and began running his other hand over her side and leg. He slid his hand under her night clothes. "You know we should not be doing this."

"Yes." She kissed his nose, his eyes, and his lips. As she did, he continued to feel her skin, running his hand over her stomach and breast. She licked his lips, and then teasingly pushed her tongue into his mouth. He slid his hand down to her pubic hair and curled it in his fingers just above the opening. She felt herself becoming moist at the thought of his touch. She wanted to push his hand down into her, but could not bring herself to do so, fearful of what he would think of her. She tried wiggling up higher, making herself more easily available for him, hopeful that he would avail himself of her. Her hand went down under the covers to his member and she found it firm. When their kiss broke, she slid down in the bed. His hand moved up to her breast. She leaned down and kissed the tip of his penis, and then ran her tongue around the head and up and down the hard shaft. She felt his body relax, giving himself up to her mouth as she continued to alternate between licking and sucking on him. Suddenly moaning, he grabbed her, pulling her up over him, kissing her mouth as he pushed her wet opening down onto his throbbing penis. He started moving her up and down until she found the rhythm he had started. Together, they moved in time until both felt the explosions. She collapsed on him and he held her tightly as the last of their convulsions subsided. Eventually, they rolled to their sides, wrapped around each other. He remained within her as they dozed off.

About an hour before dawn, he woke her. They kissed and she tiptoed back to her room. Her door was closed, but not tightly. Briefly, she thought it odd, sure that she had closed it all the way. She told herself that she must not have as she had been trying to be careful not to make any noise. It was forgotten by the time she crawled under the covers.

CHAPTER 28

When she woke again later in the morning, she stretched contentedly. She lay there thinking about the night. When she had gone to his room, she had not planned or expected that they would make love. She really had wanted to talk, yet she did not regret it. She could never feel guilty about sharing herself with him. In her heart, they were already married. It almost seemed as if they always had been. If she felt any guilt, it was about having promised to marry Ted and allowing him to touch her. She had been reviewing everything so long that she did not realize the time.

Mattie knocked on the door, and then slowly opened it, "Miz Ellie?"

"Yes, Mattie?" She spoke in a dream-like voice.

"It's late, Miz Ellie. You all right? Da mornin's 'most gone. Is ya ready ta git up now?" Mattie asked her.

Ellie looked at the bright sunlight coming in her window and laughed. "I am feeling quite amazingly fine, Mattie, and yes, I will get up now." She stretched languidly and sensually, moving slowly into the morning. Mattie watched her movements and the smile that seemed to refuse to leave her face. When she pulled the nightgown over Ellie's head, she saw the marks of passion left behind.

"Miz Ellie, either yo nightgown is rubbin' ya sore o' you been visitin' down da hallway," Mattie commented, smiling.

Ellie looked down at the red swelling around her nipples and the love bites that were so evident on her body. "Oh, lord! There are no marks on my face or neck, are there, Mattie? That is all I would need with Suzanne." She rushed to examine her reflection in her mirror.

"Dere ain't no marks what will show. Doan go worryin' 'bout dat. Ya best be worryin' 'bout wedder ya is pregnant o' not," Mattie stated, scowling at Ellie.

Ellie turned to gape wide-eyed at her maid. "Oh, lord! What can I do, Mattie?"

"Ya kin pray fer one thing. It ain't yo time ta be fertile no ways. Ya should be safe, but ya best not be takin' no chances, Miz Ellie. Ya cain't be havin' no babies without ya is married. Ya know what would happen." Mattie pursed her lips in disapproval. "Ya ain't no slave woman what kin go havin' babies whenever she wants ta."

Ellie sighed and promised herself they would not be intimate again until after they were married; however, she also knew she could not say "no" to him and wondered if there was something else she could do. By the time she was dressed and ready for the day, Ellie's smile was back on her face and the memory of the pleasure they had shared filled her mind.

She nearly skipped down the back stairs. Everyone had already finished breakfast. She was not hungry and only accepted a biscuit and a cup of coffee from Lottie. She ignored the looks that Lottie periodically gave her, not willing to allow anyone to destroy her happiness. She was determined to keep her thoughts in the present. She knew what was ahead of her, but thinking about it would only bring her sadness. Today, he was still with her. She went about her day with a lightness in her step; she found it easy to let Suzanne's snide comments pass. The joy Ellie felt stayed with her over the next few days; however, she wondered if Suzanne was in a particularly fowl mood or if her own good humor made her sister's remarks seem more obnoxious by contrast. Finally, nearly a week later, Ellie reprimanded her for disrupting their dinner.

"Well, I will not be disrupting dinner conversation much longer. I have written to Aunt Felicity telling her that I am returning to Savannah on the first of May. I can no longer abide the tedium of this boring farm. We never see anyone. We never go anywhere. I swear my brains are turning to mush sitting around here with nothing to do."

Ellie bridled at that statement. "There is plenty to do here, Suzanne, if you were not so afraid to get your lovely hands dirty. This farm belongs to both of us, yet you seem to feel that you have no obligation to help in any way."

"You would not have to work so hard had you not freed all the slaves," Suzanne reminded her.

"I was working hard before they were freed. There is a great deal to be done and all hands are needed to do the work," Ellie fired back at her.

"Well, I shall not be here to help or to hinder," Suzanne responded. "Now all I want to know is, are you going to come to Savannah with me, or are you planning to stay here with your Yankee lover?" A broad smile spread over Suzanne's face as she saw the effects of her statement on the others.

Everyone was shocked, not just because she knew the truth about Daniel, but also because of her crudeness. Ellie mumbled some denial of the statement, but Suzanne just laughed. Dramatically, she wiped her mouth with her napkin and rose from the table, leaving the room, smirking and greatly satisfied with herself.

Everyone stared after her. Her features drained of color; Ellie turned to Daniel and said, "Daniel, you have to leave, now!"

"Ellie, I promised Walker I would stay until all the foals were born."

She vigorously shook her head in negation of his promise. "We do not know what was in that letter. They could be coming for you now."

Reaching across the table, he put his hand on hers. "There are only two mares yet to foal. I will take my chances and wait."

"Nathaniel, Joey, and I will manage. You are no longer safe here." Her voice was becoming tight with anxiety.

"Daniel, Miz Ellie's right. Ya gots ta go," Peter added.

Daniel turned to the other man and stated vehemently, "I gave my word. I will not abandon Ellie!"

"Ya ever think you stayin' might hurt Miz Ellie?" Lottie interjected.

This statement seemed to stop him. Mattie noticed his hesitation. "If ya ain't here, Miz Ellie and da rest of us kin lie. If ya is here, dey woan believe ya."

Sally Ann had followed her mistress out, but had come back into the kitchen. She whispered, "Ah doan know what was in da letter, but Miz Suzanne mailt it las' Wednesday." The mail had been slower since the war had begun and some was not getting through at all, but there was no way of knowing.

Ellie realized that was the day after she and Daniel had been together. Then she remembered the door to her room being open. She turned to the butler. "Peter, will you take him to Beaufort?"

"I can find my way. You need him here," Daniel objected.

"If you are alone and come across Confederates, they will kill or capture you. If you are traveling with a man servant, they will believe you and your slave."

"She's right! Ef Ah goes ta Beaufort, Ah kin check da cottage fo' ya, Miz Ellie."

"Peter, can you be ready by dawn?" Daniel had been persuaded.

"Yes! Ah'll be ready." Peter went out the back door to gather his things and say his good-byes.

"Ah'll start workin' on da food fo' ya trip." Lottie went into the pantry; Lela quietly followed, trying to hide the tears that were gathering in the corner of her eyes.

Mattie sat there, looking back and forth between them. "Well, what kin Ah do ta hep?"

There was nothing they could say. Ellie and Daniel walked slowly up the back stairs and down the hall to his room. They hadn't expected their last night together to come so quickly or under such conditions. Ellie was finding it hard to believe. She started going through the closet and pulling things out.

"What are you doing?" he asked her, watching her activity.

"You will need some clothes," she stated, wiping tears out of her eyes with the back of her hand.

"No, Ellie. I will be back in uniform soon." Seeing the lost look in her eyes, he added, "I will take an extra shirt, some underwear and socks. That is all that will fit in my saddlebag anyway."

"You can start out in a fresh set of traveling clothes."

"Ellie, please stop!" He took her into his arms, "There are other things we must talk about now." He led her over to the chair and pulled the other one up to hers so that they were sitting face to face, knees touching.

"I love you, Ellie. As soon as the war is over, I will come back and Father Burton will marry us. That is, if you will wait for me?" He looked hungrily into her eyes.

"I will not marry another no matter when you return," she promised, leaning toward him and grasping his hands with hers.

"I also need to go home to Pennsylvania to see my family."

"Of course." She nodded, recognizing the necessity, but feeling the pain of a prolonged separation.

"I do not know where I will be when it is over. If I am in the South, I will come here first and we will go together. But if I am close to Pennsylvania, I will go home first, and then come back. It could take me two or three extra months." Daniel's voice was choked with emotion.

Ellie started desperately, "I could go with you. That is if you…"

"Ellie, they will love you as I do. We have not even had time to talk about where we will live."

Ellie gasped as she understood what he was saying. "Leave Whispering Oaks forever? I had not even thought about the possibility. We have been so happy here."

"My brother and father will be disappointed, but they will be happy that I have found such a wonderful woman. I did not think you would want to leave; however, we never talked about it. I will live and work here."

"Thank you. I love you. Now, keep yourself safe. Do not let anyone kill you. I understand now why Mother could not stay here after Father died." She leaned forward until her lips were pressed to his hands.

"I will live." He smiled and lifted her face until it was level with his. "I have four children to sire." He leaned forward and kissed her. "I have a long day tomorrow. I need to sleep for a few hours." He took her hand and led her to the bed. They lay on top of the covers, in their clothing, wrapped in each others arms.

They woke to Mattie shaking them, whispering, "It's time."

All of the ex-slaves and Sally Ann were waiting out front to say their good-byes. Daniel held Ellie's hands in his. "Good-bye, my Ellie." He brought her hands to his mouth kissing them, and then turned away.

Ellie stood watching from the porch until Daniel and Peter were no longer in sight. She spent the day in her room. She could not bear the thought of seeing Suzanne; she was afraid of what she might say to her. She hoped that Daniel would be safe in Beaufort before Suzanne even realized he was gone. When she did not come down for breakfast the next morning, Lela slipped up the back stairs and knocked on her door. "Miz Ellie, kin Ah come in?"

"Lela!" Ellie threw open the door. "Is something wrong?" She could not remember the last time the woman had been on the second floor. It was probably when they played as children.

"Yes! Ya sista's thinkin' she doan won. Ya got ta take yo place an' run dis farm. Dat lil miss gonna cause nuthin' but trouble ef you ain't in charge. Ya gots ta think 'bout the rest o' us, too, Miz Ellie. She doan lack it dat we ain't her slaves no mo'. Ah knowed her from a baby, an' she mean spirited. Ef you ain't da boss 'round here, she gonna be, an' ain't none o' us gonna put up wit her shenanigans! Now, you git ya sef up an' git on downstairs!"

Ellie was speechless for several moments. She had seldom been spoken to like that by a white adult, and never by a Negro. Then it occurred to her that it was proof that Lela thought of herself as a free woman and believed that Ellie viewed her that way as well. Ellie's expression turned from shock and disbelief to satisfaction. "Thank you, Lela. You really are my friend."

Lela just nodded and turned to leave. As she was about to go out the door, she called back, "Miz Ellie, ya need anythin'?"

"Yes, Lela, I think it is about time you stop calling me, 'Miz." You are a free woman and you have always been my friend."

Lela turned and studied Ellie's face for several seconds, considering the offer. She smiled warmly and said, "Thank ya,…Ellie." She slipped back down the stairs, not wanting to be seen by Suzanne.

Ellie hurriedly dressed and joined the others as they were finishing up their breakfast. She greeted everyone as if nothing had happened.

"Where have you been?" Suzanne's greeting was not especially warm.

"Working!" Ellie responded, her expression suggesting that it was something Suzanne would not understand.

Suzanne sniffed in disgust, and then casually stated, "I heard Daniel left. I thought maybe you had run off with him." She smirked. "I was very upset that my own sister would not even say goodbye."

"As you can see, I am still here, little sister." Ellie's smile was just barely polite, verging on a snarl.

"Daniel left suddenly." Suzanne feigned surprise and hurt. "He did not say goodbye to me."

Ellie glared at her sister in disbelief. "You insulted him, calling him a Yankee. Why should he bother to say goodbye?"

"So, he ran away." Suzanne's lip turned up in disgust at such cowardice.

"Suzanne, his work here was finished and he would not let me or my reputation be hurt by your accusations or anybody else's suspicions." Ellie's response was icy.

Suzanne chuckled as if at a joke. "I understand. You will protect your lover even as he abandons you." She shook her head in apparent disappointment at her sister's weakness.

Ellie paused before responding, considering her words carefully. "I do not understand why you dislike me so. Father, Mother, and James are all dead. We only have each other."

Suzanne thought she perceived a weakness in Ellie's defense and made a challenge. "Then come to Savannah."

"You know that is not possible without an overseer here."

"Too bad!" She shrugged, got up from the table and left the room.

Sally Ann shook her head as she followed her mistress out of the room.

The day after Suzanne left for Savannah, a letter arrived from Emmy. Suzanne had accused Daniel of being a Yankee in her letter to Aunt Felicity. However, Emmy had shared one of Ellie's earlier letters describing how Suzanne had been flirting and chasing him. She apologized for breaking Ellie's confidence, but told her parents she had overheard Daniel say he wanted to marry Ellie after the war. The Hamiltons knew Suzanne well enough to understand the source of her maliciousness. Emmy made no mention of Suzanne claiming that Ellie and Daniel were lovers.

Ellie wrote to her uncle that spring planting was well past and the mares had safely foaled. She added that two deliveries had started with foals in a breeched position, but fortunately Mr. Proctor had been able to reposition them. She ended the letter by stating that he had left to rejoin his regiment. She wrote a second letter to Emmy about how horrid Suzanne had been. She had brazenly chased Daniel, and then was nasty once he rejected her. Ellie told her cousin that it was better that the family knew her intentions to marry Daniel after the war. She hoped they would focus on finding a husband for Suzanne, instead of one for her. She ended the letter by asking Emmy about her own intended and whether he had asked Uncle Walker for her hand yet.

Peter came back, but only for a few days. He informed Ellie that they had made it to Beaufort without incident. However, after the journey, Daniel was barely hobbling. The Union officers questioned him about his whereabouts for nearly two days. The difficulty he had walking probably was to his benefit with the officers. When Ellie expressed her concern, Peter reassured her that Daniel was doing much better by the time Peter had left. The Peters' summer cottage had been taken over by some Union officers. He stated that he came back because he had promised Daniel he would let her know he was safe and because he wanted to say goodbye to everyone. There were many opportunities for Negroes in Beaufort now. Many of the houses were being sold for taxes and he hoped someday to have his own home. Ellie informed him she only had Blue Backs to pay him the wages she owed to him and she realized that, in Beaufort, they would not be accepted. She offered him a silver tray, but he turned it down. He said his good-byes and left for Beaufort.

CHAPTER 29

The summer months passed slowly. It seemed to Ellie that it was even hotter than the year before had been. She was relieved that it was uneventful, but worried about money. By fall, she decided she needed to sell a couple of horses, even if it was only for Blue Backs. Not only did she need to pay wages, but there were some basic supplies they needed before winter. She refused to touch the Green Backs that Daniel had given her for Sally Ann or any of the gold or silver she had hidden. Events had become too unpredictable. The war was dragging out and every Sunday at church it seemed that someone else from the Parish had died. Blue Backs were already practically worthless. If the South did lose, they would be worth absolutely nothing. She kept remembering what her father had told her, *"Gold and silver are the only currencies you can count on keeping their value."*

She drove into Sheldon with Joey, the two horses she planned on selling tied to the back of the wagon. She did not want to draw attention to the farm by posting another notice. She found that the cost of everything had gone up even higher than she had anticipated, including the price of a good horse. Apparently, the only thing that had not gone up was a day's wages.

Mr. Franks gave her fourteen hundred Confederate dollars for the four year old mare and agreed to consign the three year old for forty percent of the sale price. Ellie felt he was taking advantage of her on the second one, but could not risk anyone coming to the farm. She decided the extra twenty percent consignment commission was worth the price for the added safety. She returned to the farm with coffee, tea, sugar, molasses, flour, salt, and four hundred dollars in Blue Backs. The cash would be used up for wages. She felt guilty knowing how little her people would be able to purchase with their money. She was still paying them as if a Blue Back was worth a silver dollar when it was only worth about thirty cents. Nevertheless, her main concern was to feed the people and animals over the winter and keep everyone safe from scavengers and both armies.

As she and Joey returned home, she was disheartened by the way things were going. Her whole family was gone, dead or alienated; Daniel was gone, and her idealism was fading. The Negroes working for her were little better off than when they had been slaves. She thought of the family of runaways she had met so long ago, and hoped that the freedom of those who had chosen to stay on the farm gave them some sense of dignity as that man so long ago dreamed of having. As they drove along the border of the farm, she realized that the fencing was barely noticeable. She thought, *At least, something is going right.*

Ellie had never been much for visiting her neighbors in Sheldon as she had in Beaufort. She had always found too many things more interesting to occupy her time on the farm. Since Ted had died nearly two years ago, and then her father and brother and more recently her mother, she had used being in mourning as an excuse not to socialize. It had not yet been a full year since her mother had died. It seemed the way the war was going she would never be out of mourning. Still, when she heard at church that young Mark Dubois had lost both legs in battle and had returned home, she decided to visit. The wheel chair Old Joe had made for Daniel was stored in one of the vacated slave cabins. She would take it to him.

After loading it onto the wagon, Nathaniel drove Ellie to their neighbors. The Dubois family was delighted to receive the chair and quickly assisted Mark into it so that he could try it out. Ellie was invited to stay for lunch so that they could catch up on the latest news. Mark had recently received a letter from one of his friends still in the army. His mother quickly brought it out so that Mark could read it to Ellie. The news was not good.

From the end of May until July 4, 1863, General Grant and his Union troops had laid siege to Vicksburg, Mississippi. The Union wanted to take the town in order to gain control of the Mississippi River. General Pemberton had finally been forced to surrender to Grant. Shortly afterwards, the Union troops captured Port Hudson, Louisiana, and had effectively cut the South in half. On the other hand, in the east, things had been going well for the South. General Lee had become so confident that he had decided to press into Northern territory and had crossed over into Pennsylvania. His troops were pursued by Union troops under the command of General Meade. Both armies met, mostly by accident, at Gettysburg, Pennsylvania and the fighting had gone on for three days—July 1, 2, and 3. Meade had won the battle, but both sides lost an incredible number of men. All told, more than 50,000 men were wounded, missing, or dead. Meade failed to pursue Lee's army after the battle and so lost the advantage he had gained. This battle proved to be the turning point for the Confederate Army. Their fortunes waned after that. Word came that the South would not gain recognition from England, France, or any other foreign power.

In September, General Braxton Bragg had defeated the Union troops after a brief battle at Chickamauga. The Union troops retreated to Chattanooga, Tennessee, leaving the Southern troops in command of the railroads that crossed in that area. However, by the end of November, Union forces had pushed the Confederate troops away from the Chattanooga area and were again in control of the railroads. This was terrifying news as it left the deep South vulnerable to attack by Union troops that could be brought in swiftly and be kept well supplied. Everyone was greatly disturbed by this turn of events. Ellie left soon after lunch, and found herself engrossed in thought all the way back to the farm.

CHAPTER 30

Suzanne had decided to remain in Savannah for the winter. Ellie thought it just as well since she was not looking forward to seeing her sister or having her around. Although her aunt and uncle had been insistent that she join them for Christmas, she had continued to refuse to leave Whispering Oaks. She had decided that she would continue the tradition she and Daniel had created the year before for Christmas Eve. It would be terribly difficult without him, but she had a future to look forward to with him. She believed they would be together again. She decided that, whenever she felt sad and lonely, she would imagine the Christmases they would have with their own children gathered around the tree.

Lela and the household staff helped to decorate the tree. They had slaughtered one of the pigs and cured most of it. Flour and tea had been the most expensive items; corn meal and chestnut flour were substituted to make the sweets and breads. Ellie had rummaged through the attic as well as the rest of the house for trinkets to give as Christmas gifts. In the process, she found a box addressed to Ted at Whispering Oaks inside the armoire of the guest room he had frequently used. She had not known it was there. She passed over it, unsure if she would ever open it.

Ellie and the house staff served the others. At first, they seemed uncomfortable with Ellie serving them, but as the evening progressed the laughter and good will over came any discomfort. Tears came to Ellie's eyes as she listened to the sweet voices raised in Christmas songs and spirituals. She did not notice the lack of a piano. When the party broke up, Joey drove with Ellie to church. She felt badly having to leave Joey outside and walk in alone, but once she sat in the pew she fantasized about the day Daniel would be sitting next to her again. When the Beals invited her for Christmas dinner she politely refused. However, she could not turn down young Mark Dubois sitting in the wheelchair, especially once the family insisted they would send a carriage for her.

Christmas morning, Lela joined her for breakfast. She was glad of her company, realizing she would have been totally alone in the house. She knew Lela had her own family to spend time with and saw Lela's relief when she told her she was going to the Dubois' for Christmas dinner. Once Lela left, the house was silent. She had hours to dress and needed to find something to fill her time. She went to the guest room and pried open Ted's box. It contained three bottles of the scotch Ted preferred, one bottle of red Dubonnet, a can of imported cookies and a stack of letters Ellie had written to Ted over the years tied together with a blue ribbon. She opened the can, wondering if she could bring the cookies to the Dubois' for Christmas, but the first one she picked up crumbled in her hand. They were too fragile to last over two years, even sealed up. A bottle of scotch for the men and a jar of Lottie's fruit preserves for the women would have to do. She took a bottle of scotch and the cookie can down to the kitchen. Then she brought the cookies to the pond, tossing them out for the fish, ducks, and geese. After wiping out the empty can in the kitchen, she retrieved the letters, put them in the can, and brought it along with the Dubonnet to her room. She had just enough time to prepare for her Christmas outing. As they drove away, she thought how strange, it was the first Christmas in her memory that she had ever left the family house.

In the middle of January, a letter arrived from Emmy; it had been dated Christmas Eve. She was excited to tell Ellie that Christopher had asked her father for her hand and they had agreed to be married as soon as the war was over. Her other news was more disturbing. Matthew Gibbs Fuller had asked for Suzanne's hand and the two of them were determined to marry before he finished his leave and left Savannah. The Hamiltons seemed to think that Suzanne had made a good match and would be better off marrying immediately than chasing every soldier that gave her any attention. Emmy admitted that she could not endure being in Matthew's presence. She felt he represented the worst qualities of a Southern man, refusing to even call him a gentleman.

Ellie remembered arguing with the man over dinner at Whispering Oaks. He was the eldest son of a sea-island cotton planter and rabidly pro-slavery. He had viewed Negroes as no different from animals. With her experiences of the last few years, she now recognized that Matthew Fuller knew nothing of work and was only familiar with the play of running hounds and horses.

Two weeks later, a letter arrived from Suzanne. It was dated December 26, 1863. It had taken over a month for the letter to arrive from Savannah. Suzanne stated that Aunt Felicity had insisted that she inform her of the news. She announced that the next day she would be married to Matthew Gibbs Fuller. She reminded Ellie of who he was and the dinner so long ago. Suzanne continued about Matthew having proper Southern values, not like Ellie's, and that he understood how Ellie was a foolish woman destined to be rejected by any good Southern family. She added that he had been appalled that Ellie had freed "their darkies," and assured her that on his plantation she would be served by a full staff of slaves. She ended the letter by saying she had always expected her sister to attend her wedding, but she did not want to cause her pain by forcing Ellie to witness a man who had rejected her marry her own sister.

Ellie's initial response to the news was a desire to relieve herself of her breakfast. She was thoroughly disgusted by the idea of being related, even by marriage, to the man and wished she'd had some power to prevent the marriage. Despite her dislike for Suzanne, she did not want her sister to be unhappy in life. It took her some time to acknowledge that Suzanne would probably be very happy living on a plantation with abundant servants to wait on her every whim. At last, she genuinely hoped her sister would be happy with Matthew Fuller. She wrote a pleasant congratulatory reply.

Spring passed uneventfully. To Ellie's relief, there were no foaling complications. She was somewhat concerned about how long the planting had taken. She hoped it would be a late summer, so that the heat would not come too soon and destroy the young plants. She had the satisfaction of watching the crops ripen without any serious losses as the summer passed slowly.

At church, Ellie received news of the progress of the war. The news over the summer months had become disturbing. In May 1864, Gen. William T. Sherman, commanding the Military Division of Mississippi, began his campaign to take Atlanta. It required many months and several battles, but on the night of the first of September, General Hood evacuated the Confederate troops from Atlanta. By September 8, General Sherman's troops were in control of Atlanta and were spreading out to secure the surrounding area.

CHAPTER 31

On the fifteenth of September, Ellie was sipping a second cup of coffee at the kitchen table when nine year old Lily came in the front door yelling, "Wagons an' a carriage is comin' down da drive!"

Ellie and Lela ran to the front door. Each grabbed a rifle; Lela went to Peter's old post and Ellie stepped outside onto the porch. As the vehicles came closer, she recognized Charlotte's carriage being pulled by the gray mare she had taken to Savannah years ago, followed by two wagons. She leaned the weapon against the wall and ran down the front steps to welcome her family.

Aunt Felicity, Uncle Walker, Emmy, Suzanne, their personal attendants and a Negro driver who was unknown to Ellie drove up to the house. She had never seen any of her family look so disheveled and tired. She realized they must have been traveling all night. She would ask her questions later, but was fearful that something terrible must have happened. First, she would attend to their needs. She went to the carriage and helped her Aunt Felicity down.

Joey and Nathaniel had been watching from the barn. They came running to assist, helping to unload, and then led the sweaty, tired horses to the barn. Ellie knew no instructions were necessary; she trusted these men to care properly for any horse. When she saw Sally Ann and the Hamilton slaves struggling with the trunks, she called for Lela and Jonathan, Peter's replacement, to help. Ellie walked her aunt up the stairs and to the couch in the living room. She found Mattie and Lottie already busy at work in the kitchen making preparations for the comfort of the family. Coffee, tea, breads, and jams were quickly served. Ellie noticed that no one spoke, but hungrily downed the bread and jam. She sent Mattie to have Lottie prepare a full breakfast and plenty of water for baths. Ellie instructed Jonathan and Lela to put her aunt and uncle's things in her parents' room and prepare Suzanne's and one of the guest rooms. She returned to the dining room and waited for the eating to slow down. Finally, Walker explained their sudden arrival. "Atlanta is gone. I had to get the women out of Savannah. Sherman is burning everything in his way. We drove all night."

"What about your plantation, Uncle?" Ellie was in shock.

Walker sadly shook his head. "It is on his route." He looked every bit of his sixty-five years. Ellie had never seen him look so defeated.

A sob escaped her Aunt Felicity's tightly pressed lips. "All the slaves left! How could we survive there?" She too appeared older than Ellie remembered her.

"It is good that you came here." She patted her aunt's hand. "Mattie is preparing a bath. Come! Then you can have a long rest." Ellie rose and as she led her aunt to the wash room, she couldn't help but notice that Felicity seemed terribly drawn.

Ellie went to the kitchen to find the Savannah slaves eating. Sally Ann explained the situation more thoroughly. "Dere ain't no food in Savannah. Dey stole da chickens. Dey plucked da garden clean."

"Who stole them?" Ellie asked.

"Da people's all hungry an' no one kin pay fo' what food dere is. A barrel o' flour cost ya three hundred Blue an' few dare take da Green. Only silver an' gold any good, an' den it still gonna cost ya."

Ellie sighed. "Well, Sally Ann," she looked around the table at the others, "we have food here."

Once everyone settled in for a well needed rest, Ellie went to the barn and saddled up a horse. She rode to the upper fields to assess the crops. She realized she only needed to ask Nathaniel for him to do the checking, but she needed to ride to clear her head. She hoped she would have enough food; she had not expected nine additional mouths to feed. She was also concerned how her family would treat the free Negroes on the farm. She needed them to stay and work.

By dinner, Walker Hamilton seemed to be more himself. "Ellie, by the looks of the place, it is a good thing that I have come. Why did you not write to me to tell me you were having problems?"

"What are you referring to, Uncle Walker?" she asked him, wrinkling her forehead.

"I may have been up all night, but the condition of the fencing is a sad statement...and everything is terribly overgrown. We had trouble finding the entrance."

Ellie smile, "Uncle Walker, it has been left that way purposely."

"I know you have been here alone, Ellie. I am sure you did a good job considering..."

"Mr. Proctor did not want to draw attention to the farm. He felt we would be safer from Union soldiers or scavengers if the place were better hidden," she explained, hoping that the idea having come from Daniel would give it more authority with her elderly uncle.

"Hmm...Mr. Proctor...we will speak about Mr. Proctor tomorrow after breakfast, Ellie."

Ellie paled, fearing the confrontation to come. Suzanne snickered. This restored Ellie's resolve and she turned a withering glare on her insensitive sister.

In the morning, Ellie found her uncle sitting at her father's desk pouring over the books. "Ellie, what happened to your stock? You cannot run a breeding farm with only one stallion!"

"I have two more hidden. Let me get the other breeding books for you." Ellie went to the bookcase and removed two books and handed them to her uncle.

"The Iliad?" He looked questioningly at Ellie, and then opened the first book to find descriptions of horses and breeding histories. "What is this about Ellie?"

"Soldiers came, wanting to take Princess and the stallions. The first time I was able to stop them so I divided the herd. Some are in the woods; some are in the back pasture. The next time soldiers came, they wanted twenty horses including the three stallions in the barn. Mr. Proctor convinced them to leave one."

"Over the next few days, I want to see these hidden horses. Now, you have not sold many horses in the last two years. What have you been living on?" He studied the books again, angling them to see the writing better through his bifocals.

"I have spent the Blue Backs on supplies as fast as I could before prices would go up more. Also, we grow much of what we need right here on the farm. In fact, harvesting will begin soon."

"Do you have enough slaves left to handle it?" he enquired, looking up at her.

Ellie drew herself up straighter. "Sir, I do not own slaves. The men and women who work here are free and are paid wages."

"Suzanne said that you freed them all, but I could not believe you would do something so foolish. How many have left since you gave them their freedom?" He twisted his lips tightly together in disapproval.

"One. All of the ones that left did so long before I gave them their independence. Is there anyone left on your plantation, sir?" Ellie knew she was being flippant with her elder, but she felt she had to show him she would not back down on this point.

Walker humphed at her disrespect and pulled his glasses off. "If you think they stayed because you freed them, you are mistaken. How are you paying them?"

"Blue Backs…housing…and they are allowed a small plot of land to grow their own produce and raise their own animals."

"And Mr. Proctor agreed with you about this?" he asked, raising an eyebrow.

"He saw how much harder they worked as free men." Ellie did not want to raise her uncle's suspicions about Daniel's origins.

Walker leaned back in the chair and looked at Ellie speculatively. "Is this true that Mr. Proctor wanted to ask for my permission to marry you?"

"Yes, sir."

"He seemed an honorable man. Ellie, why did you reject him?" Walker asked, unsure who to blame.

"Oh, I did not! I want to marry him!"

"Why…?" he began.

"I was afraid you would not let me stay here…"

"I certainly would not have! In fact, if Suzanne had not remained, you would not have stayed in this house with him. I may be an old man of sixty-five, Ellie, but I am not yet blind. I saw the way he looked at you." He shook his head. "You are aware that your sister thinks he is a Yankee?"

"Yes, sir." Ellie forced herself to inhale slowly and to remain calm.

"Well?" he demanded.

"You have met him, sir."

Aunt Felicity knocked, and then floated into the room to Ellie's relief. She did not want to discuss this issue with her uncle any longer. "Walker, you are keeping Ellie from us. The poor girl has been alone here without any companionship. I am sure she is tired of all this business. Come, dear!"

Ellie barely kept from rolling her eyes. She felt as if she had just been pulled out of the pot and into the fire. Her family had only been there one day and she was already feeling it had been too long. She just wanted the war to be over, so that the Hamiltons would go back to Savannah, Suzanne to her plantation, and Daniel would come back to her. With Atlanta gone, it could not be much longer.

Ellie listened to Suzanne's monologue describing the merits of her husband. She tried to show interest and ask questions. She soon realized that Suzanne hardly knew her husband. Every time Ellie attempted to ask Emmy or her Aunt Felicity something, Suzanne would interrupt. No one asked about Daniel, and Ellie hoped that no one would. She did not want Suzanne to see her loneliness.

CHAPTER 32

In the year and a half since he had left, she had heard nothing of him. Until this war was over, no letters would cross the lines, nor could either risk exposing themselves or each other. When she feared him dead and her eyes began to water, she would remind herself that she could expect nothing until the war was well over. She had lost so many people she loved; she told herself to trust him to survive. She prayed for his safety, for peace, and for his quick return.

Ellie and Walker rode most mornings. Each day, they would check a different part of the farm: the hidden herds and the progress of the harvesting. Walker knew little of the workings of raising and selling horses, but they both agreed it was time to sell off more horses. Ellie was concerned about feeding nine extra mouths, especially when four of them were unaccustomed to eating the simpler fare that the farm produced. After much discussion, they picked out four horses to take into town. Lela and Nathaniel's wife, Becky, asked that they be allowed to send some of their own produce with them in the wagon to be sold. Ellie questioned the wisdom of not canning everything they could get their hands on, but Lottie informed her that she was getting low on canning jars.

Mr. Franks' store was still the heart of the town. Everyone congregated there to discuss everything that was happening in the parish. Word was that Sherman was still in Atlanta, resting his troops before moving on. No one knew for certain where he would go next. Some speculated that he would go up through Augusta, and then cross over into South Carolina, marching to take Charleston. Others said that he would go to Savannah. The uncertainty was maddening. Some of the local farmers reported that there had been several robberies by scavengers, probably Confederate soldiers absent without leave. Mr. Franks stated that several men had come into his store one evening near closing and had threatened him with guns. They wanted his money and food. "They would have succeeded, too, if the county militia hadn't a showed up right then," he told his fascinated audience. Ellie was appalled by the prices of everything. Coffee and tea were ridiculously expensive; however, Walker insisted on buying as much of the necessities and luxuries as they could afford. There was no kerosene for the lamps, only terebene, a smelly, smoky oil made from turpentine. Ellie also bought more jars for canning. She estimated that they were getting about ten cents on the dollar. Ellie wondered about how a soldier could survive and support his family with prices the way they were. A private only earned $8 a month, and a pair of boots now cost $500.

They sold all the fresh produce for as much as they could get, loaded their purchases into the wagon, and headed back home. On the way there, Ellie commented on the cost of everything and stated that she hoped Lela and Becky would not be too disappointed with what they got for their labor.

"Surely, you are not going to give those women the profits from this sale," Walker stated incredulously.

"Of course I am, Uncle Walker. It was their work that produced the food. It was grown on their patches of land. They should have the profits from the sale." She stared at the man as if he had suddenly arrived from another planet.

Walker just shook his head at such foolishness.

After the supplies were unloaded, Ellie slipped into the kitchen to speak with Lottie. The shelves at Mr. Franks' general store seemed to have been nearly barren. Ellie did not expect to be able to re-supply many of the basics, especially things like coffee, tea, sugar, and candles. They discussed adding chicory to the coffee to make it last longer and mint or herbs to the tea. She also told Lela and Lottie about the wayward men in raggedy Confederate uniforms and the need to go back to limiting day time fires and night time lights. She asked that they inform the others.

At dinner that night, Ellie attempted to explain to the family the need to take certain precautions in order to keep everyone safe.

"Stuff and nonsense, Ellie! No Southern gentleman would harm noncombatant Southerners. Nor would they ever consider stealing from them. It must surely have been Yankees. I can readily believe they would not be above doing such things," Felicity declared with indignation when Ellie explained what she was doing and why.

"If the Yankees are in the area, there is little we can do to prevent them from robbing us," Walker stated. "I will certainly do my best to protect all of you and the farm, but I am only one man. I cannot be everywhere at once and could not fend off more than a handful of invaders."

Ellie could see that he was trying to conceal his fears for their safety. "Uncle Walker, I know you to be a singularly brave man, but you will not have to defend us alone. I am quite adept at shooting now, and I have armed and trained Lela and a few of the men here on the farm. There are others here to assist you and me in protecting our home and property," Ellie tried to reassure him.

"What?" Felicity exclaimed. "You have armed the slaves? Are you mad, child?"

"Ellie, what were you thinking?" Walker demanded.

Ellie took a deep breath, trying to calm herself and prepare for the battle she feared she was about to have with them. "Father showed me where the guns were and told me to select those slaves I felt I could trust with weapons before he left. He knew there might come a time when I would need them to help defend the farm and our lives. I have been very careful in making my choices. I have no doubt of the loyalty of the men I selected and they have proven over and over again that my faith in them has not been misplaced. Had they intended to murder or betray me, they have had the opportunity many times over already. I assure you they will not be a problem." She sat straight and firm and stared down the objections of both her aunt and uncle.

Walker looked uncertain, but seemed to accept the situation as it existed. Felicity still seemed anxious about slaves having weapons, but she saw that her husband, whom she trusted implicitly, was not going to argue the point. She fanned herself rapidly and tried to feel complacent about the situation.

Ellie went on to explain that Daniel had suggested further precautions for protection; actions that would keep the chances of their being detected by outsiders to a minimum. Walker nodded his agreement to the wisdom of these measures, and Felicity sighed at the thought of cold meals and cold baths.

Suzanne, however, declared, "That Yankee is just setting you up, Ellie. Mark my words. He wants you to feel safe and secure here, until he can send his friends riding in to steal everything out from under your misguided Southern nose. I am certain he has told them exactly where to find you and your precious horses. We will be left with nothing!" She curled her lip in disgust and marched out of the room. Watching her leave, Ellie sighed in frustration and helplessness. Emmy walked over to her and put her arm around Ellie's shoulder.

"Do not worry about her, Ellie. She will comply with everything if the rest of us do. She is just very frightened, as are we all." Emmy squeezed her shoulder reassuringly. Ellie responded with a watery smile.

Over the next few weeks, Ellie began to understand more about Walker Hamilton. She realized she needed to continue to run the farm herself; however, she needed to give her uncle the illusion that the ideas and orders were coming from him. By November, they were working fairly well together, although at times Ellie and the freedmen were extremely frustrated with Walker's attitude toward women and the Negroes. Over the course of November, more and more troops seemed to be coming into the area. Walker was annoyed that they were not in Georgia protecting his plantation and Savannah.

The last week of the month, Walker came back from Mr. Franks' with a tin of tobacco and a copy of the *Charleston Mercury*. His agitation was palpable; no one dared ask him about it until dinner. Felicity finally demanded that her husband tell them. "Whatever is wrong, Walker?"

"That damn Jeff Davis wants to arm and free our slaves!" he said with extreme disgust, waving his newspaper in the air.

Felicity looked shocked, but not about the President's ridiculous notion. "Walker, such language, please!"

"Father, that is just not possible!" Emmy protested, nonplussed.

"It is right here in the *Mercury*," he stated, and began reading. "November seventh, President Davis spoke to the Confederate Congress asking the government to buy forty thousand slaves for the military and give them their freedom after a period of honorable service."

"He must be very worried to suggest such a thing," Emmy responded.

Walker laughed humorlessly. "Fortunately, the Congress has more sense than our President. They refused his request."

"I should think so!" Felicity exclaimed.

Ellie remained quiet throughout the conversation. She thought about Daniel's prediction. At the time, she had thought he was being true to his cause.

Now, she realized he had been correct; the South did not have enough men to win the war. She could not help think what fools surrounded her. Their determination to keep men enslaved not only caused the war, but would lead to the downfall of the South.

CHAPTER 33

On November 30, 1864, Ellie woke late to the muffled sound of gun fire in the distance. She heard female screams coming from downstairs. Ellie had been through this before; she was frightened, but knew that the sounds were in the distance. She threw on her robe and quickly went downstairs to try to calm the others.

The gunfire was more intense than in the past. Lottie and Mattie were reassuring Sally Ann when Ellie reached the kitchen. Ellie checked to be certain that everything was under control there. Lottie assured her they were fine, but Sally Ann flinched and stared wide-eyed at every report. It wasn't long before they heard Suzanne's angry voice screaming for Sally Ann to come and help her dress before the Yankees came and raped and robbed and killed them all. Ellie looked at the poor, frightened woman and knew she would not be able to deal with Suzanne's temper and anxiety in her current state. She asked Mattie to go up and help her sister to dress. "I will manage as much as I can on my own. I know this is asking a lot, Mattie, but Sally Ann is in no condition to help her right now." Mattie reluctantly nodded and made her way up the stairs. Ellie offered some reassuring words to Sally Ann and hurried upstairs to dress herself, knowing that the rest of the family would be down soon and would need her support as well.

When they were assembled in the dining room for breakfast, Walker was smiling bravely and trying to put on an air of confidence. Felicity was pale and jumpy, but also trying to look brave. Emmy appeared nervous, but accepted Ellie's word that the fighting was far away from them, and that they were in no immediate danger. Suzanne, on the other hand, showed her fear and expressed it through anger at everyone. She would not allow herself to be reassured and several times exclaimed that she expected them all to be dead by nightfall.

The day dragged on with no letup of gun and cannon fire. As the sun began to set, the house seemed as chilled as the atmosphere. Emmy bundled Felicity up with blankets. She flinched when the cannon fire sounds were especially loud, but tried to look calm following Ellie's example. Suzanne whined that her head hurt, but refused to leave the other women in the living room when it was suggested that she go to bed. Walker paced the house, obviously frustrated with his helplessness in the situation. Ellie tried to look busy, but thought about the last battle nearby and the comfort that Daniel had given her. She wondered if he was one of the soldiers firing at her countrymen. She wanted it to stop! With what had happened in Georgia and President Davis' desperate ploy, she could not understand why they had not surrendered. She did not know how President Lincoln would punish the South, but she could not imagine it being any worse than all these deaths.

It seemed the battle was only to last the one day. However, over the next several days, there was sporadic gun fire. After a couple of days of quiet, Walker took the carriage into town. Ellie rode to the woods with Joey; she wanted to check on Princess, Daniel's gelding, and the other horses. Afterwards, they rode out to the back pasture to check on the other herd.

She was in the barn when Walker came back. When he stepped down from the carriage, Ellie could see that he was upset. She hurried to greet him and find out what had happened.

"Those damned Yankees! Pardon my language, Ellie, but you will not believe what they have done. With Sherman marching to the sea, and no way of knowing if he is going to Savannah or Charleston, that damned Major General Hatch marched out of Hilton Head with his troops and tried to cut the railroad lines at Pocotaligo. Colonel Colcock and his men did their best to stop the Yankees from moving further north and cutting off our supply lines. He tried to hold them at Honey Hill. Hatch failed to take our entrenchments and he high-tailed it back to Boyd's Neck after dark." He was pacing in agitation as he related the story.

"Well, that is wonderful news, Uncle. I do not understand why you are so upset. The Yankees did not succeed. Our boys sent them back." She looked quizzically at her uncle, waiting for some explanation.

"Our boys certainly did chase them off, but that is not what was so upsetting. Those insufferable Yankees have got their freed niggers dressed up like trained monkeys in Union uniforms. The damned niggers are carrying guns and shooting at white men! Can you imagine that? Turning our people on us and telling them it is right for them to raise their hands against their masters!" He was stomping about furiously by this point. "Giving a nigger a gun and turning him loose with it. That is like arming a child and telling him he is allowed to shoot his parents if they anger him. I can just imagine those colored bastards marching around with their holier-than-thou airs, laughing and joking about killing the white man!"

"Uncle Walker, I understand you are upset by this, but I do not think it appropriate to speak of the Negroes in those terms and certainly not in front of our own people. They have done nothing to deserve your vilification. I would thank you to hold your tongue," Ellie reprimanded him within the hearing of several of the ex-slaves, some of whom had appeared to be getting upset with Walker over his language and attitude.

Walker looked about him for the first time, suddenly realizing what he was saying and where. He paled, and then blushed. Ellie hoped it was because he was ashamed of his behavior, and not because he had just remembered that some of these men were armed.

He cleared his throat, and then said, "My apologies for my behavior, Ellie, men." He nodded in their direction, and then turned and hurried away from the barn.

Ellie shook her head in despair that the South might be torn apart for generations because of attitudes such as her uncle had just expressed. She smiled sadly at the men as they continued their work and walked toward the house.

Suzanne announced at dinner that night, "It is time to begin preparing for the Christmas Eve party." She bounced with delighted anticipation at the thought of the party they would have.

Stunned faces turned to look at her. "Suzanne, this house is still in mourning!" Felicity seemed shocked by her niece's statement.

"Mother always loved Christmas; she would have wanted us to do it," Suzanne stated defiantly.

"Suzanne, we do not have the food for such a party, and even if we did, it would not be right," Ellie tried to reason with her.

"Could we do something to celebrate Christmas?" Emmy as always tried to smooth things over.

"The last two years on Christmas Eve, our Negroes came to the house to celebrate with me!"

Felicity tried to put a stop to this plan. "You are not alone now! We understand you had no one else here last year. There is no need for such fraternization this year."

"I had never heard such beautiful singing of Christmas carols." Ellie was not willing to give up the new tradition. "My father always gave them gifts. It will not be affordable this year, but a special meal in the house would mean so much to them."

"We will have a late family dinner and go to church." Walker's statement was accepted as the final authority.

Ellie sat at the table fuming, but also knew she could not win. She had no desire to eat Christmas Eve dinner with these people she called her family. Immediately after the meal was complete, Ellie excused herself and went to her room. When she did not return, Emmy knocked on her door and walked in without waiting to be invited. She found Ellie pacing back and forth, muttering to herself.

"What are you going to do?" her cousin asked, knowing Ellie's determination.

"I am not sure, but I will do something for these people. They work so hard, and the pittance I pay them is not enough for a pair of boots." She sat down on the edge of her bed, frustrated.

"What about the barn?" Emmy suggested, sitting down next to her.

"What do you mean?" Ellie cocked her head at her cousin.

"We could decorate it and bring the food down there." Emmy tried to force a smile. "I should not say this, but we have already lost this war. It is time to start changing our ways."

Ellie gave her cousin a hug. She was surprised and happy to hear her cousin's change of heart. Maybe, she would have an ally in Emmy after all. Maybe, all the years of lecturing to her had finally made a difference in her cousin's thinking. At least, Emmy was willing to face reality.

While Suzanne and Felicity worked on decorating the house, Emmy and Ellie decorated the barn. Once they were satisfied with their work, Emmy also accompanied Ellie to the kitchen, and helped her and Lottie with the food for the party and the family dinner. Emmy was kneading the chestnut dough and Ellie was coring apples when they heard Walker slam the front door, and then yell for

Jonathan to get him some scotch. The two women knew that he had gone into town and realized something else must be very wrong. They dried their hands and abandoned Lottie for the living room.

"Father, what is wrong?" Emmy asked, her voice filled with anxiety.

"Savannah surrendered to Sherman!"

"When?" Ellie asked.

"Did he burn it, too?" Emmy demanded.

"No! Major Arnold offered up the city under a flag of truce." Walker's expression was disgusted and bitter.

"When?" Ellie asked again.

"Three days ago! The twentieth of December! The day before, all our troops and about a third of the citizenry abandoned the city over a temporary pontoon bridge into South Carolina."

"They are coming this way?" Emmy demanded.

"Yes, there are tired, hungry families and troops looking for food and shelter," Walker stated.

"We have to help them." Emmy looked to Ellie for confirmation of this position.

"I am not sure that it would be a good idea, Emmy." Walker looked at Ellie as he answered his daughter.

"I am afraid, we barely have enough food for the people living here, now," Ellie responded, reluctantly shaking her head. She saw that her cousin was about to object. "Emmy, you were helping in the kitchen. We are already diluting the tea and coffee, using chestnut flour and molasses where we can, instead of wheat flour and sugar. We do not even have any rice."

"Mother and Suzanne should not be told," Emmy sadly said, "about the food and the refugees."

Walker and Ellie nodded in assent. Both realized that Felicity and Suzanne would be upset if they were to fully realize the situation.

Christmas Eve, Ellie had the family dinner served at sunset rather than later as Walker had demanded. No one seemed to notice the unspoken change in plans. Ellie and Emmy slipped out of the house and down to the barn as soon as the dishes were cleared.

Ellie noticed that her cousin seemed to have caught her excitement about the party for the Negroes. She wondered about Emmy's reasons. It was so unlike her to do something against her parents' wishes. The barn looked festive with the decorations and the lanterns. Lottie, Mattie, and Lela had laid out the foods on tablecloths that had been spread over bales of hay. As the barn filled up with people, it started to warm up. Ellie was delighted to see that some of the ex-slaves had their own musical instruments with them. Emmy followed Ellie's lead in helping to dish up plates of food. Her own maid started to help, but Emmy handed her a plate and shooed her away. The Hamilton slaves were obviously uncomfortable; however, the freed men and women reassured and cajoled them until they laughed and talked along with the others. As the eating slowed, one of the men began to play the fiddle; some joined in with song. They began with the traditional carols so many had heard coming from the house over the years. Ellie realized it was to please her and Emmy. Once the spirituals began, nearly all joined in singing. At first, none noticed Walker come into the barn; Ellie finally saw him standing in the shadows leaning against the wall. She could not see the expression on his face, but nudged Emmy indicating his direction. She watched as her cousin's smile melted into a frown. Ellie left her cousin's side and made her way over to her uncle.

"You went against me," Walker whispered to his niece.

"Uncle Walker, when have you seen such joy on these dark faces? It is such a little thing."

"Just make sure the coach is ready to take us to Christmas service."

"It will be." Ellie left her uncle alone. He stood there listening to spirituals much longer than was necessary.

The mid-night Christmas Mass was a solemn affair. There had been little for gifts and Christmas Eve dinners had been meager. The parishioners were all aware of the fall of Savannah and understood that Sherman and his ravaging Union forces would be coming their way. The one question that hung in the air was when? The Confederate soldiers were already milling in the area, many officers were in attendance at the services. Ellie could not help but notice the gaunt faces and threadbare uniforms. She wondered how the enlisted men looked if the officers were looking so shabby.

Christmas morning, Ellie rose early to start breakfast. She had given her employees the day off. Sally Ann and the Hamilton household slaves were surprised to find her alone working in the kitchen. They began helping as she apologized for not having the authority to give them the day off, too.

Felicity entered with Suzanne and Emmy on her heels. "Where is breakfast?"

"It is almost ready, Aunt Felicity," Ellie assured her, sliding another pan of corn bread out of the oven.

"What are you doing, Ellie?" Felicity asked, disconcerted.

"It is Christmas; I am fixing breakfast." Ellie wiped corn meal from the table and smiled at her aunt.

Felicity was not about to start Christmas Day with an argument with her niece. She put the coffee, cups, sugar, and cream on a tray and carried it to the dining room herself.

"Look what you have done now!" Suzanne turned and followed her aunt out of the room.

Emmy picked up a platter of freshly cooked eggs and left over ham from the previous night. Before leaving the room, she gave her maid the day off, too. Ellie joined them with a basket of hot corn bread. When Walker took one, he shook his head, "Next time you are going to give everyone the day off, please, Ellie, have your cook give you some lessons first."

"Do not worry, Uncle. Christmas only happens once per year. However, lunch will be cold and dinner will be late. I think we have to stop day time fires again."

"But it is too cold not to have the fireplaces heating the house," Suzanne whined.

"No, your sister is right. We will only heat the house and cook at night. You better let the slaves know."

Ellie did not bother to correct her uncle about the status of her help; she nodded. "Do you think we should block off the entrance to the drive?"

"I will go into town tomorrow. We will talk about it when I get back," Walker directed.

CHAPTER 34

The next morning, Walker drove to the general store. He was disappointed that no newspaper was available and reported that the rumors he heard were contradictory. The one thing everyone seemed to agree on was that Sherman was unlikely to make a move until after New Year's Day. He added that it was believed that Sherman was actually celebrating the holidays in Beaufort. Ellie and Walker agreed not to close off the drive yet, but to start having the men gather brush and fell some dead trees to make preparations. Walker, accompanied by Nathaniel, would continue making regular trips to the village to obtain up-to-date information. Each day, he became more concerned. Shortly after the New Year, he announced that Hardiesville had been taken by Union forces on New Year's Day, and then they started tearing up the Savannah-Charleston rail line. The one consistent rumor coming out of Georgia, Walker reported only to Ellie, was that Sherman's men were saying that Sherman wanted to bring Georgia to her knees, but blamed South Carolina for the war. Neither could imagine what Sherman would have his forces do to South Carolina. Walker added that some of their neighbors were leaving for Columbia. Ellie felt that made no sense. If Sherman wanted to punish South Carolina, the capital of the state seemed a likely destination for his troops. Most seemed to think he would want to capture Charleston and Fort Sumter. By the tenth of January, Union scouts had been reported to be in the area. Against Felicity's pleading, Walker supervised the closing off of the drive. It was set up so that it would be easy to remove some brush so that a single horse and rider could get out if need be.

Over the next few days, the tension grew on the farm. The days were damp and chilly; the nights were long, dark, and cold. They dared not even light a fire except when the rain came. They covered the basement windows with dark, heavy cloth; it became the one place at night where they felt secure enough to sit by a lamp to read. Then the shots began. They were sporadic. Ellie thought there was no one left to fight the Union Army; their own troops seemed to have left the area. Walker theorized that they left to prepare to defend Columbia and Charleston. No one knew what direction Sherman was coming from or going to. Smoke began to fill the air. When night fell, fires could be seen lighting up the night sky, first to the northeast of them. Each day there was more smoke; at night, the fiery orange light seemed to be moving west. Ellie tried to identify by the direction of the light what was being burned, but it was difficult to tell the distance. The only thing she was sure of was that the fires and shots were much closer than they had been anytime over the course of the war.

After nearly two weeks of confinement, Walker wanted to go into the center of Sheldon and find out what was going on in the area. They had not seen any fires at night, or any smoke during the day in a few days. Ellie was as anxious to know, but was becoming worried about her uncle. He had been losing weight and she did not think it had to do with the changes in his diet at the farm. Also, regardless of his age, she did not think he would fare well being a white man if he ran into any

Yankees. To Ellie's relief, Felicity intervened, refusing to let her husband go. Finally, it was agreed to ask Joey and Nathaniel to go to the store. Ellie walked to the barn to discuss it with them. They agreed to make the two and one-half mile trip on foot. They felt they would attract less attention, could hide more easily, and would not have to worry about anyone trying to steal the horses. Ellie reminded them to take their papers with them on the rare chance they might run into any local militia.

The family waited anxiously for their return. As the hours passed, Walker questioned whether they would ever come back. Suzanne was sure that they would join the first Yankees they saw. Felicity busied herself doting on her husband. Ellie confided in Emmy that she trusted the two men completely and was worried for their safety.

Four hours later, they returned. They reported that Mister Franks' store had been reduced to a chimney and ashes. The houses in the immediate neighborhood of the store had also been burned to the ground. Nathaniel stated, "We din't know what ta do, but decided ta stay roun' fo' a piece ta see ef anyone 'ud come."

Joey interrupted, "Da Father an' his wife come. He said dem Yankees burn down da church."

"No!" Ellie cried out. "Whatever was the point of burning the church?"

Her question was ignored. "What else did you hear?" Walker inquired.

"Folks is mostly headin' out, away from town any which a ways dey kin," Joey added. "Dem what's stayin' is skeered an' hongry. Da town is most all burned up or tored down, too," Joey continued.

"What about the soldiers? Did you see any Yankees there?" Ellie asked.

"No, 'am, dere weren't no Yankees dat we cud see, but da Father, he said dem Yankee deserters was still around, lookin' ta see what dey kin git afore runnin' off," Nathaniel answered.

"What can we do to help the people around here?" Emmy asked, empathizing with their situation.

"We cannot spare any food!" Suzanne stated immediately.

"I am not certain what may be of help," Ellie responded, giving her sister a disapproving look. "Perhaps we could collect some blankets and clothing that we could take around to them. We might assess what other needs they have then."

"I do not think it wise to be considering a trip away from the farm just yet, Ellie," Walker stated. "The area is still full of Yankee deserters. They will be dangerous and desperate men. Besides, Joey said the townspeople were leaving if they could."

Ellie heard his words and recognized the wisdom in them, but she also felt she needed to do something to help her neighbors. She resolved to give it more thought.

Ellie went to the barn and saddled up one of the mares. She could not stay in the house any longer and rationalized that she needed to make sure the horses in the woods and back pasture had not been found. She took off at a full gallop before anyone could stop her. She jumped off, tied up the mare, and then threw her arms around Princess' neck. She then went to Daniel's gelding, Victor, checking his legs and hugging him, too. The tears fell, "Our church is gone. Where will we get married, Daniel?" she whispered to his horse. Once she composed herself, she got back on the mare and rode out to the back pasture. She counted heads; relieved, she rode back to the barn. As she walked into the house, Walker bellowed. "It is too dangerous for you to go off riding by yourself."

Ellie's only response was to take the pistol out of her pocket and set it on the side table. When she did so, Felicity gasped, Suzanne shook her head in disapproval, and Emmy hid a smile.

One day, soon after lunch, Mattie and Sally Ann came to Ellie. "Miz Ellie," Mattie began, but then teared up.

"We's goin' ta Beaufort," Sally Ann finished.

Ellie took a deep breath. "When will you be leaving?"

"Tamahra mornin'. Henry says we should leave early," Mattie managed to say.

"Is Henry here?" Ellie asked.

"Yes, he in my cabin," Mattie responded, wiping tears from her cheeks.

"Ask him to come to the house. I will meet you in the kitchen." Ellie left the room and retrieved a book from her father's study. Once in the kitchen, she asked Lottie to fix some sandwiches. She then waited impatiently for Henry and the two women. She wanted to question Henry and she needed to pay the women. Daniel had left more than enough. Even paying them both generously in Green Backs, she would have a tidy sum to return to him. She had tried not to think about it, but it was hard not to wonder why he had been traveling with so much cash.

The three came up the back stairs; looking uncomfortable, they entered the kitchen. She offered them seats at the table and Lottie put a full plate in front of Henry. He sat silently staring at it.

"Please, Henry, eat. We have already had our lunch and I know you have come a long way."

The man tentatively picked up a sandwich. Ellie smile at him while she fingered the book in her lap.

"Mattie, I have not paid you in three months and I know you will need money."

"Miz Ellie, neva' ya mind. Dose Blue Backs no good anyways."

Ellie ignored her comment and tried to hide her smile. "Sally Ann, you have not been paid since you came back in September." She then handed each of them $50 in the currency of the Union.

Mattie blurted out, "Where'd dis come from?"

"Marster Daniel!" Sally Ann replied.

Other than Sally Ann, the others were surprised that Ellie had Green Backs and at her generosity considering the circumstances.

"Henry you have traveled a distance to get here. How many others were spared from the fires in the Parish?" Ellie asked him, craving news, even bad news, of the outside world.

Henry hurried to swallow the mouthful of sandwich he had been about to chew when she appeared with all that money. "Well, Miz Ellie, best as Ah could tell, most folks north an' east o' here was burned out by da Yankees. Ah seed some burned down buildin's on ever one o' da plantations what Ah crossed. An' none o' da white folks was about no mo'. Some o' da Negroes was still on da lan' 'cause dey couldn't figure where ta go Ah specks. Smaller places was spared some, but dem Yankees cleaned dem out an' busted dem up ta boot. White folks stuff was spread all over dey yards, what wasn't worth nuthin'. Weren't no animals lef' nowheres; not fo' ridin' an' not fo' eatin' neither. It sho was a sorry sight. Dat fo' sho. Mostly it jist dem Negroes what was lef' behind by dey marsters. It lack ever'body done died an' deys only ghostes lef'.

"But da Yankees done promised da free Negroes dat dey kin have forty acres o' lan' from da ol' Sea Islan' plantations thirty miles roun' Charleston an' a mule ef dey wants ta work da lan'. It gonna be all ah own. Ain't gonna be no white folks dere at all!" Henry shook his head in wonder at this marvel. "When Ah heared 'bout dat, Ah knowed we was gonna go an' git us some o' dat lan'. Me an' Mattie gonna have us a farm an' be lan' owners jist lack da white folks is," he finished proudly.

Ellie was shocked at the news that the Yankees were giving away property that belonged to Confederate families. A hint of fear entered her heart; a fear that it could happen to her beloved Whispering Oaks as well. But Henry's tale of the deserted land occupied only by the former slaves gave her some hope. Perhaps the Yankees were only taking away land that had been abandoned or lost because of unpaid taxes. She was determined to keep their land safe. If Mattie and Henry could benefit from this Yankee plan, she would not begrudge them their good fortune.

Ellie hugged Mattie and whispered in her ear, "Good fortune, my faithful friend, and please, if you hear anything of Daniel, please send word."

CHAPTER 35

The next day, Ellie was up early and joined Lela and Lottie in the kitchen. It was a cold, rainy day in early February. Ellie lit the kitchen stove; she hoped the rain would hide any smoke. She was grateful for the watered down coffee which smelled more of chicory than the dark beans. She smiled to herself thinking how things had changed. There had been a time when she would have refused the chicory coffee.

It was not long before they heard Suzanne yelling for Sally Ann. When there was no response, she came down the back stairs in her robe, "Where is that lazy girl?"

No one answered her question; Ellie shrugged and pointed to a chair. "Would you like some coffee, Suzanne?"

"Where is Sally Ann?" she demanded as she sat.

"I have no idea!" Ellie told herself she really did not know. She only knew where she was not.

Suzanne made a face as she sipped the hot beverage. "If she has run off, it is your entire fault."

"My fault? Suzanne we lost the war. The area is swarming with Yankees. What do you expect?" Ellie noticed Lottie and Lela keeping their back to Suzanne. She thought they were probably hiding smiles.

"This is the worst coffee I have ever tasted. Lottie, are you trying to poison me?" She had shifted her wrath.

"Suzanne, this is the best you will get for a long time. As it is, we are taking a risk lighting the stove to make it." Ellie drew the attention back to herself.

"We should have gone to the Fullers' plantation. I am sure things are much better there." She looked around the kitchen. "Where is Mattie?" She was becoming more suspicious.

"She went to spend some time with her Henry." Ellie explained nonchalantly, sipping at her cup. She wondered if the Fuller's plantation was one that had been given away.

"Who is Henry?"

"A man from the Mackey Plantation."

"Did Sally Ann go with her?" Suzanne was getting worried.

"I do not know why Sally Ann would want to see Henry." Ellie continued to be evasive while careful not to lie.

"Lottie, what do you know? Where is Sally Ann?" Suzanne demanded of the cook, turning toward her with suspicion.

"Ah doan seen her dis mornin'," the big woman responded without turning around from her stove.

"You all know something!" Suzanne got up from the table and started upstairs yelling, "Uncle Walker!"

After the rest of the family came down and had breakfast, Walker asked Ellie to join him in the study. He closed the door behind him. She prepared herself for the onslaught.

"You had no right to let your sister's girl leave!" he reprimanded her angrily.

"Uncle Walker, we have no power over any of them anymore." Ellie refused to be cowed by his attack.

"Ellie, you had a responsibility to tell your sister. Maybe if you had told me, I could have stopped her." Walker glowered at her, angered by her apparent betrayal.

Ellie shrugged and quietly told her uncle, "We may be losing more."

Walker shook his head, refusing to accept the possibility. "I will talk to them and point out they have nowhere to go and no skills to do anything."

"Uncle Walker, Sherman issued an order confiscating all the Sea Islands and a thirty mile track outside of Charleston. He is giving forty acres and a mule to any Negro who wants it and is willing to work the land."

Walker's face drained of color and he staggered back to sit down at the desk. "He cannot give our land away!"

"He has done it and the Yankee soldiers are telling every Negro man they see."

The elderly man rubbed his hands over his face. Ellie could see him trembling as he said. "Everything is falling apart. How will we survive?"

"Uncle Walker," Ellie patted his hand, "We have to offer them something that will make them want to stay."

Ellie believed that her father's policy of not selling off family members would help to save her farm. She knew that some of the Negroes would not leave because they would not abandon their elders. She still needed to offer them more than she had previously if she was going to get any work out of them. Planting season would begin in just a few weeks. She might need to use more of Daniel's Green Backs after all. She was determined she would replace whatever she used. She asked all of the Negroes, freed and slaves to come to the barn. She informed them of what she had heard of the availability of forty acres and a mule; she assumed that they had already heard the news. Few seemed surprised by the information. She added that while the war was still underway, the area was under Yankee control. She promised to begin paying them in Green Backs. She added that the Hamilton slaves would be included in this offer while the Hamiltons remained at Whispering Oaks. There were looks of disbelief; however, Lottie and Lela reassured them that they had seen the Green Backs. Ellie understood some would still leave, but she hoped the offer would encourage the majority to stay.

Much to Suzanne's distress, Ellie was not willing to take anyone out of the fields to replace Sally Ann, at least not until after spring planting was complete and the majority of foals had been born. Because she had pastured mares with a stallion in the separated the herds, foals were being born outside of the normal season. Joey and Nathanial continued to make periodic trips to neighboring farms and plantations that had also survived, as well as the old center. People had taken to posting notices on trees and gathering to exchange news in the area where Mr. Franks' store had been. They also risked talking to Union soldiers. They returned with news after nearly each trip. In early February the peace talks had failed. By mid-February, Columbia had fallen and Sherman had moved north through South Carolina toward North Carolina.

During March, Emmy's and Felicity's maids began to help Lottie in the house. Ellie split her time between the family vegetable garden with Lela and working with the horses. She kept meticulous records of the wages she paid and worried incessantly whether she would have enough money to keep her commitments.

Word of the war ending came quickly. On the twelfth of April, Joey and Nathaniel came back from town excited with the announcement that on the ninth of April, General Lee had surrendered to General Grant in Appomattox.

Ellie ordered that the drive be reopened; whitewashing the fence and clearing the rest of the brushy overgrowth would have to wait. Walker, Nathaniel, Joey, and Jonathan drove a wagon into what had been the center of town.

Lincoln was dead; he had been assassinated three days before on the fourteenth of April. No one knew what to expect. Some were fearful that the South would be blamed and further punishment would come their way. Others were pleased that the evil man, so often imagined with horns growing from his head, was dead and felt that his death by violence was fitting.

Suzanne and the Hamiltons were anxious to go back to Savannah. However, Walker decided he and his valet and driver would go on ahead. Word on conditions in South Carolina and Georgia was still slow to arrive; the telegraph had been damaged and the mail system was not yet in order. Suzanne feared that Matthew would not know where to find her if she was not in Savannah at the Hamiltons' home. Felicity wrung her hands, afraid for her husband traveling, her home, and her son whom she had not heard about in nearly a year. Emmy and Ellie tried unsuccessfully to contain their excitement regarding Christopher and Daniel returning.

On the first of May, the Peters' carriage arrived, driven by Walker Smith Hamilton. The young man was gaunt, with a faraway look in his eyes, but he had no apparent injuries. It was not long, however, before Ellie and Emmy exchanged looks of concern. W.S.'s natural laughter was gone. They admitted to one another their fear for him. It also occurred to each of them, for the first time, that the men they were waiting for might return changed. They had been so worried about death and dismemberment that nothing more had concerned them. They continued to watch W.S., exchanged looks of mutual understanding, and worried anew about their own fiancés.

Felicity, Emmy, and Suzanne were anxious to get back to Savannah. W.S. did not seem to care where he was, but stated he would take the women back to Savannah, and then go on to their plantation. He reported that he had passed by it on his way to Savannah and that much of it had been burned. He planned to try to salvage what he could and spend his time there. Ellie suspected he wanted the isolation it would offer him. She wished there were something she could do or say that might help him. Over the last few years, she had not sold many horses. Her stock had been protected and had grown. She gave her cousin a large, three year old bay, which she had broken for riding over the winter, for his personal use. She knew it would not heal his wounds, but she felt better for having taken some action.

Ellie watched the carriage and wagons, with the bay tied to the back of one, carry her family away. She had been looking forward to their departure, but now that they were gone the house seemed empty. She did not expect Daniel to return for another month or two. He had warned her of the possible delay. Still, she had work to do to occupy her time.

CHAPTER 36

Ellie and Nathaniel rode the farm surveying the conditions. They brought the stallion and some of the young horses that needed to begin their training from the back pasture to the barn and training paddocks. With the summer heat, Ellie spent mornings working with the young horses and in the vegetable gardens. Afternoons, she worked on the accounts and breeding records. She also held classes for the children and those adults who wanted to improve their reading. She moved the other horses out of the woods; some she returned to the barn area. Still, she was not sure how safe it was and wanted to protect her stock until she found out. She took Princess, Daniel's gelding Victor, and the stallion to the back pasture. Ellie realized she needed to venture out; she had not been off the farm in months and had been depending on second-hand reports for news.

At breakfast one morning, she asked Lottie if she had any jam or canned foods she could spare. Lottie filled a basket with a variety of jars. Ellie had Joey hitch a horse to the carriage and the two of them drove out to see what the neighborhood looked like.   Ellie stopped first at their nearest neighbors, the Bucknells. Angela Bucknell was a few years older than Ellie. She had married young and her husband, Marshall, had inherited the plantation from his grandfather. Marshall had been killed at Chickamauga. They had five children, ranging in age from thirteen to six years; the oldest felt he had to be the man of the house. Ellie left all the canned food she had in her basket with Angela and offered Michael, the thirteen year old, a job whitewashing and clearing brush from around the fencing at Whispering Oaks. She promised the family two piglets from her pregnant sow, two laying hens, and a rooster in exchange for the boy's labor. Ellie knew that the Bucknells had already eaten all their chickens and even if she had offered to pay them with gold or Green Backs there weren't any to be bought in the neighborhood. Young Michael readily agreed, and Angela gratefully accepted the offer.

Back on the road, Ellie had Joey drive to town. She was eager to see how things were progressing there. Mr. Franks was rebuilding his store and had hired several local freed slaves. The construction was going well, but he had no goods to sell. Ellie worked out an arrangement for some of their produce and eggs to be brought in for sale twice a week. She let him know that they had plenty horses to sell if he heard of any buyers in the area. The rotund shopkeeper told her about the Yankee carpetbaggers in the neighborhood, those Northerners who had come to the South hoping to make money off of the suffering of the Confederacy. He reported that several such families had purchased land in the parish and were already spending money to build fancy houses to replace what their soldiers had burned down. Mr. Franks said they were pushing white families off the property that had been handed down for several generations; buying up land at tax sales and foreclosures. Ellie felt chilled at the thought that they might try to take Whispering Oaks and resolved to hold onto as much gold as possible to pay any tax burden they had accrued. With the parish and state governments in disarray as they adjusted to new Yankee laws and carpetbagger judges' interpretations of Southern Law, there was no telling what might happen.

Ellie realized that Whispering Oaks had made it through the war in much better condition than her neighbors. She thanked the guiding advice she had received from her father and the help that Daniel had given. She continued to work hard throughout the summer months. Emmy had married Christopher; and Matthew had returned to Savannah. She counted the days, weeks and months, waiting for Daniel's return. When six months had passed since General Lee's surrender, she looked for excuses as to why he would not yet have returned. When Union soldiers appeared on the farm to buy horses, she asked if they knew him; they did not. They were still under military occupation and their presence reminded her that not all the Union soldiers had been discharged.

With the sale of some horses, Ellie was able to hire some extra hands to help with the fall harvest. Mr. Franks' store had been rebuilt and he was beginning to restock it. Emmy wrote that Suzanne and Matthew had left for the Fuller plantation and that she hoped Ellie would come to Savannah for Christmas. She wanted her to meet her husband. She also expressed her concern that Daniel had not yet returned and stated she was praying for his health. Ellie still had not told her cousin the truth about Daniel's origins. All of the surviving Confederate soldiers had returned to their families. She wanted to tell her cousin the truth, but did not know how, especially after Emmy had defended Daniel to her parents.

In the middle of November, Suzanne and Matthew arrived in Charlotte's carriage unannounced. Matthew was driving the old gray horse himself. Ellie was surprised by their arrival. While unsure about the nature of their visit, she was certain they would not be bringing good news. Ellie allowed dinner to be served in the dining room.

She tried to wait patiently through the meal for their explanation of the visit. Suzanne prattled on about how wonderful Savannah was now that the war had ended. She and Matthew both agreed that they were devastated to leave the city and all it had to offer, but it was expected that they would go to the country during the winter, and so they had come home to Whispering Oaks to assist "poor Ellie" with the drudgery of the fall harvest, and to plan wonderful parties for the holiday season, of course.

"Well, I am delighted to have you here for the holidays, but you realize the fall harvest is well past." Ellie responded as sincerely as she could, "What about the Fuller plantation? Surely, Matthew, they cannot do without your oversight at this time of the year?" She looked at her brother-in-law, trying to hide her suspicions about what was really going on with the couple.

"Oh, Ellie, you will not believe what has happened with the plantation. That demon Sherman confiscated all the Fuller property and had given it to the darkies!" Suzanne related, absolutely appalled at the idea. "Matthew's family was completely helpless to do anything about it. Then, when President Johnson rescinded the order in August, why we all expected to move right back in and boot those uppity Negroes out. Unfortunately…well…there was a bit of difficulty collecting sufficient funds together to pay the back taxes on the plantation. Those horrible Northerners took the property and sold it off to Carpetbaggers and…well, those damned northern Negroes have been coming down here telling us what to do! Can you imagine?" Suzanne was livid with indignation.

"I find it incomprehensible that a man's heritage could be stolen from him by such scalawags and scoundrels as are passing themselves off as politicians these days. We are being overrun by those damned Northern niggers coming into our cities and making rules about how we can live and vote here, and ogling our white women openly in public. Why they think they should be allowed to eat at the same table with white people and drink in the same establishments that white gentlemen have been frequenting for more than a hundred years. And the white trash Copperheads that have power are just as bad if not worse than the niggers! They should all be taken out and hung on the nearest tree. Mark my words! The Southern white men will not long tolerate such goings on as have been happening here in the South of late. Something will be done! If not by the duly appointed law, then by the men of these states!" Matthew was pounding the table in his wrath.

Ellie was stunned into silence by his tirade. Suzanne, however, smiled proudly at him for his sentiments. "Anyway," Suzanne finally continued, "we are so glad to be able to come here and say that we are now home."

"And I, for one, am eager to get started on making improvements to the farm. I have some wonderful ideas for improving this place and making it profitable. You and I shall have to have a talk tomorrow, Ellie. There is so much to be done. But, now that I am here, you will not be as burdened as you have been." He gave her a patronizing smile before calling for more wine to be poured.

Ellie wisely refrained from comment as she processed the information she had just been given. She had no problem with the idea of Suzanne taking her share of the farm and the responsibilities that went with it. However, she was not at all pleased with Matthew's apparent sense that he was entitled to have a say in, or even actively interfere in the running of the farm. To the best of her knowledge, Matthew had no concept of how to run a horse breeding farm. He probably had never even had much to do with the operation of his family's plantation. She would not willingly allow him to interfere with her plans for the farm, no matter what she had to do to stop him.

Ellie went to bed that night wishing Daniel would come soon. Not only did she miss his essence, but she felt she needed him to support and help her stand up to Matthew and Suzanne.

The next morning, Ellie sat in the kitchen; she was not going to change her way of life or give up Lottie's and Lela's companionship. The idea of eating all her meals with her sister and brother-in-law took away her appetite. While she was sipping her coffee, there was a commotion upstairs and Lily came running down the back stairs. "Miz Ellie! Miz Ellie, dat man's gonna hurt me!"

"Lily, what is wrong?" Ellie asked, rising to investigate.

The young girl was distraught, her eyes wide with fear, her heart beating rapidly. "He tried ta hit me. He say Ah got ta do what Miz Suzanne says."

Ellie led her to a chair and seated her before asking, "What did she want you to do?"

"She said ta move all their stuff inta your parents' room. Ah said Ah got ta ask Miz Ellie first." Lily wiped her tear-stained cheeks with her apron and looked at Ellie.

Ellie sat back down in her chair and patted the girl's arm reassuringly. "You can move their things. ...But, Lily, if Mr. Fuller ever tries to hit you again, make sure you tell me."

"Yes um, Miz Ellie," the girl agreed, nodding her head fervently.

Ellie was furious. She had not wanted to start her relationship with her brother-in-law with a confrontation, but she could not permit such behavior under her roof. She sat in the kitchen trying to regain her composure while Suzanne and Matthew ate their breakfast in the dining room. She joined them as they were finishing their meal.

"I know, Matthew, that you are unfamiliar with the ways of this household, but there are things that are not done here." She looked disapprovingly at him.

Suzanne fiddled with her napkin; she was unaccustomed to such displays of violence as she had observed earlier other than her own temper tantrums. Matthew looked at Ellie quizzically, obviously oblivious to what she meant.

"This morning you attempted to hit Lily," Ellie explained.

"Oh that! That stupid girl refused to follow Suzanne's instructions. She needs a good beating. If Suzanne had not distracted me, I would have caught her. I do not know how you have managed without a man in this house." Matthew shook his head in astonishment.

"We do not hit or beat any of the help," Ellie commanded firmly.

"Ellie, she talked back to me. When Father was alive, no one dared," Suzanne interjected irritably.

Ellie turned to face her sister. "Suzanne, you know very well that Father never raised a hand to any of them. It was not out of fear, but loyalty to this family that they obeyed."

"Half of them have run off. Is that what you call loyalty?" Suzanne demanded, throwing down her napkin.

"They are all free now and half of them have stayed!" Ellie countered.

Matthew pushed back his chair and began to rise. "I will not allow anyone to disrespect my wife in my house!"

Ellie rose as well and turned on her brother-in-law. "This is not your house! Whispering Oaks belongs to Suzanne and to me. And as long as my name is on the deed, your name will not be!"

"Ellie, please, he is my husband!" Suzanne begged, fearing what might happen if the argument escalated further.

"I am aware of that, Suzanne. The only reason he is here is that half the farm is yours."

"Half of the profit is Suzanne's, too. She needs some new things," Matthew jumped in, not willing to admit defeat.

"When there is a profit, Suzanne will get her share." Ellie felt her lip curling in a snarl. She could not remember ever being this angry.

Matthew sneered at her anger, becoming sarcastic in his turn. "You seem to be doing quite well. You think you can deny making a profit. I suppose without an overseer, you would have problems managing things."

Ellie had all she could do to keep from telling him to leave her property. She held her breath as she explained the situation to this poor excuse of a man. "By the end of the war, Blue Backs were worth nothing and we had much work and repairs to put the farm into the condition you see it now."

"Surely, Ellie, there is enough for a new gown for the Christmas party. We will have a party this year?" Suzanne asked in a meek, childish voice.

"Yes, Suzanne. We will have a party this year. Our neighbors are not nearly as well off as we are, that is the least we can do for them." Ellie thought how Suzanne sounded like a little girl. She wondered how her sister was feeling about her marriage since she had the opportunity to spend time with Matthew and his family had lost everything.

"You will not be inviting any Carpetbaggers!" Matthew commanded.

"Oh, Ellie, tell me we do not have any of those terrible people for neighbors."

"We do not have many. Too much was burned. There was not much in the area left to interest them…there are a couple we must invite." She was not too happy about the necessity of such an invitation either, but she needed their business.

"I remember that you had some strange ideas, but I cannot believe you would allow a Northerner in this house!" Matthew knew about Suzanne's accusation, but still could not believe it.

"There is no North or South anymore. Whether we like it or not, we are one country. Besides…we have to do business with these people and they are now our neighbors." Ellie steeled herself for what might come next.

"I told you, Matthew. That man she had here was a Yankee," Suzanne hissed at him.

"That man's name is Daniel Proctor and he was a wounded soldier near death when he arrived here." Ellie lifted her head and stared at her sister, daring her to continue berating him.

Suzanne took up the challenge, the little girl now gone, replaced by the shrew. "I thought he was coming back to marry you, Ellie. Where is he?"

"I do not know." Her vulnerability was obvious.

Matthew laughed. "So, we have a traitor in the family. No wonder this place was not burned down, too."

Ellie slammed her hand down on the table. "I am not a traitor! This place was not burned down because we hid it from view of the road."

Suzanne stood to leave. "Was it not your lover who told you how to hide it?"

"It was the man I love who helped protect our home so that you and your husband would have some place to live when he lost his. Something you should remember. If it were not for Daniel's help, you would have nowhere to go and there would be no Christmas party." Ellie bared her teeth at her selfish, petty sister.

"If he did anything to protect this farm, it was with the idea of stealing it away from you in the future, just as the Yankees stole my family's property," Matthew stated coldly.

"And if he loved you so much, why has he not returned to make certain that you did survive the Yankee invasion? He did not love you. He used you, like any other Yankee would have done. He had it good here. He lounged about and was pampered by his little harlot until I exposed him to the family and he fled like the coward he always was. And you can wait as long as you like, Ellie. He will never return for his Southern whore!" Suzanne rose and marched out. Matthew followed his wife out of the room.

Any sympathy Ellie had for Suzanne quickly disappeared; however, she would not turn her back on her sister. Her parents would have expected her to watch out for her and make sure her needs were met. She would not falter in keeping her commitments to her family. But she did not have to like her, nor would she ever like her brother-in-law. Ellie rationalized that her sister would not knowingly be cruel; she could not expect either of them to understand the depth of her feelings for Daniel and how their words could hurt her. She missed him terribly and continually questioned what the problem could be that was delaying his return. Not having received a single letter, she had begun to fear he might be dead.

CHAPTER 37

The atmosphere in the house remained strained. Ellie avoided Suzanne and Matthew. She communicated with them regarding necessities and gave Suzanne money for a new dress. She continued to eat meals in the kitchen with the house staff. While it was evident that Lottie did not approve of Suzanne's behavior or Matthew's attitude, she attempted to encourage Ellie to make up with her sister. Ellie argued with Lottie that Suzanne was sarcastic even when she communicated with them on business matters.

As the holiday approached, Ellie became sadder. Whenever a rider came in the drive she strained to see who it was, and then tried to hide her disappointment when it was not Daniel. She did, however, convince Suzanne and Matthew to hold the Christmas Eve party in the afternoon instead of late at night. She convinced them that it would be easier to prepare for it and better for their neighbors. Without a church to go to for midnight mass, the tradition would be changed anyway. The reality was that she was determined to hold a party in the evening in the barn as she and Emmy had the previous Christmas. Two parties created a lot of work, but Ellie needed to keep her mind distracted.

Ellie, Suzanne, and Matthew formed a reception line for the guests as they arrived. Of course, Matthew didn't know every family in the area, but it was apparent that he quickly discerned who the old families were and who the newcomers based upon the greetings given by Ellie and Suzanne. Ellie noticed that Matthew was warm and expansive with the Southern families, but cold and minimally polite with those he suspected of being Northerners. Ellie's stomach churned at the thought that he might offend some of the guests or create a scene that would embarrass the family. She did her best to keep him away from those people she thought might set him off, even surreptitiously asking the help of one or two of their closest neighbors in keeping him preoccupied.

It was apparent that all the guests had dressed in their finest party clothes; still, the distinction between the newcomers and the old families was fairly clear. The differences weren't in the quality of clothing. Some of the dresses worn by the Southern women were better quality material than the newer dresses of the Northern women. But the fashions worn by the Northern women were obviously of the latest design, while those of the Southern women were a few years out of date and showed more wear. While the Northern women had flashy jewelry, the Southern women had little or no jewelry at all. Taking in the atmosphere of the party, Ellie noticed the shabbiness of her old neighbors next to the stylishness of the more recent arrivals to the parish. It seemed that Suzanne had also noticed the differences. As Ellie observed her sister socializing with the "Carpetbaggers" she had not wanted invited to the party, she noticed that Suzanne was especially attentive and admiring of those women who were so obviously nouveaux riches. Over a period of about twenty minutes, Ellie watched Suzanne point and admire and fuss over the clothing and jewelry these women were wearing, complimenting them on their taste. However, when Suzanne went to chat with two young women she had known since childhood, Ellie overheard her sister commenting on how cheap and tawdry the women were. "Of course, what can you expect from Yankee Carpetbaggers?" Suzanne had commented as she finished her petty remarks. Ellie could only shake her head and be grateful that Suzanne would not say nasty things to their faces as Matthew might.

Despite the differences in people's current stations in life and the recent history of bloodshed between the two sides of the war, the guests seemed to get along fairly well with each other. At least, they were all socially appropriate and polite. Ellie doubted that any new or lasting friendships were being forged at the party. She didn't care. She just wanted everyone to have fun and feel lifted from the pain and drudgery that they lived through most of the time. At last, the party ended. Guests said their good-byes and Ellie hurried to the kitchen to see how preparations for the party in the barn were coming along.

Ellie hadn't realized how tense she had been all afternoon until she carried the last of the trays to the barn. In addition to the Negroes who lived on the farm, those who had worked during the harvest from the surrounding area had also been invited. The good humor and laughter filled the barn quickly. She relaxed and enjoyed herself for the first time since her sister and brother-in-law had arrived. When she crawled into bed, exhausted, she thought how Daniel would have been pleased with the party even if it had been held in the barn.

Christmas morning she slept late, dreaming of the Christmas three years before and fantasizing about everything she would tell Daniel when he finally came home. In her heart and in her head, Whispering Oaks was his home, too.

Ellie had felt bad about disappointing Emmy by not going to Savannah for Christmas. She had wanted to meet Christopher. She wrote, apologizing again, but added that, with Suzanne and Matthew on the farm, she did not dare leave the farm and Negro workers in their care. She invited Emmy and Christopher to visit Whispering Oaks instead.

She began her preparations for spring. The breeding plans had been thrown out of the normal cycle and lines had been mixed in ways that where not originally in her father's plan. She would need to carefully work out new plans for the upcoming breeding in order to promote the lines best characteristics. Fields needed fertilization and rotation. Many of the young stock had needed much more handling than they had received so far, breaking them would be much more difficult.

Throughout January and February, she was either locked in the study plotting out the next breeding season or planning the planting, or she was at the barn working with the horses. By the end of the day, she was satisfied to eat in the kitchen and go to bed. In this way, she continued to avoid Suzanne and her husband. Occasionally, she would over hear Suzanne whining or Matthew complaining.

Ellie hired more hands for the March planting and gave Nathaniel full authority to oversee them. She needed to spend nearly all of her time in the barn. The herd had grown and many more foals were due. Whispering Oaks had not had a spring party since the war had started. Ellie informed Suzanne that she needed to plan the spring party, write invitations, and be responsible for the guests being fed and entertained. Ellie did not have the time to do it and knew Suzanne enjoyed a party. She also felt it was about time her sister helped since she would reap the benefits as well.

Suzanne had been so bored that the work of getting ready for a big party did not upset her, but rather she actually became excited about the prospect. Matthew had taken to riding the farm, trying to look important, or going to Mr. Franks. He frequently came back with treats for Suzanne and liquor or tobacco for himself. Ellie was unaware of the magnitude of his purchases which had been charged to Whispering Oaks until one day she rode to the store to post a notice regarding some horses she wanted to sell. She discovered it when Mr. Franks handed her an itemized bill. She hid her surprise and agreed to cover it when she made her next trip into town.

Ellie was furious, but by the time she arrived home she had decided to say nothing. She needed Suzanne and Matthew to be cordial at the upcoming party. While it was a social event, it was also important for Whispering Oaks' business.

Emmy and Christopher arrived at Whispering Oaks three days before the party. With guests in the house, Ellie ate lunch and dinner in the dining room. Christopher made a pleasant addition to the family. Ellie found him to be thoughtful, open, and easy to talk with about nearly any subject. To her surprise and delight, he also seemed knowledgeable about horses and frequently wandered down to the barn.

The people invited to this party were mainly those who might be more inclined to purchase horses, in other words, people with ready cash to spend. For all of his anti-Carpetbagger talk, Matthew had quickly seen the value of making business acquaintances with the Yankees in the neighborhood. Once all the guests had arrived and were scattered in groups about the house, Ellie began making the rounds of each group, checking to see that everyone was contented and nothing was needed. When she walked into the front parlor where Matthew seemed to be holding court, she overheard one of the Yankees complimenting him on the excellent condition of the farm compared to the way so many others had fared during and after the war. She was stunned to hear him taking credit for the farm and for the breeding program as if he had thought it all up and managed it himself. Ellie was furious and just barely restrained herself from causing a scene; however, it soon became apparent that Matthew had the men eating out of his hand. She resolved to say nothing to him about his boastful claims; a few days after the party they sold fifteen horses at top dollar to men who had attended the party. Ellie was businesswoman enough to accept whatever methods helped to keep the farm in the green.

Emmy had been tactfully waiting for Ellie to bring up something about Daniel. When she hadn't and their visit was coming close to an end, she approached her cousin. Ellie evaded the overture with statements about having so much paperwork to complete. That night Emmy knocked on Ellie's door and entered without an invitation, closing the door behind her. "Ellie, you cannot avoid the subject with me any longer. Where is Daniel?"

Ellie looked at her cousin, her strength draining out of her. She needed someone to lean on, even if for just one night. Her lip trembling, Ellie quietly confessed, "I do not know!" She broke down in tears; she had been holding it in for so long that she thought she might never stop.

Emmy sat next to her on the bed and rubbed her back, patiently waiting. After handing her a handkerchief, she asked, "Have you heard anything from him?"

Ellie shook her head and mumbled, "No."

"Have you written to him?"

"I have written a million letters in my head, but I have no idea where to send one," she sobbed, looking into her cousin's sympathetic eyes.

"Do you know where his family lives?" Emmy probed gently.

"Not exactly… Oh, Emmy, I am so afraid he is not coming back and I have no way of knowing if he is alive or dead or changed his mind or…" Her sentence was choked off by another sob. She looked away from her cousin, fearing to speak.

Emmy squeezed Ellie's shoulders in encouragement. "Or?"

Ellie hung her head. "Emmy, I have lied to you. Daniel may not have been decommissioned yet. He was a Union officer."

Emmy sat silently for a moment, and then sighed and patted her cousin's hand. "You did not lie; you just did not tell me."

Ellie turned to study the other woman's face. "You do not seem surprised."

"Ellie, I have known for a long time. Sally Ann shared her Green Backs with us. She did not realize the significance of what she said when she admitted to me that Daniel had given them to her to take care of Suzanne. It suddenly made sense that he would agree with your ideas."

"You were not angry with me?" Ellie whispered, the handkerchief pressed to her mouth.

"He made you happy. No one else was ever able to do that. Once the war was over, what difference would it make regardless of who won?"

Ellie embraced her cousin fiercely. "Thank you for understanding. I was so afraid you would be angry with me, especially after I let you defend him to your parents."

"Suzanne was being so terrible; I would have defended the devil to go against her." Emmy returned the hug and released Ellie.

"She has been so cruel," Ellie stated looking down and shaking her head in sadness. "She called me a…a prostitute."

Emmy sighed and shook her head at the injustice of such a comment. "She is probably angry that Matthew lost his plantation. The life she would be living on a grand plantation was all she talked about after they were married. I should not say this about your sister, but those two deserve each other."

"Maybe they do, but I feel so responsible for her. Yet, every time I say anything to her, she just gets angry." Ellie threw her hands up helplessly.

"You cannot change Suzanne...or Matthew. Come to Savannah for the summer. You have not been out of Sheldon in nearly five years." Emmy smiled encouragingly.

Ellie shook her head and wiped her eyes. "I have to be here when Daniel comes back."

"Ellie, he left three years ago; the war has been over a year now. What if he never comes back?" she asked, quietly.

Ellie's chin trembled with restrained tears. "I do not care what Suzanne says; I know he loved me. I will wait."

"I know this is hard for you, but what if he is dead?" she asked, taking her cousin's hand.

Ellie bit her lip to stop it from quivering. She shook her head quickly. "I do not know. I cannot imagine being with any other man."

"Well, if you get tired of Suzanne and Matthew, come visit us. You can trust Lela and Lottie to tell him where you are if he should come while you are away."

"I will keep your invitation in mind. Thank you." She hugged her cousin. "Now, you had better go to your room. Christopher is waiting for you. He really seems to be a special man."

"You just like him because he can talk horses with you." Emmy laughed, hugged her cousin, and left the room.

Ellie felt better about her relationship with Emmy. She had been carrying considerable guilt over using her cousin to defend Daniel and protect herself. However, the reality of their conversation gave her no joy, only adding to her sadness. At some point, she might have to accept that Daniel was not coming back.

Before Emmy and Christopher left, Ellie made arrangements with Christopher to take ten horses with him to Savannah. With only three stallions left on the farm, she was concerned about in-breeding. She needed to start looking to bring in a new stallion from a divergent line. After discussing the needs of the farm with him, she sent out some letters of inquiry to a couple of the better known farms. He had offered to make the final inspection and bring back the best of the stallions she might find.

CHAPTER 38

Over the months of May and June, Matthew and Suzanne griped and fanned themselves. It was apparent to Ellie that Matthew did not trust her to run things right, nor be honest with the proceeds of the farm. However, he acceded to Suzanne's demands and agreed to go to Beaufort to see if they could reclaim the property there, and then on to Savannah. Ellie suspected that he was just as pleased to get out of the oppressive inland heat. She made a point of giving Suzanne a large sum from the spring sales as her portion of the profits, having her initial the books. When Matthew accused her of withholding, Ellie gave a detailed account of their overhead and what would be needed to run the farm for the next few months.

The summer months seemed to drag; there was little work to keep her occupied. She rose with the sun and worked and played with the horses until the heat was too much. She considered going to Savannah for a month, but the thought of having to be social prevented her from leaving the farm. She preferred to be with Lela and to listen to the wisdom of Mama Noli. She continued to give lessons in reading and numbers to anyone interested.

Mid-September, Christopher returned from Louisiana with a young stallion. Ellie was pleased with the animal and she was glad that she had trusted her cousin's husband. Not only had he purchased a sound horse with strong bloodlines that would strengthen those of her herd, but he had sold the ten in Savannah for a good sum.

Ellie had agreed to give Christopher ten percent of the sale of the horses he sold in Savannah and his expenses for the trip to Louisiana. She had offered to also pay him for his time in making the trip, but he had declined it. However, he reported to Ellie that before he left to pick up the stallion, Matthew demanded that he give Suzanne fifty percent of the proceeds of the sale. He stated that he had attempted to give her fifty percent after subtracting for the costs of his fee, expenses, and the new stallion. No matter how he tried to explain, Matthew would not permit him to subtract the costs relating to the stallion. He only permitted the expense of the commission.

Ellie tried unsuccessfully to hide her reaction. Christopher had expected her to be upset regarding the lack of awareness Matthew had about the need of another stallion. However, he did not realize the extent of the irresponsibility of the demand until Ellie let it slip how much she had given them after the spring sale. Ellie assure him he had done nothing wrong and sent another five horses back to Savannah for him to sell.

Ellie knew that Suzanne had no head for money and was impulsive in her purchases. Still, she had expected Matthew to be more fiscally responsible. Yet, the entire time they had been at the farm he had taken on no work, thought nothing of spending the Peters' money, and seemed to believe he was entitled to it. Other than socializing and softening up the neighborhood men to buy horses, he had not contributed to the family in any way. She started to wonder which one had gone through all the money, Suzanne or Matthew.

Matthew and Suzanne showed up back at Whispering Oaks during the last harvest of the year. Their carriage was loaded with luggage and Uncle Walker's driver was following with a wagon loaded with crates and a Thoroughbred stallion tied to the back. Matthew directed the unloading of new trunks of clothes, cases of imported wine, and boxes of cigars. Ellie went inside the house before they finished unloading; she did not want to see what else they had spent her hard earned money on or to wait to hear the explanation about the horse.

At dinner, Ellie heard that their Beaufort house had been sold for taxes in 1863. Matthew had tried arguing with the tax collector that there would have been no means for a Southerner to have paid them and that they should be permitted to pay the back taxes and take back possession of the house. His argument had fallen on deaf ears. Ellie had guessed from what Peter had told her that this was what had happened; however, the confirmation of the loss still made her angry. They chatted about the conditions and changes in both Beaufort and Savannah.

Matthew announced that, after their stay in Savannah, he had expanded his interest in horses. He extolled the potential profits of breeding for speed and raising race horses, thus explaining the presence of the new stallion. As he continued, it became apparent to Ellie he was more interested in betting on horses than in raising and training them. She realized Matthew had been raised expecting to have the easy life of the master of a plantation. He was not making the adjustment to the New South. It explained where the money had been going and who had spent it. Ellie resolved to tighten the reins on their spending.

She was surprised to hear Suzanne express a desire to invite neighbors for Thanksgiving. It was still thought of as a Northern holiday and something the Peters family had never celebrated. Ellie would not celebrate such an occasion unless Daniel was sitting at the head of the table. After questioning Suzanne about her change of loyalties, she realized it was just an excuse for a party.

Ellie finally stated that they were not in a position to hold a large party in a couple of weeks, and then host another for Christmas a month later. She was not about to say anything regarding money at dinner. She had decided to discuss it alone with Suzanne.

It was a couple of days before Ellie was alone in the house with Suzanne. Matthew had ridden out to Mr. Franks'. Before Ellie had a chance to say anything Suzanne came to her. "Have we sold any horses lately?"

"I sent some to Savannah with Christopher when he came here with the new stallion," Ellie responded, surprised that Suzanne would take an interest in the business.

"I need some money for Christmas," Suzanne stated boldly.

Ellie was truly amazed at her sister's temerity given how much money they had already received. "We need the money to run the farm. Did you spend everything?"

"Savannah is expensive and we needed so many things. You could not expect what you gave me last April to last all this time," Suzanne exclaimed indignantly.

Ellie stared at her sister, nonplussed by her demand. "What about the money you got from Christopher over the summer?"

Suzanne squinted her eyes and wrinkled her nose at the question. "What money?"

Ellie felt her frustration rising. She wondered if Suzanne was truly that ignorant or if she were trying to be manipulative. "Christopher gave Matthew half the money from the horses he sold in Savannah. He would not even let Christopher take out some for the new stallion I bought for the farm."

"You must have misunderstood. We got just enough money for the stallion," her sister responded dismissively.

Ellie was becoming angrier by the moment. "Suzanne, Matthew received considerably more than the price of one stallion. I have the receipt he signed for Christopher."

"Let me see it! I do not believe you!" Suzanne demanded, angrily snarling at Ellie.

Ellie sighed; it was worse than she feared. She believed her sister did not know. She went into the study and brought back the paper, handing it to Suzanne.

Her sister's face went pale. "He must have forgotten to tell me. He knows I know nothing about money."

"Suzanne, do you understand why I had to buy a new stallion?" Ellie asked quietly.

"No, but I do remember that father always kept at least five and Matthew did buy another one. I do not know why you sold any of them." She flapped her hands in confusion and irritation.

"The soldiers did not give me much choice; they wanted all of them," Ellie stated in disgust.

Suzanne must have begun to feel defensive as she took the opportunity to try to sting her sister. "I suppose Daniel wanted to give away all of them."

"They were Confederate soldiers!" Ellie retorted. "Suzanne, Daniel is a good man."

Seeing that she had turned Ellie's attention away from her husband, Suzanne could not resist pressing home her advantage. "Then where is he?"

Hurt, Ellie confessed, "I do not know."

Triumphantly, Suzanne derided, "When are you going to face it that he never planned on marrying you. He is never coming back."

"You do not have to attack Daniel because Matthew took our money!" Ellie grabbed the receipt away from her sister and walked out of the room.

CHAPTER 39

As Christmas approached, Ellie's moods fluctuated between sadness and anger. She resented feeling that none would have noticed if Daniel had not gone back to his regiment. The Union certainly did not need him to win the war. He did not have to put himself in danger's way; he could have stayed on the farm with her. How could she stay with her memories in the house if he were dead? What if he'd found someone else? If he did not want her, the least he could do was write and say he was not coming back. Did he really love her or was she just a convenience as Suzanne repeatedly suggested? No, she knew he had loved her; but did he still? The questions continued to repeat themselves in various forms in her head. No answer lasted long before another question arose.

She prepared for the Christmas Eve party in the barn and let Suzanne take over the preparations in the house. As she dressed and made last minute adjustments to her hair and makeup for the afternoon party, she discovered her hand-mirror was missing. She could not remember when she'd seen it last. She used the brush regularly, but dressing to work in the barn, she hadn't given much thought to how her hair looked. She searched her room to no avail. When Lily knocked on her door to tell her the first guest had arrived, she asked the girl if she'd seen it. Lily had not noticed it in the last few days. With guests arriving, Ellie gave up on the search, thinking she would find it later.

She put on her best face and greeted their guests. She forced a smile and tried to laugh. She thought of the years the family had decorated the tree together, years that were now gone. The first Christmas Ted had given any hint she was more than a friend to him, he gave her the silver hand-mirror and matching comb and brush. She remembered how much fun it was surprising her family by wearing Ted's engagement ring to the Christmas party the following year. But, she had trouble holding back the tears as she remembered the love she felt the one Christmas she had with Daniel. She was relieved when the afternoon was over and hoped the evening would be easier.

The evening in the barn began with more warmth and cheer. She was with people she felt knew, accepted, and cared about her. She relaxed and enjoyed serving them and laughing at their humor. When it was time for the music and singing, her emotions began to erupt again. She slipped into the shadows where she felt safe to let the tears flow. During the third song, she felt a hand on her arm. She looked through her tears to see Mama Noli standing next to her.

"Ah'm tire, chile. Will ya walk me home?"

Ellie brushed away the tears with her free hand and slowly walked out with the old woman leaning on her. The walk took much longer than Ellie expected. She realized that Mama Noli was in considerable pain. She knew that winters were difficult for the woman's joints, but she did not remember her ever to seem so crippled. She helped her into bed and took off her shoes. After adding a log to the fire, she kissed her on the forehead. As she started out the door, she heard, "Cry hard tanigh', den rememba ya got yo whole life 'head a ya."

Ellie did not go back to the party, but crawled into bed and cried herself to sleep.

Christmas morning, Ellie, Suzanne, and Matthew exchanged gifts. Ellie presented Suzanne with cameo earrings and Matthew with a new pocket watch. It had been difficult for her to give either of them anything, but she knew it was the right thing to do. Together, Matthew and Suzanne gave Ellie a crocheted shawl. Ellie realized it was really from Suzanne and that her sister had added Matthew's name to the gift card. Matthew presented Suzanne with a new dress that he apparently had bought when they were still in Savannah. Suzanne held her gift for Matthew until last. She was obviously very excited about it. It was a set of silver cufflinks engraved with his monogram. Ellie knew that Suzanne had no money to buy such a gift. She wondered if she would find it on next month's bill from Mr. Franks. She would make sure it came out of Suzanne's share of the profits. She was getting tired of doing all the work and supporting the two of them. However, it was Christmas; it could wait for another day.

The first of January 1867, Ellie decided that she could no longer think of Suzanne in the same way. Her sister acknowledged that she had taken the hand-mirror and sold it in order to buy Matthew's Christmas gift. She did not even apologize, but rationalized that since Ellie no longer cared for Ted, she should not care about the mirror either. Ellie thought about leaving, but where would she go? Savannah, to be the unmarried eccentric relative? Definitely not! Why should she have to leave? Suzanne liked the city better anyway. But, she really did not want to be alone with her memories. Every time she turned a corner, she could see him in her mind. She went to Mama Noli for counsel.

She found the old woman confined to her bed with a terrible hacking cough. Mama Noli struggled for breath as she indicated that Ellie should sit in the rocking chair next to the bed. Ellie watched her wince as she struggled to find a more comfortable position in the bed, her gnarled joints were twisted by arthritis. A shaft of fear lanced through Ellie's heart as she realized how much her old friend was declining.

Despite the pain and her poor health, there was still a warm smile on the toothless face. The old woman labored to get the words out. "What's ailin' ya, chile?"

"Oh, Mama Noli. I should be taking care of you and offering you comfort, instead of you doing so for me," Ellie began. Mama Noli waved her twisted fingers in negation. Ellie sighed and poured out her troubles. She told her of her frustration with Suzanne and Matthew, including her belief that they were both stealing from her, one way or another. She spoke of her loneliness and her fear about the future of the farm if she could not stop Matthew from interfering. Mama Noli listened in silence, nodding her head in understanding.

When Ellie ran out of words, the old woman whispered, "What's keepin' ya here?"

Ellie felt tears well up in her eyes and spill over as she quietly responded, "Daniel. Oh, Mama Noli, I am so afraid he is dead or has abandoned me. I have not heard from him in so very long. I have no way of finding him or finding out about him. I do not know what to do, and it is eating away at my soul every day." She dropped her head and allowed the tears to flow. There was some relief in just sharing her pain with someone who cared about her and liked Daniel.

Mama Noli stretched out her hand toward Ellie, trying to offer comfort. "Daniel wouldn' abandon ya, chile. He loves ya sure an' true." She paused to draw breath again. "He gonna come back ta ya, effin' he kin. Ah knows dat fo' sho. Ya gots ta believe dat, no madda what else happens." She nodded her head in affirmation of her words, too out of breath to speak more. Ellie slid to her knees on the floor next to the bed. She embraced the old woman as gently as she could, taking the brittle old hand and rubbing her cheek against it.

"Thank you, Mama Noli. Not just for listening to my troubles all these years, but for being such a dear and loving friend. I do not know how I would have survived without you all this time. I am so grateful to you for all the words of wisdom you have shared with me over my lifetime. I am a better person for having known you." Her lips trembling with emotion, Ellie laid her head down on the bed next to the old woman's and let more tears of loss and grief fall. She wasn't sure for whom she was crying: Daniel, Mama Noli, or herself. But she knew that she had to stay on the farm as long as Mama Noli lived.

Ellie began her annual planning for the spring planting and breeding season. She felt it was important that Matthew start earning his living and called him to the study. "I would like to discuss this year's plans with you. I think it is about time you start doing something around here."

"I plan on it," he told her smugly, crossing his legs and looking bored. "Why do you think I bought the Thoroughbred stallion? I am going to start using him to breed some mares."

Ellie's brow wrinkled in surprise and consternation. "What mares do you plan on using?"

He shrugged and gestured broadly. "Some of the ones here on the farm. I need ones that are big and fast."

Ellie was appalled at the man's ignorance. She spoke slowly, as if she were speaking to a very simple minded child. "Matthew, we are breeding riding and carriage horses, not race horses. You cannot contaminate our line with your horse. Besides, if you want race horses, your plan will not work."

"You know nothing about race horses!" Matthew exclaimed in derision.

Ellie took a deep breath, trying to hold onto her patience. "True! I do not know much about racing. I do know how to breed and make money with Saddlebreds. Whispering Oaks is known for the quality of the horses we produce. You will not destroy our reputation by breeding that horse with our mares!"

Matthew uncrossed his legs and leaned forward menacingly, no longer bored. "That horse belongs to me and half of those mares belong to my wife."

Ellie became icy in her anger. "No, actually you bought that horse with money belonging to your wife."

"We will have our race horses!" he asserted loudly, trying to intimidate his sister-in-law.

Ellie refused to be intimidated. She told him firmly, "Matthew, go buy some Thoroughbred mares. Start your own line, but do not mix the lines."

Matthew glared at her, frustrated that she was not backing down from him. "Maybe I will do that when Suzanne and I go to Savannah."

Seeing his statement as capitulation, Ellie tried to reduce the tension of their discussion. She still had business to conduct with him. "Do you have plans to go there soon?" she asked, turning away and moving to sit behind the desk.

"Not yet. However, we will not wait for the heat this year." Matthew leaned back in the chair, trying to appear at ease and in charge.

Ellie looked through some papers on the desk, letting Matthew sit in silence. When she had found what she was looking for, she asked him, "Were you familiar with the crop rotation at your family's plantation?"

He shrugged, not certain where this might lead. "I knew about it."

She looked up at him and smiled pleasantly. "Good. I was hoping you could help me with the plan and oversee Nathaniel implementing it."

Matthew nodded sharply. "I will take care of it."

Still smiling, she turned back to her paperwork. "Thank you. Just let Nathaniel know how many men to hire by the end of the month." She ignored him as he rose and left the room, appearing somewhat chastised. Ellie fervently hoped that Matthew would make himself useful and hold off on his plans to breed race horses.

CHAPTER 40

Ellie began spending more time with Mama Noli. She brought hot soup to her for lunch every day. She let Lily off early to attend to the woman in the evening. She was afraid for the old woman's health. The preparation of the fields started over the next month. During that time, Ellie was busy. Ten mares foaled, and Mama Noli was getting weaker. Ellie had hoped that, as the weather became warmer, Mama Noli would show some improvement in her health. But her hopes were not met. She spent more of her time caring for the woman, talking with her, reading to her, or sometimes just sitting by her bedside. Ellie felt strongly about the old woman. She had filled a void over the years since her parents had died. She realized she was there for Mama Noli in a way she had not been able to be for her own mother. The last thing Mama Noli said to her was, "Ah's had a good life, Miz Ellie, once Ah accep' dat da pas' was gone, Ah foun' me a new home. Now, Ah goes ta anudda new home."

When the gnarled old hand went limp, Ellie gently laid it on the quilt. Nathaniel closed Mama Noli's eyes for the last time. Ellie kissed her forehead, and then left to give the family privacy as her grandson, Nathaniel, his wife, Becky, their son, Jacob, and daughter, Lily, each took their turn saying goodbye. She walked to the house, heading for the kitchen to tell Lottie. As the words came out, "Mama Noli is dead," the tears broke through. It was not long before the wailing could be heard echoing over the farm.

The next morning, Matthew came in from the barn, angry. "There is not one colored in sight! No one is working!"

"Did the horses get fed and watered?" Ellie thought she might need to take care of them.

"Yes! You do not seem surprised! Where did they go?" he demanded.

"They are in mourning. Mama Noli died yesterday."

"When Father was here, things did not stop when one of them died." Suzanne seemed confused and annoyed.

"Mama Noli was born in Africa. None of them remember a time when that wonderful woman was not here to guide and advise them." Ellie sighed and brushed away a tear. "She was a very wise woman."

"Are you crying about that old, shriveled prune?" Suzanne snipped.

"Yes! Excuse me. I must leave to attend her funeral." Ellie started to get angry, but checked herself, realizing she could not expect either of them to understand.

Ellie joined the end of the procession. She hummed half to herself as the others raised their voices in song. Some of the songs she had heard before, but most were unfamiliar. She could not understand the words; however, the cadence she recognized as being the same as the tongue she had frequently overheard them using with one another. She stood behind everyone, not wanting to intrude, thinking about the words Mama Noli had uttered. She had learned over the years that the woman's words were always spoken to guide Ellie to look inside for her answers. She was not sure if she had the strength to go where they were taking her this time. There were no people to keep her there any longer. The only thing she had left was the horses.

Plans for the spring party and horse sale were well under way. It was the first week of April. More mares were due to foal and the breeding of others had begun over the preceding two months. Ellie walked into the barn to find Matthew hobbling a mare in preparation for breeding. "What are you doing with that mare?" she demanded sharply.

He looked at her as if she were dimwitted. "I am getting her ready to breed!"

"She is not on the list to breed this year!" Ellie exclaimed, hurrying forward to stop him.

"Exactly! It will not disrupt your plan," he said, not accepting that there was a problem.

Ellie grabbed his arm and shook it. She pointed to the mare that was showing signs of obvious distress and exhaustion. The mare was underweight and hung her head listlessly. "Look at her! She needs the year off!"

Matthew shook her off his arm, pulling it away from her. "You are too soft on your horses, just like you are on your coloreds!"

"Matthew, which horse were you going to use to breed her?" She was afraid she already knew the answer.

"Mine!" he stated boldly.

Ellie moved to put herself between the mare and her brother-in-law. "You cannot use my horses! Go get your own!"

Matthew moved forward until he was standing toe to toe with Ellie. "Half of these horses belong to Suzanne. I will use any ones I want! Do not worry, I have not interfered with your precious plan!"

Ellie was suddenly filled with a dreadful notion. "Have you already used that Thoroughbred to breed mares?"

"Yes! This one will be the fourth!"

Ellie wanted to dive at his throat and strangle him with her own hands. The only thing that stopped her was his size. She turned on her heels and ran out of the barn straight to the house, screaming, "Suzanne!"

Suzanne rushed out of the sewing room, "Ellie, whatever is wrong?" She looked closely at her sister. "You look as if you are about to pop a vein!"

"Matthew has been using that race horse to breed our mares!" Ellie was panting from exertion and rage.

"Ellie, I do not know why you are so upset. Matthew has an excellent plan that will make a lot of money for us." Suzanne looked quizzically at her sister.

Ellie couldn't believe what she was hearing. "You knew about this?"

"Of course I did," Suzanne stated, shrugging.

Ellie paced back and forth. Finally, after taking a deep breath, she firmly stated, "Suzanne, we can no longer be business partners."

Suzanne became immediately defensive. "You are my sister; this is my home. I will not sell it to you."

Ellie looked at her sister coldly. "Suzanne, after the spring sale, I will take my share of the profits and half of the remaining horses."

"You cannot take half the horses!" she exclaimed, panic setting in.

"I would be willing to sell some of them back to you," Ellie stated, still without emotion.

"What about the farm? Who will run it? You cannot make me stay here all summer!" Suzanne was beginning to wail.

Ellie shrugged, indifferent to her sister's plight. "Your husband will have to run it."

"How much do you expect me to give you for your share? I do not have the money. If you are going to abandon me, you had better just sign it over." Ellie could see Suzanne's thoughts racing as she tried to figure out a way to turn this to her advantage.

"No!" Ellie replied firmly. "I will keep my share of the farm. It is the only thing left that I can do to protect you."

"Protect me! Protect me from what?" Suzanne screeched at her sister.

"Your husband! He is a gambler and a fool! He will sell this farm or mortgage it the first time he needs money, and then you will have nothing." Ellie felt her whole body filling with cold, as if all emotion were being drained from her.

"You are wrong about Matthew!" her sister exclaimed, stamping her foot in defiance.

Ellie looked at her sadly and shook her head. "Oh, Suzanne, I wish I were."

Suzanne appeared about to cry, her lips puffing in and out with her breath. "Where will you go?"

Ellie shrugged and looked out the front door. "I do not know. West; maybe west."

CHAPTER 41

Ellie left her home of twenty-six years with a heavy heart. It was the first of May 1867. The war had been over for two years and Ellie had not heard anything of Daniel in four years. Nearly everyone in her life was dead: Ted, her brother, her father, her mother, and Mama Noli. And Daniel, she did not know if he was alive or dead; however, since he had not returned, the effect was the same. She had to accept that they would not have the life and family together at Whispering Oaks that they had planned. She needed to find a new home: one without a history of betrayal and abandonment. The horses were all she felt she could count on and were all she took with her. From the shack in the woods, she recovered the gold, her father's watch, and the diamond ring Ted had given her, and from the barn, the silver. She considered leaving the ring in the tin cookie box with the letters she had written to Ted and those from him that she had left hidden behind the baseboard in her room. However, she realized such sentimentality was foolish; she might need the money it could bring. She was not sure where she was going or how far she would need to go before she found another place she could call home.

Lela, Nathaniel, and his family left with her. She had not asked any of them to go west with her, but was pleased when Lela informed her she would be joining her. Lela had become her only real confidant and friend. She had planned to hire men to help her with the horses on her trip. She would sell off some of the horses in Augusta. While she would have preferred to keep them all, traveling a great distance with too many horses was unrealistic. When Nathaniel informed her that he and his family wanted the job of accompanying her and the horses to her final destination, she was relieved. Having people she trusted with her would make her trip easier and safer.

On the way out of town, the entourage stopped at Mr. Franks' store. Not only did she feel she should say good-bye, but she wanted to make sure he understood she would not be responsible for any of the bills from Whispering Oaks and to mail two letters. She had not been willing to listen to Emmy or her aunt and uncle try to talk her into staying in Sheldon or going to Savannah. She had written the letters the week before, but held them until it would be too late for anyone to respond to her before she journeyed west.

None of them had been to Augusta, Georgia before. They needed to find a place to stable the horses and stay for the night. Finding a suitable place for so many horses was difficult, but not nearly as difficult as locating a place for the Negroes to stay. It was a problem that had not occurred to Ellie. In Savannah, she'd stayed with family, and their slaves were housed with the Hamilton slaves. In Charleston, at hotels their personal attendants either stayed in the room with them or the hotels had some sort of dormitory for the slaves of their guests. She discovered that Negroes were not allowed in the hotels unless they worked there. Nor were they permitted in the restaurants.

She knew they needed to leave Augusta as soon as they sold the horses and that they could not settle in any of the Confederate states. She also did not like the reactions she saw and heard from the Northerners who were now living in Augusta. They looked down on her as soon as they heard her Southern accent and seemed to think of the Negroes as beneath them, although they did not say it. The irony rankled her. She realized that if she traveled with the Negroes and went north, they would all be rejected. She could not go to any of the Northern states that were involved in the war because she would be rejected for her Southern origins and the Negroes would be seen as little more than her servants. She needed to go to an area that had not been part of the tragedy of the last few years.

After four nights and three frustrating days in Augusta, Ellie had sold most of the horses with the exception of Princess, Victor, one stallion, two one-year old colts and seven mares. She led her friends and the remaining horses toward Atlanta.

Ellie found the same housing problems in Atlanta as she had discovered in Augusta. They stabled the horses; Becky, Lela, Jason, and Lily stayed with the wagons, while Ellie and Nathaniel walked to the train station. She soon discovered that there was more than one train heading west. After making the arrangements to go to St. Louis, "The Gateway to the West," and paying for their passage and freight, Ellie and Nathaniel left the station. Their train would not be departing until two the next afternoon. Ellie would need to spend another night alone in a hotel.

Atlanta was bustling. Reconstruction had been ongoing for the two years since the war had ended. There were more Northerners and unsavory looking men and women than she had seen in any place she'd ever been. She'd hidden valuables in the wagons and sewed money into her hem and waistband as she had before when she was hiding money to help escaped slaves. However, she could not afford to lose what she was carrying in her purse. Ellie stayed locked in her room, foregoing dinner rather than risk attracting any attention from any potentially dangerous characters. She had been looking forward to a warm bath to soak away the dirt and tired muscles from sitting and driving the wagon for days; but she found the tub dirty, as well as the linens. She settled for washing herself down with one of the cleaner towels and water. She put the pistol under the pillow and stretched out on top of the bed in her underwear. It was too hot to pull the sheet up.

She woke hungry, dressed and, gathering all her belongings, went to the dining room for breakfast. She drank weak coffee and ate lumpy porridge and corn meal biscuits. She slipped the ham into her napkin and ordered another helping which she also slipped into the napkin. It was not much, but she wanted to give it to her traveling companions. It was a small gesture to ease her guilt for being the only one to sleep in a bed and sit for a meal. She went back to her room thinking to hide there until Nathaniel came for her at eleven. However, by ten it was too hot and the air too stifling; she went downstairs to the lobby with the few possessions she had brought with her and waited.

While the train had made frequent, but usually brief stops, Ellie was relieved to debark and stand on solid ground, only then to have to board a ferry to cross the Mississippi River to St. Louis. Standing on the deck of the ferry, Ellie was stunned by the long expanse of the levee, which extended for six miles along the Mississippi

River. There were dozens of steamboats docked there, and room for many more. The city was larger than she had expected. She had thought that anything so far west would have been merely a small town, but it was a thriving city. She recognized that the decision as to their final destination could no longer be delayed. She discussed with the group the need to stay in St. Louis for a few days in order to obtain information, so that they could decide on the direction for the next leg of their journey and restock their supplies. She was also insistent that they obtain some sort of lodging and not have to sleep in the wagons. This could be their last opportunity for hot baths, cooked meals, and beds for a long time.

Nathaniel refused. "Jason and Ah's stayin' wit da wagons! Da ladies kin go."

Ellie was taken back. It was the first time Nathaniel had ever defied her. The others were surprised as well.

"Nathaniel!" Becky began to chastise her husband.

"Ya wan' ya hosses an' our thin's o' ya wan' dem all gone?" Nathaniel looked from face to face.

"Ah stays wit ya. Da chillen kin go wit Lela," Becky stated firmly.

"'Spose we takes turns," Lela suggested.

Ellie stood by quietly. Nathaniel had been right; she decided to let them work out the details.

"Dere's got ta be a man here," Nathaniel asserted.

"Ah's a man now, Daddy. Ah'll take a turn," Jason proudly stated.

"Ya cain't be here alone!" Becky declared.

"It's betta ta have two o' us here," Lela added.

Once the group had worked out how they would protect their belongings, Nathaniel approached a Negro porter and asked for information about stables and hotels.

Ellie had not wanted to waste money on her accommodations; however, after her experience in Atlanta, she felt it was necessary to stay in a better hotel. She wanted someplace clean and safe for a woman traveling alone. She wanted desperately to change her clothing. She had changed underwear whenever possible, but she had to protect the outfit she had been wearing with the money sewn into it. She knew no other way but to wear it. She resigned herself to the added expense.

Ellie checked into the newest hotel in the city, the Southern, and told the desk clerk to send a maid up to fill a tub with hot water immediately. As soon as the woman left the room, she stripped and slipped into the tub. She sank down into the water, wetting her hair. She had expected to completely relax; her body did, but her mind kept going. She hoped she had not made a mistake leaving home. They had come so far and she still did not know where they were going. The others had been trusting in her judgment, yet she had nearly made a major mistake and would have if Nathaniel had not stopped her. She needed to push Lela and Nathaniel to voice their opinions more. She had been making decisions in areas where she had never been prepared or advised. After scrubbing from head to toe, she wrapped herself in a towel and tossed her dirty clothes into the tub, money and all, and scrubbed as much dirt out of them as she could. She rinsed them in what clean water was left, wrung them out, and laid them over the furniture in the room to dry. She dressed for dinner, enjoyed a hearty meal, and slept soundly.

The next morning, Ellie rose and retrieved the ring and watch, placing them in her purse so that she could get to them easily, went downstairs and had breakfast. Her first stop was the stable. She checked to be certain everyone and everything had come through the night successfully. Nathaniel reported that there had been no trouble and that they had all had a good breakfast. She commandeered Jason to accompany her on her errands, leaving the others to watch over the wagons and horses.

Both Ellie and Jason were amazed by the size and bustle of the city. The downtown business district was several blocks long. All the streets were paved and lined with gas lamps for night. Jason stared, mouth agape, at the buildings and the horsecars that ran on tracks down the streets of the business district. Ellie, who had been to big cities, was still impressed by the number of people moving about. She was more surprised by the voices of the crowds. They didn't sound like the people she had grown up with, their speech faster and more nasal than she was accustomed to. And there were strange accents; foreign sounding. She thought they must be German and Irish immigrants. A shift in the wind brought the smell of the many breweries from the various parts of town.

Giving Jason's arm a tug, Ellie hurried them across the street before they could be mowed down by the wagons trundling by at what seemed an inordinate rate of speed. They moved purposefully down the sidewalk, looking for a jewelry store where she could sell the ring and watch. She wanted to get the cash before going to buy the supplies they needed. Becoming frustrated with meandering about, Ellie stopped a small group of women and asked if they could point her in the right direction. She felt they looked at her with some disapproval upon hearing her Carolina accent, but they politely guided her toward what they assured her was a very reputable establishment. Ellie thanked them for their help, but walked away thinking that she needed to get still further away from the east and the bad feelings about the war if she was to find any peace and contentment.

The owner of the jewelry store, a stout, affable German man in his late fifties, proved to be a very honest gentleman who gave Ellie a good price for her valuables. He also made some suggestions about where she should go to purchase her supplies for her journey. Ellie was so satisfied with the outcome of her sale, that she stopped at a bakery nearby and purchased some cookies and baked treats for Jason and the others. Jason happily munched on a cookie as they walked toward the western side of the city where the wagon outfitter was located. Ellie allowed herself one longing glance at the horse car, but knew that Jason would not be allowed to ride with her. She steeled herself for the long hike, took a cookie from the sack, smiled at Jason, and marched on.

They walked past German and Irish saloons advertising beer for five cents a glass and a free lunch thrown in with it. Even at that time of day, these establishments seemed to be doing a booming business. With the sounds of music and laughter pouring out of them, Ellie had her hands full keeping Jason from peeking inside. Ellie wasn't sure what he might see, but she feared it wouldn't be appropriate for a boy his age.

They found the outfitter in a part of town that seemed raw with so many new buildings and ongoing construction. The crowds were smaller in this part of the city, but the noise and smell had not improved. There was an odor from the iron works that was blowing in their direction. Ellie was eager to get inside and get away from it if possible.

The men inside initially stared boldly at Ellie, seeming to wonder what a woman alone with only a boy to accompany her was doing there. Ellie ignored their stares and sought out the owner of the store. She was impressed with the quantity and variety of items he had on display. Ellie had never seen a store that was as large as this one, not even in Savannah or Charleston. She explained her needs to the owner who quickly began writing up a list of articles she would need. He asked her where she was heading and if she had signed up for a wagon train. Ellie explained that she had not yet decided on a destination, only knowing that she wanted to get away from all of the pain and bad feelings of the war. The man nodded sympathetically and told her about the various destinations that most of the wagon trains headed for.

"But if you're willin' to take a chance and ya don't need a whole lot of amenities, I'd suggest you think about the Dakota Territory. They've just started homesteadin' up that way in the past few years. You could get your land for free if you can improve it and stick out the winters. The army's been building forts up along the Red River Valley. Supposed to be some nice farmin' country up that way," he told her.

Ellie thanked him for the information, assuring him that she would certainly consider it and would talk it over with the rest of her party. She paid for the supplies and made arrangements to have them picked up the next day. Hurrying out of the store, Ellie wondered where she could find out more about the Dakota Territory. Certainly a city the size of St. Louis would have a library. Maybe she could learn something there. There might even be a land office in town. She knew she had some research to do before making the final decision, but she felt suddenly rejuvenated by the idea of the Dakotas.

That afternoon, after lunch at the stable with the others, Ellie sought out the library. She found a fairly new atlas that showed the Dakota Territory and all the area they would have to traverse to get there. She looked through the archived newspapers for stories on that region. There wasn't much information available, but from what she could glean, there was some very fertile land available, and lots of it. She realized that it was still very new to settlers, and there were still Indians in the area that were hostile to white people. On the other hand, there were some new forts being built that would offer settlers some greater protection. Generally satisfied with what she had found, Ellie returned to the others to share her information and discuss options.

She arrived to find a cold meal prepared and everyone waiting. Happily joining the group, she began by telling them about the Homestead Act and what it meant for them. "As head of a household or as an adult twenty-one years of age or older, Nathaniel and I can claim as much as one-hundred-sixty acres of land each as we are both over twenty-one and," she smiled at him as she said the next part, "citizens of this country. We would have to live on the land we claim for a minimum of five years and make improvements on it such as a house and barn. And we would have to cultivate the land in some way. But we will want to plant crops to sustain ourselves, so that will not be a problem." She took another deep breath and continued, "If at any time after the first six months either one of us so decides, we could buy our land for a cash sale of $1.25 per acre. The land would be free to us if we remain on it and continue to improve it for the full five years." Ellie looked around to see if the others were following what she was saying.

"A hunnert an' sixty acres is a lot o' land fo' one man…o' one woman ta farm, Miz Ellie," Nathaniel stated, frowning and rubbing his stubbled chin in consideration. "Does we have ta take dat much?" He looked at her with concern in his eyes.

"No, Nathaniel. You could claim less. They offer some half sections, that would be eighty acres, and they have quarter sections as well, that would be forty acres. But, you have to consider growth potential. Jason is growing fast; some day, he might want land of his own. And you might have more sons and daughters. If you take the full one-hundred-sixty acres, you will have more land to leave to your children and grandchildren when you pass on." Ellie watched as he contemplated this. "But, you do not have to decide right now. What we all need to decide is, do we want to go all that way up north to a wilderness. There will not be any big cities or even many small towns to go to when things get difficult. We will be very much on our own there. I have been told it gets frightfully cold in the winters, far more than any of us has ever experienced. It will be a hardship, but we will be free of the prejudice of the states that fought in the war. And we will know that it was our own hard work that won our places for us, that we will have earned what we have."

"Ef we doan go up ta da Dakotas, where else kin we go, Miz Ellie?" Becky asked, concerned about the weather. "Is dere anywheres else what would give us da lan' fo' free?"

"I am sure there would be other territory available farther west, but it would be just as difficult, if a little warmer. And there are a lot of people heading to those areas already. Almost no one is going to the Dakotas as yet," Ellie told her.

"An' jist why is dat, Ellie?" Lela asked suspiciously.

Ellie knew she would have to answer that question at some point, but she had hoped to avoid it a bit longer. "Well, for one thing, the land is very flat up there, without a lot of trees. Water can be scarce if you do not live near a stream or river.

I was told that the wind blows almost constantly. I have already mentioned that there are not many settlements there, but there are new forts going up."

"An' jist why would dey need ta be buildin' dem fo'ts, Ellie?" Lela demanded, very suspicious now. She stared at her former mistress through squinted eyes.

Ellie sighed and nodded. "The Indians in the area, the Sioux, seem to still be hostile toward the white settlers in the area. Just five years ago, there was a big Indian uprising in Minnesota and many whites were killed. But the soldiers have pushed the Indians out of the area and onto the reservations. We would have to find land outside of the reserved territory and fairly close to one of the forts in the area. I still need to find out more about what is available and where, but I did not want to proceed without discussing it with you all first." She looked around at the others and waited for them to respond. The women seemed anxious. Ellie could understand that. The idea of hostile Indians in her back yard made her rather fearful as well, but she was determined not to show this fear. She didn't want to be thought prejudiced against the red man like so many of her acquaintances had been against the Negroes. She would meet these people and decide for herself if they were ignorant and dangerous savages, or just people with a different way of living.

"Miz Ellie, what does you think 'bout dis Dakota Territory?" Nathaniel asked.

"I believe it will be a challenge…a very difficult one. But it will be our best chance of escaping all the prejudices of the South and the North. And we will be building something new for ourselves and for future generations. I like the idea, but I will abide by the decision of the group. Tell me what you all think, please." She looked at each of them, willing them to take their destinies into their own hands and not wait for her to decide it for them.

"Ah spec's we kin buy us some mo' warm clothes b'fo' we gits dere," Becky stated. Ellie smiled at her. She was the most timid of all of them. If she was willing to take the chance, the others would follow.

"Certainly we can. We can buy things here, or there may be somewhere between here and our destination. As I said, there is much more I need to find out before we commit to this venture wholeheartedly." She smiled encouragingly at them again.

"Ah think we should find out mo' 'bout dis Dakota Territory," Lela pronounced. "Dat free lan' sho does soun' good ta me. Ah'm over twenty-one an' a citizen, too!" She stood proudly straight. "Even ef Ah doan have me no fambly as yet."

"Ah guess ya best find out what ya kin, Miz Ellie. It seem like we all in agreement on da Dakota Territories soundin' good," Nathaniel stated, a grin spreading across his dark face.

"I will find a land office tomorrow and see what I can learn from them," she promised. She finished by discussing with Nathaniel the supplies she had ordered and arranging with him to take Jason and the wagons with Jason's help to pick the things up the next day.

CHAPTER 42

Right after breakfast, Ellie got the location of a land office from the desk clerk of her hotel and hurried off. The man in the land office showed her maps of the surveyed lands in the territory. He was kind enough to answer many of her questions about how to best travel there, suggesting that she sell the wagons in St. Louis and purchase new ones in St. Paul, Minnesota. She could pay for shipping everything else, but would save significantly on the freight she would have to pay for traveling by steam wheeler up the Mississippi. The new wagons would cost her more than the old ones would get, but it would still be less in the end than if she shipped the old ones. They would also have the advantage of being new.

St. Paul had long been a major trading post and stop over for settlers in the area. From the city, there was a well-established wagon trail that headed across Minnesota to Fort Abercrombie on the west side of the Red River of the North. Once across that river, they would be in the Dakota Territories. She could get more information about available land in the area at the fort. Ellie thanked the man for his excellent advice and left the office. She agreed that selling the wagons would be the best thing to do, but they would need to keep them until the last possible moment. She would have to make the sale and arrange to have the wagons collected after they had transferred their possessions to the boat.

Rather than go to the docks alone to book passage, Ellie returned to the hotel for lunch and a rest. She would go to the docks in the afternoon with Nathaniel as her escort. Ellie hoped there would be a boat going to St. Paul soon. The hotel and stable bills were expensive and she wanted to keep as much of her money as possible.

After eating, she returned to her room and dropped on the bed. It was a very warm and muggy day; the kind of day that drew the very life from you. Ellie felt her anxiety rising. She couldn't help but wonder if she was doing the right thing. She felt responsible for the lives of the others. They trusted her to make the right decisions, but she didn't want to make the choices for them. She didn't own them anymore. They should be deciding on their own. Ellie caught a glimpse of herself in the mirror over the dresser in the room. She realized that she was letting her feelings run away with her. None of them had waited for her to make the decision. They had asked questions, received information, and then had reached an agreement. They were more than carrying their own weight, she reminded herself. She just felt so lonely in all this. Why wasn't Daniel there to help her think things through and advise her? What had happened to him? Why hadn't she heard anything from him in all the time she waited? He had to be dead. Nothing else would have kept him away from her for so very long. And she absolutely refused to think that he had just used her, and then abandoned her. He was not that kind of man, no matter what Suzanne had said. Ellie felt overwhelmed at the thought that she had lost him for all time, just as she had lost Ted. But this loss was a million times worse for her. She lay on the bed, sobbing into the pillow until she fell asleep from emotional exhaustion.

When she woke an hour later, she had a dull ache in her head. She rose and washed her face, straightened her clothes, and left the room once more. At the stables, Nathaniel and Jason were covering the new purchases with a tarpaulin and lashing down the load. She quickly explained the plans and they made their way to the booking office for the paddle wheelers that plied up and down the Mississippi. It took most of the afternoon to arrange everything, but Ellie was relieved to learn that they could leave in two days for St. Paul. Their next task was finding a buyer for the wagons. When she asked the blacksmith at the stable if he knew of anyone who might be interested, he said that he would be willing to buy all of them. They haggled over the price and Ellie was grateful for her experience at selling horses.

Their last day in St. Louis, the entire group went sight seeing through the city. It was a marvel like they had never seen before and were unlikely to see again. They passed a restaurant advertising strawberry ice cream as a special that day. Ellie went in and persuaded the owner of the restaurant to allow her to bring bowls of ice cream outside to her friends. However, they had to consume them in the rear of the building so that his other customers would not see the Negroes using the bowls and spoons that he intended to wash and use again. Lily's eyes nearly popped out of her head when she experienced this treat; even the adults expressed their excitement over this incredible concoction. None of them had ever eaten ice cream before in their lives. Ellie wondered if it would be possible to find an ice cream maker to take along. How much space could it take up? It would be so wonderful to be able to have such a treat once in a while. Finishing their treat, they returned the bowls and spoons to the back door of the restaurant and continued their exploration.

They found a part of town that seemed to have more Negro families in it than other parts had. Ellie could see it was a poorer section of the city, but the inhabitants seemed to be doing their best to keep the area as nice as possible. There were retail stores here and the others could go inside and shop without causing a stir. They found a clothing store and went in to see if there were any winter clothes in stock. The Negro owner of the store brought out heavy woolen coats, long underwear, scarves, gloves, boots, and other winter wear. He was happy to discount the merchandise in order not have to keep it stored until fall broke into winter. Ellie even found some clothes for herself. Lela and Becky talked about the purchases they had made and how remarkable it was to see a colored man running his own store.

"Kind a makes ya feel proud, don't it?" Lela commented and Becky nodded her head in agreement.

They curtailed the rest of their sightseeing so that they could get their purchases back to the stable and store them in the wagons for the next day. After dinner, they strolled through one of the local parks, admiring the flowers and enjoying the warm summer evening. They agreed that they would bring the wagons to the hotel in the morning after breakfast to pick up Ellie and her luggage and then go on to the docks to get everything secured onboard the boat.

Ellie got little sleep that night, thinking about the journey they were about to undertake. She was up, dressed, and packed by first light. She went downstairs to have breakfast and arrange to have her bags brought down. It seemed the others were as eager as she to get under way, as they appeared shortly after she had taken a seat in the lobby.

The children were both very excited about getting onto a big paddle wheeler and traveling up the biggest river they had ever seen. Neither of them could comprehend that it would take days to travel to their destination. Almost everything in their lives had been just a few minutes away. This trip from South Carolina was a glorious adventure to them and the river journey was just one more part in the story.

The riverfront was a scene of chaos, color, crowding, and noise. Long before they could see the ships, the air was filled with the sound of steam being released and ships' bells being rung. Nearer to the landing, musicians played their fiddles, sang and danced, trying to pick up a few coins from the passers-by. The blacksmith had sent a couple of his hands along to deliver the party to the landing and bring the wagons back. This was fortunate, as it left Nathaniel and Jason free to walk along the string of horses and keep them calm in the noisy crowd. Ellie rode on the first wagon, pointing out their boat where it was tied up on the riverside. It was a one hundred ton side-wheeler, with three decks and a pilot house. The smoke stacks on the boat showed no steam at the moment, but it was apparent that the ship was being hurriedly loaded, as colored stevedores hustled back and forth carrying cargo and herding livestock up the gang plank.

Nathaniel and Jason stayed to watch as their property was stowed aboard and to see that the horses were taken care of properly. Ellie, Lela, Becky, and Lily went to the passenger section of the huge boat, seeking out their accommodations. Ellie had booked a suite on the boat for all of them. It was one of two on the boat and she got a good price for it as there wasn't much demand for a suite among those traveling up river to St. Paul. All six of them would travel in luxury and have meals provided to them for a grand total of only $20. Granted, this was a lot of money to most people, but it was more reasonable than traveling by train had been, even if it was slower. The others would travel as her servants for appearances' sake, but would at least have decent, comfortable accommodations for this leg of the journey. Lela would share a bed with Ellie, Nathaniel and Becky would have some privacy, and the children would sleep in the drawing room on cots. Ellie thought it ironic that her father's watch was paying for the pleasure and luxury of his former slaves. She arranged to have their meals served in the suite, so there would be no problem about the former slaves eating in the dining room with the white passengers. Ellie wondered how her friends, her former slaves, would react when they were served by other Negroes.

There was some delay as the passengers waited for cargo to be stowed. It was the middle of the afternoon by the time the big paddle wheeler pulled out from the dock and began making its slow progress up the river. They all went out on deck to watch their progress and to see the sites as they moved north. Sighing, Ellie said an anxious farewell to the life she had known and tried to convince herself that everything would turn out for the best.

Their journey remained uneventful. Traveling the river was slow and peaceful. Most people were pleasant. Those who weren't were ignored as much as possible. Ellie remained with Lela and Becky instead of venturing into the salons on the boat. Although she might have found some society there, she didn't want to leave her friends. Besides, she had seen some disreputable looking types enter the well-appointed rooms and felt certain that she was safer with the women out on the deck or in their suite than she would have been inside. It was a noisy crowd of card-playing, hard-drinking types in there.

It took ten days to make their way up river to St. Paul, and another half day to get all their property offloaded and the horses settled. They easily found carts to transport their supplies to a stable, and herded the horses along on foot. After St. Louis, St. Paul was a bit of a letdown. It was large enough to be termed a city and was the capitol of the state. Still, it could not compare with the amazing sights in St. Louis.

Their next mission was to find some place to spend the night. It was quickly agreed that the same system of guarding the horses and supplies would be followed. Lodging was soon procured for all and they took time to eat before breaking up into work details. Ellie and Becky went looking for the place that the blacksmith had told them about where they could purchase wagons. Ellie was pleased that they had decided to purchase the new wagons, as they were in much better condition than the old ones from the farm. The outfitter also provided them with a new plow and a grinding wheel for sharpening knives and tools, since it wouldn't be easy to obtain such services where they were heading. Lela and Lily had gone, cash in hand, to purchase beans and grain, they would need to supplement the diets of humans and horses alike. They also bought chickens, a milk cow and her calf, seeds, and dried goods. Ellie was impressed with Lela's bargaining skills when they later detailed their tasks. It was decided that, if the weather held good, they would leave the next day on the trail to Fort Abercrombie.

It took four days to make the trip across state to the Red River. Although sparsely inhabited, they saw some settlements along the way. Jason eagerly looked out for Indians, but saw none. Ellie didn't have the heart to tell him that no Indians were allowed in Minnesota any longer on penalty of death. When they finally reached the river, they found the water level was low enough that they could ford across it without much difficulty. It was a short distance to the fort from the river, and they were soon within its protective stockade.

As a cavalry outpost, there were many who could appreciate beautiful horse flesh and Ellie's horses received a great deal of attention. The travelers quickly introduced themselves to the commander of the garrison and requested to be allowed to stay for a day or two until they could establish where they would be homesteading. The captain, a ruggedly handsome man, was quite gallant and a bit flirtatious with Ellie. He readily offered her party the protection of the fort and invited her to dine with him and his fellow officers that evening. Ellie hesitated, but Lela nudged her to accept the offer.

At dinner, Ellie was the center of attention for the captain and two lieutenants who had not seen so sophisticated a white woman in some time. Ellie was relieved that there didn't seem to be any animosity toward her or the South. They all chatted about the loss of civilization and the pleasures, or lack thereof, of living on the plains. By the end of the evening, Ellie had learned of an abandoned homestead that had some improvements made on it. The captain thought he recalled it had a cabin and a barn already constructed. He showed her on one of his maps where it was located and gave her directions, describing some landmarks she could follow to find it if she were so inclined. Ellie thanked them all and excused herself for the night, retiring to the wagons with her friends. She told them what she had learned. They agreed the land with a cabin would be worth looking into. Since it was nearly a day's journey from the fort, they also agreed to take all their supplies and livestock with them. That way, if it turned out to be acceptable, they would simply stay on rather than having to return to the fort, and then retrace their steps. Everyone turned in so, they would be well rested for hopefully the last part of the journey.

CHAPTER 43

Ellie looked down at the directions she had taken from the captain in Abercrombie, and then gazed back up the gentle incline toward the ramshackle cabin. Next to it was a tiny, forlorn outhouse. It was the first of August, 1867. There would be no time to find another location or to build a new house. They would be lucky if they could prepare the cabin sufficiently before the winter set in. There was a small barn about fifty yards from the house, off to the west and down toward the stream. One of the barn doors was missing and the other open. Even from a distance, she could see that boards were missing from the roof. Winding behind her was a trickling stream. The bed was much wider than the water course, and she guessed it was probably at its driest.

Sighing, she turned to her companions, "I guess we are home."

The others exchanged looks of uncertainty, and then Nathaniel started his wagon up toward the house. Ellie followed with the one she was driving; Jason drove his toward the barn.

"Miz Ellie, we gonna unload yo stuff here an' take da rest ta da barn for da night."

"Nathaniel, if you do not stop that, I will call you 'Mister' from now on. As far as putting your things in the barn, I think it would be better if we all stayed in the house together. It is going to be a very difficult winter to adjust to for all of us. None of us will get through it unless we stay together."

Becky looked at her husband, and then at Ellie. "We wants ah own place," she stated firmly in protest.

"Oh, Becky, I understand that. And you will all have your own land, but how will you build a home for your family before winter? This is not South Carolina," Ellie stated, concern filling her voice.

The women climbed down from the wagons and began unloading without making any further comment. Ellie was unsure if they were just tired of traveling or understood the wisdom of her statements. She was unsure herself what a North Dakota winter would be like; however, what she had heard and read frightened her that they might not be prepared for it.

The Gephardts, the former homesteaders, had obviously put a lot of hard work into building the cabin. It had been built into the slope. The foundation and cellar were made of stones plastered together. The upper portion of the one story structure had been built of wood with an open uncovered porch; the second and fourth steps of the six leading to the porch were broken. The front door was hanging loosely by one leather hinge. The windows were shuttered closed. Ellie helped unload, piling things on the ground near the steps, and then drove the empty wagon to the barn.

Jason had tied the lead horse and was inside the barn exploring. He yelled out, "It doan seem bad in here, 'cept da hole in da roof. Jist needs a good cleanin'."

Ellie walked in and wrinkled her nose, smelling mold, dung, and something she could not identify. It was dark inside, other than the light coming through the roof and the doorway. She went back outside and started pulling at the closed shutters. The first set fell off with the first tug. The next two, opened with little resistance. She was unable to open the last. There was another small door on the back side of the barn; however, dirt had built up on the ground, making it impossible to open.

Jason had been working on clearing out the barn with a shovel and broom and had already cleared out one corner. Ellie backed the empty wagon into the barn to block off the cleared area. She unhitched the mares, removing their harnesses, and then tied them to the side of the wagon. By the time Nathaniel came with the third wagon, half the barn had been swept clean. They roped it off and let the six horses that had been hitched loose in the area along with the rest of the horses.

Ellie left Jason and Nathaniel in the barn, confident that the horses and cows would be watered, fed, and sufficiently settled at least for one night. The chickens could remain in the coops on the wagons that were inside of the barn. The third wagon was left outside blocking the doorway. She walked to the house, wondering what she would find. The other women had opened the shutters and were looking around inside the house. They had taken a broom and knocked down cobwebs and swept out some of the dust and debris that had collected inside. There was no glass in any of the windows and apparently there never had been. There were two rooms inside with one fireplace in the center of the building opening into each room. It was made of the same stone as the walls of the cellar below. In one of the rooms, there was a crudely built, square wooden table with three chairs, part of a fourth, and a cast iron stove on the back wall. There were two narrow, wooden pallets strung with rope, about two feet off the floor. At the back of the room, a door opened out at ground level. In the other room, there was one double size, wooden bed frame, also strung with rope, and a small table.

Although the roof appeared to be intact, there were spots in both rooms indicating leaks. The smell of mold permeated the house. Ellie began stomping on the plank floor, checking for weak spots and rotten boards. She did not want to risk anyone falling through to the cellar. She moved the broken chair over the one area where the flooring felt spongy and was under a leak. Then she suggested to the others that they have something to eat before doing more cleaning.

While eating, they discussed how to attack the rest of the moving and settling in. They agreed they wanted to be able to get their things off the ground and sleep inside. Ellie knew she could not sleep outside in this open country. She did not voice her fears, but she could not help but wonder what kind of wild animals might be about at night.

They sent Lily to the barn with food for the men and started working as soon as they finished eating. After finding no ropes or pump at the well, Becky took two buckets and went down the hill to the creek to fill them. Ellie started the mindless task of scrubbing the bedroom floor while Lela worked in the other room with Lily. Becky made more trips for water.

Ellie's mind wandered as she scrubbed. She started making mental lists of what needed to be done to make the house ready for winter. She could not imagine how the Gephardts had made it through even one winter in the house. The outer walls were exposed on the inside and light could be seen through numerous cracks. Any heat generated by the fireplace or stove would have gone right out the roof and through the walls. She wondered about the condition of the cellar and the well, but that would have to wait for another day. She was beginning to understand the difficulties that lay ahead of them for the first time. She chastised herself for not taking a fourth wagon load of household goods from home. She had led her friends to what felt like the end of the world; she just hoped it would not lead to the end of all of them.

As the sun began to set, their work was not nearly done. The women continued cleaning; the men had not yet returned from the barn; Lily brought in candles and lanterns. Darkness had already fallen by the time Nathaniel and Jason came up to the house and began helping the women in carry their possessions onto the porch and into the house. The team had been moving together well until Nathaniel started to drag one of Ellie's trunk's into the bedroom.

"No, Nathaniel, leave that out here," she called to him, halting his progress.

He looked at her, puzzled. "Doan ya wan' it in yo room?"

"You and your family should take that room. Lela and I can sleep in this one."

Nathaniel continued to be confused. Shaking his head, he pointed out, "You has allas had yo own room. We's used ta sharin'."

Ellie turned to Lela, asking how she felt about the suggestion. "Lela, do you mind sleeping out here with me?"

"Ah don' mind, but you sho 'bout dis?" Lela's wrinkled brows indicated her skepticism.

Ellie nodded firmly. "Yes, they are a family of four. They should have their own space. We can fix a changing area for you and me."

Nathaniel and Becky continued to object, but as the debate proceeded, Jason and Lily had been quietly moving the family's meager possessions into the bedroom. Once the arguing stopped, Ellie found a blanket, her pillow, and a mattress. She spread it on one of the bed frames, wrapped herself up, and lay down. She was too tired to do anything more or care how the others settled in for the night. She was asleep before the lights were even blown out.

Ellie woke in the morning to a chill in the air. It felt more like an October morning at home than August. She was stiff and cold as she stood, thinking she would need to make major adjustments. She had hoped the physical work during the war and the deprivation of basics would have prepared her for her new lifestyle. Still, the thoughts of what would need to be accomplished over the next couple of months left her questioning her strength and abilities. The front door was still hanging partially open; she slipped out, wrapped in the blanket, to use the outhouse. She then went to the barn to check on the animals; she threw some hay to the horses and cows and some feed to the chickens. The cow was nursing her calf, so she might not need to be milked. Ellie knew they'd have to get the calf weaned before the cow stopped producing milk naturally. The grass was waist high; she needed to get the animals out of the barn and pastured for as long as the weather would last. She could picture fencing and numerous paddocks from the back side of the barn leading all the way down to the stream. Nevertheless, she knew she was dreaming, at least for the near future.

As she began walking toward the house, she realized she must have stayed in the barn longer than she had thought, spotting Lily and Jason re-entering with armloads of brush and dead branches. Nathaniel was on the roof of the house, reaching down the chimney and pulling out a bird's nest. At least, they'd be able to use the fireplace. The thought of a hot bath crossed her mind. She pushed it aside, knowing it was not possible and not wanting to miss that ordinary luxury even more.

Ellie piled her linens on the pallet she had used the night before while she waited for breakfast. She was determined to make it more comfortable than it had been the previous night. She quickly saw that her efforts were making little difference. Becky passed around coffee and Ellie opened the discussion about their first day's chores. Nathaniel agreed that they needed to get the horses out to graze on the high grass, so that they could save the grain for winter and added he and Jason would work on it. Becky reported on the condition of the well, offered to work on their water problems, and asked Lily to collect whatever materials she could find to burn in the fireplace and stove. Lela volunteered to clean out the cellar.

Ellie began by helping pull the wagons out of the barn. It was a slow process, but she and Jason managed to line them up at the ends of the barn, and then strung ropes making a temporary paddock the length of the barn and width of the wagon lengths. It was not much, but she could let a few of the horses out at a time, rotating them until they all got out into the sunlight, fresh air, and tall grass.

Ellie went back to the house and began sorting household articles. She loaded many of the kitchen items and her dirty clothes onto the wheelbarrow they'd brought along and took them down to the stream to wash. The days passed quickly as the group worked diligently cleaning, building, and organizing.

CHAPTER 44

By the end of August, they had fenced off ten acres with ropes, boards, and stones for the horses to graze. They left the back door of the barn open during the day so the animals could go in and out. The pasture enclosed a small stretch of the creek so the horses could drink. They had cut fields of grass and gathered it after it had cured in the hot summer sun and dry winds. More would be needed to get the horses through the winter. The barn roof had been repaired using the wood steps from the front of the house. They rebuilt the steps out of stones and clay from the riverbank.

Ellie and Nathaniel decided they would need to make the long trip into Abercrombie soon. Nights had been getting colder, and there were numerous supplies they would need to get through the winter. Nathaniel felt they only needed one wagon, but Ellie insisted they take two. She did not expect to be able to go into town again before winter. They left at sunrise with empty wagons; they hoped to cover the twenty miles and get into the trading town early enough to complete their business and be able to start back first thing the next day.

Ellie asked around and found there was a man who would ship wagonloads of wood for fires. It seemed like a good idea to get a couple loads in. They didn't have any significant timber to cut on their land, and what wood they did have would be used up very quickly in a cold winter. Ellie knew that having firewood shipped in from Minnesota was not going to be a good long term solution. They would have to find other sources for burning in their fireplace and stove. She inquired about this and found that many people collected and burned the dung from their cows and horses because of the high grass content it carried. The smell wasn't all that pleasant, but it would burn and would stretch the wood supply. Others made up tight bundles of hay that could burn for up to four hours. Some people also searched their property for buffalo dung which would burn better than the horse or cow dung.

That task done, they headed for Mulcayhee's General Store where Ellie purchased a barrel of flour, several bushel bags of oats for the animals, a ten pound bag of sugar, ten pounds of corn meal, five pounds of coffee beans, a two pound bag of salt, a bushel of apples that had just come in, twenty pounds of bacon, ten pounds of dried beans, two bushels of potatoes, and a bushel of tomatoes that Michael Mulcayhee, the store owner, said he was having trouble selling. It seemed that many people from the northern European countries still viewed tomatoes as strange, he explained, shaking his head. Ellie eagerly bought them, thinking of fried green tomatoes as a special treat. She rationalized that they could keep some of the tomato seeds and plant them in the spring. Finally, she looked at the stock of tinned cans to see if there were any foods they might want or need. She purchased several cans of fruit to offer their diets some variety. While they had a fair supply of jars that Lottie had put up, she wasn't certain that they would last through the winter and spring until other foods could be gathered and prepared.

Having made her food purchases, Ellie inquired about glass for the windows. The store owner stated he only had enough glass on hand for two of the windows. He had it because someone had ordered it and never picked it up. The man refused to order more glass for Ellie, telling her to come back after the winter. If she made it through and still planned on staying, he would order the glass for her then. Ellie scowled at him, but recognized it was useless arguing about it. Instead, she continued ordering; she needed sufficient lime to make plaster for the entire interior of the house. She purchased several sawed planks to make repairs on the structures. Then she saw two buffalo hide blankets. They looked so thick and warm she had to purchase them.

While Mr. Mulcayhee and Nathaniel were getting the supplies loaded onto the wagons, Ellie began to experience some remorse over how much she had spent; however, this passed when she realized that money wouldn't matter very much, if they didn't live through the winter. This made her think about the possibility of deep snow and ice cold temperatures and the long walk out to the outhouse. She decided they needed at least one, maybe two chamber pots.

Once the wagons were loaded and Ellie couldn't think of anything else they would need, Mr. Mulcayhee asked if they had met any of their neighbors as yet.

"No, we have not," Ellie told him. "We have been extremely busy trying to prepare the place to face the winter. However, I would not even know which way to go to find neighbors out there," she added.

"Well, seems ta me yer nearest neighbors would be the Andersens, Eric and Elsa. They'd be about an hour's ride northwest of ya. Nice folks. From Sweden, I think. Ya ought ta drop by an' say hello," Mulcayhee suggested, and then turned his head and spat a wad of tobacco juice into the dirt.

"Thank you, Mr. Mulcayhee. You have been most helpful." Ellie gave him her most winning smile and slapped the reigns against the team's rumps to get them started.

"See ya in the spring," he called after them. Ellie thought she heard him add, "If ya make it." She just raised her hand and waved good-by.

Both wagons were loaded down; progress was slow and the drive back took considerably longer, but they made it home well before sundown.

The next day, Ellie saddled up Princess for herself and Victor for Jason. They rode northwest to the closest farm. She brought some apple muffins that Becky had made. She hoped she might be able to buy a couple of hogs from her neighbors. She also felt it was important to start to get to know them. Not only might she need help, she hoped for some conversation.

As they rode onto the Andersen property, Ellie first spotted a tall, heavy set woman with blond hair braided and pinned up around her head, hanging laundry. Two young children were running around her and a girl of about eight years was helping hang the clothes.

The woman stopped her work, shielding her eyes from the late morning sun, squinting at Ellie and Jason as they rode up. The children stopped their activities and stared. As they came into better view, the woman seemed to relax. A tall, sturdy man with a sun burned face came out of the barn carrying a rifle under his arm. Two blond boys stood behind him; a third, nearly his father's height was at his side and also armed.

Ellie quickly assessed the situation and realized that they rarely received company and were unsure if she was a threat. She walked Princess slowly up to the man, "Mr. Andersen, I am Ellie Pe…Proctor and this is Jason. We have moved into the Gephardts' old place." Ellie saw Jason give her a startled glance when he heard what she had said, but he kept his surprise well hidden. She would have to thank him on the way home.

The man handed his rifle to his son and walked forward extending his hand. With a heavy accent, he greeted her. "It's good to have neighbors. Elsa, come meet our new neighbor."

Ellie dismounted, as did Jason. The family introduced themselves and invited them into their home. Ellie handed the muffins to Elsa. She was surprised to see that the interior roof was wood since the outside had sod on it. The woman's English was broken, but she managed to communicate well enough for Ellie to understand her meaning. She explained that the first winter they had lived in a sod house, cutting turf from the area of the house and stacking it up for walls. They had roofed it over with boards and tar paper, and laid sod on top for insulation. She explained further how the process was done, adding that they had decided to sod the roof when they built this house as the sod kept the heat in better than just plain wood.

Ellie noticed the younger children staring at Jason. As they became more relaxed around the strangers, one of them asked if she could touch his skin. Ellie realized that the little ones had never seen a Negro before. The eight year old girl also stared, but at Ellie. Finally, she blurted out, "I have never seen such a beautiful dress." Ellie had worn a relatively plain dress that she might have worn into town to go shopping in Beaufort or Savannah.

The Andersens had been there for four years. As the conversation progressed, Ellie realized they had not understood the need to register their intent to homestead the property. Apparently, none of them read or wrote English. She did not want to frighten them, but only casually mentioned that when she went to register hers the next spring they might travel in to do it together. Ellie also offered to teach the children to read and write and invited them to visit any time. After they finished lunch, she brought up the subject of buying hogs. Elsa seemed reluctant, but Eric turned to his wife, saying something in their native language. To Ellie's relief, the woman agreed.

Ellie and Jason walked their horses home, herding a healthy looking boar and sow ahead of them. By the time they arrived, Nathaniel had already used some of the planks to build a stall for the stallion and one to keep the cows separated from the horses while they were in the barn. Ellie asked him to build pens both inside and outside for the hogs as well, suggesting they be moved away from the paddock for the horses. They had decided to try to house all the livestock in the barn to increase the warmth during the winter months. The chickens were closest to the door where they got some sun light. Nathaniel had built a chicken coop inside the barn with sufficient perches for six brooding hens and their one rooster. The birds were given free range during the day. They wouldn't wander too far, since they knew there was a guaranteed meal if they stayed nearby. Ellie surveyed the improvements they had made with satisfaction.

Ellie told the others about the sod on the roof of the Andersen house and how well it insulated their home. She suggested they try it on their home as well. Nathaniel quickly acknowledged the value of the suggestion, stating that he would like to learn how to build a sod house, too. They could live in one sooner than having to wait to build one out of wood which was very scarce. The next day, they began digging and cutting sod for the roof. It took some experimenting to get the right depth so that the grass roots remained intact. Live roots would keep it from dying and blowing away. Jason loved the idea that the house would have a living roof over it.

The rest of September and into October was spent cutting and gathering the dried grasses for winter feed. Mornings, frost covered the ground, making their work slower and harder. By late October, Nathaniel stated they had stored enough hay to feed thirty horses. They had already seen snow flurries one night. The morning cold was already worse than anything they had experienced in South Carolina. They had filled the loft with hay, but they had not begun to insulate the walls of the house.

CHAPTER 45

Lela and Lily sat on the front porch protected from the winds out of the northwest. Together they worked on weaving grass matting. Becky showed Ellie how to weave the straw. They had decided they could nail it to the walls to set the plaster and to hang panels of it as a curtain to create a private area for changing and bathing. The work was slow. By sundown, their hands were stiff and all had blisters.

"Dat wind doan never quit," Lela commented.

"It lack it be talkin' ta ya, but ya cain't never quite unnerstan what it saying. It lack it whisperin' somethin' all da time out dere in dat grass," Lily said with a shiver. The other women all agreed with her that it was rather eerie hearing the continuous susurration of the grasses in the constant wind.

They continued their work the next day. Early in the afternoon, a wagon came carrying Elsa, her teenage son, and the two smallest girls. Elsa presented Ellie with two freshly killed wild rabbits. Jason and Nathaniel came up from the barn to see who was visiting. Kort Andersen had been impressed by Princess and asked to see her and the other horses. Jason accompanied him to the barn while the rest went into the house. Conversation was awkward at first. Ellie turned the conversation to the work they had been doing, the topic loosened Elsa's tongue. Lela and Becky had many questions and the women laughed over their struggles to understand one another. Ellie became distracted watching the little ones. It made her sad to think of the little ones that she would not have with Daniel. After a couple of hours, Elsa excused herself, stating she wanted to get back before dark.

Through the next couple of days of weaving, the progress seemed faster as they became more adept at their tasks. However, it was the end of October, the work was not yet complete, and the snow started falling. The only part of the cabin that seemed to have any warmth was between the stove and the fireplace. Nathaniel and Jason came back from feeding the animals and began complaining that the barn was warmer than the house. They were all cold and discouraged. It was not even November. How were they ever going to get through January and February?

Ellie felt responsible for dragging these loyal people out of the warmth of the South. She felt guilty for giving up on her home. What if Daniel had been wounded? Maybe she should have gone to Pennsylvania in search of him? But she knew she could not face him if he did not want her or had married someone else. If she had not been so afraid of running out of money, they could have gone to California. The only thought she had was that they were trapped in this cold cabin for months to come. She sat holding a hot cup of coffee, trying to warm her hands. She shivered, feeling the draft on her back. At first, she thought it was because she was facing the fireplace, but it did not seem as if her back was simply colder. She stood and lit a candle. It flickered, but the flame decidedly was leaning away from the northwest corner of the cabin.

"Look! Look at the candle! No wonder it is so cold in here."

"It's col' in here, 'cause it's col' out dere," Lela snapped.

"We can stop the wind from coming in." Ellie understood Lela's reaction. She had been having the same thought.

"What kin we do, Ellie?" Becky asked.

"We can start by nailing up the straw mats we wove and plastering the walls."

"We don' have enough for da whole house," Lela complained.

Ellie shrugged and grabbed up one of the mats. "We will start where the wind is strongest and keep weaving more."

Lela was incensed by the suggestion. "It's too col' ta weave out dere."

"We will weave in here." She looked around.

"Ah'll go ta da barn an' git da nails an' hammer." Nathaniel got up, threw on his coat, and went out the front door.

Jason followed and began bringing in the mats that had been finished. Ellie and Lela went out the back door and into the cellar to get the lime and dried clay from the stream that they had stored there to make the plaster.

Nathaniel nailed while Jason and Lela held the mats in place. Ellie mixed plaster and Becky and Lily wove. The mats went up quickly. They had previously made enough to cover the entire west wall and the north wall from the west corner to the back door. Ellie started slopping the plaster onto the mats. It was rough and lumpy, but it was only the first coat. She was not concerned about the look of it. The point was to keep the wind out and the heat in. Jason and Nathaniel took over the plastering while Ellie made up another batch. They did not stop for lunch, but worked until late in the afternoon. With only the light from the one south facing window in the room, it became too dark for further weaving. The women worked on preparing food and the men went to the barn to tend the animals. At the end of the day, when Ellie crawled into bed, she was thankful that she was not alone; she might have given up.

The next day, Ellie joined in weaving with Lily and Becky; the others put up the mats as they were finished and plastered them. They continued along the north wall into the other room. They soon realized that some kind of curtains needed to go up over the shuttered windows and the doors. Jason made a run to the barn and brought up two burlap bags, having emptied them into a wooden bin. Nathaniel nailed them over the two northern windows. A blanket covered the back door. Although it remained cold in the cabin that night, the wind no longer came through.

Ellie woke to the sound of dripping. The sun had come out and was melting snow off the roof. By afternoon, it was warm enough to work on weaving mats on the front porch. The wind had not let up, but the newly plastered walls blocked it and they were relieved to be able to get outside. Ellie started to understand the importance of getting outside whenever possible. Only two days of being trapped, even while constantly working, had left her feeling sad and alone. She wondered if it would have felt different if Daniel had been with her. She smiled at the thought of his humor and what he might have brought to their group.

The men went hunting for the first time and returned with a brace of grouse and an antelope. Nathaniel was so proud of having been out with a gun and feeling the freedom, power, and authority that represented. The women praised their accomplishments and quickly dressed the meat for storage. Ellie envied them the freedom of activity they had experienced. She wished she had gone with them.

By the end of November, they had spent more days inside than out. They had lined all the interior walls with woven mats and a heavy coat of plaster. As it snowed again, they sat trying to busy themselves within the cabin. Ellie noticed Lily's slim figure shivering as she sat on the foot of Lela's bed. She stirred the fire, and then wrapped the teenage girl up in one of her blankets.

Lily looked at her with misery in her eyes, "Why's it still so col' in here? We fixed da walls!"

"I am afraid, Lily, that most of the heat is going up the chimney and even with the sod on the roof, the heat is still escaping."

"Cain't we cover da chimbly?"

"I wish we could. But we would choke to death if we closed off the chimney." She shook her head helplessly.

After a few minutes, Lily spoke up again. "Can't we put da straw bundles up on da inside of da roof?"

Everyone stopped what they were doing. Without a word, each looked at the ceiling in concentration. Finally, Nathaniel broke the silence. "Ah thinks dares a way we could do it!"

Conversation erupted as they each shared their ideas and discussed how they might be able to do it. Eventually, they agreed on a plan. By tying the bundles together, they would create long strips that could be used to build a ceiling inside of the cabin. They did not have enough rope for what they needed and had to unravel it to have enough lengths of heavy string to attach the bundles together. Nor did they have enough bundles of straw completed. As they began work on the new project, their spirits seemed to lift. Ellie believed the straw ceiling would hold some heat in, but she was unsure if it would make enough of a difference. However, the hope it brought would in itself be worth the effort.

Christmas came with little fanfare. They made a special meal of roasted rabbit, potatoes, gravy, and applesauce. They sang Christmas melodies and went to bed. Ellie did not want to think about the day. It was the first time in her life that she did not have even one gift to give to anyone. She vowed that next year, she would again have gifts to give.

January was bitter cold. The days were short. The winds were unrelenting, howling throughout the day and night. However, the inside of the cabin was no longer freezing. Although it was cold by morning, there was no film of ice to greet them on top of the water bucket. By the end of the month, Ellie wanted to scream. She could see that the others were restless as well. They needed to find something to fill their time. Their accomplishments had been efficient, but it looked coarse. Ellie debated with herself whether she was being frivolous thinking about a second coat of smooth plaster or whether the job would help get them through the winter with their sanity. She finally asked Nathaniel and Jason if they would be willing to put another coat of plaster on the walls. Before either could answer, Lela jumped up, stating she would get the supplies and start mixing. Ellie smiled to herself; now she would need to come up with more tasks for the rest of them.

Ellie had brought bundles of material. Some of them had been left over from the time when she was helping escaped slaves. She had stored them under her and Lela's beds. She picked a roll of flowered cotton. She suggested they make curtains for all the windows out of it, hoping it would remind them that spring would come. She picked a heavier material to make a draw curtain for the corner, replacing the blanket that had been hanging to block off one corner for privacy. Each time they completed one project, she tried to come up with another one.

By the end of February, even the ceiling had been plastered; curtains had been completed, as well as a new dress for Lily. None of them knew when the winter would begin to let up; however, the days seemed to be getting slightly longer. The cold winds and periodic snow continued into March. Ellie suggested they begin weaving mats for the house that would be built for Nathaniel and Becky and their children. Ellie hoped that Lela would stay with her for at least another year. Realizing that the growing season would be much shorter than that to which they were accustomed, they started to germinate some of the seeds and plant them in small containers in the house for the vegetable garden. The snows were finally beginning to melt. The temperature outside had become bearable during the day. As the weeks passed, their moods began to lift. They'd made it through their first North Dakota winter!

CHAPTER 46

While the other women planted, Ellie worked with the two year old colts. Both needed training. As each of the mares came into season, they were bred to the stallion. She had relatively little money left, even though the others had made financial contributions to the maintenance of the homestead, and she worried how they would make it until she had horses ready to sell. They would need to grow extra of everything in order to use hay and vegetables for trade or sale. They extended the pasture areas, leaving little to do for the horses over the summer months.

The men went out hunting and fishing whenever they could find the spare time. Everyone appreciated the addition of meat and fish to their rather monotonous diets. The chickens were producing plenty of eggs; enough so that Ellie decided to allow some of them to be hatched. That required the expansion of the chicken coops and a bigger area for them to run in. They had lost several hens to foxes and coyotes before deciding that they could not give the birds totally free range. The hogs produced a litter of six, which delighted everyone. Separate pens were constructed for the boar and the sow with her young. Lily developed an affinity for the boar and herded him out to the stream to root for additional food to supplement his diet. The sow was contented with wallowing in the dirt while her shoats ran about squealing and chasing each other.

Nathaniel and Becky had decided to stake out a piece of land across the stream from Ellie's acreage. They chose to build their house and animal shelter out of sod due to the lack of trees in the area. Ellie gave them a share of the tools and seed they had purchased or brought along with them from South Carolina. Once the litter of hogs was weaned, Ellie gave the couple a male and female as a house warming gift. She also sold them the heifer at a modest price and allowed Nathaniel to rent a pair of horses for his wagon by cutting hay for her later in the year and doing some of the work around her farm until she could find some farmhands to employ. Ellie moved into the bedroom and Lela continued to sleep in the main room.

Once the weather seemed fairly stable and the garden was well in hand, Ellie, Nathaniel, and Becky visited with the Andersens and planned their joint trip to Abercrombie to file their intent to homestead. The Andersens were grateful to Ellie for helping them to understand and deal with the bureaucracy involved. It was agreed that they would set out the following week. Ellie, Nathaniel, and Becky traveled in one wagon.

They had been discussing the two homesteads and what progress was being made on each, when Nathaniel changed the subject. "Ellie, Jason done tol' us how you done called yo'se'f Ellie Proctor. We ain't challengin' ya on dat o' nuthin', ya unnerstans. But...well, me an' Becky, we bin talkin' 'bout what name we was gonna use. We'd be mighty proud ef you said we could call us da Peters fambly. Ah knows dat's wha' mos' udder colored folks does, takes day marster's name fo' dares. We ain't slaves no mo', but you an' yo daddy was good ta us. We doan know what udder name we could take. What do ya think, Ellie?" Nathaniel and Becky both looked at her to see her response.

She looked away, biting her lip for several seconds, and then turned back to them and said, "You are both loving, strong, honorable people. My family would be honored by having you as members of it. If you would like to use Peters as your name, I would be very proud." She smiled at both of them, tears in her eyes for the honor she felt they were doing her and her family.

Once they had all finished registering their homestead claims, Ellie made sure they stopped by Mulcayhee's General Store. She wanted to show him that they had indeed made it through the winter and she wanted her panes of glass to finish the windows in her home. Mr. Mulcayhee congratulated her on her success and wrote up the order for her. Nathaniel and Becky bought some penny candy treats for their children which motivated Ellie to do the same for herself and Lela. Ellie enjoyed the taste of the peppermint melting in her mouth on the trip back home.

As spring progressed into summer, the two women spent more time outside enjoying the warmth. Lela delighted in the beautiful wildflowers growing all about them and picked bouquets of black-eyed Susan, purple coneflower, prairie clover, larkspur, and Indian paintbrush. They watched colorful butterflies flit about the fields and listened to the songs of the meadowlarks and the screeching of the magpies.

In the warm evenings, after settling the animals safely in the barn, they chose to eat their dinner outside as well, remembering the claustrophobia of winter and knowing they would have to endure it again. Sitting out until the sun had set and the sky filled with stars delighted them and that was how they happened to see the shimmering play of the Northern Lights in the night sky. Initially, Lela was frightened by the strange array of colors undulating above them, but Ellie recalled reading about them and reassured Lela that they were not at all supernatural. Once Lela accepted that they weren't ghost lights or a sign that the world was about to end, she began to appreciate the performance. Both women were filled with awe at the sight.

But they were always driven back inside by the late evening wind blowing through the grass, whispering to them in words they could not understand. Sometimes, to the loneliness of that sound was added the howl of a coyote or even a wolf. On such nights, Ellie would go to sleep with tears sliding down her cheeks. She felt like howling out her own loneliness as well.

One morning, as Ellie and Lela sat on the porch shelling peas and plucking a chicken for dinner, Lela noticed several men on horseback riding toward them from the west.

"Now what ya s'pose dey want?" Lela asked, pointing out the approaching strangers.

Rising, Ellie said, "I do not know, but perhaps we had better be ready for trouble." She ducked into the house and brought out one of her father's revolvers. She sat back down on her chair and put the bowl of peas on top of the gun. The two women watched nervously as the riders drew closer. Both were relieved to see that it was a detachment of cavalry. Ellie quickly slipped the revolver into her pocket.

An officer and six enlisted men rode up to the house. The officer tipped his hat and introduced himself. "Good morning, ladies. I am Captain Stephen Nielson. My men and I are on patrol from Fort Ransom. We have been looking for renegades from the reservation. I trust you ladies have not had any problems with the Indians." He smiled warmly at Ellie, obviously admiring her.

"Good morning, Captain, gentlemen. Won't you stop to water your horses and accept some refreshment?" Ellie invited, rising from her seat.

"Thank you, ma'am. It would be a relief and a pleasure," the captain responded, dismounting. "Sergeant, have the men water the horses, and then you may all come back up to the house," he commanded, and then returned his attention to Ellie. "I do not believe I caught your name, ma'am."

"I am Ellie Proctor, Captain. And this is my friend and companion, Lela...Peters." Ellie looked at Lela to see her response to the surname. Lela just nodded to the captain.

"A pleasure, Mrs. Proctor, Mrs. Peters." The captain again tipped his hat to the ladies. He had made the assumption that they were both married and Ellie chose not to disabuse him on that point. "Is your husband about, Mrs. Proctor, or is he off hunting? I do not see him about the house or barn." He seemed to wait breathlessly for her answer.

"I am a widow, Captain. My husband died in the war," Ellie hastily blurted out. She sensed Lela's surprise once again, but again the other woman kept quiet. "Lela, would you mind preparing some coffee for our guests? Or would you and your men prefer some tea, Captain?"

"Coffee would be much appreciated, Mrs. Proctor, if you can spare it." His eyes continued to travel over her face and figure; his smile suggesting it was a most pleasurable excursion.

Turning her back to the captain, Lela gave Ellie a knowing smile and went inside to make enough coffee for all of them. Ellie invited the captain to come up onto the porch and have a seat while he waited. The young man swiftly leapt up the stairs to take the seat next to her.

"This is a mighty big place for just two women to tend to, Mrs. Proctor. It must be very difficult for you...both." Captain Nielson tried his best to look empathetic. Ellie had to restrain a giggle at his expression. She was flattered by his attention, but really was not interested.

"It is difficult at times, Captain. But it is well worth it. My horses are thriving. In just a few years, I should have a herd that would impress even the cavalry. Perhaps you could get the Army to buy from me then? You will never find a more comfortable riding horse than the American Saddlebreds. Are you familiar with the breed?" She smiled politely, trying not to give him any encouragement.

"I cannot say that I am, ma'am. But I would appreciate a chance to see them," he stated, insinuating that she should be the one to show the horses to him. The captain's men began congregating in front of the house, thus saving Ellie from having to maintain the uncomfortable conversation. Before long, Lela brought out the coffee and some sandwiches she had made. All the men were very appreciative. They consumed their lunches and said good-bye to their benefactresses.

Lela gazed after them and said, "Ah doan think we seen da las' o' dat captain." Ellie did her best to make a disapproving face at her friend, but she couldn't help laughing.

The summer went by too quickly for Ellie's liking. She had made acquaintance of some more of her neighbors. Winter preparations began in early September. Watching the early winter growth of fur on the animals, it seemed that the winter was to begin ahead of schedule. Ellie had lined up projects for Lela and herself. She was determined to make Christmas gifts this year. She had decided to make the oldest Andersen girl a pretty dress by cutting down one of her old ones. The two women also agreed to cut up one of the antelope hides they had succeeded in tanning and make gloves for each member of Nathaniel's family. The two cabins were close enough that they were able to get out and visit each other often.

The third week in November, Captain Nielson rode up alone. He presented Lela and Ellie with four Ring-necked pheasants for Thanksgiving. "I know most Southerners do not celebrate Thanksgiving, but..."

"My Daniel was from Pennsylvania!" Ellie interrupted as she accepted the gift. "Won't you come in, Captain. It is far too chilly to be visiting on the porch."

The captain gratefully accepted her invitation. Once inside he sniffed the air and asked, "Goodness! What smells so delicious? Could that be apple pie?" He looked at Ellie, smiling broadly at her.

"It is. Could I offer you a piece, Captain? It is freshly baked," Ellie asked, indicating that he should take a seat at the table and make himself comfortable.

Seating himself and slipping off his great coat, he responded, "It would be the high point of my day, no, my week to have a piece of your delicious smelling apple pie, Mrs. Proctor." He continued to smile and watch her every move.

"Would you like a glass of fresh cold milk with that or a cup of tea?"

"Tea to warm me up, if you don't mind; although just being in your presence does a great deal to warm me." His smile broadened to a grin.

Ellie pretended not to have heard the flirtation as she handed him a cup of tea and brought out the apple pie she had just made. She had become a much better cook with a lot of coaching from Lela. Ellie cut a large slice of the pie and served their guest. Lela busied herself at preparations for their dinner.

Groaning appreciatively, the captain stated, "Oh, it has been far too long since I had such delectable cooking. I surely have missed the taste of food prepared by a woman's hands. I thank you for this, Mrs. Proctor." He continued to heartily enjoy the pie. When he had finished, Ellie offered him a second slice which he also accepted.

"Speaking of missing things, there must be a great many things you have been missing living out here without a man's company." He looked at Ellie speculatively.

She knew what he thought she had been missing, and was not about to satisfy him on that question. Instead, she stated that the thing she missed the most was a good book. The captain, though caught off guard by her response, took it in stride, agreeing that it was a trial to the spirit not to have access to decent literature. They continued their conversation for a while. Finally, the captain rose, announcing that he had to get back to the fort. He thanked both women for their hospitality and wished them a good Thanksgiving.

As soon as he left, Lela burst out laughing. "Dese soldiers all git it bad fo' you! Fust Marster Ted, den Daniel, now dis un."

"You are being silly! Stop it! He is no more interested in me than that chair. The first time he saw me I was wearing that stupid braid with dirt on my face and under my nails. Maybe he came to see you!" Ellie swatted at Lela with the damp kitchen towel.

Lela jumped back, laughing and shaking her head. "Naw, he sees me as yo maid."

"Well…if he ever comes back, I will set him straight before he can even open his mouth to say hello," Ellie stated firmly, beginning to clear the dishes from the table.

Lela laughed. "Ah'm sho ya will."

"He did bring some nice fat birds. There are enough for all of us. Should we ask Nathaniel to come with the family tomorrow?"

"Oh, yes! We kin have a real Thanksgivin'. We got a lot ta be thankful fo'."

"I wish we had a bigger table and enough chairs for all of us to sit together." Ellie was finding it hard to be thankful for anything. Lela's reminder of Ted and Daniel made her think of death. The idea of another man in her life made her sad. She knew she would never be able to give her heart to anyone else the way she had to Daniel. She could not settle for "good enough" as she had with Ted. Captain Nielson seemed like a nice man; it would not be fair to him. She would accept his friendship if he offered it, but nothing more. As she looked toward her future, it would be nice to have someone to be her partner and help her; however, the guilt would be too much. She would always feel as if she were cheating on Daniel.

Lela walked to the sod cottage to extend the Thanksgiving invitation. Ellie went to the barn to do the late afternoon feeding and watering. She was in no mood to go back to the house and face Lela. She took the time to brush down Princess and check her over. She had bred her for the first time and was especially concerned about her progress. She then took the brush to Daniel's Victor. It had become her custom to talk to the horse about their common friend. The conversation ended as she sobbed with her arms around the animal's neck.

As Christmas approached, Ellie asked Lela if she would be willing to venture out with her to the Andersen's. They had made apple cakes, ornaments for each member of the family with their given names on them, and a dress for Birgetta. Lela responded, "Col' o' not, it ud be good ta git out a here fo' a bit."

On Christmas Eve, Ellie went to the barn to get the horses ready. She brought Princess and Victor to the house, saddled and ready to go. When Lela came out of the house, Ellie could not hold back the laughter at the expression on Lela's face.

"Ya think it's funny? Ya knows Ah never been up on one a does animals!"

"The gelding is very gentle," Ellie told her persuasively.

"Why cain't we ride in da wagon?"

"Do you want to get stuck in the snow?" Ellie watched her friend's face.

"No, I did not think so. Let me help you on. You just squeeze with your legs and hold on to his mane. He will follow Princess."

Both women started laughing at the clumsiness of their attempts to get Lela up onto the horse, which stood patiently still. As they rode off, Ellie tried to hide her laughter at Lela's frequent squeals and exclamations. Once their ride became quieter, Ellie became somber, thinking about the excellent job of training Daniel had done with his horse and how she longed for his companionship.

The Andersens were surprised to have company, but welcomed them warmly. Young Kort took the horses to the barn out of the wind while they visited. The women warmed themselves by the fire with hot tea, holding the mugs to thaw their hands. After breaking into the apple cake with the family, Lela took out the ornaments and distributed them to each member of the family. She pointed out their names and explained the letters and how they spelled out their first names. They had no Christmas tree, but seemed glad of the festive decorations. The children began searching for special places to display their personal ornaments. The sounds of their youthful voices and laughter gave Ellie pleasure and she noted Lela's smile as well. It reminded her of home. Ellie brought out one more package, much larger than the rest. She turned to Elsa, "I am sorry I could not give more to all of the children, but I have something else for Birgetta."

Elsa looked questioningly at Ellie, and then called out, "Birgetta, come here!"

The child was quick to obey, but kept looking back at her ornament and her siblings playing. "Yes, Mama?"

"Mrs. Proctor has anudder gift for you."

The child's eyes lit up. She curtsied to Ellie, accepting the package. "Danka, Mrs. Proctor."

The child carefully untied the string around the burlap package. She seemed unsure. Ellie wondered with so many siblings in this desolate land whether the child had ever had a present for herself before or not. The girl finally pulled out the dress. The smile that came across her face was all the thanks that Ellie would ever need. However, what surprised Ellie the most were the tears she saw Elsa wipe away from her own eyes.

Christmas day, Ellie and Lela went to Becky and Nathaniel's home for dinner. They brought the antelope hide gloves they had made for them. Becky and Lily had made hats woven of strips of material taken from a dress that Lily had outgrown for both Ellie and Lela. The day was pleasant and Ellie was thankful for the friends she had. She tried not to think about the Christmases she had dreamed of sharing with Daniel and their children that would never be.

CHAPTER 47

On New Year's Day, there was a surprise knock on the door. The snow had begun during the night and it seemed as if neither the snow nor the wind would let up soon. Thinking it must be Nathaniel or Jason, she quickly opened the door.

Seeing the look of surprise on her face, Captain Nielson greeted her with, "I could have been an Indian."

"I believe most Indians have too much sense to be traveling around in this weather."

Captain Nielson stood on the uncovered porch with his hat in his hand. Lela looked at the two frozen statues in the doorway, "Ellie, invite da man in. You is lettin' all da heat out!"

Ellie stepped back from the door and gestured for the officer to come in, and then blurted out, "Lela is my friend. She has never been my maid."

He seemed confused by her statement, but took it well when he heard Lela giggle. "I…I just came by to give you this." He pulled *A Tale of Two Cities* by Charles Dickens out of his coat and handed it to Ellie.

She stared mutely at the book in his hand for several seconds. "Oh. Thank you." She took the book from his hands. "We were about to sit down to some soup. Will you join us?"

"I would like that very much, Mrs. Proctor." He began to remove his coat, but Ellie stopped him.

She indicated the door and said, "Go put your horse in the barn while we set the table."

Nielson looked at her a bit uncertainly. "She is fine, ma'am."

Ellie became immediately indignant. "You think it is fine for her to freeze in the snow while you warm yourself? I think not!"

Seeing the look of anger in her eyes, the captain quickly reconsidered his position. "I will be right back." He put his gloves and hat back on and left the house.

Ellie mumbled as she spread out the tablecloth. "What kind of man would leave his horse out in this weather?"

Lela giggled as she set the table, "Ya do enjoy givin' men a hard time."

It did not take long before Captain Nielson was coming back in the door. He brought news of the outside world. By the time he left, she had to admit to herself that it was pleasant to have conversation with someone other than her regular companions.

Lela and Ellie tried to keep occupied as the winter days dragged on. They were pleased with the small braided rug they had made for Ellie's room. They decided to begin another larger one for the main room. Ellie savored the book Captain Nielson had given her. She rationed out how many pages she would allow herself to read each day, trying to make it last as long as possible. In the middle of March, they began the process of germinating seeds. They had prepared better this year, having made flower boxes out of wood and filling them with dirt before winter. They had stored them under one of the beds. Once the seeds had started to germinate, they pulled the flower boxes out and planted the sprouts.

Finally, the winter was over and April brought the beginning of spring. They anxiously awaited the birth of six foals. Two of the mares had not taken the year before; they attempted to breed them again. They did not transplant the delicate plantings until well into May, not wanting to risk a late killing frost.

She and Lela began constructing another soddy to be used as a bunk house for the farmhands she planned to hire in the future. Nathaniel and Jason helped with the place and dug a second latrine nearby for it. The sod house didn't have a stove, but she thought she and Lela would do the cooking for the help. All they would need was a fireplace for heat. They managed to collect enough stones out of the creek bed to construct another chimney, but they had to go a half mile down the stream before they had a sufficient supply. They left the floor bare dirt, but compacted it as much as they could. There was one small window in the wall that would give some light to the interior. Ellie brought the old table and three chairs the Gephardts had left behind and set them up in the soddy. They would have to construct bed frames as well and make some mattresses to stuff with grass for the beds. Ellie made a mental note to buy more rope to construct the beds. The small sod house could hold two or three beds, since they wouldn't need to put any other furniture in it.

With six new horses on the farm, Ellie realized they would need to stock up considerably more grain and hay. Also, the barn was going to be too small to house all the animals throughout another winter. Not only were there more horses, but more chickens, and pigs as well as the milking cow. She took to riding one of the mares that had not taken. She had been saddle breaking the two colts that were now three year olds, but they were still unpredictable. She did not want anyone to see either of them misbehaving. She would not actively try to sell the mare, but if she got a good offer she would let her go. She also hoped to sell off some of the pigs. She'd need the money to hire some men to expand the barn and cut more hay. There were other supplies she would need to replenish before the next winter. She counted out how much money she had left, and then went to the pasture to bring in and harness Daniel's gelding and the mare she thought to be barren.

Ellie and Lela drove out in the direction of Abercrombie, planning to stop at any farms they would pass, looking for men to hire on the way. One of their neighbors along with his teenage son offered to help out for a couple of weeks working on the barn.

In Abercrombie, the two women went directly to Mulcayhee's to stock up on flour, sugar, coffee, salt, and other necessities. Lela used some of her money to purchase cloth to make some dresses. They intended to rip some of their old ones to finish making the rug for the main room. Mr. Mulcayhee wanted to know how things were going on the farm, and Ellie quickly filled him in, telling him about their need for some hired help in expanding the barn and getting in the hay. Initially, he couldn't think of anyone locally who would have sufficient free time from their own place to hire out to her. Then he remembered two Santee Sioux men who had come to town from the reservation in the south. "They were looking for work and seemed nice enough, peaceable men," he told them. "They'd give ya an honest day's work fer yer money."

Lela was appalled at the idea and tugged on Ellie's arm, indicating she wanted to discuss this idea. "Doan you even think 'bout takin' on dem Injuns. Dey'd kill us in ah sleep!" she whispered harshly to Ellie. "Ever'body knows dey ain't no good Injun 'cept a dead un."

Ellie acknowledged to herself that she felt rather anxious about the idea, too. But she refused to allow her concerns and prejudice to get the best of her. She put on a brave smile and whispered back, "Lela, neither of us has ever met an Indian. We have heard terrible stories about them stealing and killing, but we have no firsthand knowledge of this. It would be wrong of us to judge them before we even speak with them."

"An' ef dey kills us da fust time what dey talks to us, what we gonna do den?" Lela hissed back. "Ever'body knows dat da Injuns is crazy savages!"

"And everybody knows that Negroes are lazy and stupid animals, and all the white masters in the South raped and tortured their slaves! We need to talk to them before we decide we cannot trust them." Ellie turned back to the storekeeper. "Where might we find these gentlemen, Mr. Mulcayhee?"

"I reckon they'd be down ta the stable. You never seen such people crazy about horses as the Injuns are. They're pro'bly down there right now, looking over the animals. I'll bet they'll git real excited about your horses, Mrs. Proctor." He smiled, just a bit wickedly, Ellie thought. None the less, she decided she would go talk with them.

Just as Mr. Mulcayhee had said, they found the two men standing by the corral looking at the horses. They seemed to be discussing the qualities of each animal. Ellie walked up to them, Lela hanging back a bit, and introduced herself.

"Excuse me, gentlemen. Do either of you speak English?" she asked them.

"We both do," one of them responded, turning to look at her.

"Oh, good. I am Mrs. Ellie Proctor. This is Miss Lela Peters. We are homesteading not far from here. I am looking for some men to work for me, building a barn. I would pay you ten cents a day and food and lodging. I heard from Mr. Mulcayhee at the general store that you were looking for work. Would you be interested?"

Ellie could feel her heart pounding. She had never been so close to someone who appeared so alien to her. Both men were dressed in buckskins with beading on them. One man wore his hair pulled back and tied, the other let his hang loose and it fluttered around his face in the wind. While their skin was dark, it seemed more the color of aged wood than the dark brown to tan skin she was used to seeing among the Negroes. Each man stood very straight, their knees a bit bowed as if they rode horses when they were young and the bones were still forming. They discussed the offer in their own language for several minutes. The man who had spoken to her seemed to want to take the job, while the other man seemed reluctant. Finally, the second man seemed to give in to his friend's persuasion.

"We'll take the job. When do ya want us ta start an' where?" the first man asked.

Ellie told them to be at her farm first thing the next morning and gave them directions. She would not admit to anyone that she was glad Nathaniel would be around to supervise them. She was not sure how the Indians would behave alone with two women. She would return to sleeping with a loaded pistol under her pillow.

CHAPTER 48

The two men showed up on time the next morning on foot. Ellie wondered if they had walked all the way from town. If so, they must have started right after she had hired them. She told herself she would have offered them a ride if she had known they would be walking, but there was a sense of relief that she had remained ignorant of their plight. She walked down to meet them, Nathaniel at her side.

Ellie smiled as they approached, calling, "Good morning. You must have gotten an early start."

Both men smiled, but didn't bother to respond. Ellie introduced Nathaniel as her neighbor and the man who would be supervising the work. It was then that Ellie realized she didn't know either of their names. She apologized for this and asked what they were called.

The taller of the two, the one with his hair hanging loose, stated that his name was Little Dog Barking and his friend was He Runs Along. Ellie smiled a bit awkwardly at their names. She wasn't sure how to address them.

"Well, Mr. Barking and Mr. Runs Along...Uh...Nathaniel will show you where he needs you to begin working. I will see you both later. And...uh, thank you for coming." She smiled at them again and hurried away.

The neighbor man and his son arrived shortly after that, and construction of the barn extension got under way. First the ground on the west side of the barn was cleared and leveled. The structure would be built of stone. Not only was stone more available than wood, but it would also be a better block against the winds. Ellie and Lela had been collecting rocks for several weeks. It had been very hard work and she hoped there would be enough to complete the structure. She didn't want to have to make another long excursion up or down the creek bed to see what had washed out of the top soil.

Ellie went to the barn to work the colts and check on the work that was being done. She overheard her neighbor's son tell Nathaniel to mind his own business. She stopped her work and stood just inside the door, out of sight. Nathaniel repeated himself, "You gots too much water in da mixture."

The boy ignored him. Ellie came out where she could see what was going on. Even she could tell the mixture was too thin. "Leif, you need to add more clay."

"Mrs. Proctor, that nigger of yours don't know nothing. It will thicken once it dries," the teen responded, waving his hand dismissively toward Nathaniel.

Ellie walked up closer to the young man. "You will not call Nathaniel a nigger; he is a free man, not my possession; and I assure you he knows exactly what he is doing."

"I'm sorry, Mrs. Proctor, for my son's language, but we're not used ta takin' orders from his kind. It just don't seem right," the boy's father said, entering the conversation.

Ellie struggled to keep her temper, not wanting to alienate a neighbor she might need some day. "You might actually learn something from Nathaniel," she said simply and went back into the barn, angry and frustrated. She had thought she had escaped such nonsense. She realized she was too angry to work the colts and put the young stallion she had started to saddle up into a stall. Instead, she went to the vegetable garden and started pulling weeds. Once she worked off some of the anger, she washed the dirt off her hands and joined Lela in bringing lunch down to the men. As they passed around the food, one of the Indians quietly asked, "Miss Peters, why won't them other white men take orders from the boss man?"

Lela was surprised by the question. "What happened, Little Dog?"

"That white man said it wasn't right taking orders from his kind. It ain't like the boss was an Indian or even part Indian like me," he explained, obviously confused.

Ellie overheard and saw the look of disbelief on Lela's face. She smiled realizing that these Indians did not see the difference between herself and Lela or Nathaniel and the white men. She did not want Lela to say anything that would make them think any less of either Nathaniel, Lela, or any Negro. She interrupted, "Lela, could you give me a hand?"

"Yes, Ellie." Turning back toward the man. "'Scuse me." She walked over to Ellie, "What you need?"

"Come here for just a minute, please." Ellie led her friend into the barn. Suppressing a smile, Ellie looked at Lela and said, "You are a white person with dark skin to that man. Do not teach him the prejudice we moved so far to escape."

"Oh, but he thinks…." Her voice trailed off.

Ellie noticed that Lela seemed to be finding excuses to go the barn, bringing the men drinks of water, cakes, or just to see if they needed anything. Once the barn was completed, Nathaniel asked Ellie if she wanted to keep the two Indians on to cut hay. He added that they were both good workers and did not seem to have a problem taking directions from him.

Ellie knew that Nathaniel had his own place to work and she needed to get in as much of the tall grasses for feed as she could. She met with the two men on the front porch; Lela and Nathaniel stood by her side. After much discussion, the Indians agreed to work throughout the rest of the season. However, the amount Ellie was willing to pay was not enough by itself. She had to agree to feed them through the winter and provide them with a warm shelter. She was nervous about the prospect, but had no choice. Without their labor, she could not make it through the winter and it would still be another couple of years before any horses would be ready to sell. Even through her anxiety and desperation, she could not help but notice the way Lela and Little Dog kept stealing looks at one another. She had to admit she could understand Lela's attraction to him. Not only did he treat her with the respect expected by a white woman, he had a straight nose, high cheek bones, soft brown eyes, and bulging muscles. When Lela and Ellie went back into the house, it was Ellie's turn to tease.

Grabbing an apron full of potatoes, Ellie sat down at the table and began peeling them. She watched Lela move about the kitchen humming to herself.

"I wonder what has you so very cheerful these days," Ellie began.

"Ah ain't so specially cheerful. Ain't a body 'lowed ta hum ta dey se'f? Dis here is a free country, so Ah heard," Lela responded. But she couldn't banish the smile from her lips.

"Hmmm. I do believe you have a beau, Miss Lela. Yes, Ma'am! A tall, handsome, hardworking beau." Ellie peeked up at Lela to see how she was responding to the teasing. Lela just shrugged, noncommittally, and swayed from side to side while scraping carrots into the bucket in the sink.

"Mrs. Little Dog Barking. Lela Barking. Lela Little Dog? Just what will your name be? Have you thought about that?" Ellie was getting frustrated from the lack of intense response from her friend.

"Ah doan s'pose it'll matter none what Ah'm called, long as Ah have dat han'some man ta curl up next ta on dese col' Dakota winter nights," Lela replied smugly.

Ellie dropped her paring knife into the bowl on her lap. "Has he asked you to marry him?" She feared to hear the answer to that question. She wasn't ready to lose Lela's company along with everyone else's'.

"Naw. He ain't axed, an' Ah ain't sho Ah'd say yes ef he did," she said, much to Ellie's relief. "It ain't lack we got so much in common. An' where would we live? Ah ain't gonna go live on no reservation lack Ah was a slave agin. But would da white folks let us live aroun' dem? Most dem hates Negroes an' Injuns 'bout da same." She sighed.

"You will work it out if it is right for you. I, for one, would be delighted to have you as my neighbor. Do not let that kind of fear enter into your decision making. There are plenty of other things to worry about. Believe me!" Ellie had spoken with such vehemence that Lela turned to look at her.

She studied her friend's face for several seconds. Finally, she asked, "Ellie, what is it dat's worryin' you?"

It was Ellie's turn to shrug. Lela walked over and laid her hand on Ellie's shoulder. "You kin tell me. How long we been frien's? Ah knows dey is sumpin wrong wit you."

Ellie drew in a deep breath, laid the bowl on the table, rose, and walked to the stove where the pot of coffee was kept on the heat, so the men could come in and get some when they needed it. Pouring herself a cup, she returned to the table and offered Lela some, which the other woman quickly accepted. They sat at the table just as they had so many times back at Whispering Oaks, sipping their coffee and talking. Finally, she began. "I left the farm with a large sum of money. But most of it is gone now. I have enough to pay the men for their work as I promised, but it is not going to go much beyond that. There will not be any horses ready for sale until at least next year, unless I sell that barren mare. She is a good saddle horse, but that money would not go far either. I have no idea what to do."

"Ellie, Ah has some money from da time when you was payin' us back on da farm. Ah should be hepin' ya out here more wit some da 'spenses, instead a waitin' ta buy some lan'." She seemed to be determined to have her way in the matter.

"Lela, I could not take your money. You worked far too hard for that little bit of savings. No, I will find a way." Ellie picked up her bowl and knife and began peeling potatoes again.

"Well, den. Ah guess Ah jist have ta move on out a here. 'Cause Ah ain't gonna be no burden ta you no more. Mah slave days is over. Now Ah gots ta care fo' mah se'f." She set down her coffee cup and rose, moving toward her bed.

"What do you mean, Lela? What are you going to do?" She watched as Lela pulled out her old trunk and began filling it with her own possessions.

"Ah'm leavin' here. What's it look lack Ah'm doin'?" Lela responded, thumping things into the old trunk.

"Lela, no, please. If I said something that hurt you, I did not mean to and I apologize. Just please do not go this way. Please." Tears were beginning in her eyes. She could not believe Lela's intense response to her refusal.

Lela hesitated. "Ah ain't no slave no mo'. Ah doan need you o' nobody else takin' care o' me. Let me hep roun' here!" she demanded, hands on hips.

Ellie sniffled loudly. "I am so sorry, Lela. I did not realize this was so important to you. If it means that much, of course you can contribute financially." She wiped her eyes with her apron.

Lela scowled at Ellie. "Ah bin livin' here mo dan a yeah now. We shoulda done dis long ago." She began taking her things out of the trunk and putting them away again. "Ah buy da supplies next time we goes ta town," Lela stated, pointing her finger at Ellie for emphasis. Ellie just nodded her agreement. Lela gave a satisfied smile and brushed her hands together as if to say, that's done.

CHAPTER 49

A few days later Captain Nielson and a couple of his men stopped by the farm. "Good day to you, Mrs. Proctor." The captain tipped his hat.

"It has been a long time since we saw you last, Captain." Ellie smiled warmly, but tried not to put anything into her smile that he might interpret as encouragement.

"I was away from Fort Ransom for a while helping out at one of the new, northern forts. It looks as though you have been doing well. I see you have extended your barn."

"We have six new foals," Ellie proudly stated.

"I see you have a couple of Sioux working for you," he stated, frowning toward the men off in the field cutting hay. "Be careful. We have had a rash of livestock gone missing in the area."

"I thank you for your concern, Captain. They seem to be good workers." Her tone was short.

A faint frown of irritation crossed his face. "I am not suggesting your Indians are responsible. I just wanted to warn you."

"They are not my Indians, but thank you for the warning." Her tone was polite, but blunt.

Nielson looked at Ellie for several seconds without saying a word. She wasn't certain what was going through his head. At last he said, "I need to be leaving now."

Ellie nodded her head at him. "Good-bye."

He turned his horse abruptly and rode off without looking back.

Both Indians proved to be worth their pay. By the end of fall, they had stocked up enough feed for the winter. A routine had been established; Ellie brought breakfast to the barn, watered and fed the animals while the men ate, and then returned to the house with the empty plates. Lela brought lunch to them. The men frequently showed up at the house with fish, wild game, or fowl that they had hunted. Ellie fed the animals and the men the late afternoon meal. However, Lela accompanied her, insisting that she needed help carrying the dinners to the bunk house.

As the weather became colder, to Ellie's relief, she realized that the barn seemed to be warmer than the previous year. Between the stone addition on the windward side and the additional body heat from so many more animals, the temperature stayed warm enough that she could spend more time handling the weanlings. Spending more time in the barn also gave her the opportunity to get to know the men better and, as a result, become more comfortable with them.

As the temperatures and snow fell, Lela insisted the men eat in the house. She argued with Ellie that she had eaten with the help in Sheldon and that the food was cold just from the short walk from the house to the barn. Ellie initially gave in for just the noon day meal. She felt more comfortable having men in the house during the daylight hours. Also, she did not want them to end up spending their time in the house. She had become accustomed to the privacy.

The first meal was awkward. Neither of the men had grown up in the white man's culture, even though they spoke excellent English. They were accustomed to sitting on the ground or on logs, not chairs. Their usual grace evaporated while sitting at the table. They ate with their fingers or with a spoon. Rather than cutting their meat on their plates and using a fork to bring it to their mouths, they picked up the slices of roasted venison, biting into them. If their fingers were greasy, they wiped them on their clothing or their skin. Ellie tried not to stare, but Lela could not stop herself.

"The food is very good. You are good cooks. Your husbands must have been happy fat men," He Runs Along stated, smiling as he bit into a warm biscuit.

"Thank you, Runs Along. I am so glad you are enjoying the food. And you, Little Dog? Is everything to your liking?" Ellie asked his companion.

Little Dog belched loudly, and smiled, nodding his head. "It is very good food. You have done very well. The deer meat is cooked just right."

"Little Dog, ain't you never learned 'bout usin' forks and napkins? Folks doan pick dey food up wit dey fingers an' jist chaw on it. Ya s'posed ta cut it up on da plate, lack dis." Lela demonstrated holding the fork and knife and slicing the piece of meat. She used the fork to convey it to her mouth, slipping it in, and then chewing with her mouth closed.

Little Dog and Runs Along both tried to copy what she had done. Runs Along managed to fling a piece of roast across the table, striking Ellie in the face. Runs Along was embarrassed when Little Dog began laughing at him. He said something in Lakota that seemed to be rude, but made Little Dog laugh even harder. Runs Along pointed at his friend and indicated that he should try the trick himself. Little Dog held the fork awkwardly, but managed to get the meat cut. But he stabbed the piece he had cut as if he were trying to kill an enemy. In trying to convey the food to his mouth, he realized he had the fork going in the wrong direction, but could not quite figure out what was wrong. Despite that, he persevered and delivered the meat to his mouth. He smiled broadly as he chewed.

In response to his friend's success, Runs Along stated, "A man could starve to death trying to feed himself in this way." He dropped his fork in disgust and picked up the slice of meat once more. He smiled happily as he chewed away at the big chunk.

Little Dog informed them that he was interested in learning more about the white man's culture. He explained that his father was a white man, but he had grown up with his mother's people. He added he had always wanted to know and understand more about his father, but because he looked like his mother, no one ever seemed willing to teach him.

Ellie had been trying to hold back her laughter at his behavior. However, she was touched by his story. She asked him if he would like to learn how to read. He was excited about the possibility, but insisted he do something in exchange. They agreed that he would feed and water the animals over the winter.

CHAPTER 50

The next morning, Little Dog came to the house with a bucket of fresh milk. He had fed the animals and milked the cow. Lela took the bucket and told him to get his friend for breakfast. After they ate, he stayed for his first reading lesson. Runs Along grumbled and quickly left.

Over the winter, Ellie watched the romance progress between Lela and Little Dog. She was pleased to see the respect that the man showed her friend and the changes that Lela showed. She even felt a bit jealous when Little Dog stood outside of the house in the evening and played his flute for Lela while she tried to go to sleep. Ellie listened to the lovely, exotic music that seemed to be accompanied by the wind rather than being hindered by it. When Lela would go out to him, Little Dog would drape his blanket over both their heads and they would sit or stand for hours huddled together under the cover. Ellie speculated on what happened under there, but never asked.

When spring of 1870 arrived, the two announced that they were going to establish their own home. Lela proudly stated that she was a citizen and could register their intent to homestead. Ellie was happy for her friend, but she realized that she was going to be totally alone for the first time in her life.

Lela and Little Dog built a one room sod house on land about two miles south of Ellie's property and began clearing a field to plant. Ellie's old friends were now tied up with their own work on their own land. Other than an occasional visit or invitation, they had little time for her. She needed to hire regular help. The summer passed quickly; her days were spent working the gardens, handling the young horses, and directing the hands; her nights were spent working on the farm accounts and the lineages of the horses. She had little time to think about herself or her life. She fell into bed exhausted every night.

When winter arrived, Ellie found out what it meant to be alone. She cooked for the couple of hired men who stayed on; she re-read the few books she had; she sewed; she waited for spring. When it finally came, the outdoor work began all over again. While the year before there had only been one foal, this year she had the excitement of five mares foaling. Two of the men from the previous year returned, looking for work. She found two more for a total of six hired hands. In August, Lela gave birth to a baby boy. Ellie, Becky, and Lily took turns helping her. At the beginning of winter, Ellie tried to get out more often visiting her neighbors. She hated being alone all the time and she was not looking forward to being confined to the cabin once the snows became too deep and the temperatures too cold. Lela understood Ellie's sorrow. She tried to encourage her to look for a man. Ellie listened politely as Lela shared the joy of motherhood and suggested that, while Ellie might not find a man like Daniel to love, she could have a decent man and be able to give her love to their children.

Captain Nielson came by before Christmas with another book for Ellie. She sincerely appreciated the attention he showed her, the news, and conversation, but she had no interest in him and felt it only fair to let him know. Ellie cried after he left, but her tears had nothing to do with Captain Nielson.

That spring, Ellie finally had some horses to sell. She had five three year olds and the colts were old enough to breed. She decided to sell the mare that had not produced, two of the three year olds that she had the men geld, and one of the three year old fillies. The other two fillies she would keep on to extend her breeding stock. The captain did not return, but another officer from Fort Ransom came by. The lieutenant reported that a friend had told him she had horses equal to General Lee's famous mount, Traveller. Ellie explained about the American Saddlebreds that she was raising, touting their versatility and smooth ride. She enjoyed showing off her livestock and sold him one of the geldings for more than she expected. After he left, she realized that these mid-level and junior officers would be her best customers. They wanted well broken animals that would make them look strong and important. Additionally, they had regular pay and few places to spend it.

More officers came looking for horses over the next few weeks. Some were all business, others rude, and some flirtatious. Ellie held her tongue; this was business. She refused to be taken and eventually sold all four. While it would be years before she could sell enough horses to be making a profit, it felt good to replenish her coffers some. The summer fled by. When she stocked up for the winter, she treated herself to some fabrics to make gifts and a new dress. She hoped to keep herself busy during the winter months of confinement. Winter passed slowly. While her hands kept busy, her mind wandered, reminiscing about Whispering Oaks, Daniel, and what could have been.

In the spring of 1873, it had been five years since she had registered her intent to homestead. She and Nathaniel rode to Abercrombie, stabled the horses, and took the paddlewheel north to Fargo to file their claims and obtain their deeds. As they walked out of the claims office, deeds in hand, she felt triumphant. She had succeeded. Nathaniel was excited and beaming. She shared his joy and thought back to a time when she thought such things would be impossible for the Negroes her family had owned.

She now truly felt established as a resident of North Dakota. It was time to write home. Before this she was afraid she might fail and, if she did, she did not want her family to know. She bought some paper and sat down to write Emmy. She was the only one she would want to hear back from anyway. Any important news of the farm or Suzanne, Emmy would tell her. She told of their struggles and the successes. She did not mention her loneliness, but asked about everyone back east. She explained that the mails were not yet well established, but if she wrote back in care of Mulcayhee's General Store in Abercrombie, North Dakota, she would eventually receive it. She posted the letter, hoping it would find everyone well. It had been six years, since she had left home. On the trip back to Whispering Creek, her excitement faded as she wondered whether Emmy or Suzanne had any children. She was thirty-two years old with no children and no prospects of ever having any. She had given Lela's advice consideration, but recognized she was not one to compromise. She realized if Ted had lived they would have been miserable together. She laughed to herself; Daniel had spoiled her. She could no longer accept anyone less. She would love to have a partner, a companion, someone to lean on and hold her. But, she would not allow someone into her life whom she could not love the way she had loved him. There were more than enough men to choose from in the territory and few available women. Even with the hard work, sun, wind, and cold taking its toll, aging her, she could have someone if she wanted. She cringed at the thought of anyone else touching her. No, she would rather be miserable and alone.

Ellie found herself making excuses to go into Abercrombie more often. She was hoping for a response from home. While no letter had arrived, she discovered a copy of the Bismarck Tribune. She was thrilled to have a newspaper to read that talked about the issues important to the residents of North Dakota. She asked Mr. Mulcayhee to save a copy of every issue he received. She would pick them up each trip into town. She smiled to herself; she'd have reading material stocked up for the winter. She was also pleased to discover that the railroad now went all the way to Bismarck. This would improve the mails and the availability of numerous products. The following year, The Fargo Express came out. Ellie had Mr. Mulcayhee save them for her, too. The newspaper covered the Red River Valley more closely.

Ellie wrote Emmy again; when she still received no response, she broke down and wrote to Suzanne. While Emmy and her husband might have left Savannah, Whispering Oaks still belonged to Suzanne and she would be there at least part of the year.

The years continued to pass. The only thing that seemed any different for Ellie was the years of drought. They followed cold, dry winters. While it was pleasant not to have as much snow, she had learned it would result in a summer with a dry well. Lugging buckets of water from the creek up the hill, no matter that it was a small a hill, was slow and time consuming.

As time went by, there was still no response from home. She stayed involved with her neighbors and old friends. She attended Jason's and later Lily's weddings. She watched their children grow. By 1881, the railroad had made it to the Montana border. More people had settled in the area. With the success of a couple of bonanza farms, those huge farms created by the sale of acreage by the Northern Pacific Railroad to its investors to cover its debt, she had new customers that wanted the best horses. A few of the women tried to introduce her to men. She realized she had been right to lie and say she was a widow, when one of the women stated that, "As a widow, you are still marriageable. It is not as though you have never been married. That would scare off any decent man." She understood it would have scared off the women, too.

Lela and Becky remained close to Ellie, visiting as often as they could, and including her in their family gatherings, but they both worried about her being alone. None of them were young anymore, and they reminded her of that one pleasant fall day as she sat with them in the yard, watching the butterflies float over the last of the season's blooming flowers.

"You ain't gittin' any younger o' prettier, ya know," Lela told her. "Now, you is still a fine lookin' woman, even ef ya is a bit skinny an' mo' wrinkled dan ya was twenny years ago. Ya could still git a man ta warm ya covers. Ah bet Little Dog could find ya a good lookin' Injun man. Ah kin tell ya dey makes good husbands an' real good lovers." She smiled and nudged Ellie with her elbow. All three of the women laughed, and Ellie swatted at Lela playfully.

"Do not worry about how warm my blankets are! I have not gotten frostbite yet, and I have been through enough of these Dakota winters without a man in my bed to know I can continue to survive them. Tend to your own knitting!" Ellie told her, but smiled to take the sting out of her words.

"We all worry 'bout ya, out here all alone, Ellie. Who gonna hep ya when ya gits old? Sho ya kin do it now, but what about when ya gits all bent an' gnarly lack an ole oak tree? Ya needs ta fine a man ta be a hep ta ya, too," Becky stated, no smile hiding her true concern for her longtime friend.

Ellie reached out and patted Becky's arm as it rested on the wicker chair. She gave her friend a sad smile and just shook her head. Ellie had long since given up on ever loving again. Even if a suitable man came into her life, she would feel she was cheating on Daniel. She leaned back in her chair, looking up into the broad blue sky, and watched a red tailed hawk circle and swoop toward its prey. Life didn't always turn out as one had expected.

Ellie knew that she would end her days on Whispering Creek Ranch alone. There was no one else with whom she wanted to share it. No one had ever even piqued her interest since Daniel. However, she decided that she did need to make preparation for her future and the future of her land. In response to their conversation, she drew up a will leaving everything she had to the heirs of her sister Suzanne.

Christmas of 1894 was especially difficult for Ellie. She chastised herself that she had what she wanted and had striven for. She remembered having told her mother so many years ago that all she needed was to raise horses, and how she would rather be alone than to settle. That was before she had become engaged to Ted. She was sad her mother had not lived to meet Daniel or to know she had found happiness, even if it had only been for the one year they had been together. She had bought or made special gifts for all the children and grandchildren of her friends. She had expected to enjoy their excitement, but instead she was reminded of how alone she was.

As winter passed, the cold weather seemed to make her stiff and uncomfortable. She was relieved once the weather started to warm. She found excuses to stop while planting the vegetable garden. For the first time since the hot summers of Sheldon, she was tiring before she finished her work. She was surprised when the well went dry in September.

It was 1895, she was fifty-four years old, and the hired hands were in the fields cutting the last hay of the season. She had been getting short of breath carrying the buckets up even the smallest incline, and sometimes there was a tight band of pressure around her arm afterward. Nonetheless, she was determined to remain independent. She needed the water to cook the evening meal. She could not wait for someone to return nor would she ride a horse out to the fields to ask for help. She took two empty buckets and went to the creek. It was not that low and she thought how there must be a problem with the well. She filled the buckets and started back toward the house. Before she had gone very far, she had a shooting pain in her left arm causing her to drop the bucket. Frustrated, she put the other bucket down and went back to the creek with the one she had dropped. After refilling it, she continued back up the hill. She could not understand why the pain kept getting worse. Her breathing became labored and, as she reached the other bucket, she collapsed. She rolled onto her back, clutching her chest, the sky seemed to darken as she thought:

I am alone with no one to help.

CHAPTER 51

"I am sorry I was so long on the phone," June stated. When Jillian did not respond, she moved closer. "Miss, are you all right?"

Jillian saw a shadowy figure behind her. She was confused by the setting in which she found herself and exhausted by the journey that she had just experienced. All she could think to say was, "Lela?"

June was startled by her response and walked closer, moving into the sunlight from the window. "What? Did you just call me Lela?"

"I'm sorry?" Jillian was still feeling confused and could not remember this woman's name. She turned around to face the other woman, somehow expecting to see a black woman standing there.

June cocked her head to the side and extended her hand toward Jillian. "How did you know about Lela? When I was a little girl, I used to tell everyone that was my name."

Jillian leaned back, shaking her head. "I don't know."

"My mother still tells the story of how I would ask her if she remembered when I had dark skin and was called Lela." June appeared to be lost in memories of her childhood.

Jillian started to get up, but the woman stopped her. "You better sit for another moment. You look terribly pale."

Jillian sat, still cradling the brush in her hand. She looked at it more closely, brushing her fingers over the bristles. "It is amazing that it is still here."

June moved to the side of the vanity, touching the other pieces. "I am glad you came looking for them. The set really belongs together."

"Did you find the letters behind the baseboard?" Jillian was still dazed and did not realize that her question would seem strange.

"What letters?" June asked, looking at her quizzically.

Jillian stood and walked to the spot where Ellie had hidden Ted's letters. She pointed. "Right here; there was a cookie can."

Seeing the matching mirror for the first time and being called Lela by a complete stranger had made June more curious than suspicious. "Let me get a screwdriver." She was back in no time to find Jillian returning the brush to the dressing table, next to the comb and mirror. She slid the screwdriver behind the baseboard and worked it loose. Jillian watched, afraid there would be nothing there. June finally pulled it off. "There is a cookie can in here!"

"It's full of letters." Jillian was relieved that she was not crazy. It was the first real proof she had that the memories were real and not just a fantasy.

June carried the can to the bed and opened it. "How did you know about the letters?"

"You don't know me; you'll think I'm crazy." She looked down, hesitating. "Those letters are between Ellie Peters and Ted Campbell. This used to be Ellie's room."

"Charlotte Peters Hamilton wrote about Ellie and Daniel. It was a sad story. But she never said anything about a Ted." June looked at the letters. "How did you know about Ellie?"

Jillian sighed; she did not know where to begin. "Remember, you said as soon as you saw this place you had to have it, and that somehow you knew this room had always looked this way?"

June nodded.

"The old lady was right. There were slaves here. One of them was called Lela."

June gasped. "Charlotte referred to a woman named Lela in North Dakota in her journal. Wait until I tell my husband. He thinks I'm crazy."

Jillian laughed with relief at June's response. "You're not any crazier than I am."

June waved the can gently. "You still haven't told me how you know all of this."

Once again, Jillian hesitated, fearing the other woman's response to what she was about to say. "I believe...I was Ellie."

It was June's turn to hesitate. She looked at the stranger standing in her home for several seconds, and then handed Jillian the can of letters. "I believe these are yours."

She accepted the can and gently opened one of the letters. She laughed. "Ted really was a scoundrel."

June smiled, but was more interested in the part of the history she knew about. "What about Daniel?"

"I don't understand how he came to own the farm. I thought he died in the war." Jillian wrinkled her brow, trying to make the connection from her own recovered memories.

June nodded, understanding Jillian's confusion. "Charlotte wrote the story that Daniel told her." She slipped her hand under Jillian's arm. "Come. It's in my room."

Jillian stood and allowed June to lead her.

June looked back at the silver items on the vanity. "Don't you want your mirror and the rest of the set?"

Jillian glanced back at it. Sighing, she said, "No. It belongs here. But I would like to keep the letters." June nodded and led the way to the master bedroom.

There had been some changes to the room. It now opened into one of the old guest rooms that had been converted into a master bathroom and walk-in closet. June noticed Jillian looking at the change. "I've become..." June began to explain, or maybe excuse what she had done.

Jillian patted her hand reassuringly. "I would have done the same thing."

June took the journal gently out of her night stand drawer. As she turned the pages, she explained, "Charlotte was Suzanne's daughter. After the family received a telegram that Ellie had died, she discovered that she had been left a farm in North Dakota. Daniel traveled with her to claim her property. On the trip, he told her their story." She handed the book to Jillian, opened to the beginning of the trip.

Jillian's hands were shaking as she took the book. She wanted desperately to know what had happened to Daniel; she wanted to know if he loved her and why he had not returned. She corrected her own thoughts. Why it took him so long to return? Why did he wait until she was dead to go to North Dakota? She was afraid of the answers she might find. She stroked her fingers over the aged leather cover.

"May I read your letters?" June asked.

Jillian nodded and handed her the cookie can. The two women sat side by side on the bed carefully handling the fragile paper each of them examined.

On the train ride out to North Dakota, Charlotte was able to corner Mr. Proctor about Ellie. It was apparent from her writing that she knew little of her aunt and did not understand why a woman she had never met would give her a horse farm. If it had not been for her cousin Emmy, she would have known nothing of her. Her parents refused to hear the name and blamed Ellie for losing the farm to Mr. Proctor. And he became so sad whenever she had asked about her aunt; she quickly learned not to ask. He had been kind to her, made her laugh, and allowed her family to remain in their home. She did not want to hurt him, but she had to have answers.

Jillian continued to read the account of Daniel's description of Ellie and of their relationship. With the details Charlotte relayed, Jillian could almost hear Daniel's voice in the telling. Her eyes brimmed with tears as he proclaimed his love for Ellie. Charlotte realized the trip to North Dakota was as much for him to get answers as to accompany her. He blamed himself for waiting so long to return and questioned Ellie's love for him. However, he knew the depth of Ellie's love for Whispering Oaks and her horses, and did not understand why she had left. Emmy and Christopher had given him hints and claimed she had loved him. He had waited, believing she would someday return to her home. By the time they got off the train in North Dakota, Charlotte reported that she understood why Ellie would will her property to the family, but she could not understand why Aunt Ellie had not given anything to her own sister.

Charlotte continued to describe the journey. They stayed in Fargo and hired a carriage the next morning to take them to Whispering Creek Ranch. She gave a detailed account of the landscape. It was the end of September, only three weeks since Ellie had died. She continued by describing the charm and modesty of the barns and house. She stated how sad and touching it was when she caught Mr. Proctor embracing Ellie's pillow, smelling it as if it were a rose. They were not in the house long before one of the men came up from the barn. He seemed to be expecting them. Charlotte registered the shock of both herself and Mr. Proctor when the man stated, "You must be Mrs. Proctor's niece." She could barely hear him as the stranger continued to speak of the kindness and generosity of his employer.

Jillian stopped reading for a moment. She found herself blushing. As Ellie, she had never expected Daniel or her family to find out about the lie she had been living.

June noticed that the woman had stopped and looked over to see where she was in Charlotte's journal. "I hope you can tell me more about the people who built and lived in this house. But you look as if you could use a break."

Jillian nodded, "I still have so many questions."

June nodded her head toward the door. "Come downstairs." Jillian started to hand the journal back to June.

"No, bring it with you." June held the cookie can close to her, obviously not ready to give it up.

Jillian followed her down the back stairs to the kitchen. June refilled their iced tea glasses and they sipped in silence. Jillian had to face her fears and know the truth. She opened the book to where she'd left off and continued to read.

Charlotte reported that the workman started up the stove, also informing them that Mr. and Mrs. Peters had been running everything since Ellie had died and that Mrs. Peters would be there soon to start the evening meal for the workmen. After the farmhand left, it was the first she saw Daniel smile since they had arrived.

"Your aunt was always full of surprises."

Charlotte's frustration that he would explain no further was apparent. She described her surprise when a slender, slightly stooped, Negro woman with gray around the temples introduced herself as Mrs. Peters. She wrote, *Mr. Proctor, ever the gentleman, stood immediately. The two stared at each other. You could not imagine my shock when the woman blurted out, "Daniel, 'member me? Ah's Becky, Nathaniel's wife." They actually embraced.*

Jillian giggled, thinking how any daughter of Suzanne and Matthew would be confused to see such an emotional interaction between a white man and a black woman. She continued reading.

The journal indicated that she had wondered what he was getting them into when he accepted her invitation to dinner, but it did not surprise her. After all, she had heard her parents call him a Carpetbagger enough times behind his back. She added, however, that he probably knew in that not much got by him.

In the next section, Charlotte bemoaned the lack of amenities and the chill in the air as the sun began to set. Then she wrote, *I expected, as Ellie's niece, to be the guest of honor at the Peters' home, but all the attention was directed toward Mr. Proctor. He was greeted as a long lost friend.* She began to wonder why she had only heard him called Mr. Proctor when everyone here called him by his given name. *These people had obviously been slaves owned by my family, yet they treated him and he them as equals. The lighthearted banter that seemed so natural to them continued until the end of the night.*

Daniel asked Nathanial Peters where Ellie was resting. My confusion mounted when Becky and Nathanial looked at one another as if they did not want to tell him. Finally, the woman told her husband to tell. I could not imagine what the problem could be, especially when they first stated she was on top of the hill behind the house. But they both seemed so uncomfortable. Then Nathanial added, "She's buried next ta two hosses: Princess an' yo ole geldin'." My first reaction was that my aunt may have been mad. I had never known Mr. Proctor to be peculiar, but when he burst out laughing and stated, "That would be just like Ellie." I questioned his sanity, too.

Charlotte still had not understood the depth of Daniel's feelings until she heard him go out the back door with a lantern in hand. *At first, I thought he was on his way to take care of personal necessities, until I saw the light going up the hill. I wrapped myself up in a blanket and, not wanting to lose sight of his light, ran up the hill behind him in my bare feet. I saw him standing with the lantern on the ground. I could hear his voice, but I could not make out his words. When he suddenly fell to the ground, I became fearful for his health and started to approach. However, I stopped when I realized he was lying on Ellie's grave, sobbing. No one other than you, dear journal, shall hear of his pain.*

Jillian wiped her eyes before turning the page to the next day's entry.

Charlotte wrote, *I believe everyone in this state is a lunatic. We never should have admitted them to the Union. The Peters had stated that Mrs. Little Dog Running had been keeping the books, and had the will, and all the important papers. I should have known better; however, I was expecting an Indian woman. Instead, a tall Negro woman opened the door. Without even looking at us, she invited us inside. When she did look at me, she started shaking her head. "Ya look jist lack yo Grandma Charlotte."*

I never knew a Negro could turn white, especially one as dark as any I had ever seen; but when she looked at Mr. Proctor, it was as if she had seen a ghost and I suppose for her she had. When she blurted out, "You dead! Dead!" It was the least of my surprises. Mr. Proctor laughed and, with that so familiar smirk, responded, "I am sure plenty wish I were, but Lela, I assure you I am quite alive."

I had never seen an old woman move so fast, so you can just imagine my amazement when she lunged across the room and started flailing her arms at Mr. Proctor, screaming, "If ya had been dere, she wouldn't have died!" He stood his ground, allowing her to hit him until she started to calm down. He actually held her while she cried. His only reaction was to say, "I am sorry. I am so sorry. You know I loved her."

My interests were not addressed at all that day. However, the things I learned about my family, love, and sacrifice were more important than taking possession of my inheritance. The questions those two had for one another spanned a lifetime. It had been more than thirty years since they had seen one another. As a spectator, I learned the truth. We sat at the table in awkward silence as Lela prepared the tea. She set the tea before Daniel, prepared the way he always takes it. While putting a cup before me, she asked him about Lottie.

I will try to repeat their conversation as closely as I can remember it. "Your grandmother passed peacefully, three years ago." He sipped his tea.

"We thought ya was dead. Where was ya all does years? When ya din't come back, we was sho ya was dead." The old woman just stared at Mr. Proctor, shaking her head.

Mr. Proctor looked so extremely sad as he explained, *"I had responsibilities to attend to first."*

"What respons'bilty? What respons'bilty greater dan Ellie? Ya knew she was waitin'!" she raged at him, tears slipping down her cheeks.

"I told her I would go home to my family, and that it would take awhile before I could be with her."

"Months ya said. Two years da war had ended afore we lef'."

"My brother had died during the war. When I arrived home, my father was on his death bed. I needed to let my mother grieve before sending her to my sister's in New Jersey and selling the farm for her."

Lela stared coldly at Mr. Proctor. *"Had ya forgotten how ta write?"*

Mr. Proctor looked down into his tea cup, his face lined with the pain of the choices he had made and now regretted. *"Time just went by, a month turned into a year. I gave all the money from the farm to my mother. I could not show up at Ellie's doorstep with nothing in my pocket. She had cared for me once; I could not expect to live off of her."*

She looked at him with the weight of all those years of grief and hurt in her eyes. *"You men is all fools! We thought ya was dead. Ya should a writ!"*

He looked up at her, the tears beginning to fill his eyes as well. *"I thought of it many times. But then...I could not tell her when I would be there. I wanted to have good news."*

"Three words! Three words! 'I is alive!' Dat would a been good news enough."

"I promised I would not die. I promised I would come back," he proclaimed in his defense.

Lela shook her head, denying him that comfort. *"Ya knowed 'bout all da people dat died on her."*

Mr. Proctor's hurt and grief rose up in rebellion. *"She promised to wait. She promised not to marry anyone else."*

"She waited. She neva knowed no udder man. Plenty dat wanted her. She say it would be cheatin' on ya. Ah axed her, 'How ya cheat on a dead man?' She jist cry an' cry."

Imagine my shock. Had they really known each other? Was that why my aunt called herself Mrs. Proctor? Had they secretly married?

"Lela, why did she leave?"

"Ever'body was dead and den does two...." She looked at me. I am sure she would have preferred that I leave. However, I had never heard a Negro talk to any white man the way she did, and I was sure she knew more about my family than anyone, or at least anyone would willingly tell.

"Why ya wait 'til she was dead ta come?"

Mr. Proctor refused to be distracted from his question. "Do not change the subject!"

Lela shook her head vehemently. "Answer me!"

He glared at her, obviously debating whether to insist on his answer or give in to her demand. Then he sighed heavily and capitulated. "I did not know where she was. I could not believe she would never come home."

Lela's forehead creased with confusion. "She wrote Emmy in Savannah an' Suzanne at Whispering Oaks!"

I could not figure out why she would write to our cousin in Savannah. Everyone knew she lived in Atlanta.

"Damn her!" *He slammed his fist against the rough wood of the table, rattling the dishes, and pushed himself away from the table.*

Lela drew herself up very straight and stiff. I felt as if the wrath of God were about to descend upon us. "Don' ya use dat talk wid me 'bout Ellie!" *She compressed her lips into a thin, angry line.*

Even I knew that was not who he was referring to, but rather my mother. I watched Mr. Proctor pace the room. I had thought he was angry until I saw him wipe away the tears. I could not imagine my poor mother being so cruel if she had known of their romance.

"What did they do to my beautiful Ellie?" *he asked, looking at the old woman.*

"She din't complain when dey stole; she jist worked harder ta replace it. But dey went against her ever' step o' da way. Marster Hamilton try ta hit Lily. He bred dat horse a his to da mares. Dey try ta take da farm. Dere was nothin' lef ta stay fo. Why ya think we all lef' wit her? Still she try ta protec' dat woman. He want ta buy her out, but wit his habits an' all, he'd a lost it."

Mr. Proctor made a sad laughing sound. "They lost it anyway."

Lela stared at him, appalled. "Oh no! Dat would a broke her heart agin."

"I bought it for the taxes. I wanted her to have it when she came home..." *He turned to look at Lela.* " I want to take her home."

"Dis her home now. She work hard ta make it her home. Ya would a been proud a her. She want ta stay here wit dem two hosses. She talk ta dat ole hoss a ya's as ef it was you. Ya gonna take da hosses, too?"

Mr. Proctor seemed to slump under a great weight. "Oh, Lela, I made a mess of things."

"Ya sho did! But it seem lack ya had some hep...jist lack when ya had ta leave da fust time!"

The woman actually glared at me as if I had done something terrible. My parents had accepted Mr. Proctor's charity; they must have known it was for Aunt Ellie. Were they afraid that, if she came back, she would throw them out? She did not seem to be that kind of woman. Why did they dislike each other so? I could not hold back any longer. "Maybe my mother did not get any letter. Why would she not tell Mr. Proctor if she knew where Aunt Ellie was?"

"Ah's sorry chile, but yo mother was a hateful thing. She was allas jealous o' Ellie since she was little. An' yo' father was a cruel, selfish man. Dere. Ya had ta hear it."

Jillian stopped reading and looked at June. "Poor Charlotte! June, are you still so out spoken? Charlotte did not need to know how terrible her parents were. She seemed like a nice girl."

"Yes, I am, and that girl needed to know. Years later, it saved her. Her father wanted her to mortgage the farm to give him money in his old age, but she remembered that conversation and she didn't do it. She wrote about it again years later."

"It wasn't all his fault. I should have written more letters. I should have…I should have tried harder." Jillian wiped her eyes, and then read on.

"I still do not understand. My Ellie was a fighter. She would have won. If only she had stayed..."

"Daniel, she had loss too much. Dere was too many mem'ries. Thinkin' ya was dead, she couldn't bare da mem'ries."

Mr. Proctor seemed to consider all that he had learned. Then he turned to me and said, "Charlotte, you can stay, but your parents will be leaving as soon as I get back."

I was shocked at this turn of events. How could I stay if my parents had nowhere to go? But how could I leave the only home I had ever known? I certainly do not have my Aunt's strength.

"No, Daniel! Ellie could no longer live wit Suzanne an' Matthew. But it was important dat Suzanne always have a home. Ya cain't turn Suzanne out."

"Mrs. Little Dog Barking, why did my aunt leave everything to me and not to my mother?"

"She hoped the children would be ole enough ta keep Whispering Oaks safe from Matthew and take care of Suzanne."

"And Whispering Creek?"

"Ya don't have ta keep it. She didn't know how many chillen yo mama had. You's jist one. Ya cain't run dem both."

I have to admire my aunt's courage and sense of family. I have always missed the commitment to one another that I have seen my cousins' share. I may have never known Aunt Ellie, but somehow I now feel it from her. I missed much of what they said after that. I became too involved in my own thoughts. I do not know how I will face my parents when we get back. I do know, if it is acceptable to Mr. Proctor, I would like to start calling him, 'Uncle Daniel'.

Jillian stopped reading. She was curious about Charlotte and Daniel. However, she already knew that Daniel died ten years later and had willed the farm to Charlotte. Her most important questions had been answered. She would need time to process all that she had learned and was acutely aware that she was not really in her own kitchen. She looked over at June, who was refolding one of Ted's letters. "Thank you. Charlotte answered many of my questions."

June smiled at her. "I hoped it would help. Would you mind answering some of mine?"

Jillian opened her arms. "Ask away!"

"Who was Ted and what happened to him?"

"Ted and Ellie were good friends until they were pushed together by their families..." Jillian began explaining.

The two women fell into conversation about their lives then and more recent events. There was a natural flow to their understanding and comfort with one another. The passing of time had no apparent meaning until June's husband walked in, followed by a sulky pre-teen girl and a teenage boy. June invited her to stay for dinner, but Jillian refused, stating she had a lot to review. June understood; she also had more reading and thinking to do. Jillian gave her a business card and promised to return before flying back to Ohio. She left the mirror and the letters, knowing that June would want to show her husband the letters. She borrowed the journal; she needed to hear about the rest of Daniel's life.

CHAPTER 52

Jillian drove back to the Rhett House. She had missed the cocktail hour, but was in no mood to socialize. She walked down to the waterfront, stopping for a sandwich to go. She sat on a rocking bench along the walkway. The breeze off the water was a bit chilly, but she didn't mind. After a North Dakota winter, this was absolute paradise.

She nibbled on her sandwich, only eating half before rewrapping it. She sat peacefully watching the reflected lights glimmer off the gently lapping water. She smiled, feeling content, recognizing that for the first time in her life she was alone without distraction and did not feel lonely. She started laughing; she wasn't crazy. Wait until she brought Ted's letters back and showed them to Anna and Sally. She wasn't going to settle for Peter. He was a good person; however, not for her. She had plenty to thank him for. She would need to let him know that their relationship was not going to grow. Ellie had been right not to settle, but she did not appreciate the love she had from her friends. Maybe if she had not become estranged from her family, or had so many years of hearing she needed a man, she would not have had to feel so alone.

The word grief came to mind. Grief; the sadness was grief. Ellie had started to grieve the loss of Ted, but once her father died, she could no longer allow herself the luxury. She lost everyone, her father, brother, mother, and Mama Noli. In their estrangement and failure to respond to her letters, she lost the remainder of her family, Suzanne and Emmy. Although Lela remained her friend, their relationship could never be the same after Lela had her own family. She had lost her home and way of life. It was not until she was completely alone and no longer needing to struggle to survive that she was able to feel the greatest loss of all: Daniel, and the hopes and dreams for a future with him.

The tears flowed down Jillian's cheeks as she realized that the goals of independence and professional and financial success she shared with Ellie, they had both achieved. Yet, she continued to carry Ellie's feelings of emptiness. Her mother's shared belief with Ellie's mother that she needed a man to survive and be safe, reminded her spirit of the pain of Ellie's loneliness. For the first time in her life, she felt she understood the source of it. She stood to walk back to the Rhett House, hoping she'd be able now to figure out what to do about it.

She stopped by the kitchen and had a gooey, chocolate brownie and two cups of coffee. She had decided to stay up and read the rest of Charlotte's journal. She barely heard the other guests' conversation and excused herself early. She wanted to know what had happened to Daniel and the rest of her family.

Jillian settled into bed with the delicate book. Having put the North Dakota farm up for sale, Daniel and Charlotte took the train back to South Carolina, taking Ellie's dog and the best of her horses with them. She reported watching Daniel shut down as they approached home. *"It was almost as if a wall went down over his eyes. Ellie's dog became his only companion."*

Charlotte married a year later; her husband, Jonathan, was a lover of fine horses and saw the potential in the horses they had brought back from North Dakota. As her husband took on a stronger role and turned to Daniel for advice, the tension between Suzanne and Matthew and the rest of the household increased. After Charlotte's first child was born, Suzanne complained incessantly that the baby was disturbing her sleep. Jonathan and Matthew nearly came to blows, resulting in Suzanne and Matthew leaving to visit Emmy in Atlanta. They never returned to the farm.

She reported that, once Suzanne and Matthew left the house, the wall over Daniel's eyes came down, but the old spark was gone. He seemed to enjoy Charlotte's two children and the horses, but after Ellie's dog died, he appeared to give up his own life. He died quietly in his sleep one winter night. His will stated that he had bought and saved the farm for Ellie and that he was following her wishes by leaving everything to Charlotte.

Jillian realized that Daniel had never married or had any children. Due to his lack of communication and Ellie's impatience, the two lived solitary lives, missing the love, friendship, and family that had been so important to both of them.

That night she dreamed of being held in loving arms and staring into Daniel's eyes.

The next day, Jillian drove back to Whispering Oaks. She was no longer fearful of what she might discover. Other emotions arose on the way; there was still sadness for a lost love, anticipation of seeing June again, and the comfort of being home.

June greeted her as an old friend. They discussed what each had learned from their reading. Jillian sadly returned the journal, and offered the broken mirror to June to complete her set. June gave her a bag to wrap the cookie can and letters in to be certain they stayed dry and protected. They said their good-byes with promises to keep in touch. Jillian returned to the Rhett House and packed. The next day she returned to Ohio, looking forward to sharing what she had learned with her friends.

Jillian had Sunday to get ready for work. She had plans with Peter, but was not yet exactly sure what to tell him. She begged off, claiming to have too much to do. She then called her parents when she knew they would be at church, leaving a message that she was home. After she hung up, she remembered it was Mother's Day and she would have to go see her later. The next call was to Anna. Without saying hello, Jillian reported, "I have something to show you. Will you be home for a while?"

"Yes…" Anna responded, a question in her inflection.

"I'm on my way." Jillian grabbed the tin can and ran out the front door.

The twenty minute drive seemed like forever. She had proof. She rang the bell, waiting impatiently, holding the can out in front of her.

Anna looked at the eager expression on her friend's face, and then down at the old can. Quirking an eyebrow, she asked, "You came over to show me old cookies?"

"It's proof! Proof of Ellie and Ted! I have so much more to tell you. Wait until Sally sees these letters!" Jillian was literally bouncing with excitement.

Anna put her hands on Jillian's shoulders to calm her. "Slow down. Come in."

Jillian continued talking excitedly, telling her about how she had used the mirror to get into the house and how, as she sat at Ellie's dressing table, she had slid back in time and remembered the rest of Ellie's life. She showed her the letters and explained how they were still behind the baseboard, right where she'd left them. Once she finished, she continued by talking about the immediate connection with June, and about Charlotte's journal. Anna interrupted, "You still have not told me what happened to Ellie!"

Jillian became less rushed and more serious as she told Anna the story of Ellie and Daniel.

Anna had been leaning forward in her eagerness to hear the whole story. With the tension broken, she flopped back against the cushions. "That certainly explains your fear of dying alone."

Jillian nodded her agreement. "Yes, but I'm still not sure what to do about it." She fiddled with the edge of a throw pillow.

Anna considered her response. "Ellie lost everything, except the horses. She passed up opportunities not to be alone. You don't have to do that."

"Ellie refused to compromise. Her mistake was being impatient, not waiting for Daniel. I don't want to settle. If I don't find the right one, well...then I don't. I want a love like Ellie and Daniel had, nothing less."

"I take it Peter is not it?" Anna asked sympathetically.

Jillian gave a small laugh and shook her head sadly. "No, he isn't. I know we haven't been together long enough to really know each other. But, I do know I would rather go to a horse show alone than be with him."

"You may be looking for a fantasy," Anna cautioned her.

Jillian looked calmly at her friend, understanding what she meant. "I don't expect to find Daniel."

"Good! Jillian, don't be unrealistic. Daniel obviously wasn't perfect. No one is." Anna reached out to touch her friend's hand.

Jillian nodded again, looking down at the pillow she continued to play with. "I know, but I certainly can find someone that I can love, who will love me, and share my interests and goals." She raised her eyes to look at her friend. Anna realized that real determination glittered there.

They spoke for a while longer, and then Jillian realized the time. She still had to buy a card and gift for her mother and go out to the house to see her. She gathered up Ted's letters and headed out.

It was a pleasant family gathering, for the most part. Her mother nagged her minimally, pressing for details about how things were going with Peter.

"About Peter, I don't think things are going to go any farther with him. As a matter of fact, I've decided that I'm going to break things off," she told her parents.

"But why?" her mother demanded. "He's a great catch! And he really likes you so much. Don't you enjoy his company? Has he done something wrong?"

"No. He's done nothing wrong," Jillian replied.

"Then why are you doing this? Do you want to spend the rest of your life alone? You know your father and I won't be here forever. And your friends are married and having families of their own. They won't always be available for you." Her mother stared at her as if she had lost her mind.

"We just want to know that you're safe and taken care of, sweetheart," her father added.

"Just because I'm in a relationship or married, for that matter, doesn't mean that I will be safe or taken care of. I think we all saw that with Drake. No, I don't want to be alone the rest of my life, but I am no longer willing to settle for good enough. I want to be in a relationship with a man I love and respect. One who will love and respect me just as much. I deserve that. And if that means that I'm going to be alone for a while, then so be it. I have a career I love. I have my interest in horses that I want to pursue even farther. I'm going to buy my own horse, instead of just borrowing other people's. And if I meet the right man, I will become involved with him. Until then, I'm going to enjoy my life and all the wonderful people in it." She looked at her parents, pleading with them to understand and accept that she had grown and had a better idea of what she needed and wanted from her life. Jillian could see that they weren't completely convinced, but they stopped arguing with her.

Her father hugged her, saying, "We just want whatever will make you happy. You know that."

Her mother sighed and reached out to her daughter. "That really is all we want for you."

Jillian went into her mother's arms and hugged her tightly. "It's all I want for myself, too, Mom."

Not long after that, Jillian said good night and headed home. She resolved that she was going to get more involved with the horses. It was something that she loved now as much as she remembered Ellie loving it. She would go to as many horse shows as she could, and she would find just the right mount for herself.

As she fell asleep she thought, *if I don't find the right mate, I hope I will appreciate the love of my friends and family and remember I can be fulfilled without a man in my life, regardless of what everyone else tells me.*

CHAPTER 53

Jillian had a busy first day back at work. As she drove home, she realized she was pleased to be there again; she enjoyed the work, but no longer needed it as an escape from the rest of her life. She headed for the remote as soon as she walked in the door of her condo, as was her habit; but she put it down without turning on the TV. Today, she felt no need for the background noise to fill her home and drive away the sense of emptiness. No need for another form of escape!

Jillian and Ellie had fought for their independence. Ellie had attained her autonomy; however, she was never able to fully let go of the ingrained belief that she could not succeed without a man at her side. She had allowed her grief and disappointment to overshadow any potential for joy. Jillian was determined not to do it again.

Wednesday night's riding lesson couldn't come soon enough. She brought home a schedule for the next couple of months of horse shows. She tried avoiding Peter's calls; he finally caught her and she agreed to a late dinner on Friday after yoga class.

Jillian met Peter at the restaurant. She was not ready to completely sever the relationship, but by the end of the meal she realized she had no desire to go to bed with him again. He was a pleasant dinner companion and conversationalist; however, they had little in common and she felt she could not share who she really was with him. She watched his eyes glaze over when she spoke of her work or riding. She had learned from him that sex could be pleasant. Now that she had Ellie's memories of Daniel, she understood that making love could be much more. She wasn't sure if it had something to do with being in love or the talents of the lover.

Lana invited Jillian to stay with her at the horse show on Memorial Day weekend. It was the first out of town show since she'd returned from her vacation. She wasn't sure how it would be sharing a room with Lana, but the opportunity to go away and save on expenses was a plus. Although she had been avoiding Peter, he had this long weekend off and wanted to spend it with her. When she turned down his invitation, stating she was going to another horse show, he became annoyed. When he accused her of caring more about horses than their relationship, she did not deny it.

She took Friday off from work and met Lana at the stables. They drove together in Lana's hybrid Escape to Indianapolis. They went straight to the show grounds. Lana didn't have a class until Saturday, but she wanted to check on her horse and see who was going to be there from some of the other stables. Jillian wasn't sure whether to laugh or to admire Lana's single mindedness. She was on the prowl for a new boyfriend. Lana explained to Jillian that she had tried dating men who were not horsemen, but they could never understand or accept her passion. Eventually, the men got fed up or asked her to choose. Jillian understood and told Lana about Peter.

After saying hello to everyone at their stable, they went to the exhibitors' tent. Lana informed her that it was one of the few shows that had an exclusive exhibitors' area that was open throughout the show times and beyond. Between the afternoon and evening classes, they served hors d'oeuvres, wine, and beer for no charge. Saturday night, there would be a live band and cash bar. Every exhibitor received two passes; Lana handed Jillian her spare one. They grabbed a light snack, and then went to the ring to watch the late afternoon classes.

Lana suggested they skip dinner and fill up on hors d'oeuvres. Her primary interest seemed to be looking for available men. She was just as determined to find one for Jillian as herself after having heard about Jillian's last conversation with Peter.

The lines were long, so the two women split up. Lana headed for the food and Jillian for the wine. Jillian was still somewhat uncomfortable alone in large social gatherings, but as she got in line, she stayed focused on the goal of obtaining two glasses of white wine. She didn't pay much attention to the tall man in front of her until the group behind her bumped her into him. He nonchalantly turned around. "If you'd like to get in front of me, you only have to ask."

"I'm sorry. I…" She mumbled, chagrinned. She gestured to the people behind her, having trouble finding her voice.

He motioned for her to get in front of him. "Please. It seems you could use a buffer."

"I guess maybe I could," she laughed. Looking up at him, she was taken by his warm, lopsided smile.

"Are you riding tonight?"

Jillian realized she was staring and tried to look away as nonchalantly as possible. "No, I'm not showing at all."

The man squinted slightly at her, as if trying to remember something, and then said, "You're with Misty Glen Stables, aren't you?"

Jillian's eyes were pulled back to his face. She was surprised and flattered that he would know that much about her. "Yes. How did you know?"

The man shrugged. "Oh, I've seen you around with that crowd."

"Are you riding?" She did not know how to respond to his comment, implying he had noticed her.

He nodded affirmatively and indicated she should move forward. "Open Jumper, tomorrow afternoon."

They had reached the front of the line. Jillian picked up two glasses, handed him one, and then took another.

He raised an eyebrow at her two drinks. "That's one way to avoid the line." There was a question in his tone.

Jillian looked down at her hands, blushed, and quickly explained, "No, this one's for Lana. Do you know her?"

"Yes." There seemed to be a tone of disapproval in his voice.

She was caught off guard by the brevity and brusqueness of his response. She paused awkwardly, but when he didn't continue, she decided she'd better move on. Lifting her glasses to him in a brief salute, she stammered. "Well...good luck tomorrow." She did not know what his tone was about or how to respond to it. She smiled a bit hesitantly at him and turned to go.

His only response was, "Thanks," and then he stood watching her as she left.

Jillian walked away with her heart in her throat. There was something about the lopsided smile, the timbre of his voice, and his sparkling, gray eyes that she found exciting. She didn't even know his name and hadn't thought to tell him hers. She sat down with Lana, still shaken.

"What did Tate Bradley say to you?" Lana demanded when Jillian handed her the glass of wine.

Jillian looked back to where the man had been standing, but he was gone. "Is that his name? Not much. He seems nice." She hoped she'd get a better reaction from Lana than she had from him.

"Tate Bradley? Arrogant maybe, but nice?" Lana humphed her disbelief.

Jillian cocked her head and studied Lana's expression. "He certainly didn't seem arrogant. What's his story?"

Lana took a sip of her wine and shook her head. Swallowing, she stated, "Don't waste your time."

Jillian scowled at her friend. "Well?"

"OK. OK. He is one of the top jumpers, not especially social, but there are a number of guys from his stable that hang out with him."

"Is he a professional?"

"Rider? No, he's kept his amateur status. He makes his money in stocks or something. I think there's family money, too." She shrugged indifferently and took another drink.

Jillian looked back toward the line to see if she could find him again, but he wasn't in sight. "Is he involved with anyone?"

Lana leaned back and put her feet up on the empty chair next to her. "I haven't seen him with anyone in about a year." She pointed her finger at her friend, commanding, "Jillian, don't get any ideas. Between his looks, his money, and his riding skills, there are probably fifteen women chasing him at any one time. He fluctuates from being polite to dismissing them with a sarcastic remark."

Jillian slumped back into her chair, sighing. "He seems so nice. Too bad! How does he know you?"

"The messy breakup I told you about a couple of months ago? He's a friend of that trainer."

"Oh!" That explained his reaction to Lana. Jillian silently promised herself she was going to watch the open jumper class anyway. She couldn't get those gray eyes out of her head. She would need to keep reminding herself that he was just being polite. She believed that she would have no chance with him, so she would not even try to let him know how interesting he was to her.

CHAPTER 54

Saturday morning, the two women watched the Junior Exhibitors' Three-Gaited and the Fourteen to Seventeen Year Old Equitation Class. Lana then took off to prepare for her afternoon class. Jillian picked up a yogurt for lunch and was walking back toward the rings when a large chestnut mare trotted up next to her. She heard a pleasant male voice say, "Lose your side kick, Jillian?" He trotted off before she had a chance to respond. She almost choked on the yogurt, realizing he knew her name. She tried to be calm, remembering Lana's words. However, they did not stop her from finding a spot on the rail to watch the open jumpers.

Jillian was intent on watching each contestant and listening to the announcer, trying to understand how the points and positions were counted. She didn't notice when Ed came up to her. "Jillian, you're not thinking of switching on us, are you?"

She turned and gave him a welcoming smile. "Definitely not! Don't you know I'm crazy about five-gaited horses! But I am curious. How do they judge them?"

Ed patiently explained about points, faults for the knock downs and times, and how the lower the number the better the round. He continued to explain about jump offs for the ties of the best rounds. He then noticed her becoming distracted from his lecture when Tate entered the ring. "If you're watching the riding, he's one of the top jumpers. If it's the rider, watch out."

"Huh?" Caught off guard by his comment, Jillian tried to sound casual, "What's his problem anyway?"

"I don't know. He's just so standoffish. When he does show up at a social event, he doesn't mingle. Maybe I'm not being fair, I really don't know him. Other than the people from his own stable, I don't know if anyone does."

Ed stayed with Jillian throughout the class, answering her occasional question. Tate and his mare won the class. The friends found a seat on the bleachers once the crowd cleared out and caught up while the jumps were being taken down. Jillian told him of her hopes to find a horse of her own over the summer.

Lana's class was next and was quite large. Ed and Jillian agreed that Lana's second place in a field of twenty-two horses was a triumph. Yet, Jillian knew Lana would be disappointed. Although, her friend worked hard and was nearly always pinned, she rarely won a class. They walked to the stable area to congratulate Lana. Ed took off to prepare two of his riders for their class. On and off throughout the rest of the day and evening, Ed seemed to be everywhere Lana and Jillian went.

Jillian and Lana had changed for the party which started at nine. As they walked into the tent, Ed greeted them with a couple of glasses of wine. After finishing her glass, Jillian excused herself to get her sweater out of Lana's car. Ed stated he would accompany her, but she insisted he stay at the party. As she walked to the car she thought how Ed was a nice guy, but he was getting in the way of her or Lana talking with anyone else. She hurried to the car, feeling chilly, but strolled back enjoying the crisp night air once she had her sweater. As she approached the tent, she could see the silhouette of a man sitting on a bench to the side of the entrance. When she got closer, she recognized Tate.

"Congratulations! That was a great ride." Jillian felt her heart speed up. She really wanted to try to get to know him, but she was waiting for him to brush her off. She stood hesitantly, still turned toward the entrance.

He nodded his head in casual acknowledgment. "It was nothing, but thanks…. Do you always wander around alone in the dark?"

"Not if I can help it." She laughed. "I just went to get my sweater." She expected that his next response would dismiss her and she began taking a step away from him.

However, his next comment quickly drew her back. "Ed certainly isn't doing a very good job."

"Ed? Oh, Ed is just a friend." Jillian scuffed her shoe in the dirt of the pathway. She was flattered and startled that Tate had noticed her and Ed together.

"The way he follows you around, I don't think that's what Ed has in mind."

Jillian wished she could see his face more clearly. "He knows I'm not interested."

"Poor Ed, always the friend." He shook his head in pity.

Jillian felt a twinge of guilt that seemed to require some explanation. She didn't want Tate to think she was judgmental. "He really is a sweet guy, but he's so…so…"

"Goofy?" He cocked his head, giving her a lopsided smile.

"Sssh!" She laughed. "Remember, you said it. I didn't."

He gestured to the bench, "Would you like a seat?"

Jillian sat sideways on the bench in order to see Tate as they talked. "As long as you're criticizing my friends, why don't you like Lana?"

Tate pulled back his head in surprise. "Where'd you get that idea? Lana?"

"No, you!" she stated.

Tate shrugged and shook his head in denial. "I personally have no reason not to like her!"

Jillian turned her head and gave him a long sideways look. "You're not going to answer my question, are you?"

A little smile spread across his face as he tried to sound surprised and innocent. "I didn't answer your question? I thought I did…hmm…. You're not riding; what are you doing here anyway?"

"Learning, watching, looking." She looked down at her fingers as they played with the edge of her sweater, trying not to stare at him too obviously, but her eyes were drawn back to his face against her will.

Tate expressed his incredulity. "From Lana and Ed? I could suggest some better teachers. What are you looking for?"

"Maybe a three year old, not fully trained yet."

He quirked an eyebrow and looked startled. "Kinky! So you're into robbing the cradle?"

Jillian gasped as she realized how he had twisted her words. She swatted at him playfully. "You're terrible! A horse!"

Tate clutched his chest where her hand had lightly struck him. "I'm hurt."

"No, you're not." She laughed. "So what are you doing out here? Don't you like to socialize?"

It was his turn to look down at the bench. He shrugged, stating casually, "I'm not very good at small talk."

"You seem to be doing just fine." Jillian let a teasing note enter her voice.

Tate snapped his fingers in feigned embarrassment. "Ah, shucks."

"I suppose you don't dance either?" she stated in a tone that implied he was pretty useless.

"I dance!" he responded defensively, drawing himself up straight. "I'm actually quite good at it; just not to that stuff." He indicated the music coming from inside the tent.

Jillian smiled at his attitude. "And what kind of stuff do you like?"

Tate quickly shook his head in negation. "You'll laugh."

"No, I won't...well, maybe I will. Tell me! I won't tell anyone else." She boldly reached out and put her hand on his knee.

Tate hesitated. "My favorite is the waltz," he stated shyly.

Jillian squeezed his knee in surprise and approval. "I love waltzing! I haven't been in such a long time." She sighed, thinking about how she had always enjoyed dancing the waltz.

The conversation continued as they faced each other on the bench, knees touching, discovering more interests, likes and dislikes they had in common. Lost in time, they heard the bartender from inside the tent yell, "Last call!"

"Your friends must be wondering what happened to you." He stood and without another word headed toward the parking lot.

Jillian was baffled. They'd just sat talking for nearly three hours and yet he left without even saying good-bye. She got up and went into the tent. She didn't mention the conversation to anyone. After Lana's comments and Tate's abrupt departure, there was no reason to believe the conversation was anything more than an evening's distraction. She didn't, however, believe he was arrogant.

The next day, she saw him once. He tipped his hat to her as he trotted by. He passed too quickly to even see her smile in response. Monday morning, Lana had one class. Jillian went to the exhibitors' tent for breakfast by herself. As she stood in line, Tate came up behind her. "I know a really great place for breakfast. Let's get out of here!"

"I have to get back in time for Lana's class. It should come off at about eleven."

"No problem." He nodded toward the exit and started walking away. Jillian followed him out, asking herself what she was doing. He opened the car door for her and handed the seat belt strap to her once she sat down. The drive to Café Lena's was only about fifteen minutes. The conversation was slightly awkward on the ride, staying strictly to the weekend's events. Jillian was unfamiliar with many of the hunter and jumper riders to whom Tate referred. As she asked him questions about them, he seemed to become more relaxed and the humor she had noticed when they previously spoke began to come out. They sat at a patio table in the courtyard of the small restaurant. They both ordered lightly, starting with rich French roast coffee and fresh fruit. They spoke of their families, their jobs, laughing with one another at some of the anecdotes. Jillian felt as if she were catching up with an old friend. Before they knew it, two hours had gone by and it was a quarter to eleven. Tate flagged the waitress and paid the check; they hurried to the car, still talking and laughing. The traffic was heavier on the way back and Lana's class had already started. Tate dropped Jillian as close to the ring as possible and drove off to park the car. She saw him once, later, talking to members of his stable. He smiled sheepishly at her from the distance, and then continued his conversation.

CHAPTER 55

Back at home, Jillian called Anna to discuss her feelings about this confusing man. "Yes, I'd say he's cute. He has the most gorgeous gray eyes, and a lopsided grin that just gets to me. We talked for hours together, and it was like old friends who hadn't seen each other for a while; like we were just getting caught up. It felt so familiar and comfortable," Jillian told her friend.

"Well, that all sounds very positive. You certainly seem to be attracted to him," Anna responded.

"Oh, I am attracted. I get butterflies when I see him. I feel like I want to touch him, put my hand on his arm, or brush up against him, so that there's some physical contact with him," Jillian shared.

"So what's the problem?"

"Despite all that time together, I don't know if he's even interested in me. He never says good-bye, he just walks away. And he never even asked for my phone number. He didn't try to touch me or hold my hand. And he certainly didn't ask me out or even imply that he cared whether or not he ever saw me again." Jillian felt her frustration rising.

Anna heard her friend's unhappiness. "Well, Jilly, there's not much you can do about it right now. You don't know much about him, either. Maybe it's better if you just wait to see if things change between you. You're sure to see him again, now that you're going to all these horse shows. If he's interested, he'll pursue you. If he isn't, you have a lot of other things going on in your life. You're the one who said that you didn't want to feel you needed a man in your life to be complete. Enjoy yourself. If it's meant to be with Tate, then it will be. Just be patient. Wait to see what happens. Besides, you don't have any other plans right now."

Jillian sighed. "You're right. I need to be happy with me; man or no man. Thanks, Anna. Every now and then I need a reality check." She laughed as she felt some of the pressure lift from her.

"My pleasure. Any time," Anna replied.

The following weekend passed quietly. She rode on Saturday, had lunch with Lana, and spent the rest of her time alone catching up on housework and the necessities of living. To her relief, Peter had not called. Wednesday night after riding, she noticed on the caller ID that someone had called, but she did not recognize the number and there was no message. She wrote it off as a wrong number. Thursday evening, the same number appeared as the night before. Expecting it to be a wrong number, she picked it up. "Hello?"

A male voice stated, "I tried calling you last night, but you weren't home."

Jillian took a second to identify the speaker. "Tate?"

"Were you expecting someone else? If you were, I can hang up."

"No. I was just surprised." Jillian still sounded a bit tentative, not sure what to say.

Tate must have picked up on her hesitance, because he asked, "Is it a problem?"

"No, not at all," Jillian rushed to reassure him, making sure that her voice sounded welcoming.

"So, were you out dancing last night?" His voice was insinuating.

"I was at the stable," Jillian told him, picking up on the innuendo. "I have a five-gaited lesson every Wednesday after work."

"That's one of the problems working for someone else. Your time's not your own...."

Four hours later, Jillian got off the phone to go to bed for the night. It was one in the morning. She lay in bed, staring at the ceiling, replaying the conversation in her head, remembering the twinkle in his eyes and his crooked smile. It seemed she had done this before, and then she realized it had been Ellie in bed thinking about Daniel.

CHAPTER 56

Another uneventful weekend went by. Wednesday, she went straight to the stable from work. After her lesson, she headed up to the observation lounge to retrieve her work clothes.

"You're pretty good with those shaky tails," a familiar masculine voice told her from a seat in the dark corner.

"Tate, what are you doing here?" She smiled broadly, pleased to see him.

"Josie suggested I sit up here if I wanted to watch. I don't think she wanted any distractions."

"She didn't even mention you were here." Jillian thought she was glad she hadn't; she would have been too nervous to pay attention to what she was supposed to be doing if she had known.

He leaned forward, smiling wickedly. "She was definitely surprised and a little annoyed. She probably thinks I'm here to convince you jumping is much more exciting."

"Well," she laughed, "I'll just have to tell Josie you're thinking about riding gaited."

"Oh, right! Like anyone would believe that one!" He rolled his eyes and snorted derisively.

Jillian propped her fists on her hips and challenged him. "You can't tell me you don't like Saddlebreds. That mare of yours may be trained for jumping, but that's not her breeding. She is pure Saddlebred and you know it."

"Well...you caught me," he laughed.

"It just proves their versatility and superiority of breed." Jillian wiggled her head and pointed her nose into the air.

"You are committed," Tate replied, shaking his head.

Jillian laughed at her silliness, and then slid into a chair next to Tate. "Why are you here?"

He spread his hands and explained, "I'm a little slow sometimes. When you told me you loved waltzing and hadn't been for a long time, was that a hint for me to ask you?"

"I...I hadn't meant it that way." Jillian could feel the heat starting to rise in her neck and face.

Tate cocked his head and asked hesitantly, "So, you wouldn't want to go out dancing with me?"

Jillian was flustered. "That's not what I meant."

He leaned forward. "So...then you will?"

Jillian blinked in confusion. "If you are asking.. yes."

"That shade of red is very becoming on you." His eyes were laughing. "Saturday, nine o'clock?."

"Fine!"

He stood to leave. "I do like that color."

"You're terrible!" She laughed and gave him her address and directions off I-71.

He laughed and started down the stairs.

She called after him, "Bye!"

There was no response. Over the next couple of days, she found she was a nervous wreck. She called Sally; she called Anna; she finally broke down and called Lana. She had to find out if this was his pattern of seduction.

Lana sighed, realizing that it would do no good to tell Jillian to forget about Tate once again. "So that's where you disappeared to during the party on Saturday night and Monday morning. I wondered what you had found so interesting. I knew it couldn't be Ed."

"Lana, get to the point!" Jillian demanded, having all the frustration she could deal with.

"Well, to the best of my knowledge, the last woman he dated he was with for about a year. She cheated on him. He found out and they split up. In the past year, he hasn't really had any relationships. When women chase him he just jokes with them, but he never calls any of them, and he never takes them out. He might socialize with them at the stable or on the show grounds. But that's it."

Jillian humphed. "That doesn't sound so bad. He seems like he's fairly stable in relationships and doesn't just get into chasing skirts. Good qualities, as far as I'm concerned."

"Well, don't get too excited. He's probably a lousy lover."

"Good-bye, Lana, you party pooper! I'll see you Saturday." She hung up the phone, feeling a bit better about Tate.

After riding Saturday morning, Jillian picked up Sally to help her buy a new dance dress. She had not gone waltzing since she had lost weight and she wanted to look stunning. They found a dusty rose colored, waltz length, satin gown at a specialty shop downtown. The neckline was low enough that it would show off her assets without shoving them right in Tate's face. Her shoulders would be bare as well, but there was sufficient movement in the sheer sleeves that the dress wouldn't cut into her. The skirt was full enough to have some sweep to it, but not so much that they'd have to struggle to get it all into the car. Jillian twirled in front of the shop mirror like a three year old dressed up for a party.

She was ready at quarter to nine. At ten after, she started pacing. *Did he change his mind? The least he could do is call. Is he lost? Was he in an accident?* The thoughts and feelings spun in her head until she felt she would be sick.

Twenty-five after nine, the doorbell rang. Relief swept over her. Jillian took a deep breath as she walked to the door. She opened to see a single, long stem yellow rose in his hand. Accepting the rose, she invited him in. Tate followed her to the kitchen to put the flower in water. He picked up the linden green silk shawl that he saw lying on the couch and gently placed it over her shoulders. He opened the condo door and the car door for her, again handing her the seat belt strap. She liked the way he showed his consideration.

Jillian had found a new place to go dancing. She didn't want to spoil even one minute of this night with thoughts of Drake. Tate led her to an empty table where they dropped her shawl, and then he quickly swept her out into the flow of the other dancers. He was remarkably light on his feet and much better than she had hoped. Jillian felt dizzy and breathless by the third waltz. She wasn't sure if it was due to Tate's expertise at reversing her or just the physical contact with him. She tingled everywhere he touched her and feared her sexual response to his proximity would be communicated to him. However, if he was aware of his effect on her, he continued to be a perfect gentleman the entire night. He was playful in a way he had not been before, teasingly stroking her neck or shoulders, twining a lock of her hair around his finger. There was more physical contact, both casual and deliberate, than there had been between them previously. Jillian thought she might burst with the tension she felt building inside. She commanded herself to stop thinking about her desire to slide her hands inside of his shirt and stroke his chest and back. She reminded herself that sexual attraction was not sufficient basis for a relationship and she was not interested in anything less with this man. It was Tate's humor and warmth that helped keep her emotions under control. He was the best company she had ever had, and she could state unequivocally that this was the best date she had ever been on with anyone.

When they got back to her condo, Tate walked Jillian to the door. He raised her chin so that they were looking into each other's eyes, and then kissed her on the lips, gently parting them with his tongue. He took the keys out of her hand and unlocked her front door. Once she stepped in, he turned and sauntered off to his car.

Jillian closed the door, leaning against it, trying to catch her breath. She felt as if she were a school girl having been kissed for the first time. Yet, his touch, the kiss felt so familiar. The crooked smile, the sense of humor, the twinkle in his eyes; could he be the man she had been waiting for since the Civil War ended or was she projecting Daniel onto him, the memory being so fresh in her mind? Her head was spinning. She could not remember having such a physical reaction to a man. She turned out the lights, threw off her clothing, and flopped down on the bed. It had been a wonderful night. She hoped she would hear from him soon.

Tate called Monday night and Tuesday night and they stayed on the phone for hours. He knew where she'd be Wednesday. He called again on Thursday and asked her out for Saturday. "My sister's in town. I promised her all day Saturday for fittings and Saturday night is a girls' night out. I plan on spending the night at my parents," she explained, the regret apparent in her voice.

"Hmm…How about a movie Sunday night?" Tate suggested.

"Yes." They discussed the movies that they wanted to see.

"I'll call you with a time." There was a pause on his end as he waited to hear her confirm the plan.

"Call my cell," she instructed quickly, before he just disappeared from the line in his usual abrupt way.

Jillian spent the weekend with her sister, Donna, and her sister's friends. Fran made a brunch on Sunday, thrilled that all three of her children were in the house. As usual, Fran started on Jillian. "Have you seen Peter?"

Jillian cringed. "No, Mom. I told you we have nothing in common. I'm not seeing him anymore."

"I just thought you might have changed your mind." Fran sounded long-suffering.

"Mom, he was last month. Why don't you ask Jilly about Tate?" Donna smiled broadly.

"Tate?" Fran's attention perked up. She turned to look quizzically at Jillian.

"I've only been out with him once," Jillian stated, diving into the refrigerator to try to find an escape from the third degree she was about to receive.

Donna smiled at her sister's discomfiture. "I'd count it as three times. And what about the hours on the phone?"

"Donna!" Jillian threatened through clenched teeth.

"Tate? What kind of name is that for a man anyway?" Bill Jr. decided to get in on teasing his big sister.

The banter continued until Jillian heard her cell phone ring, jumped up from the kitchen table, and grabbed her phone off the counter. Everyone at the table was laughing at her as she answered the phone.

It was Tate. Jillian tried to muffle the sound of laughter in the background as they agreed on a movie and time. Tate teased her about her sexual allure until she started blushing. Once she hung up, Bill Jr. started, "Jilly's got it bad!"

"I've never seen you like this. You mustn't have told me everything," Donna chimed in.

"Yes, I did!" Jillian snapped back defensively.

"Who is he anyway?" Bill Sr. asked her seriously.

"He is someone I met through the horses." She heaved an exaggerated sigh, knowing what would follow.

"What does he do?" her father demanded.

Donna leaned over and threw a sympathetic arm around her sister's shoulder. "Sorry, Jilly. I didn't mean to start them off on you."

Jillian produced a smile that said her sister would pay a terrible price for what she had done. "That's OK. ...He owns his own business, something to do with stocks and acquisitions. He must do all right; he owns his own horse and travels to shows. That takes money."

"Where'd he go to school?" the examiner continued.

"Northwestern and Yale business."

"Has he ever been married?" her mother put in.

"Mom, you're forgetting, I've been married, but...no!"

"When are we going to meet him?" her mother asked, ignoring the other intrusive comment.

"Maybe in a couple of months. Maybe, never. I don't know!" Jillian almost shouted. She was getting fed up with this cross-examination. After all, she was an adult and had been for a number of years now.

"Jillian, don't use that tone with your mother," Bill Sr. admonished.

Jillian rolled her eyes, but said nothing more. When she left, Donna hugged her, "I hope he's as special as he sounds. After Drake, we worry about you."

Jillian hugged her back, "I hope so, too." As she drove back to her condo, she realized she had already fallen for this man whom she hardly knew. It was frightening and exciting at the same time.

She fussed for two hours changing outfits. She wanted to look casual, but sexy, but not obviously sexy. Again, he was late. Extreme thoughts echoed through her mind. The rare times that someone she was dating had been late, she had never had such intense feelings of fear. She had been annoyed with the others, but not fearful. The closest she had ever been to this was with Drake; she had been afraid he would reject her or die driving drunk and never come back to her. She could not allow anyone to treat her the way Drake had. And she could not put herself through the same torment in response to someone else's behavior. Yet, she did not want to make the same mistake Ellie made. She would not give up on him and run away. How could she explain to him without sounding histrionic or completely crazy? This was only the second date, or fourth by Donna's reckoning. She did not want to scare him away. Yet, with the hours of phone calls, she felt such closeness that she'd never even felt for Drake. The doorbell rang. They wouldn't make the movie anyway. She would have to talk to him.

"Are you ready?" He smiled, oblivious of his faux pas.

"It's too late to make the movie!" she stated, letting some of her frustration and fear show.

He looked askance at her, but continued, "We could go to a later showing and get something to eat first."

"Fine!" Jillian would not make eye contact with him as she bit her lip to keep from speaking.

Suddenly, understanding seemed to dawn on him. "Oh, the lady is not happy."

"Come on in!" She turned and walked to the kitchen and pulled a bowl of grapes, cheese, and an unopened bottle of white wine out of the refrigerator. To this she added half a loaf of French bread.

Having followed her into the kitchen, Tate asked, "Does this mean you are going to feed me before throwing me out?"

She pressed her lips together, and then said, "I have no intension of throwing you out. Could we talk?"

He didn't say anything, but picked up the grapes, wine, and bottle opener and followed her back to the living room. They sat on the couch and he opened the wine, pouring two glasses. As he handed her one, he stated, "You're angry with me."

"No, I'm more upset than angry," she stated, curling her legs under her and turning to face him.

"Is this about me being late or something else?"

"Being late."

Tate had the good grace to look a bit sheepish. "I've never been very good with time, but we can catch another movie."

Jillian shook her head. "It's not about missing the movie. It's about not knowing what happened to you."

Tate seemed rather surprised by that answer. "I never thought about it being that important or that seeing a later movie would upset you."

"Maybe it isn't to other people. This may sound ridiculous to you, but to me you being late with no call means something terrible has happened and you are never coming." She turned her hands over, palms up, showing him her helplessness and fear.

Tate gave a small laugh, reaching out and taking one of her hands. "Nothing will happen to me. I am too stubborn to die."

She squeezed his hand hard. "None of us knows that! I need you to call me if you are going to be late. You don't have to explain. Just tell me how late." Jillian tried hiding the tears that were coming to the corner of her eyes.

Tate reached forward and twirled her hair between his fingers. "You really are upset." He wiped away a tear from her cheek. "I'll try. Be patient with me. I'm really not good at this, but I will work on it."

Jillian offered him a small, trembling smile. "Thank you."

"There's no need to thank me." He slipped his hand behind her neck pulling her forward to kiss her. She parted her lips for him. As the passion of the kiss mounted, he played with her hair, slipping his hand from the back of her neck and wrapping his other arm around her, pulling her into him. When the embrace finally ended, they were both a bit breathless. Jillian leaned back on the couch while Tate reached for a grape to feed her, teasing her lips and tongue with the fruit and his own soft lips. They nibbled on the grapes and cheese while talking between kisses.

Jillian realized she needed to slow things down. While he had not tried anything besides kissing, she had no desire to stop him if he did try; still, it was too soon to let it go any farther. "Maybe we should leave now, if we're going to make it to the movie."

He started to release her, but caught his hand in her hair and began laughing. "I think you'd better brush your hair before we leave."

She attempted to run her fingers through it and found it to be all snarled. By the time she got a brush through it, they barely had enough time to make it to the movie just as the credits were beginning. Afterwards, he walked her to the front door, kissed her, and said, "I don't trust myself to come in." He turned and walked to his vehicle.

She closed the door thinking, *Good! He wants me, too!* The next two nights, they had three hour phone conversations. Wednesday night, he unexpectedly showed up at Jillian's stable.

Slipping his arm around her waist, he said, "I waited to eat with you. Is there a decent place nearby?"

"Decent? I guess that depends on your definition of decent." She laughed. "There's an all-night diner?"

"All night? Mmmm. Sounds good!" He leered at her and nuzzled her neck.

Laughing, Jillian pushed him away. "I have to go to work in the morning."

They took their own cars to the diner, ate, and talked until midnight. As they were leaving, Tate said, "I'm leaving for Springfield in the morning. When will you and Lana arrive at the show?"

"Probably not until late Friday night."

"I'll see you then at the hotel". He opened her car door, waiting for her to start it up, and then leaned in the window to kiss her quickly, turned, and hurried off to his car. She wondered what his aversion was to saying good-bye.

Lana and Jillian checked in just before eleven that Friday. There was a message at the desk for Jillian. It read, "I'll be in the lounge."

Seeing the grin come across Jillian's face, Lana grabbed it from her hand. "Tate?"

"I've never seen his hand writing, but I don't know who else it could be." She laughed, "Or maybe I should say scrawl."

"Let's dump our stuff and go to the lounge for a drink. It was a long drive. Besides, I really want to see if Tate can talk as much as you say he does."

The two women stopped just inside the door to the lounge, giving their eyes time to adjust to the dim light. Tate walked up to them, "Lana, Jillian, I have a table over here." He put his hand on Jillian's back, guiding her to the table. They had just sat down when Joe and Mike from Tate's stable came over with three beers. "How do you do it? We just left the table and you were alone."

Tate made the introductions, asked Jillian and Lana what they wanted, and then went to the bar. Mike monopolized the conversation until Tate came back. Tate put his hand on Lana's shoulder. "Don't listen to a word he says; his wife is upstairs sleeping."

It quickly became apparent to Jillian that the men related to each other by teasing and joking. They all left together when the lounge closed at two. Tate walked the women to their room. With Lana standing there, he kissed Jillian on the cheek. "I'll see you at the show; I need to get there early."

The two women watched him walk away. Once he was out of sight, Jillian said, "See, I told you he talks."

"He certainly has a dry sense of humor. He can be very entertaining."

Jillian realized her friend was still unsure of him.

CHAPTER 57

Saturday went by quickly. Lana got a third in her class and Tate won his. Tate showed up next to Jillian while she was watching a Fine Harness Class. They agreed to meet at the exhibitors' party at seven. It was being held at a restaurant about half-way between the show grounds and the hotel. Mike, his wife, and Joe found Jillian and Lana before Tate showed up. Joe tried flirting with both women and had them laughing by the time Tate arrived. By nine, it seemed that the party had become extremely loud. Yet, Jillian and Tate had become quiet. He leaned over and whispered in her ear, "Let's get out of here."

Jillian got Lana's attention to let her know she'd meet her back at the hotel. Once they got outside, she stated, "It was too loud in there."

"That's what happens when you have too many drunks together. I like a drink, but sometimes this group gets carried away."

"I'm glad to hear you say that." Jillian had told him a little about Drake, but she had learned enough at Alanon to know that if Tate was a drinker he wouldn't have missed the excuse to drink.

They'd both had enough of loud noise and drunks, which left them few places to go. Without either saying where they were going, they went back to Tate's room. He tossed her the remote, suggesting she see what was on TV. He opened the mini-bar and pulled out a couple of bottles of Pellegrino. She was sitting on the bed with her feet up, slowly flipping through the channels, when he sat down next to her, handing her an opened bottle. She moved over on the bed, making room for him to relax with her. She was thinking how much she wanted him to kiss her, but considering the environment, did not want him to get the idea that she was ready for sex.

He sat self-consciously next to her. Both were leaning against the headboard with their feet up. Finally, Tate broke their silence. "Jillian, I don't want you to get the wrong idea. It's just there's no place else to go and I wanted to be alone with you."

"If I thought you were going to try something, I would have insisted we stay downstairs." She took his hand in hers and turned toward him, leaning forward to kiss him. He responded first closed mouthed, and then pushed her back. They stared into each other's eyes. Jillian felt as if she were melting into him. He wrapped his arms around her, pulling her to him, and began kissing her. His hand slid down her side to her waist, and then slowly, gently back up, brushing the outer part of her breast with his fingers. When she did not move away, he risked covering her breast with his hand and gently moving his thumb back and forth over the nipple. She responded to his touch. Not only was his gentleness exciting, she realized there was a sense of relief that he did want her sexually and that his behavior thus far had been out of respect and not a lack of desire for her. She felt she had been missing his touch her entire life. As he kissed her neck and slid his hand down her side, they both slid down on the bed. He moved one leg over one of hers and their bodies became entwined. They continued kissing, touching, holding.

She felt a bulge through his pants against her. Then he suddenly stopped. He held her in his arms, eventually whispering in her ear, "We better find something on TV."

He flipped through the channels finding an old black and white movie. Jillian fell asleep in his arms. She woke at five, fully dressed, under the covers, spooned with Tate. She sighed and fell back to sleep. The next time she woke, he had obviously showered, shaved, and dressed and was sitting on the edge of the bed offering her a cup of coffee.

She had hoped to slip back into her own room without waking Lana; however, her friend was up nursing a cup of coffee. "Well, was he any good?"

"Huh?" Jillian responded, blushing. "Oh! Nothing happened. We fell asleep watching TV."

"Right!" Lana did not seem to believe her.

Jillian took a shower and dressed for the show grounds. Fortunately for Lana, her class was not until late in the day, but Jillian was anxious to get there to watch Tate ride. That night she slept in her room with Lana, but she and Tate rode back to Cincinnati together. They continued to see each other two or three times a week, talking on the phone for hours in between.

As Donna's wedding approached, Jillian debated with herself what to do about Tate. She wanted him to come with her to both the rehearsal party and the wedding, but she was unsure how he would feel about it. She did not want him to think she was trying to give him a message that she wanted to get married. She knew he would be uncomfortable with so many strangers, especially since he'd never met her family, and part of the time he would need to be alone because she was in the wedding party. By August first, she decided she just needed to discuss it with him. The wedding was only two weeks away. As they sat at dinner, Jillian was trying to decide how to bring the subject up, when Tate asked, "What's going on?"

"My sister's wedding..." She paused, unsure how to proceed.

"And?"

In one breath she blurted out, "I don't want you to get the wrong idea or be uncomfortable, but I would like you to come with me."

"Jillian, I would have wondered about where this relationship was going if you hadn't asked me."

She leaned back in her chair, sighing with relief. "Thank you. Will you go to the rehearsal party the night before as well? It will just be the bridal party...and their spouses or dates...and the parents." She realized she was putting pressure on him.

Tate looked at her intently. "Are you sure you want me there?"

"Don't worry, no one bites." She laughed. "And this way you'll get to meet a few people before the wedding."

He smiled, reaching out to touch her hand where it lay on the tablecloth. "Jillian, if you really want me there, I will be there."

She grinned at him, her eyes half closed. "On time?"

Tate snatched his hand back and pretended to pout. "Come on! I've been pretty good, haven't I?"

"You're always pretty good." She reached across the table, taking his hand.

"I'm glad you noticed." He covered her hand with his, stroking her palm with his thumb. Jillian smiled warmly at him and enjoyed the intimate contact.

The evening of the rehearsal and party, Jillian nervously dressed. She was not nearly as concerned about how she looked, but rather how she could ease the situation for Tate. She knew him well enough now to understand that Lana had been wrong; he was not arrogant, but rather shy. She hoped her parents would not interrogate him in front of so many people. She was actually less concerned about the wedding. There would be too much going on for them to focus their attention on Tate. She had told him to meet her at the restaurant. She was not going to torture him with the rehearsal as well.

The minister made them run through everything a second time. Jillian started checking her watch. She was worried they would be late to the restaurant. She knew the feeling of waiting for someone when she was already nervous. When they finally arrived, Tate was sitting at the bar, drinking a cup of coffee. Jillian walked up behind him, slipped her arms around his waist and whispered in his ear, "I'm sorry we're late."

"Hmm. What's sauce for the gander is apparently not sauce for the goose," he quipped, but she felt the rumble of his laughter. He turned to face her, giving her a quick kiss.

They joined the others who were just seating themselves at a table set for eighteen in the back of the restaurant. Jillian introduced him to the group. As he held her chair for her, he whispered, "Do you really expect me to remember everyone's name?"

"Absolutely..." she laughed, "...not."

He seemed relieved as he sat down in the chair next to her.

With the first question Bill Sr. asked Tate, Jillian rolled her eyes and Bill Jr. jumped in before Tate could mutter a word. Mimicking his dad, he turned to his future brother-in-law, "Now, Son, are you sure you can afford my daughter?"

Others joined in teasing Donna and her fiancé, Greg. The razzing went on until the food was served. As they quieted down to eat, conversations evolved in small groups around the table. Bill Jr. was sitting next to Tate and began telling tales of Jillian's youth, embarrassing her and entertaining Tate.

He grinned at her discomfiture. "Well, Jillian, did your brother tell me all your secrets?"

"Oh, I still have one more," she stated with exaggerated mystery, widening her eyes. Jillian was thinking about Ellie.

Tate tilted his head to study her face, narrowing his eyes. "Only one more? Or only one more that a little brother would know?"

Jillian turned her profile to him, grinning mischievously. "Wouldn't you like to know?"

After the party, Tate and Jillian stood in the parking lot talking for sometime before Tate kissed her good-night, and then they each drove their own cars to their own homes.

The morning of the wedding, Jillian packed an overnight bag and drove to her parents' house. As one of her sister's bride's maids, she would need to dress there and ride with the family to the United Methodist Church in Sharonville.

Donna had been kind to her bridal party by choosing dresses they looked good wearing. They were apricot satin sheath dresses with a short, contrasting bolero jacket they were to wear in church. The problem was, the dresses were strapless and the women had to wear a corset to fit into the dresses properly. Still, they would look great once they were dressed. There were a few death threats made toward the bride as they struggled to get each other cinched into the corsets, but Donna refused to take any of them seriously. And they all loved what the corsets did for their figures when they saw their reflections in the mirror.

When they arrived by limo at the church, Jillian spotted Tate's SUV in the parking lot. The bride's entourage was escorted into a small room to wait, while Donna and Greg's guests were seated in the church. Jillian tried to peak to see if she could spot Tate, but the wedding planner chased her back into the nursery to wait with the others. As Jillian walked down the aisle, two ahead of her sister, she scanned the two hundred guests looking for Tate. She was relieved to see that he was standing next to Bill Jr.'s girlfriend. While she did not know the young woman very well, she was sure that she had corralled Tate when she spotted him, probably standing awkwardly on the sidelines.

The ceremony began a few minutes after four. To Jillian, it seemed too solemn for what she had come to expect from her sister. If she were ever to get married again, she could not imagine going through it this way. However, she would not want to elope again as she had with Drake. She would want her family and close friends present. She now understood she had married Drake only because he had needed her; next time, she'd do it for the right reasons. She was so involved in her own thoughts that she'd missed their vows and only came back from her reverie to hear the minister say, "I pronounce you husband and wife."

Greg kissed Donna and the witnesses applauded. A reception line formed at the exit of the church. Tate leaned in and whispered to Jillian, "I know this is supposed to be the bride's day, but I'd rather kiss you."

Jillian smiled and blushed. "I'll see you at the reception. I have to go with them for pictures first."

It felt as if the pictures were taking forever. It was a full hour from the time they had left the church until Jillian was able to join Tate at the banquet room at the Marriott. She gladly accepted a glass of wine while they mingled before dinner was to be served. After the champagne toast, Jillian picked at her meal, and then left the head table to sit with Tate. The bride and groom's first dance was called as soon as the head table finished the main course. Jillian had been looking forward to dancing with Tate. She did not wait for him to ask, but took his hand, leading him to the dance floor. In his arms, she forgot there was anyone else in the room. While no waltzes were played, they danced every slow dance. The last dance, they spent staring into one another's eyes.

The Whites' had reserved a block of rooms for the bridal party and out of town guests. Many of the guests were moving the party to the cocktail lounge. Jillian had previously suggested to Tate that he bring some casual clothes to change into after the reception, warning him that the party would probably continue into the night. He retrieved a saddlebag from his car and joined her in the lobby. Together, they went to her room to change.

Jillian kicked off her shoes the second she walked into the room. Tate took off his jacket and hung it in the doorless closet. He took her hands in his and pulled her toward him. Eyes locking, he ran his fingertips over her arms, up to her neck, and then traced along the edges of her neckline. The gentle movement sent chills throughout her body. She wrapped her arms around his neck; stepping in to him, she initiated a kiss. She had been waiting for this moment alone with him. As she did, he unzipped the back of her dress. He gently pushed her back, allowing the gown to fall to the floor. As he resumed his explorations, she undid his tie and began unbuttoning his shirt. When she reached his belt, she unbuckled it, and then the button of his pants and the zipper. She slipped her hand within his pants and felt his enlarged penis through his underwear. He reached for her hand, removing it and bringing it to his lips, "Are we going to change and go back to the party?"

"I'd rather be alone with you." She stroked her fingertips across his lips, feeling their silky texture and the warmth of them.

He broke the embrace, taking off his shirt and hanging it next to the jacket. As she stepped out of her dress and was about to throw it over a chair, he took it from her and hung it. She stood in her corset and stockings in shocked amazement, watching as he removed his trousers, hanging them, too. For a brief moment, she remembered Daniel, neatly folding his clothing. He caught her staring at him, "What? Is something wrong?"

"No, no, not at all." She assured him as she continued to stand and stare.

He laughed and waved his hand in front of her eyes. "Aren't you going to change?"

Jillian grabbed a tee-shirt and entered the bathroom. She removed her stockings, and then started to reach back to unhook the unfamiliar garment. She came back out laughing; she stood before him in her panties and corset. "I don't know how to get out of this thing!"

"You do have a problem, don't you?" He laughed, but made no move to assist her.

Jillian waited several seconds for Tate to rescue her. When he didn't, she flapped her arms helplessly, and pleaded, "Will you help me?"

"I don't know. I kind of like the look." He watched her flush. Smiling, he added, "Such a beautiful shade of red."

"Oh, please. I'd like to breathe again," she begged, twisting her arms behind her in another attempt to unhook the corset.

Daniel walked toward her, smiling lasciviously. "I suppose it would be pleasant to free your breasts."

As he approached, she turned her back to him. He worked on the hooks slowly and laughed when she took a big gulp of air. He slipped his hand around her waist, still standing behind her; he removed the corset and slid his hand over her bare stomach to her breast, fondling the nipple. Jillian leaned her head back on his shoulder sighing. Tate leaned down, kissing the side of her neck; she could feel herself melting into him. He released her, taking her hand in his, flipping off the lamps in the room with one switch, leaving on only the light in the entrance way to the room. He led her toward the bed and, with his free hand, pulled down the cover and blankets. Wearing only their underpants, they sat together at the foot of the bed. He resumed kissing her and fondling her breasts. She let her hands roam over his back, his chest, and his stomach. She realized she was becoming wet between her legs without him even touching her there. He kissed her neck, her breasts, running one hand over her legs, gradually bringing his hand between them and slipping his fingers into the bottom of her panties. As he touched her opening, the moisture increased. He pulled his hand out of her panties and, grabbing her by the waist with both hands, lifted her up into the center of the bed. He swept his hand down off her waist, removing her panties. He leaned down, kissing her flat belly, slipping his fingers down through her pubic hair, searching for the opening. She lifted herself slightly wanting his touch, his fingers to enter her moist cleft. As his fingers slid in, his lips went lower until his tongue found her clitoris. Her shoulders sank back into the bed as her hips lifted, moving in rhythm with the movements of his fingers and tongue. As her breathing increased, so did the movement of his fingers and he began gently sucking on her clitoris. Her response was explosive. Once her body began to relax, his movements relaxed with her and he moved up, kissing her stomach, her breast, neck, and face. She looked into his eyes and reached down, pushing down his underwear. Not only did she want to give him as much pleasure as she was experiencing, but she wanted him in her. She felt his firm erect member; she ran her hand over it. He grabbed her wrist, "Are you sure you're ready? I can wait."

Her eyes glazed with pleasure and her voice husky with passion, she groaned, "I'm absolutely sure, and I can't."

He pulled his pants off the rest of the way. She opened her legs for him, raising her hips to him as he slipped himself into her. Their eyes locked. As he moved slowly in and out, she continued staring into his gray eyes. Her hands moved over the muscles of his arms and back, needing to feel the heat of his body, its strength. Their momentum mounted until she lost control, her eyes rolling back, and together they released all that had been building for months. Finally spent, they rolled to their sides, falling asleep with him still in her.

During the night, Jillian woke cold from the air conditioning. She reached down, covering them, snuggled back into his arms and fell back to sleep.

CHAPTER 58

Having gone to the horse show with Lana, Jillian had missed the annual Memorial Day barbeque with her college friends. Since her relationship with Tate had moved to a new level, she felt it was time that he meet her best friends. Both Sally and Anna had been hearing about Tate from Jillian on the phone, but neither had seen her for a while. Between riding, work, horse shows, and Tate, Jillian had not been able to get together with either of them. The weekend after her sister's wedding, the group was convening on Sunday afternoon at Anna and John's house.

Tate had spent Tuesday and Thursday nights at Jillian's condo. They talked half the night away, falling asleep in each other's arms. She asked him if he would go with her Sunday. His reaction surprised her. "I'm finally getting to meet your friends."

She was pleased that he was willing to become more involved in her life. He picked her up Saturday night to go dancing, and then returned to her condo for the night. She had been amazed by the feelings she'd had their first night together. But, as they spent more time with one another, she was feeling more comfortable with him and her own emerging sexuality. For the first time in her life, she felt she was with a man who truly found pleasure in her pleasure and was not just trying to prove or satisfy himself. As he drove them to Anna and John's, other than telling him where to turn, she sat quietly, staring at him, taking him in; she was so absorbed she nearly missed pointing out her friends' driveway.

Tate seemed more relaxed than he was meeting her family, having heard so many stories about her friends; he felt he already knew them. Jillian made the introductions and John handed him a beer, "So you're Tate! We were wondering when we'd get to meet the guy who was taking up all our Jilly's time."

"Guilty!" Tate accepted the beer.

Jillian suppressed a giggle, wondering if Tate caught what John was saying. This group would be much more perceptive and tougher critics of anyone she was dating or with in a relationship than her family had been.

It had been two years since the picnic where Drake had so embarrassed her. She winced at the memory of how naïve and insecure she had been during her marriage, allowing her husband to belittle her in public, in front of her friends…making excuses for him! How different this new relationship was. Tate seemed to fit in very well with these people she loved so much. She smiled as she watched him rolling around on the ground, chasing the two little girls, making them squeal with delight.

Sally brought her an iced tea and sat down next to her. "He seems like a nice guy, Jilly. He's great with the kids. That's a good sign," she said with a wink at her friend.

"Don't start any rumors, Sally. I don't know where this is going yet, myself. But he does seem to like the girls, and they're already mad about him." Both women laughed as the two toddlers flopped on the reclining Tate and began climbing on him.

Marie and Peggy joined the two women where they sat at the table watching the wrestling going on in front of them. Marie called to her husband, Tom, to rescue Tate from the onslaught, but Tom refused to interfere. "I've had my share of pummeling for a while. Let him get broken in. I can use the break."

Finally, Sally and Marie decided that Tate had been broken in enough and retrieved their daughters. Tate collapsed on the ground, panting and laughing. Jillian went over to him, offering her hand to help him up. Tate took hold of her outstretched hand and pulled her down on top of him. Jillian squealed with surprise and laughter of her own. "So, you like wrestling with girls, huh?" she demanded, pinning his shoulders.

"Beats the hell out of wrestling with boys," Tate responded, slipping his arms around her waist and pulling her against him. Jillian enjoyed the impromptu embrace, but felt the intently watchful eyes of her friends upon them and began to blush.

"I think dinner is ready, and I'm starved," she told him, pushing herself up.

Sighing in exaggeration, Tate rose as well, brushing the grass and dirt off his clothes. "Well, I guess I could sublimate my passion in a good burger." He slipped his arm around her waist and walked her to the table where the others were busily trying not to have observed the intimate moment.

Jillian watched with great pleasure as the men got to know Tate and seemed to enjoy his company. She mentally compared his quietly engaging humor with the attention seeking things Drake used to do as he got drunk. There was no need to be the center of attention in Tate's behavior. He teased her girlfriends, flirting with them in pleasant ways that they reciprocated without any sense that he was really hitting on them. But Jillian really felt the tug on her heart strings when Tate offered to hold Marie's two month old infant. He had given the baby her bottle, and then laid her over his shoulder to burp her. As babies will sometimes do, she spit up on his shirt. Jillian held her breath, waiting to see how he would respond. Marie hurried to take the baby from him, apologizing for the mess; but Tate just laughed it off, saying, "I'm honored. She's marked me as a member of the family." Jillian kissed his forehead as she dabbed away the milk on his shirt.

As they drove back to Jillian's, Tate asked, "Well, did I pass all the tests?"

She laughed, "What makes you think you've had all of them yet?"

Shrugging, he exclaimed, "What's next? I'm ready to take it on!"

She knew he was only partially joking. She answered him seriously, "I'm the only one who has to approve, and I should think you would know by now that I do." She reached over, squeezing his shoulder as he continued driving.

He seemed uncomfortable with the compliment and just smiled shyly.

"Now, you haven't told me what you think of my friends." It was more of a question than a statement.

Tate laughed quietly. "They were great. I don't think I've ever felt so comfortable so quickly with any group of strangers before. But I should have expected it. They're your friends, and I felt pretty comfortable with you right away." Jillian smiled and reached over to stroke his arm as he drove.

Labor Day Weekend, Jillian flew up to Syracuse to meet Tate, who was showing at the New York State Fair. Her family was not holding the annual reunion, having gathered for Donna's wedding so recently. It was the farthest she had gone for a horse show. Although Misty Glen was not showing, there were a number of Saddlebred classes. Jillian was sitting, watching a Five Gaited class by herself when Ed joined her. She was glad to see someone else she knew.

"What are you doing here? I didn't think Misty Glen was here," Ed commented, sitting down next to her.

"They're not. I came up to spend the weekend with Tate Bradley."

Ed paused to absorb this information before responding as casually as he could. "Ah, so the rumors are true!"

"Rumors?" Jillian turned to look at him, frowning at the thought of being the subject of gossip.

Ed waved a calming hand at her. "Just that you two are an item."

"Oh...I guess you could call it that."

"As long as he treats you all right. Oh, I was going to call you. I was checking out a Fine Harness horse for one of my people. The mare wasn't what we were looking for, but I thought of you. She's a three year old and doesn't have the right confirmation for harness. She's not saddle broken yet, but if you're willing to put in the time, she might make a nice pleasure Five Gaited."

Jillian felt her enthusiasm rise. Ed had a good eye for horses. "Where is she?"

"She's at a small place in Kentucky. Stop back at my tack room later and I'll give you the name and phone number." He started to walk away.

Jillian called after him. "Thank you. Oh, Ed, what are they asking?"

"Eight. But, they know she'll never make it as a Fine Harness horse. I should think you can get her for less." He offered her an encouraging grin and turned to walk away again.

"Thank you. I'll stop by later."

Jillian was excited. So far, the horses Josie had checked out had either turned out to be duds or too expensive. She couldn't wait to tell Tate, but she knew it would have to wait. He was warming up for his class. She wouldn't be able to talk with him until it was over. She'd learned that, when he was competing, he thought of little else besides the next round. She understood. Although she did not compete, when she rode nothing else crossed her mind.

Tate went with Jillian later to Ed's stable area. He was friendly with Ed, asking more questions about the horse Ed was recommending. Jillian smiled, realizing that not only was Tate concerned for her welfare, but he was also making it clear to Ed that she was with him. She had never seen this side of him. He knew from the first night they spoke her opinion of Ed, but apparently she was one area of his life where he did not want any competition.

They skipped the exhibitors' party and rode the rides on the midway. Tate won an overpriced stuffed animal at one of the games and presented it to her with great pride for his athletic prowess. On Monday morning, they left early for the long drive back to Cincinnati. The last part of the trip was slow due to the holiday traffic, but Jillian didn't care. She was sitting next to the only person she wanted to be with. The more time they spent together, the more she wanted to be with him and the greater the understanding between them. Out of the silence, he suddenly asked, "We've been spending all our time at your place. Work nights it probably makes sense; the condo is much closer to both our offices than my house. But, would you consider coming out to Lebanon next weekend?"

"I'd love to see your house. Saturday afternoon?"

"Yeah, I don't want you missing Yoga," he stated, a lecherous grin on his face at the thought of her contorted body. "Gotta keep you flexible." Jillian swatted him, but shared his grin.

She was excited that Tate had invited her to his house. She had been curious about it for sometime, but felt uncomfortable inviting herself. For all she knew, he had a one room hut and all his money went to his horse. She had thought about asking Mike's wife if she'd ever been there, but she did not want to sound too materialistic. She hurried straight home after her morning riding lesson to shower and change. She had already spent the previous evening organizing her things. She called before leaving to see if he needed her to pick up anything on her way. He responded, "You! I have everything else covered."

She followed his meticulous directions. The house was on a half-acre of land and was set back from the street. The driveway was paved with cobblestones set in concrete. As she pulled into his driveway, she saw a two story, nineteenth century farmhouse flanked by two huge oak trees that seemed as old as the house itself. Jillian pulled her car into the wide parking area next to the house and stepped out, looking at the expanse of lawn. There were bare patches in the grass where trees had cast too much shade for the grass to grow unless it was given special attention. There was an old rose bed in front of the porch, but it, too, looked like it could use some work. It appeared that Daniel was too busy or disinclined to put a lot of effort into his landscaping. She walked up the front steps onto the porch and rang the bell. Tate yelled, "It's open. Come on in!"

As Jillian opened the front door, she felt as if she were stepping back in time. The entryway had an antique coat rack and hat tree with a seat where someone could sit to change shoes. It was in great condition and appeared to be the right period for the house. Jillian slipped out of her coat and hung it on the rack. She set her purse on the seat, and then turned to look at the rest of the furnishings. The floors were beautifully polished hard wood. She peeked into the first room on her right. There was no furniture in the room, but there was wainscoting half way up the walls that seemed to be original. In the far corner was a door, opening into another room in the back of the house. The room on the left side of the hallway was furnished with more antiques. It was a living room with the stereo set up, but no

TV. The double doors in the back were closed, but Jillian guessed that there would be another room back there of equal size. Straight ahead of her, the hallway continued to the back of the house, running parallel with a staircase that went to the second floor. Jillian began walking toward the stairs, wondering where Tate was.

"I love the house. Where are you?" she called to him.

"I'm back here!" he responded.

Jillian followed the voice down the hall to the kitchen. Her first reaction was to burst out laughing. He had flour all over his face and hair. He was standing at a butcher block table in the middle of the kitchen, rolling dough.

"What's so funny? Haven't you seen anyone make a pie crust before?"

She watched his movement; this was obviously not the first time he'd made crust. "Your face is covered with flour." She suddenly remembered having said this to a man before as Ellie.

He laughed self-consciously, picking up a clean towel, and began wiping. Jillian walked over to him, took the towel from him, and finished the job. Having scrubbed his cheek, she gave him a kiss on the cleaned spot, and then moved to kiss his lips. Tate returned the kiss, hugging her tightly to him.

"Mmmm. You taste like coffee and baked goods."

"And you just taste like heaven. So, welcome to my humble abode. Let me show you around." He started telling her the history of the house. "This house used to stand on a two hundred acre farm. The property was first settled in the early 1800s. The house was built in the 1850s. It's the original structure. By the time I saw the property, it had been broken down into parcels. They had already torn down the out buildings and were selling the farm in five acre plots. As soon as I saw this house I knew I had to have it. There's just something about the middle and late nineteenth century that appeals to me.

"I had to pull down a lot of the interior walls, but I managed to save some of the original moldings. I've been doing most of the work myself. There are four bedrooms upstairs, but three of them are still a mess. I finished the dining room, but I haven't had a chance to furnish it yet. I want to try to keep most of the furniture from the period; but I did give in to comfort in the den...the back parlor to you, Ma'am. I've got a contemporary couch in there. That's also where I've got the TV and computer. I'm not totally lost in the past," he finished, laughing at himself. After they finished the tour of the first floor, they returned to the kitchen. Jillian sat down at the table while Tate returned to his pie dough preparations.

Jillian smiled, thinking how she couldn't get away from the 1800s no matter how hard she tried. She had gone against her own desire to buy antiques for her condo, trying to leave Ellie and Ted behind. She wondered what she would have done if she had remembered Daniel at the time. She sat at the table, watching. "Do you need any help?"

"No, everything except the pie has been prepared."

"If you iron too, I think I'm in love!"

"I have many talents." He blushed.

"You're blushing! You do iron, don't you?"

"You'll just have to come around more often to find out."

CHAPTER 59

They left for work early Monday morning. They developed a routine; Tate spent Tuesdays and Thursdays at Jillian's and she spent Saturdays and Sundays at his house. There was only one more show that Tate was attending before the end of the season. Jillian had a business conference the same weekend and could not go. While she missed his companionship, she did not feel the loneliness she used to experience, trusting he would be back.

Josie had been tied up with shows and preparing her young riders for the finals. She had been unable to make the time to check out the mare Ed had suggested. Jillian was getting anxious; she was concerned that someone else might buy her. When Josie informed her it would be at least another month until she would be free to check out the filly, Jillian's disappointment and anxiety was obvious. Josie suggested, "Go take a look at the horse yourself. Ed's not going to send you off to look at something that's lame. If she handles well, isn't too skittish, and you like her, go ahead, on the condition we use my vet to check her out. I did look up her bloodline. If you had to, you could always breed her. But, Jillian, don't pay the eight no matter how much you like her. Walk away. I'll talk to them later on the phone."

"When can I go?"

"Let's give them a call and set it up."

Jillian was excited, but the anxiety at buying her first horse alone overwhelmed the pleasure. When Tate heard what she was about to do, he was furious with Josie for suggesting such a thing. It was the first time Jillian had seen him angry over anything. He insisted on taking the day off from work and going with her, stating, "I may not know anything about Five Gaited horses, but at least I can make sure she's sound and not crazy."

Jillian and Tate took Tuesday off from work and headed south into Kentucky. The directions led them over three hours of two lane highways, running through farms and small towns. Jillian tried to enjoy the picturesque landscape, but her anxiety continued to interfere. She finally closed her eyes and tried to do some Yoga breathing, hoping to get her anxiety under control. Silently, she said, "I know what to look for, I just have to remember. Ellie would know. Ellie would know. Trust yourself." As she repeated the mantra, she could picture looking out on a paddock full of young horses grazing, listening to John Peters identifying the qualities of the stock.

Her reverie was interrupted by the sound of Tate's voice, "Just because you want one, doesn't mean you have to buy this one. If she's not right, we'll keep looking."

Jillian reached out to stroke his arm. "Thank you for coming with me."

Tate smiled at her. "I wouldn't miss this first for you."

"You've given me more firsts than you realize." Jillian was thinking about their sexual relationship.

Daniel tilted his head and raised an eyebrow. "I hope you mean that in a good way."

"Oh, yes!" She smiled broadly at him.

"There's our turn off." He slowed the vehicle, turning right onto a long drive. "Don't let on to them if you absolutely have to have her."

"I know." She flapped her hand at him impatiently.

They pulled up to the barn area, parking next to the one other vehicle. Jillian took a deep breath as she unbuckled the seat belt and opened the door. The owner of the small farm came out of the barn to greet them. "Jillian? I'm Tom."

"Hi! This is my friend Tate."

"I spoke on the phone with Josie; she said you're interested in My Princess."

"Princess?" Tate almost choked.

"'My Princess' is her registered name. She's a three year old. We've been working her for Fine Harness. Old Joe is getting her ready now."

Jillian went silent, thinking; *it's just a coincidence nothing more.* Tate asked, "Could we see her now?"

Just then a short man with dirty blond hair led a brown and white painted mare out the side door of the barn; she was harnessed to a training cart.

"There she is now. I'll warm her up for you."

Jillian tried to hide her giggles. Ed hadn't told her the mare was a paint. She hadn't thought to ask her coloring, but was expecting a chestnut or bay. She hadn't even considered a paint, yet she found the look surprisingly pleasing. Tate leaned over and whispered, "What are you laughing about?"

"She's not what I was expecting. Neither is Old Joe for that matter."

He nodded, in agreement, not taking his eyes off the mare.

Joe came over. "She's really a sweet little thing. I'll miss the old girl if you do take her."

"How old is she anyway?" Tate asked.

"She's a three year old. An April foal."

"Tom, could you take those rattlers off? I'd like to see her natural gait," Jillian requested.

Joe took off the rattlers and Tom took her around the ring a couple of times in both directions. He pulled her up for Jillian to take a closer look.

"She's kind of long in the back," Jillian commented.

"She'll grow into herself."

Jillian knew better, but thought under saddle it would not be a problem.

Tom jumped out of the cart, "You take her around."

"I've never driven."

"It's easy. Come on. I'll tell you what to do!"

Jillian climbed in and followed Tom's instructions. She was surprised by how natural it felt. "Have you ever had a saddle on her?"

"No, hadn't planned on saddle breaking her."

"Could we put one on her, just for looks?" Jillian thought it would be a good test of the mare's temperament to see how she handled something new and give her a chance to see how she looked under saddle. She hoped it would hide the long back.

Tom unhooked the cart and started taking off the harness. Joe ran into the barn and came out with a four-inch cutback saddle.

The young horse stood quietly while the saddle was attached. As Joe backed away, the mare bent her neck as far as she could trying to sniff the strange thing on her back. Jillian could not help but laugh aloud at her; she liked her curiosity.

Tom moved her out, running behind her, directing her with the long harness reins. Once around half the ring, he brought her back and stretched her out. Jillian thought she'd have to remember not to stretch her as far. She then went up to the mare and began running her hands over her body, focusing on her legs. Tate joined her, picking up each foot, waiting to see the mare's reaction as he checked the condition of her hooves.

Tom turned to Jillian. "What do you think?"

"She's not exactly what I was expecting?" Jillian was trying to hide her excitement.

"Come on up to the house. I'm sure we could all use something to eat!" He led them up to the house and into a country kitchen.

"Could I see her papers?" Jillian wasn't sure what to look for, but thought it would sound like she knew what she was doing.

Tom handed her a photocopy of the papers and started passing out sandwiches. "What were you expecting?"

"Ed hadn't mentioned that she was a paint. I guess I'd never considered one. She's very long in the back, even under saddle."

"She'll fill out and it won't be noticeable. She's young yet."

"She may be young, but her confirmation is not going to change," Tate interjected. "What do you want for her?"

Jillian nodded at Tate.

"Eight, we've put a lot into her."

"Now, let's be realistic!"

Tom and Tate went back and forth, leaving Jillian out of the conversation. Finally, Tom said, "Write me check for forty-five now and you can have her."

"We'll give you a thousand to hold her and, after our vet checks her out and approves, we'll pick her up and give you the balance."

Tom reached out to shake Tate's hand. Jillian sat in amazement. She would have been happy to pay seven. Tate turned to Jillian, "Do you have a check?"

Jillian nodded, "Tate, may I have the keys? My purse is in the car."

He handed her the keys. She nearly ran to the car before Tom could change his mind. She was excited, but wondered if there might be something wrong with the mare that he'd be willing to let her go so cheap. She pulled out her cell phone and called Josie. After describing the situation, she asked, "Is something wrong?"

"No, she can't make it in Fine Harness; they don't want to feed her over the winter and, while paints are becoming popular, not everybody likes them. If you like her, go ahead!"

They left the farm with the copy of the papers and a receipt spelling out the agreement. Jillian asked Tate to pull over once they were out of sight. She threw her arms around his neck, kissing him. "Thank you. You're fabulous. I would have paid way too much. I don't think even Josie would have done so well." She kissed him again.

"I can think of some more ways you can thank me."

"Hmm..."

CHAPTER 60

Josie made arrangements for the mare to be vetted and had her picked up the following week. As an owner with a horse in full training, Jillian's schedule changed. Fortunately, her annual raise came around the same time. She realized, with the added horse expense, she would not really be bringing in any additional money. Between board and training, most of it would be used. The money Tate had saved her was also spent. She had to pay the vet and trucking as well as buy her own saddle, bridal, blanket, cooler, leg wraps, and various other supplies.

The show season was finally over and Jillian was glad to have Josie's attention working with her horse. As she got to know the mare better, she found herself thinking of the flashy, young, painted mare as fun and her personality as charming. While Anna did not appreciate horses, she was the one person who did appreciate the significance of the horse's name.

As November progressed, Jillian felt she should ask Tate for Thanksgiving Dinner at her parents. Her mother had already started asking if he would be joining them. While fixing dinner together at Tate's house, she brought up the subject. "I'd like to talk about Thanksgiving."

"I'm glad you brought it up. I keep thinking there's plenty of time."

"Yes," she laughed, "we both know about you and time, but it's the weekend after next."

Simultaneously, they said, "My mother..." They both laughed. He put his finger to her lips. "Jillian, I would like you to come to Lake Forest with me for Thanksgiving and meet my family."

She looked up into his eyes and saw how important it was to him. Smiling, she replied, "I'll tell my mother we'll be going to your family's." Jillian knew that, although Daniel called his family regularly, he had not been home since Christmas. She hoped she would not be seen as an intrusion; but he had asked and she was not going to miss the opportunity to know him better.

Tate handed her the phone. "Now! Before you change your mind."

"Yes, sir." She took the phone and punched in her parents' number. "Hi, Mom."

Tate pushed the speaker button.

"That's not nice!" Jillian exclaimed, laughing.

"Jillian? What's not nice?" her mother's voice asked, confused.

"Mom, Tate's not coming for Thanksgiving."

"Oh, Jillian, I'm sorry. He seemed so nice. Did something happen?"

"No, Mom, and I won't be there either."

"Are you two running off someplace? It's not right to spend Thanksgiving away from your family." Jillian was trying not to laugh.

"We're going to Tate's parents."

"Oh..." her tone changed, "Oh..., well, we'll miss you both. Maybe you can come for dinner some Sunday?"

"We'll talk about it. Got ta go. Bye."

"Bye, Dear."

"Your mom took it pretty well."

"Now, call your mother." She handed him the phone.

"They're probably at the club."

"You're not getting out of it that easily."

"OK. OK." He pushed the automatic dial for his parents.

"You're home!"

Jillian pushed the speaker and made a face at him.

"You just caught us." Tate's father had answered.

"Tell Mom I'll be home the day before Thanksgiving."

"Are you sure I shouldn't say Thanksgiving Day? You know how she worries when you're late."

Jillian covered her mouth trying to silence her laughter.

Tate shook his head, "No. Jillian will be coming with me, so we'll be on time."

"She must be pretty special if she manages to get you to be on time." His father started laughing. "I'll let your mother know. She'll be pleased. I have to go or you'll make us late, too. Bye, Son."

Tate hung up without saying good-bye.

"What is it with you about saying good-bye?"

"I don't know. Even when I was little I wouldn't say it... It just seems so final."

The day before Thanksgiving they left early for the Chicago suburbs, hoping to be ahead of the worst of the traffic. It took them seven hours. The driveway was lit with imitation gas lanterns leading to a circular area in front of the center portico. The house was well lit and Jillian could see a two story brick house with wings extending in both directions from the portico. A four car garage was off to the left, with an enclosed walkway to the end of the left wing of the house. Jillian had resisted the urge to investigate Tate or his family on the internet or through her banking connections. She had felt it improper and that he would tell her more as he became more comfortable. She was also afraid she might slip and say something he had not told her and, if he confronted her about it, she could not lie to him. She wondered if she had made a mistake not preparing herself better.

Tate pulled up to the front door. She wanted to say something, but did not know what without sounding overly impressed. Before she knew it, he was opening her car door and walking her up the front steps. The front door swung open and Tate greeted the family butler, introducing Jillian to him. Tate then pointed out a bathroom to Jillian. When she came out, he had already retrieved their luggage from the SUV.

"Mom...Mom!" Tate yelled, stomping into the foyer and dropping the luggage.

Tate's mother came down the hall wiping her hands on a dish towel. "Tate, you're here early." She kissed her son on the cheek. "Jillian, we're so glad you could come." She kept drying her hands and went up to Jillian, brushing her cheek against Jillian's. "Please, you've had a long ride; you must be hungry and tired. Dinner is not for a couple more hours, but I'll have Rosie bring something out to the living room."

"Mother, I'm sure Rosie has enough to do. Jillian and I are quite capable of helping ourselves." He put his arm around his mother, directing her back to the kitchen. Jillian followed the Bradleys down the hall.

Tate gave Rosie a big hug and teased her about getting younger, and then introduced Jillian. She soon found out the woman had worked for the family since Tate was two years old. It quickly became apparent that Tate was more comfortable in the kitchen than his mother was.

Sara Bradley nonchalantly began asking Jillian questions about her life and background. Jillian had been answering questions for half an hour before she even realized that she was being interrogated and that Tate had disappeared. Mrs. Bradley then showed Jillian to her room, suggesting that she would need time to prepare and change for dinner. Jillian had no idea what she would need and was glad she had decided to over pack. She was shaking out her clothing and hanging them up when Tate slipped into the room. "Your mother said dress for dinner?"

"She'll wear a cocktail dress; I'll wear my jeans and my father will still be wearing his business suite. Just be comfortable."

Jillian chose a tailored linen dress that she would normally wear to work. Sara and George Bradley were sitting in the living room having a cocktail when Jillian came downstairs. Tate came out of the kitchen when he heard his father greet her. She quickly understood where Tate got his dry sense of humor. However, George seemed most comfortable talking about business matters and seemed relieved when he found out Jillian worked with a VP at Midwest Bank. It meant he could actually have a conversation with her. They turned in early, going to their separate rooms.

Waking early, Jillian threw on a pair of jeans and a tee-shirt and quietly went down to the kitchen. The coffee was on and a man of about twenty-five with bleached blonde streaks in his hair and blood shot, gray eyes was hovering over a cup of coffee. A tall, bleached blonde with pierced earrings running up her ears, a midriff-less top over silicone breasts, a belly ring, and hip huggers was pouring coffee. Jillian guessed the man was Tate's struggling photographer younger brother, Albert. No one had mentioned that he would be coming in from California. By the looks of them, Jillian guessed they had flown in on the red eye from LA.

"Good morning. I'm Jillian."

Albert looked up, "Al, she's Sabrina."

"Coffee?" Sabrina asked.

"Please!" She took the cup from Sabrina and sat at the table across from Albert, trying to clear her head.

Albert stared at her through drooping eyelids, "It's your fault I feel like shit right now!"

"Mine?" Jillian was flabbergasted.

"Yes. By the time I found out you were coming for Thanksgiving, the only flight we could get left at 11:30 last night."

"To meet me?" Jillian felt even more amazed.

Sabrina smacked her boyfriend on the head. "Al, she doesn't know."

Albert started laughing. Jillian looked back and forth between the two of them, confused.

"Tate has never brought any woman home for a family gathering or holiday dinner." Sabrina explained.

"Oh... Never?" The significance of this visit and Sara's interrogation started to make sense. She was glad she had not known at dinner the night before or she would have felt extremely self-conscious.

Al grabbed a last piece of toast and drained his coffee. "Never! We're going to catch some sleep now." The two picked up their knapsacks and a camera bag and headed upstairs.

Jillian sat at the table by herself until Rosie showed up. She worked side by side with the older woman, helping to prepare breakfast and stuff the large bird that needed to be cooked. Laughing and chatting with her, she heard stories of Tate's childhood. Eventually, the rest of the house started stirring. Before long Tate joined them and gratefully accepted the coffee he was offered. George and Sara followed soon after.

"Good morning, everyone. Jillian, I hope you had a good night's sleep," George said with a smile.

"Yes, thank you, Mr. Bradley. It's a lovely room and a marvelous bed," Jillian responded, handing him a cup of coffee.

"Please call me George. 'Mr. Bradley' makes me feel like I'm in the office," he responded, accepting the mug from her.

"All right, George. Thank you."

"What time did Albert and Sabrina get in? I can't believe they came all that way at the last minute. That boy is so impulsive. I swear, Jillian, sometimes I just despair about the men in this family." Sara stated, shaking her head, but smiling to take the sting out of her words.

"Speaking of arrivals, what time are Darcy and Andrew getting here?" Tate asked.

"She said they'd be here after lunch. The kids have some sort of program to attend this morning." Sara told him.

"Great! Maybe, we'll have some time to play before dinner," Tate stated enthusiastically. "You'll love my sister's kids, Jillian. Brittany, who's eight, wants to be a ballerina when she grows up, and Kevin, four, wants to drive trucks. They're bright children and a lot of fun." He smiled at Jillian and she smiled back, thinking how amazing it was to find a man who was so excited by the idea of having two young children around.

After breakfast, Rosie and Sara began preparations for the dinner. Jillian insisted on pitching in with the work and was pleased when Tate also began helping out. She enjoyed sitting at the table, pealing and chopping vegetables while the other women told embarrassing stories about Tate when he was growing up. Tate seemed to take the teasing in stride and laughed good naturedly.

Albert and Sabrina emerged around lunch time, looking a little less bedraggled. Lunch was a casual affair with a great deal of laughter and teasing among the family members. Darcy and Andrew arrived around one with their two children who quickly ran to see their Uncles Tate and Al. They regaled them with reports of the Thanksgiving Day parade they had attended and all the excitement that entailed. Kevin was delighted to report that he got to ride on a fire truck and planned to be a firefighter when he grew up. Brittany described the costumes she had seen some of the women and girls wearing in the parade and bemoaned the fact that she did not have such clothing. Al and Tate were dragged away from the others to play games with the children. Jillian went to watch their interactions and was delighted with the rapport that existed between Tate and the kids. She watched him regress to childhood, acting far more uninhibited than she had ever seen him. Of course, she couldn't help but feel that Tate would make a wonderful father once he had children of his own.

When dinner was at last announced, Tate helped Rosie serve the other family members, and then insisted that she join them for dinner. Jillian stole a peek at Sara, who was sitting next to her, to see how she would respond to having the servant sitting with the family. Sara seemed surprised by the idea, but politely joined her son in urging Rosie to join them. A place was quickly made for her.

Once the meal was finished and all were completely satiated, Rosie stood and began clearing away the dishes. Tate rose and began helping her with the task. Jillian also began pushing her chair back to join in the task, but Sara laid a hand on her arm, pushing her gently back into her chair.

"It's all right, Dear. You're company. They can handle the job. Just relax and enjoy yourself," Sara commanded softly. Jillian considered protesting that she didn't mind, but thought better of it. She didn't want to offend her hostess and she was sure that Rosie and Tate would understand.

CHAPTER 61

Friday night, Jillian and Tate went out in Chicago with Albert and Sabrina. The two couples tastes in music were very different. Tate broke up the revelry early, stating they had a long drive back to Cincinnati on Saturday. They arrived back at Tate's house late Saturday night. Jillian had never felt so contented as she snuggled into his arms and fell asleep.

Sunday morning, Tate suggested they go to the Golden Lamb for brunch, and then to the supermarket. They arrived at the inn by ten, and found the restaurant almost full. They were lucky to get a cozy table in one of the four dining rooms. Jillian was charmed by the nineteenth century antiques on the walls and scattered about the room. The hostess offered them menus and sent a waitress to take their drink orders while they decided what else they wanted.

Tate studied Jillian as she examined the menu. After several seconds, he tentatively asked her, "What do you want?"

"I don't think I want much. I'm still stuffed from all that food at your parents' house."

Tate seemed surprised by that. "Really? You'd certainly be cheap to maintain. Actually,...I meant for yourself...for your life."

"Oh. Well,...I want to finish my MBA. ...I want to ride My Princess across fields of wild flowers..." She hesitated, wondering where this conversation was going.

Tate continued to study her face, a small smile tugging at his mouth. "Is that it?"

Jillian laid her menu down, realizing he was being serious. "No, I'd like to have a family someday."

Tate seemed to become more alert. "So, you would get married again?"

Jillian shrugged and nodded. "To the right man."

He leaned in toward her across the table, smiling even more. "To the right man, huh? And who would that be?"

She tilted her head and studied him for a moment. "Well, we'd have to have the same interests, the same goals and values. He'd have to not only want children, but want to be involved in raising them...a partner...."

He interrupted, "Is that it?"

Jillian laughed. "No, there'd have to be great sex." She smiled at him. "You've spoiled me..."

A mock frown creased his brow. With concern in his voice, he asked, "I've spoiled you for sex, have I?"

Jillian blushed and looked around them at the other diners before responding in a whisper, "Not for sex, with sex!"

Tate leaned back, genuinely surprised and a little smug. "I'm that good?"

Jillian tried to straighten her countenance, but felt a laugh bubbling beneath the surface. "Oh yes, but do you want to hear the rest of my list?"

Raising an eyebrow, a look of mild trepidation on his face, he responded, "I'm almost afraid to?"

Jillian shrugged in what she hoped was a nonchalant way. "Well, you asked."

Tate leaned forward and nudged her arm. "Go on!"

"Let's see...He'd have to be sensitive to my feelings...and, of course, I'd have to be madly in love with him and he'd have to be absolutely crazy about me."

"Anything else?"

She shook her head. "That's the gist."

"And if anything is missing?"

"Well, then I guess it wouldn't work. ...And what about you?"

"Moi?" he responded, his hand gesturing to his chest.

Jillian responded with feigned indignity, "You started it!"

"Well, of course, she'd have to be beautiful, want me in bed all the time, blush a lot..."

She swatted at him playfully. "Be serious!"

"I am! Sex is important! You said so yourself."

"Go on!"

"She'd have to love horses or we'd end up fighting all the time."

Jillian nodded in agreement. "True."

"She'd also have to be patient and understand that no matter how hard I try, sometimes I'll be late and that does not mean I'm dead."

"Ouch," Jillian responded, wincing.

"Is that a deal breaker?"

Jillian was startled by the serious expression on Tate's face. "I didn't know this was a negotiation." She was getting nervous.

Tate waved a reassuring hand at her. "It's just a conversation."

"Oh...good...that's what I'd thought it was." Jillian felt herself relax a little.

Sensing the tension, Tate asked, "How's the training going with Princess? When do you think you'll be able to ride her?"

"She seems to be catching on quickly..." she replied, grateful that Tate had changed to another subject. The breakfast was eaten without any more deep conversation.

For the rest of the day, whenever Tate was about to say anything even remotely serious, Jillian would direct the conversation to safer topics. She now understood why he had taken her to his parents' home for Thanksgiving and that he had been feeling her out regarding marriage. She knew that, if he asked, their relationship would be changed forever, no matter what her answer was. If she said no, she would never see him again. If she said she was unsure, he would be terribly hurt. He'd probably never ask again and they'd drift apart. However, she was not going to say yes unless she was absolutely sure. After the fiasco of marrying Drake, she was not going to make another mistake. She wanted to make sure that, if she ever got married again, it was for the right reasons and to the right man.

They'd been spending nearly every night together. She needed some time to think, to talk with friends, to be alone. She did not want him to feel he had frightened her, yet he had. She had been enjoying the closeness as it slowly grew. She did not want to lose it, but she would not agree to marry anyone out of a fear of being alone or a fear of losing him. She had learned; she would not repeat the same mistakes again. Nor was she willing to make new mistakes out of old fears.

She called Anna from work to see which evening they could go out for dinner and conversation. Jillian changed her Wednesday night lesson for the first time since she had started riding. Of all her friends and family, there were only two people she could count on not to try to push her into something, Anna and Joan. She was unsure what to tell Tate about skipping riding to meet up with Anna. She thought about not mentioning it, but realized it would be worse if he just showed up there, as he sometimes did, and she was not around. She finally told him that she had talked to Anna; they had not been together in a long time, and that they needed to catch up with each other. It would be a girls only night.

She met Anna at the restaurant. It didn't take her friend long to see that there was more to their meeting than just catching up with one another.

"Okay. What's up, Jilly? You look like a month of wet Mondays. Has something gone wrong with Mr. Right?"

"I guess that's the problem. Is he Mr. Right? I just don't know. I mean…he's probably the closest anyone has come to being everything I want. But am I just settling for the first offer to come along? Am I so afraid to be alone that I've built this relationship up into something it's not? Oh, Anna, I'm so confused!" Jillian sighed with helpless frustration.

"Jilly, it's been two years since you divorced Drake. You've dated other men and very quickly realized none of them were right for you. I think it's safe to say that you aren't rushing into anything. Nor are you afraid to be alone, for the same reasons. So, the questions really are, how do you feel about him? Do you want to be with him? Is he good to you? Do you share common interests and hold similar values? Would you be sadder if he were gone?" Anna raised her eyebrows and let her friend think about the issues she had raised.

Jillian acknowledged that Anna was right; but she couldn't answer those questions and feel that her other concerns were not legitimate.

"Well, Jilly, you know I'll back you no matter what you decide. Just don't over think this one. There are no absolutely right answers, just choices based on hope."

Friday after yoga, Jillian spoke briefly with Joan. The only advice Joan would give was, "Don't let your head get in the way; trust yourself."

Sunday afternoon, Jillian went with Tate to his stable. He'd been complaining all week that his mare had been off stride and he needed to be working her more. Jillian stood in the center of the indoor ring watching Tate warm up the mare and take her around the course. A couple of teenage riders raised and widened jumps for him. Jillian was trying to hide her laughter at the way the boys ran to assist him. They were junior riders and looked up to Tate. When he finished working, one of the boys asked Tate if he would stay around and give him some pointers with his own horse. The other boy offered to cool out the mare and put her up for him so that he could help his friend. Tate asked Jillian if she'd mind hanging out a little longer. She agreed, wondering what kind of teacher he'd make. How would he teach their children? Would he guide them with patience? She hadn't fully made up her mind what she would say if he asked, but she knew she loved him.

The teenage boy brought his horse out and mounted up. Tate had lowered half the jumps and suggested to the young man that he warm up his horse, and then take him over the lower jumps. He added that he wanted to get a sense of their style. He stood next to Jillian, intent on the horse and rider, counting out strides, moving in place with him. He called the boy over to him and spoke softly with the rider about his timing and becoming one with his mount. Tate sent them back around the ring and began lowering the remaining jumps that he had not yet lowered. Tate called out, "Slow him down a little. He's getting away from you."

As Tate turned his back on the horse and rider to walk to the next set of jumps, the pair came crashing through the jump at Tate's back. Rails went flying. Tate went down. The horse scrambled through the obstacles trying to stay on his feet. Jillian went running to Tate.

He was not moving. He was on his side and there was blood on his head and face. A rail had fallen across his legs. The boy was still trying to get his horse under control. Jillian fell to her knees at Tate's side, touching his face, wiping away blood with her hand. "Tate Bradley, I love you! Don't you dare leave me again!" She felt a lump of despair in her throat. There was blood all over him, but he was still breathing.

Coughing, he choked out, "Oh, Jillian, I've told you...I'm too stubborn to die." He squinted through the blood and dirt to see tears streaming down her face. "I love you, Jillian. ...Do you love me madly?"

More tears fell, "Oh yes, madly!"

"Does this mean you'll marry me?"

"Yes! Yes!"

He pulled her down to him, kissing her. He tried sitting up. Jillian put her hand to his chest, pushing him back down. "No, let me get some help." She moved the rail off his leg. "Please, just wait. I'm going to get some help."

Jillian ran into the barn looking for someone to help. She had Tate's blood on her hands, her jacket, and her face. Tate's horse was on the cross ties and the other boy was brushing her. When he saw Jillian, he grabbed a clean towel and ran up to her. "What happened? You're covered in blood!"

She grabbed the towel from him. "It's not mine! It's Tate's!" She called over her shoulder as she ran back toward the ring. "Come!"

Two other people were there and they all came running. Tate had gotten up on his own. Jillian arrived back at the ring to see him walking toward her. She stopped in her tracks. She watched him limping with one hand holding his leg. Suddenly, everything came together. *He is Daniel! ...Someday, I'll tell him. This time nothing will keep us apart.* Jillian rushed forward to offer him support, wrapping her arms around his waist. Tate allowed her to support him; as he hung on to her, he whispered in her ear. "I'm not going to let you get away from me this time. We're not going to lose another lifetime."

Authors' Note

The authors have attempted to present an accurate account of life in nineteenth century America.   Descriptions of food, clothing, furnishings, transportation, and entertainment are representative of the time.   Specific descriptions of the churches, businesses, streets, and homes in Beaufort are correct.

The names of some of the characters are actual historical persons; however, their lives as presented are largely, if not completely fictitious. None of the other characters in this book is a real person. The political events of the time have been presented with as much accuracy as possible. The language used within dialogs approximates that used at the time and was gathered from published diaries, "Journal of a Residence on a Georgian Plantation in 1838-1839" by Frances Anne Kemble, edited by John A. Scott, 1984, by Brown Thrasher Books, The University of Georgia Press, Athens, and "Mary Chesnut's Civil War" by Mary Chestnut, edited by C. Vann Woodward, 1981, by Yale University Press.   While Gullah would have been spoken by the African-Americans of the South amongst themselves at that time, it was felt attempts at reproducing it would have been more distracting than beneficial to the reader's understanding of the period.

Made in the USA
Charleston, SC
03 December 2013